Paul Park left his job and Manhattan apartment in 1983 to travel in Asia – hiking in the Himalayas, touring India, Burma, Nepal, and Southeast Asia. *Soldiers of Paradise* was written then, on notebooks and loose pieces of paper, in cheap hotels and rented rooms from Rajasthan to the Golden Triangle, from Mandalay to Jogjakarta. He has no fixed address.

PAUL PARK

Soldiers of Paradise

The Starbridge Chronicles

GRAFTON BOOKS
A Division of the Collins Publishing Group

LONDON GLASGOW
TORONTO SYDNEY AUCKLAND

Grafton Books
A Division of the Collins Publishing Group
8 Grafton Street, London W1X 3LA

A Grafton UK Paperback Original 1989

Copyright © Paul Park 1987

ISBN 0-586-20419-9

Printed and bound in Great Britain by
Collins, Glasgow

Set in Caledonia

For my sisters

Prologue

To those who remember starlight, the spring sky over Charn is one of the most desolate sights in all the universe, for by the second hour after sunset there is not one star in all the sky. During the first few thousand days of the new season, the canopy of heaven dwindles and grows dark, until by midspring the night sky is so black it almost glows, and the eye plays tricks, seeing color where there is none – iridescent clouds of indigo and mauve.

On winter nights the sky is full of stars. But as the season changes, a stain of darkness overtakes them from the east, a microsecond earlier each night. There at the galaxy's edge, staring out over the brink of space, the citizens seem grateful for any clouds or mist which might cast a veil between themselves and their own loneliness. Twice each season Paradise fills up the sky for a few dozen rotations, and then the people crowd into the temples, praying for clear weather. But otherwise they hate it, and they line the streets with bonfires, for comfort's sake. On clear nights the city burns like a candle far out over the hills, and to refugees and pilgrims coming down out of the country, it shines like a beacon under the black sky. At waystops and lodges high up along the trail they swing their bundles to the ground; and on benches set into the rock they sit and hug their knees as evening falls, and watch the temples and the domes of Charn light up against the dark, each one outlined in neon or electric bulbs.

And as they watch, the whole river valley seems to fill up with fire, for at dusk the lamplighters come out in Charn, and with long prehensile hooks they pull down the corners of a web of ropes slung between the roofs. Acetylene lanterns hang suspended from long pulleys, and they sway slightly in the evening wind as the lamplighters hoist them back into a firmament of nets.

The lamplighters are small and semihuman, with soft blobby faces and bright eyes. They stand barefoot in the muddy street, dressed in the green overalls of their caste, listening to the temple bells, to the cadence that directs their labor. They are listening to the music. And on the ridge above the city, a traveler hears pieces of it too. He has wandered down from the courtyard of the hillside shrine where he has left his blanket. Grimacing, kicking at the stones, he has clambered out onto a pinnacle of rock. There, looking out over the lights, he turns his head a little, straining to hear. It is what has brought him to this place. He has heard wisps of it along the trail, even in far lands where the prophet's name is never spoken, perhaps in the mouth of some begging preacher or some thick-lipped merchant in the marketplace humming over his pile of salt. But in Charn, the prophet's birthplace and the center of his worship, he hopes to hear the music in its purest form. Down below, it fills the mind of every citizen – harsh, rhythmical, sedate, issuing at sunset from the doors of all the temples, mixing with incense and yellow candlelight, coiling like smoke above the town.

On Durbar Square, the doors of the temple are thrown open. At the altar, the priest conjures to the image of Beloved Angkhdt, and then he steps down towards the kneeling rows of worshipers, a basket in his hands. It is piled high with packages of artificial flour, each one enough for one man for one day. In the city, all is quiet for an obligatory count of four, but on his rocky pinnacle above the walls, the traveler paces nervously. He has heard about this part of the ritual. His enormous frame is gaunt with hunger, because in spring it is the starving time in Charn and all those northern dioceses. The melted snow of twenty thousand days' accumulation has scoured the hills to their foundations and stripped the pastures clean. The trail that he has followed south has run through red rock canyons full of broken timber, and valleys full of stone. He has passed through ruined villages, and hunted for garbage in the burned-out shells of factories. Other travelers on the trail have stood aside to let him pass, and spat into the dust, and made the sign of the unclean. He has not sung a song in many months. But on the pinnacle above the city, he smiles as if for the first time. He shakes the hair back from his face, black hair with a streak of white in it. He squints out over the city, smiling to himself. He takes a · wooden flute from the pouch at his side, and as the music rises up from all the temples of the town, he plays a few notes of another darker melody and hums a few notes of another song. On the hillside above him at the shrine, the keeper puts her fingers to her ears.

In spring of the year 00016, scattered families of antinomials started to appear in Charn, and they hid from the police in a neighborhood of abandoned warehouses between the river and the railway yard. Immense, sulky, powerful, they had drifted south over the course of a generation, down seven hundred miles from their villages in the farthest north, victims of religious persecution and the driving snow. They were a silent, terrifying race, unfit for any kind of work. But in time they became famous for a sad ferocious music of their own. Rich people risked their lives to seek them out. And one night towards the end of July, in the eighth phase of spring, Abu Starbridge and his cousin made the journey through the slums to a deserted warehouse built on pilings out over the river. They had difficulty finding it, though the prince had been there once before. But finally they came in under the cowl of a long building, and inside it was black as night, save for a small fire at the far end, past a row of steel pillars stretching up into the dark. There, a gigantic antinomial sat cross-legged on the floor, holding a wine jar in his hands. But he didn't even raise his head when they got close. He didn't even look at them, though they had brought a basket full of chocolates and fruit. And he had started to sing already, even though at first there was no one else around. From far away they could hear him. 'There had been others before,' he sang. 'Of course there had been. There had been others.'

1

Rangriver Fell

There had been others before, of course, traders and travelers – our house was full of things only barbarians could make: glass and steel, products of slavery and the burning South. The first barbarian I saw with my own eyes, my brothers and sisters were coming back from somewhere, down from Rangriver, where we lived in those days, when we were still free, before the soldiers burned us out. That's not fair. We would have gone anyway, soldiers or not. The world was changing, and we changed freely – from the time I speak of, I cannot now remember anything but snow. From farther north, whole households had already ridden through, searching for food.

This barbarian was on muleback and alone. We followed him along the cliff's edge, singing and throwing snowballs. He was taller than I expected, though not so tall as a man, and he smiled and gave us sugar candies wrapped in real paper. His teeth were black. There are barbarians who pull their children's teeth in babyhood, canines and incisors – they leave gaps on both sides, and later they smoke cigarettes. Their speech is slurred and indistinct. Because they are closer to beasts, they love them more. They eat no meat, raw or cooked. They wear no leather or wool, for their own bodies are hairy past belief. How can they live where it is hot? When I was young I never asked. I was still free, nothing in my mind, wisps of things, snatches of songs, clouds in the sky. We capered around him, grabbing at his stirrups and the heels of his rubber, spurless boots, looking for his tail. 'Is it a rat's, a rabbit's, or a dog's?' we sang, each in a different mode. He reached down to pat our heads. He was keeping it hidden in his pants.

At the top of the gorge, we came up through cinder pines, and here it started to snow again. And here we found people waiting, in from hunting, the horses steaming and blowing, and kicking at the snow. I can identify the time, because the horses still looked sleek. Later, they ate bark from the trees. Bears and lions, unnamed from hunger, came down to find them in their pens.

My sister stood away from the rest, and when she saw us, she turned her horse. Not knowing whether the barbarian had been among us before, I hummed a word of possessiveness and pride, for this was how I would have chosen my people to be displayed before a stranger. A woman on horseback, her shoulders wrapped in bearskin, the rifle on her back, her long hair matted and tangled, she looked so transient. The dead buck hanging from her saddle. Child as I was, I felt her beauty in my heart. But barbarians are a practical people. This one felt nothing. He dismounted and walked towards her, talking, and we could hear behind the words of her reply a hint of music, tentative welcome, as was proper, in a mode of strength to weakness. Not that it mattered, because though like all barbarians he knew everything, there was something the matter with his ears. He could hear our speech, but not our music. In his country, the sun has bleached out melody from rhythm – they know all languages, and speak them in dry cadences that mean nothing to us. They hit the bald words like drums. They never try to listen, they only try to understand. He looked so puzzled. He couldn't hear that in her music she was offering a place to stay, freely, gladly. She meant no harm. Our town was close by, over the ridge. It seemed so easy in those days.

Two ponies pulled a sledge piled with gutted animals, and when he saw it, the barbarian spat, and touched his nose with the heel of his hand, and ducked his face down into his armpit. It is your ritual of hatred; seeing it for the first time, standing in the snow, I found it funny. My brother had climbed up onto the mule, and he was kicking his boots into its ribs, while I kicked its backside. 'Look how he hates death,' sang my brother, as the barbarian muttered and prayed. 'He hates the sight of it.' A strutwing goose trailed its beak along the snow from the back of the sledge, its feathers dripping blood. 'He hates it,' sang my brother.

My lords, how hard it is for me to tell you this. To tell a story in the mode of truth from beginning to end, a man is chained like a slave. We were a free people then. This means nothing to you, I know. To me it means my memories from this time are wordless. The beast on the mountain, what is in its mind but music? Chained, it understands each link. It fingers them, it memorizes the feel. Barbarians have their prayers, their work, their things, their names, their families to think of. But we had nothing. No names for ourselves. No words for so many things. No future and no past. Good – here, now, I can be proud of that. But it makes it difficult to begin. Difficult to remember a whole world. But I remember the death of this barbarian; he was a scholar. He was studying a place familiar to us all, unnamed in our tongue, Baat – or Paat – Cairn, something like that, in his: an empty city high up between the mountain's knees, where the river runs out. I used to go so often. And of all the places of my childhood I remember it the best, because I know that now, right now as I speak, it is there unchanged – the great stone walls and staircases, the fallen columns and carved figures many times my height – unchanged, just as I remember it, in that eternal snow. We were a transient people then, dancers, musicians, hunters on horseback, sloppy builders.

13

We were in love with things that disappear: the last note of the flute, the single flutter of the dancer's hands. And in that old barbarian city, people had lived and disappeared. They would never be back.

The scholar went there every day. And at night he stayed in our town and studied us, stayed in our houses, took up no room, made no trouble. He played with his books and papers, his camera and tapes. He had brought his own food, dried vegetables and fruits. Real food disgusted him. And at first my sisters were careful where they slept and how they dressed when he was by, for they had heard barbarians were sensitive to human women, and they had no wish to kill him. But nothing came of that; he slept heavily on the mats and rugs we gave him. And by nightfall he was always drunk. Every evening he would find a corner in the longhouse, and watch and drink until his eyes burned. And I paid close attention. I said to him, 'Stranger.'

'Yes, boy,' his voice a dry drumbeat.

'Stranger, what do you see?'

But one night, I thought he hadn't heard. I was squatting beside him. He lay in the dark among the outer circle of watchers, among the children and the cripples. Although it was a frozen night, he wore only a cloth shirt, heavily embroidered, open at the neck, his chest hair like a blanket, I hoped. The liquor numbs your senses, I know now. He was very drunk. My face, so close to his, ignited nothing. I saw nothing in the mirror of his face. Fascinated, I stuck my hand in front of his nose. Nothing. His mouth sagged, and I could smell his ruined teeth.

In the silence behind me, in a circle of torchlight, my sister started to dance. She was new to it, and nervous, her gift just large enough to hide her nervousness. And she danced passionately, as if she were looking to deny what we all knew, that she had not yet heard the song of her

14

own self, that her movements were stolen, mixtures of copies, and she was too young and hot to be anything but formless, anything but molten in her heart's core. She danced, and from time to time in her flashing hands and feet an older dancer in the hall might catch the flicker of something as personal to him as his own body, performed with a dextrousness that he, perhaps, no longer had. This was why old and younger dancers were able to summon up the pride necessary to perform. Their greenness or their dryness gave their work a tension missing from more perfect work, the tension of their bodies and their spirit in unequal struggle. And when later we would watch a dancer in full flower, his death would dance around him as he danced.

I saw this without looking, but the barbarian stared and stared. My sister raised her naked arms. What did he see? I had heard wonders of drunkenness, stories of hallucinations, burning fires, men turned into beasts, whispers to thunder. I had seen a woman so in love with death that she had cut her foot off and died of the wound, not allowing the biters to come near. But this man didn't look at me. Impatient, I stuck my fingers into his face, poking his uneven cheek. He jerked his head away.

Behind me, a musician had begun to play. She had built a new instrument, a kind of guitar that I had never seen before. Envious, I turned to listen, but she had just started when the barbarian got up and stumbled forward under the lamps. Ignoring me, he pushed his way into the center of the hall. My sister crouched over her guitar. The barbarian covered her shoulder with his hairy fingers, and she looked up at him and smiled. The rest of us were too surprised to move, though some of my brothers and sisters were violent and loved bullying. Others had not forgiven him for having brought his camera into the hall one night, or for having tried to sketch them. But most of us were free from that, and we would have been happy to hear him

15

out. And I especially, for some reason, I felt my heart beating as I watched him in the torchlight, leaning on my sister's shoulder, closing his drunken eyes. And when he started to sing, I was caught by a kind of sound that I had never heard before, the uncouth melody, the words like vomiting. His voice was harsh. It made me listen and remember, so that much later I would recognize, in a language that I didn't know, the beginning of the Song of Angkhdt, which is barbarian scripture. 'Oh my sweet love, oh God my love, God let me touch you, and feel the comfort of your kisses, for you are my light, my life, my joy, my cure, my heart, my heartache . . .' The language was dead before time began, abandoned by decree. It was decreed a sacrilege to use the holy words for common purposes. Now no one can tell how they were once pronounced, and barbarians fight wars over their meaning.

Of all that I knew nothing yet. But I heard the delirious conviction in the drunkard's voice; it rang the rafters. This was the first song I had heard – I mean with words. Among us words were thought to muddy music, for the notes themselves can mean so much. That was not at issue here, in a language none of us could understand. But some could not endure even the sound of your religion, the vicious ecstasy, the sound of faith. I didn't mind it. I thought they were jealous of a new thing. Anyone should be able to stand up and sing. But we had habits, though it hurts me to say it, for yes, that was slavery too, of a kind. You must understand, not all of us were gifted. But some sang every night, and their music and their pride was the only law we had. One of my brothers, a bully and a dancer, took the barbarian by the throat, and struck him down, and threw him out into the snow.

Late at night I got up from the sleeping room and went out. He was lying in a snowbank, breathing softly. I thought his body hair might keep him warm. There was no

16

wind. The stars hung close. I had brought a bearskin, and hoped not to offend him, but I did. By morning he had thrown it off. He was a slave to his own faith, and I suppose he smelled the leather even in his sleep. By morning he was frozen dead.

The antinomial paused to spit into the darkness, and wipe his lips, and wipe each one of his enormous fingers on a rag before he picked his flute out of its case. He nodded to his guests. He said:

My lords, our world must appear cruel and incomplete. We knew nothing about love. That is a barbarian lesson I learned later. But at that time we were a free people. We called each other brother and sister, but we were always alone. Because what is freedom more than that – the need to hear your own music always, even in a crowd? When the barbarian died, I felt stifled, watching the biters cut his tail off up on the high ground above the river, watching them cut his body into pieces, the vultures huddling in a circle. In the morning I took a pony and some skis, and rode out through the gates of our town, out over the hills, far out towards the abandoned city, where the barbarian had had a camp. I felt unhappy, but not for long. The snow stretched unbroken all around me, and in a little while I had forgotten. My mind felt empty as the snow, and I found myself humming and making little gestures with my hands, because I loved that journey. You rode in over a high span of stone, the river booming far below you at the bottom of a ragged gorge. Birds flew underneath the arch, and at the far side the remnants of a huge bird-headed statue broke the way. Its head lay in a rubble of chipped stone, as long as my body, intricately carved, its round eye staring upward. I had to lead my pony over it, and in through the shattered gateway where the bridge met the sheer cliff face, the clifftops high above me. I rode up through a steep defile cut into the rock, lined with broken columns in the shape of trees. Their stone branches mingled into arches, and I rode up through another gateway where the rough walls around me rushed away, and out into a great open space, where the wind pulled at my clothing and swept the stones as clean as ice. From here you could see the sun, rising as if behind a paper shield, the sky as white as paper. And in the middle of this stone expanse rose up an enormous pitchrock fountain, a giant in chains; that city must have been a great center of slavery, the stonework is so good. His hands and feet are chained behind him, his eyesockets are hollow. The water must have come from there and dribbled down from wounds cut in his chest and arms and thighs. In the old days, he must have stood in a pool of tears and blood.

I went on and entered streets of empty palaces, their insides open to the weather, their doorways blocked by drifting snow. I turned the corners randomly and wandered in and out of being lost, but the pony knew the way, slave to habit. So I dismounted, and left it sheltered in a ruined porch, and climbed up into an older section of the town, where massive pyramids and temples of an older, gentler design stood like a ring of snowy hills. And in an open space near the largest of these, a tumbled hill of masonry, I found the barbarian's camp. He had discovered something, a hidden temple where the rock seemed solid, and he had come up every day to work on it, and come back every night to live with us and drink and sleep in our houses in the valley. He had kept maps and papers here, in a black tent standing in a ruck of fallen stones. He had kept a fire outside, the black smoke visible from far away. Once I had come to watch him work.

Now the fire was scattered, but there was a horse tethered outside. I had seen its footprints in the snow, and dog prints too. I could hear dogs barking, and in a little while they came running towards me over the snow, long-legged hunting dogs, but the tent was empty. I stood outside, the dogs jumping and cleaning my hands. I opened my coat to the white air and sucked the cold air through my teeth. I was so happy. I had no way of guessing then, my lords, that the future of my people lay in a barbarian city like that one had been, full of sweat and noise and slavery. Our tails would grow long, and we would never eat meat any more. My lords, here in your hard streets, hunger forces me to make up answers to your questions and sell my memories for food. It is a biting habit to think about the past. But I have no pride left; it hurts me to say it, for humility was something far beyond my childlike imagination as I stood in that abandoned city in the snow. Then my heart was empty as the air. I stamped my feet and shook my arms, and saw as if for the first time where the barbarian had found a flaw in the gradual surface of the pyramid, and rubbed it with gasoline and blasted out a hole the size of a man.

He had discovered a rough passageway into the heart of the stone hill; I entered it, and stopped on the threshold of a round chamber. To my right and to my left around the wall stretched a row of statues in a ring, facing inward to the room. They sat and stood in lifelike poses, some stiff, some slouching, and some leaned together as if talking. Some were gesturing with open mouths, as if they had been cut off in the middle of a word. The one beside me touched his neighbor lightly on the arm, as if to draw his attention to something happening across the room. And they had all been carved by the same hand, that much was clear, a hand that took delight in complicated clothes and simple faces. For though some were old with stringy necks and some were young, they all had qualities in common. Their faces were unmixed. Each had hardened over a single mood – pride in one, stupidity in another, malice, innocence. An old man was biting on a coin. Another pulled a stone cork from a stone bottle, his face contorted in a drunken leer. Another hid the stiffness in his lap under a fold of cloth and scratched forever at a bleeding sore. For a free man, the joy of living comes from knowing that it won't be long, that all flesh dies and disappears, but these barbarian kings and princes, it was as if the god they worshipped had turned them into stone. They would live forever, as doubtless they had begged him in their prayers.

A man stepped out across the room opposite from where I stood, a biter. I would have known him by his clean clothes even if I had not known his face. He had been a strong musician once, and I have memories of him standing in the torchlight of the hall, bent over his violin, my brothers and my sisters packed like slaves to hear him. Or even when he played alone, by himself in the high pastures, I remember children running out to find him, and they would sit around him in the snow. But by the time I speak of, that was past. A man had cut his hand off in a fight, I don't know why, and he had given up and taken to biting in a house by himself. Let me explain. Our kind of life was not for everyone. Some found it hard to give up everything for freedom's sake. They had things to occupy their minds. They were addicted to some work, or they had friends and children. We had given them a name. We called them betrayers, literally 'biters' in our language, and we hated them. The pride of our race was so hard to sustain. The rest of us had sacrificed so much to music, to emptiness and long cold wandering, that we could only hate them. And we hated them the more because we needed them. The biters were our doctors, builders, makers, parents. It gave them happiness to do things for themselves and other people. Without that, life falls apart, no matter what your gifts. Babies die, houses fall down. We needed someone to preserve us, to preserve a spirit they themselves could never share, a spirit to fill us with hunger every morning as we broke snow on the mountains with our horses and our dogs, a spirit to fill us every night and every morning with reasons to be up and to be gone.

But I am wandering: that day, in that stone chamber when I was a child, a biter stood in the middle of a circle of statues, with a carbide lantern in his hand. He said, 'Is that you?' in an empty voice, and then something else. I didn't understand him. Biters often know peculiar words. But the dead man, the barbarian scholar, had had a name and that was it. Mistaking me for him, the biter called me by his name, a word that referred to him as if he were a thing, fit to be used, like a blanket or a bed. My brothers and my sisters had no names.

I took up a loose piece of tile and skipped it across the floor. It made a circle round the biter's feet. He laughed. 'Little brother,' he said, and he came towards me. 'Little brother, what are you doing here?' This was common biting, not worth a reply. I spat on to the floor and turned away. There was a statue in the center of the room, different from the rest – a stone table and the figure of a man astride it, his legs hanging down on either side. He had a dog's head, dog's teeth, dog's eyes, and the hair ran down his back under his rich clothes. And from his groin rose up a stiff enormous phallus, which he held in front of him between his hands. It was so thick his fingers couldn't close around it, and so tall it protruded to his chin. Along its naked sides long lines of words were cut into the stone, and single words into the spaces between his knuckles.

The biter stood behind me and reached out to touch its bulbous head, where it swelled out above the statue's hands. 'It is Angkhdt,' he said softly. 'Prophet of God. The dog-headed master. It's sad, isn't it, that it would come to this?'

Questions, hard tenses, gods. I hated him. I hummed a

few phrases of an anger song, a melody called 'I'm warning you', but the biter took no notice. 'Where is the barbarian?' he asked.

I turned to face him, furious. How could he force me to remember? The man was dead, gone, vanished out of mind. Time had closed its hand. In those days we were in love with a lie, that objects could disappear into the air, that there was no past, no future, that people needed the touch of my hand in order to exist, the image in my eye.

It was a lie I cherished rather than believed. In fact, I remembered very well. And I wanted him to know what had happened. I wanted him to know the man was dead. And so, though I said nothing, through music I put a little death into the air, a song called 'now it's over', but in a complicated rhythm because I could not cover in my voice a small regret.

The biter listened carefully, tilting his head. With his forefinger, he stroked the underlip of the stone phallus, and his face took on a strange gentle expression. 'They murdered him.' he said. 'Which one?'

How I hated him! Him and his past tense. Him and his questions. Yet there was a power in his hawklike face that made him difficult to resist, a keenness in his eye. I dropped my head and muttered part of a song, my brother's music, the man who had first struck the scholar down.

He recognized it. It was a beautiful song, spare, strong, proud, like the man himself. At the second change, I heard the biter hum a part of it himself, as if in reverie, frowning. He brought his wrists together, and with his whole hand he caressed the angry stump where his other hand had been. 'It is he,' he said softly. 'It is always he. Little brother,' he said, and stretched his hand out to touch me, only I ducked away. 'Little brother,' he continued. 'Don't you see how men like him can kill us all?'

I started away, my face full of disgust, but he smiled and

called out to me: 'I'm sorry. I apologize. No biting. Or at least, only a little. Because I am talking about the future. Don't pretend you never think of it.'

I turned to face him, because I was pretending. He was right. He said: 'I see you. You are different from the rest. I see you. Before. I saw you. The others cannot think. You can.'

I stood appalled. He was trying to seduce me, I could tell. It was the biter's slough of reason, of cause and effect, so easy to fall into, so hard to climb back out. I could feel tears in my eyes, and I bent to pick up a loose stone.

The biter smiled. 'I'm insulting you,' he said. 'Listen. Use your mind. We are beginning to starve. There is no meat left in these mountains. Every day the hunters bring in less. There is none left.'

I listened, hardfaced. This made no sense to me.

'Don't you understand?' he said. 'We have to do it. Something. All together, for the first time. Not just alone. Together.'

I stared at him. This made no sense.

'South of here,' he said. 'Way south, there is no snow. There are deer on the hill. Fish in the water. Listen – every day I talk to the barbarian. The dead barbarian. Every day I come here. I listen to his stories. He is teaching me so much. Now he is dead, yet it is still the truth. He was . . . He told me about it. There is food to eat.'

'I prefer to starve.'

'That's stupid.'

'Yes,' I cried, furious. 'But I am not a slave of my own mind. I am not. I prefer to die. My brothers and sisters are too proud.'

'But I don't meant that,' he said. 'We are not beggars. I mean to take what we want. Steal it. These barbarians are a race of hairy dwarves. Free men and women would burn

23

through them like a fire. And I can make it happen. He was teaching me a trick. A way of singing – don't you understand?'

Bored, I turned away. But there was a peculiar music in his words. He brought his fist crashing down on the tabletop. 'But I can force you,' he shouted. 'I can force you to follow me. There is a power in this room, if I knew how to use it. There is power in these empty gods.' He came towards me, grinning savagely, and I backed away. 'I will do it,' he said. 'I hate your stupidness. And I hate myself.'

He lied. His self-love rang in every word. His voice was like two instruments in conflict, one ferocious, one insinuating. He had been a strong musician, and this music was a storm in him. 'Do not laugh at me!' he shouted, and shook the stump of his arm in my face as if it were a weapon. He was a little crazy, too, I thought, with his bony face, his eyebrows, his dark eyes. In the light of the carbide lantern his shadow made a giant on the wall, reeling drunkenly.

In those days I was easily bored. I knew so few words. And this biter was talking about something. He was using words as a kind of action, and that made me uncomfortable. So I left him, and outside it had begun to snow again. The sky was full of wordless snow. It blunted the edges of the mountains and the buildings, blunted everything, relaxed and calmed me. The dogs were stifled as I slogged away. It was very cold.

'What is he talking about?' whispered Thanakar Starbridge. 'What did he call us, a race of hairy dwarves?'

Prince Abu wiped the sweat from his fat face. 'It's perfectly true,' he muttered, giggling. 'At least in your case.' He was already drunk, staring down into the bottom of his winecup with unfocused eyes.

Thanakar stretched out his leg and looked around the

24

dark interior of the warehouse. Shadows flickered among piles of cinder blocks and garbage. 'It's a bit much, him calling us barbarians,' he yawned, touching his wristwatch. Nearby, a woman squatted over the fire, feeding it with handfuls of dung.

'Shhh. Quiet!' whispered the prince. 'He's beginning again.'

The antinomial had dozed off momentarily, but now he roused himself. He sat for a while, nodding and fingering his flute, and then took up his recitation near the place where he had broken off. And when he started, he spoke in the guttural singsong which of all his modes was hardest to understand. He said:

My lords, that night a volcano burst up on the ridge somewhere, and my brothers and sisters and I went up to see – nothing, as it turned out, nothing but smoke and steam. It rained, and in the valley you could hear the trees exploding like distant gunshots, like gunshots where the hot stones spattered on the ice. The clouds reflected a dull glow from far away, that was all. We froze. I thought the night went on forever. That night I thought the world had changed, and perhaps it had, because in the morning the sun was late in coming, I could tell. It rose late out of a smelly mist, and we shivered and whispered, coming home over the ice. From far away we could see a fire burning in our town, and we laughed and ran down the last ridge, in through the gates, under the belltower, up past the longhouses and barns. In those days before the soldiers came, our town was built of logs and mud, among the ruins of an older place. The stone walls, the tower, the eternal well, all that was ancient barbarism. We had built our windowless, dark halls on their foundations.

Outside the dancing hall, the biter had made a great bonfire. With biter friends he had slaved together a wooden wagon with heavy wooden wheels and had pulled the stone table and Angkhdt's statue from the mountainside, all the way down from the empty city. He had drawn his cart up to the bonfire, the open end facing outward, and the firelight shining through the braces and the wooden spokes. He stood in it as if on a stage, the fire at his back. Beneath him, my brothers and my sisters shambled around the stone table, and they admired its blunt surface and the lewd god astride it.

We heard the biter's voice. He had been a great musician once, but now he used his voice to bite us. He used the thing that he had learned from the barbarian. He had combined barbarian magic with a new way of singing. He could make pictures in the air. And he was using them to bite us, for in those days nothing could bind my stupid family like fire, like dancing; he capered above them in a black flapping robe, his mutilated arm held crazily aloft, and they stood in the slush with their mouths open. At first I didn't listen. For I was watching for the sunrise, and as I stood on the outskirts of the crowd, pushing towards the heat, I saw a little way in front of me the neck and shoulders of my sister, wedged in between some others. She was close enough to touch, almost, a girl almost ripe, older than I. I could only see part of her head, but I knew that it was she, because around her I always felt a sad mix of feelings, so I wriggled forward until I stood behind her. Her yellow hair ran down her back. My mind was full of it, full of the barbarian luxury of it. Yet even so the biter's melody broke in, and I looked up to see him dancing and reeling. He was a powerful man. He could make pictures out of music. In his singing I could see the barbarian city on the mountain as it was when men still lived there, the paint still fresh on the buildings. His voice was full of holes. Yet even so, I saw that barbarian city so clearly, and a crowd of people standing in the square. I saw the colors of their clothes and the lines of their faces. In a central square of yellow stone, of high, flat buildings, lines of open windows, hanging balconies, a group of huntsmen dismounted. They were dressed in leather and rich clothes, red and brilliant green. A huge horse stood without a rider, and beside it, chained by one wrist to the empty stirrup, naked and dusty, his great dog's head bent low, knelt the barbarian god. He had careful, yellow, dog's eyes. Nearby, a pale boy, wounded in the chase perhaps, lay dead or dying on the stones, surrounded by slaves and sad old men. The sun burned, and the god waited, sweating in the dirty shade around the horse's legs, until they brought a wooden cage and chained his hands and feet, and prodded him inside with long thin poles; he lay in one corner and licked along his arm.

This is a story from the Song of Angkhdt. As we listened, standing near the fire with our mouths open, people said they saw the statue move, and some claimed that the lines of symbols on its swollen penis seemed to glow. I know nothing about that. But as stupid as it sounds, my lords, I did hear a voice out of its stone head, for the music had stopped suddenly, and the vision had disappeared. It was a curious, airless kind of voice, and either the language was unknown to me or else I was too far away to understand. But I understood the biter. He was speaking too. 'Listen to God's laws,' he said. 'Love freedom. Love freedom more than death. Be kind to one another,' things like that, laws and hateful rules. That biter was a crazy man. So much loneliness, so much gnawing on his biter's heart had made him mad. He was searching for a god to make him king, to force us to follow after him, yet how could he have thought that we would stand still and listen to that kind of song? In fact, he must have quickly realized his mistake, for all around, people were moving and touching themselves, the magic broken. In front of me, the girl had turned away and put her fingers to her head.

I was bored and angry, but not for long, because the biter started to sing again. In his voice I saw the god lying in darkness, in a wooden cage. It was empty night in the barbarian city, and I saw him raise his silver head just as a dog would have, for towards him over the flagstones flowed a rivulet of water – down one street, down another, out into the open square. He was waiting for it. And as it came, a gentle wind ran through the city, starting out of nothing, then subsiding. The god yawned, and passed his hand along the bars of his cage. He rubbed it slowly, rhythmically, coaxing some greenness back into the dead wood; slowly at first, imperceptibly, he sealed the wounded bark, he rubbed it whole. Under the cage the flagstones split apart as roots spread down. And in the iron joints the first leaves appeared, one, and then more, tiny and weak at first, but gathering strength and number until the cage had disappeared and Angkhdt lay as if in a leafy thicket or a wood, a gentle wind stirring the branches, while in the houses women woke next to their sleeping mates, and shook themselves awake and looked around.

Again the vision broke. I heard the statue speak again, louder this time, and this time I could understand, for I was looking for the magic, and so was everybody else. That way it claimed our minds. It said: 'You are my chosen people. Free men and women, free as fire. Like the fire you will grow and spread. For I have chosen a way . . .' It went on for a long time, telling us to take our things and leave our town, telling us to follow this biter and make war with him. In the crowd, some stood without listening, warming their hands, but others shouted angrily, and one climbed up into the open cart. He grabbed the biter from behind, one arm across his stomach, the other on his throat. He lifted him up off his feet, lifted him up kicking, and dropped him over the side of the cart into the crowd. Then there was quiet. My brother was in the cart, standing up alone. We were used to him, watching him dance, so we just stood there, watching. He raised his arms above his head and clenched his fists, and leaped the distance from the cart on to the tabletop. He kicked the dog-headed statue in the chest, and it turned on its base and fell heavily to the ground, legs in the air. The biter cried out and struggled forward through the crowd, but nobody looked at him because my brother, limping and twisting on one foot, had raised his hands above his head and started to dance. It was tentative and slow, a dance we all knew, a dance which belonged to us, part of all of us. All of us could dance it in our different ways. It was the song of freedom, of namelessness, the triumph of our race, and so poignant, too, to see him dancing with his broken foot, it gave each step a special transience. My brother danced, and the crowd spread out away from him, because this was the kind of dance that tells you not to stand together in a group, thinking the same thoughts.

My brother pulled a knife out from his clothes and danced with it, and now from the crowd came up a kind of music, hesitant at first, but stronger and stronger as it became clear to us what he was going to do. Our voices, young and old, rough and smooth, searched for a common music, making it out of nothing, and some had carried their instruments with them, and some ran to fetch theirs, and all clapped their hands and sang – we didn't know this music. But like the dance it came together as we sang, more sure with every motion, every note. It sang of freedom, sang of emptiness, and it came together as if out of our own empty hearts. My brother danced a long time. And in the end, everybody knew it; we forced him with our voices, we built him to a climax, and at the end of it he drew the knife around his neck, once, twice, in perfect rhythm to the dance, a scarlet string around his neck – too tight, for he tried to sing then and couldn't, for his mouth was full of blood. He spat it out, and summoning his strength, he sang a song that was not like singing nor like anything.

And as he sang, a shadow rose, and it got dark. The sun was hidden in a cloud of frozen dust, remains of the volcano we had seen the night before. Sticks and pieces of dirt fell from the sky. Horses cried out and kicked their stalls. People gathered together, cursing in the filthy dark. We ran inside out of the storm, and then the biter spoke again, and said in plain language that he was running south with others of his kind, to bring some war into the cities there. He said the storm was some barbarian god. He said it was a sign. People clustered around him, desperate and afraid, but more prepared to go off by themselves, according to our custom of leaving and never coming back. They prepared to ride out north, perhaps, alone. They had no maps. They prepared to ride out into the unbroken snow. For some it was as if they had found a sudden reason to do as they had always wanted. The mud lay inches thick on all the beds. It seemed pointless to clear it all away.

My lords, a child's mind is not to be relied on. If I thought that you were interested in the truth, I suppose I would keep silent. Yet I have carried these images with me, and now I unpack them, some for the first time. And always I am tempted to describe my life as if to an empty room, as if the words could simply disappear. Tempted and not tempted, for the bitterness is that I have changed and not just gotten older. Here in your sad city I have let a world collect around me, opinions, objects, thoughts; I have found a name. Nor can I claim compulsion. I have made myself a slave, and now I look around me through a slave's eyes, that's all. Therefore I have become very fine in my distinctions, and I think I was mistaken. I think now the volcano and the mudstorm came some other time. Reason tells me now there must have been a period when people came to their own conclusions and rode out, too hungry to stay, but how could we measure time in that blank winter, with our blank minds? When my mothers and fathers were growing up, there were still seasons in the lives of animals, but in that last phase of winter, when I was a child, there were no more fawns, no cubs, no colts, no pups, no calves, no goslings, no sweet lambs, and after that the hills were empty. We went hungry. Why would people stand for it, who had a choice?

I remember a full town and an empty one. And there was a mudstorm, yes. The sky was black; stones fell from the sky. I huddled in my muddy bed. People yelled and ran. And I remember waking up one morning to new snow. New snow was falling. I walked out to the open space in front of my house. The stone table was there, and the dog-headed statue on its back in the new snow. Our town was empty. Or rather, the children were left. Those who hadn't had the strength to go. They came out one by one, my brothers and my sisters, with white, muddy faces. There was not a sound.

I walked over to the gate. Broken instruments littered the ground, sifted over with snow. Departing during the storm, people had stood shouting over the noise of the wind, their baggage around them in fat bags, the horses kicking and stamping in the frozen mud. One by one, men and women had pulled on their knapsacks and swung themselves up into their saddles, leaving what they could not carry. And as they walked their horses through the tower gate, their instruments in their hands, some would bend down and break them on the stone gatepost, and others would stand up in the stirrups and break them on the arch above their heads. I kicked through fretboards, mutes, and reeds.

Some older children had been able to seize the strength

to go, and women had taken the youngest ones, their own or someone else's, for tangled reasons. Those left behind were of the age which no one loves, and I was one of these.

We took our blankets from the abandoned halls and all moved into one, except for a few of the proudest. But these soon took horses and rode out, not knowing where, I suppose, or where else but to their deaths. The rest of us lived together in one hall, and kept a fire burning. For nothing reduces people to barbarity quicker than hunger. We developed barbarous habits. We sat together and discussed things. Looking back, that seems like the worst part. Then, the worst part was going to bed hungry, was the interminable waiting to grow up.

There was a girl with yellow hair, as tall as I. How can I describe my feelings? They were a source of shame to me. She lit a fire in the hall and danced for us a little. I scraped the mud away from part of the floor and built a pile of pillows next to her bed. I should have stayed away in the farthest corner. She was not musical or strong, a great hunter or a great dancer. But I wanted her, even though I knew that wanting is a trick of the mind. It is like stooping to believe a lie. For days I would go off alone, hunting in the snow, fishing, yet at night I would sit and watch her shake her hair loose down her bare back. She had a face – how shall I say – unmarked by pride. That is our flaw, in general, the way barbarians are hairy, with rotten teeth and foul breath. Our men and women had proud faces, and if they laughed it was for a reason: because after a cold day they had brought a buck down with one shot. Or because another had missed. Or because in the midst of day they could hear nothing but their own music. Yet this girl would laugh about nothing. She saw no stain in kindness, and perhaps she was adapting to new circumstances, but I thought rather it was something true to her. The men and women of our race have hungry bodies – clean-limbed and hard – but already hers was made for giving. She had full breasts, wide hips, round arms and legs.

The snow went on forever, and then a new season came, a dark, false season. It was the Paradise thaw, the last phase of winter, though how could we have known? The sun barely shone. The snow melted, for a while. The grass grew white and yellow, but it did grow, and in a biter's house we had found a store of corn. The taste was poisonous, but I was glad to be alive, because the world was strangely beautiful during the thaw. The trees never recovered their leaves. In the valleys, in the white grass, they stood up dead with naked arms. And it was always dark, for at this time the sun crept blood-red along the horizon all day, rising and setting between the jagged peaks, the colored clouds like sunset all the morning and midday, the shadows long and heavy. At night it was almost brighter – you could ride all night, because during the thaw a new planet appeared, Paradise, you call it, another world, and it burned with a dead light above our heads. That first night it took up half the sky. The dogs howled and cried out. Barbarians worship Paradise, but I knew nothing of that yet. At first I was afraid.

The air was still. There was not a breath of wind. There was no rain, although the ground was wet with stagnant water everywhere. No dogs gave birth. Plants grew, yes, but the stalks had lost their stiffness – they grew flat and tangled on the ground like the hair on a man's head. The air seemed hard to breathe and full of queasy echoing. There was no nourishment in it. Noises close at hand seemed far away. And in the high pastures our ears buzzed and rang; we walked our horses and held on to their manes. It was a different kind of living. People slept all day, and even awake they were part asleep.

It is easy to describe these things as if the world had died overnight. But soon we remembered nothing different. These changes, though they sound tremendous, came subtly and gradually. I thought I was growing up. My body had changed more than the air. And though every day I was filled with sleepy awe, though in everything I saw the promise of my death – the stark trees, the plants twisting along the ground – I was more concerned with hunger, and more concerned with sleeping next to that girl every night. I wanted there to be a way of touching her, but it was impossible. I would sit awake, looking at the heap of blankets next to me. Perhaps she would have responded to my touch. Yet I was afraid I was not capable. I had seen it often enough. And barbarians can copulate like animals, but I thought I was not yet quite enough of a barbarian for that. There were physical differences, I had heard. Besides, what should I do? Should I say . . . something, should I reach out my hand? Men and women drank to frenzy before they could surrender to desire. They drank a wine we had, and then they dreamed a numb, erotic dream. In the morning they remembered nothing and could look at each other without shame. Women had no men, children no fathers. The slavery would have been intolerable, for in this act of loving there is always slave and master, victory and defeat. We were too proud for that – too proud for love, for tenderness.

But the temptation made me bitter, and I saw her sweating like a pig that season, her and a few others, planting and digging. I told myself she had surrendered to a biter's foresight, finding a biter's comfort in the dirt, the sweat, the feeble grain. It was not food for human beings. But with a biter's caution, she saw that soon we would be so hungry we would be eating dogs and horse meat. She had found a taste for choices. She took corn and ground it to a pulp, and mixed it with hot water – edible, perhaps, but deadly to the heart. We blamed her for it. We would slink up to the pot and put our hands in it, angry and sullen because we found ourselves grateful, I suppose. We would have starved on what human food we had. Or we would have had to kill our animals. Horses, always docile, had learned to eat grass, though it made them sick and listless. But our dogs had higher stomachs. Already they fought one another and devoured the carcasses, and in this we might have seen a wild premonition of ourselves, had not my sister showed us we were more like horses.

And in time I came to admire her for her serenity, her way of laughing at our sulkiness. Besides, I had begun to notice biting tendencies in myself. I discovered the importance of things I never would have noticed. One of the younger children was very sick. He had started to die. He was a sniveling little boy, with a sniveling weak face, but it was as if I found a strange compulsion to memorize everything about him, every sickness, every change. I could feel I was robbing him of his own death, for it was as if I had clenched my hands around his spirit, and as if his spirit was escaping not from another room, not from some private place, but from between my fingers. But finally he escaped me.

That day the sun shone blood-red on the pale grass, and I was walking with my horse among some trees. I will describe the place. Among dead trees a brook widened into a clear pool, a small thing, water coiling on a cold rock. I found a single, leather, child's boot. A boot like many others, but with the biter's part of my mind I recognized it. It had belonged to the little boy.

In winter, a field of snow stretches unblemished to the horizon, but you have only to look behind you to see your own trampled mark, ephemeral and confused, a dream in the pure wilderness of sleep. I thought, what difference can it make to me where the child is? If he were dead, then he was on that hillside where the snow never broke beneath his feet, not in front of him, not behind. He had become part of the world's intolerable beauty. Where was the sadness in that thought? Where was the sadness in death? Yet I was not happy, because no matter how hard you try to be free – and when I was a child we did try – people have dark in them as well as light. They have deep, biting instincts in their heart of hearts. They are like the dark world with Paradise around it.

I reached for the boot. It was a good one, fur-lined, but with the remnants of some decoration. I held it in my hand, trying to forget, until above me on the hillside, a boy came running down. Dogs were with him, barking and excited. He carried dead animals from the end of a long pole, and now he swung the pole up over their heads and kicked them as they snarled and jumped. He capered down the hillside out of breath, the dogs around him. And when he passed me, he stopped and swung the pole above my head.

I saw the naked tail hang down from one of them. 'Rabbits,' I said.

'Rabbits,' he repeated proudly.

'Look what I have,' I said.

He seemed doubtful. I held the boot out by the heel, and he took it, saw it was too small for him, cast it on the bank. I admired the sparseness of his mind. 'Boot,' he said.

I explained what I was feeling as well as I could. He understood me, or rather understood the words, the music, the sense, but not the point. I could tell he thought me strange to concern myself when there must be other children still alive who fit my vague descriptions. But he retrieved the boot, examined it more closely, threw it down again. And, sick of listening, he said, 'Come eat,' and leapt away from rock to rock, brandishing his pole, humming part of a song called 'I forget'.

I did not follow, even though the smell of dead meat swinging near my head had lit in me a burning hunger. I turned and walked up to where I had left my horse. I knelt by the stream and ran my fingers in the water. It had gotten dark, but even in the darkness I could see the shadows of the trees. And when I stood up to lead the horse away, I saw that he held between the cruel ridges of his beak a child's severed hand. He was sucking on it the way barbarians eat candy. I reached up, and he pulled his head away and glared at me; he had been scratching for toads in the flaccid grass and had found something better. I let him be.

The air was perfectly still. The grass grew thick where I stood in a bowl-like indentation in the slope, lined with trees and slabs of stone. Paradise had risen, once again, up over the mountain crests, and rinsed the grass with silver light. And from one tree there came a drip, drip, drip. Something hung from a rope among the lower branches. It circled quietly in the quiet air.

I walked up the slope until I stood beneath the tree. I reached out and caught some of the drops. In that light they had no color of their own, but it was blood, of course. I knew it by the feel and smell and taste, and it awakened in me a hunger like the smell of my brother's rabbits – blood past its first freshness. I stood admiring the light until a little pool had formed in my palm. Beneath the tree, the grass lay crushed, as if an animal had rolled in it.

A child's body had been tied up like a package. It rotated slowly at the end of a rope, and I saw the rope was barbarian-made, because of its contemptibly high quality.

I climbed up into the tree. A child had been strangely mutilated, his eyes dug away, his tongue cut out. Only his torso and his head remained; his arms and legs had been severed at the joints and carried away. His strange, empty head fell loosely from side to side as the rope rotated. His neck must have been broken. Standing on a low branch, I reached out to shake the silken rope, to make the body jerk and dance. It was my little brother.

I climbed down. My horse was already nosing at the grass, but I pulled it free, down the slope. There was no space to ride, but in a little while the trees gave out into a grassy meadow. And there I swung myself into the saddle. Paradise was bright like day, and the horse uneasy, pulling at his rope. At first I thought it was from horsey love of open spaces, until I smelled what it smelled: once again, the smell of death. The grass had been trampled in a muddy track down towards the town, as if a troop of men and horses had passed together. That was unusual enough. But in the middle of it lay the body of dog, a great noble brute, silver in the gleaming starlight. His silver fur was seething, alive in the shadows of the grass. But he was stone dead, lying on his side, his heavy head stretched out in the mud. I walked my horse around him in a circle.

Farther on, over the next hillside, I found my brother's body, the boy whom I had seen that evening, running down the mountain, full of laughing plans for dinner and the love of running.

I dismounted. He had been shot with an expanding bullet through the back and had fallen with his arms in front of him. His stick had broken under him, and the rabbits were trampled in the mud. They had shot another dog there too, shot it in the side and disemboweled it later, it seemed. And again, the boy's face was mutilated, as if they had tried to carve a letter or a sign into his features.

I gathered together my brother's scattered arrows. There was no bow, but that morning I had taken mine, taken my knives and steel sling-shot – tools for hunting. And when the track of horses broke away uphill again, I followed it up into the fields beneath a mountain slope of red volcanic stone. It was a place I knew well. At one time, biters had brought their sheep up here to graze on insects incubating in the snow; they had lit fires and stayed for a long time. I had come, too, with my childish music, or with some childish problem only a biter could resolve – an earache, a hole in my boot. And now the grass lay thick and white, and it dragged at my horse's feet. His claws got stuck in it, and sometimes he came near to stumbling, for I spurred him hard, driven by my anger, until we broke the crest of a steep hill, and I saw in the valley underneath us a bonfire.

I dismounted and ran down through the fields. The fire seemed enormous. Close at hand, I could only see outlines and shadows, but on the far side, the hot light painted their faces and their clothes. They were barbarians, small hairy men in black uniforms, squatting near the fire. They had heated up some orange mash of vegetables in a metal pot and were eating out of metal cups. I was happy not to smell it close. But I could hear them talking, and I was amazed to realize I could understand what they were saying, though the accents were harsh and ugly, the verbs unfamiliar. There was no music in it, yet even so there was something more than words, for they shouted and laughed and seemed content. I saw that they were drinking. They were drunk. I crept closer. One said, 'Even so, you shouldn't have shot the bitch.'

'It tried to bite me.'

They were talking about the dogs, I thought, though it was hard to tell. I felt a strange thrill listening to their voices, watching their clumsy movements. They were so small, so ugly, with flat, hairy, intelligent faces, full of thoughts and knowledge. Dark skin, dark eyes, dark hair hanging down their backs, gathered at their necks in metal rings.

They finished their food, and they sat drinking, smoking cigarettes, talking about places I had never heard of, things I didn't know. It made a kind of sense. One played the

guitar in a way I had no words for. He said, 'Let's see if
she will dance for us. I'd like to see her dance.'

'You let her be. You know what our orders are.'

'Our orders are to kill them as we find them. I could
report you both for keeping her alive.'

One laughed: 'That's all right. She's just a girl.'

'Yes, that's right. She's a meat-eating bitch. And an·
atheist. You leave her be.'

One laughed: 'Admit it, you like her.'   .

I found it hard to understand who was talking. Yet even
so it made a kind of sense. There was a fat, older man. He
said: 'Well maybe she does look more like a woman than
some others. I don't care. She's still built like a bear. She
still stinks like dead bodies. She stinks like the bodies she
eats.'

'I hear they are beautiful dancers,' said the one playing
the guitar. He plucked out a series of low peculiar notes. 'I
find her attractive,' he said.

There was much I didn't understand. But I was fascinated. The older man rose to urinate outside the circle of
light. He was a leader, perhaps. He stood facing me, his
legs apart, staring outward blindly, and I thought I could
puncture his fat stomach like a bag. The other man put
down his guitar and got to his feet. Not far away, on the
other side of the fire, they had tied their horses in a group,
And they had a girl there, my sister, a prisoner. They had
tied her hands in front of her, and the guitar man went and
got her. I could hear him talking, and she got up from the
ground. I saw her shadow cover his. Yet he must have
been stronger than he looked, or braver, or stupider. He
pulled her roughly by her knotted wrists, down the bare
slope from the trees where they had left her with the
animals, until she stood in the firelight, humiliated, her
shoulders bent. I recognized her, though they had tied a
cloth bag over her head. I recognized her body – naked

40

from the waist, her wide hips. Her legs were spattered with mud, and she was bleeding from a wound on the outside of her thigh. Her feet were bare.

They had built their fire in a space between some large rocks, and I was watching their shadows on the uneven surface. At first the flames were high, their shadows long and menacing, but now the fire had settled somewhat. And when I saw my sister with them, they no longer seemed so fearsome. Without thinking, I had thought that there were lots of them, but there were not. Barbarians have names for any kind of quantity; they are in love with numbers. But such things are difficult for us. There, that night, there were not many: the fat man, the musician, and another with a long gun standing up between his knees. I could see the shadow of it on the rock.

The musician pulled the bag away from her face, and I saw her tangled yellow hair, her nose, her heavy lips. She was beautiful. He must have thought so too, for he put his fingers to her face and to her hair, catching at the tangles, pulling them back from her forehead. And when he forced her face into the light, I felt a sudden surge of joy. I was happy to see her. Happy to see her proud and unafraid, for there was nothing in her eyes but hatred. I could almost hear the song of it, but the barbarian could not. He pushed the hair back from her face, and she let him touch her without moving, touch her bruised cheeks, her torn and broken lips. He said, 'Don't be afraid. We won't hurt you. Understand?' She made no movement. 'Don't be afraid,' he repeated. 'Here, drink,' and he brought a cup of something to her mouth. She swallowed it in silence. She finished it. 'Here,' he said, and squatting, he pulled a square of cloth out from beneath his shirt. There was a plastic bucket on the ground; he wet the napkin and stood up again to clean her face. 'There,' he said. 'We mean you no harm.'

41

One sat on the rocks, fingering his gun. 'There's no point in talking,' he said. 'It can't understand you.'

'I think she can. Can you?' he asked her. 'Would you like something to eat? You must be hungry.' She shook her head. 'You see?' he said, gesturing to his companions. 'You see? She understands. My name is . . .' something, he said, pointing to himself.

The fat one laughed. He was squatting near the fire, poking at it with a stick.

My sister brought her hands up to her face. I saw the cords had cut into her wrists. 'Free me,' she said, her voice naked, empty of significance. She thought that otherwise they wouldn't understand.

They stared at her. 'Free me,' she repeated carefully. 'What do you want from me?'

The man with the gun stood up. 'Beloved Angkhdt,' he whispered, and even the other one, the musician, took a step back from her uncertainly. And then he smiled and stuck his tongue out of his mouth. 'She understands,' he said. And then he turned away. 'I think I love her,' he said to the fat man.

The fat man laughed. He was drunk.

'No,' the other said again. 'I think I do. She's beautiful. She's like an animal.' And he turned back to face her, and showed her his tongue, and said something I didn't understand. But later I would come to recognize that famous verse of scripture which begins, 'Oh my sweet love, let us be free as wild beasts, free as dogs, and let us kiss one another mouth to tail, like the wild dogs . . .'

He stuck his tongue out of his mouth. The fat man laughed. 'You're disgusting,' he said.

'No. Nothing like that. You have to take what you can find. I think she's beautiful. Look at her. Look at her arms.'

'Yes, look at them. Just be careful. Female or not.'

'She's a female all right. You'll see.'

'I'm warning you. Don't be a fool.'

The musician shrugged. 'I think she's beautiful.' And then he paused and smiled, and said to her, 'We heard you were a dancer. That's why we captured you.'

She shook her hair back from her face and brought her joined hands up to show him. The rope was biting her cruelly; I could see it and could hear it when she talked. 'Free me.' They were too deaf to hear the mixed intentions in her voice.

The musician licked his lips. He was standing in front of her, between her and the fire, looking at her body, her naked legs, her sex. She wore the remnants of a sheepskin shirt, and her arms were bare. And yes, she was beautiful, yes, and he thought so too. He was a slave to beauty. He reached to touch her, cupping his palm around the bone of her hip. 'We mean you no harm,' he said. 'We'll let you go, don't worry about that. You're safe with us.' He was smiling, and working his thumb into her skin as if to soothe her, staring up into her face. Even in his smile I could see his nervousness; still, he met no resistance when he slid his hand, so slowly, down along the bone of her hip, across her leg, down to the hair between her legs. He plucked at it and curled it between his fingers. And then he brought his hand up to his face, to sniff it and spit from his smiling mouth into his palm, but I could see he was still nervous, nervous when he put it back between her legs, nervous as he rubbed his spit into her sex. He was standing close to me, for I had crept so close. He faced away from me, the fire between us, and I could see the fingers of his other hand gripped tight behind his back, gripped tight around the handle of a knife hung upside down between his shoulder blades, and he gripped it nervously as he was rubbing spit into her sex. The other men were excited too, one standing with his long gun, the fat one sitting forward, smoking. Paradise was down, and the fire was low, neglected. And I also was excited. I knew that she was going to kill him if he freed her hands. I took an arrow from my belt.

She smiled. And this was hard for me to believe: the barbarian went down on his knees in front of her, turning his face to inhale, and then burrowing his face between her legs, kissing and licking her. And in a little while she opened her knees, and he passed his hands under her, hidden from my sight, but I felt something just by looking at her face. She had drawn her lips away from her teeth. And she had let her wrists, tied together in front of her, sink slowly down, her fingers stretched, grasping at nothing, until she put her hands on to his head, burying her fingers in his hair. I heard her breathe. And then she let her neck sink too, until she was looking down at him and I could see her eyes. She was crying, making no noise. But quiet tears were running down her cheeks and down her chin, down her neck and into her hair. Crying is not common among us. But she thought she was going to die, and perhaps a little softness is best, at the end. She worked her fingers into his hair. And then she pulled him to his feet, softly, gently, because he was eager, too; he stumbled to his feet and stood in front of her, still smiling, and he passed the back of his hand across his lips. Then she touched him. She put her hands down to touch the front of his pants, and then she looked him in the face, her eyes shining with tears. She smiled. This was the moment, and he hesitated. But she stared at him, the yellow hair around her cheeks, her wet eyes – she was so beautiful. And I suppose he must have known it too, in his own way, because again he reached behind his back and loosened the knife there. He hesitated, and then he drew it out, the short cruel blade, and he brought it around between them and tested the cruel edge along his palm. But she was still standing with her legs apart, the dew of some moisture

44

shining on her sex, and she had bent her shoulders to hide the difference in their heights. For whatever the reason, for the sake of his own pride, he pulled the blade under her wrists and cut them apart. The ropes fell away; I had crept close, I could see the marks. And I could see her tense the muscles in her hands, testing their strength, opening and closing her fingers. She slid her hand into his pants. I waited for his yell, even though it took a little while – she was caressing his forearm below the hand which held the knife, running her fingernail along the vein. He had given away all of his power. And in a little while he realized it. He had closed his eyes, but then they started open; he cried out and raised his knife, and she grabbed him under the wrist. The others were slow to respond, because they understood the noises he was making in another way, at first. But she was squeezing his testicles to jelly. And I saw the one who had been standing still as stone, holding his long gun, come suddenly to life. I shot him in the throat, in the chest, in the arm, and he fell over into the fire.

The fat man didn't move, though I was waiting for him. I had nocked another arrow and had pulled it back. Yet he just sat there, his fat stomach in his hands. He was afraid. I came close into the firelight, and I could see him – he was afraid of death, and it made it hard for him to think. He had no weapons, yet he reached for none, nothing, not a movement, though his body was tense. Nothing, only he had opened his eyes wide, opened his mouth, and he had dropped his cigarette. His hands were shaking, grasping stiffly at nothing as I squatted down in front of him. I was not a frightening sight – hungry, barely grown, old clothes, ripped leather, filthy fur. Nothing to be afraid of, except death like the black night around him, and the fire burning low. I stuck my knife into his face, hurting his cheek with the ragged steel. 'Holy beloved God,' he croaked, 'don't hurt me,' but it was as if he wasn't really paying attention. And maybe it was hard for him to think because his friend was screaming hoarsely, without pause. Not that it mattered, for he was already finished: she had bent his hand back over his shoulder, cracking the bone, and his knife was useless. Yet still he kicked at her with his feet and hit her with his free hand, with his head, but it didn't matter, he was finished. The hand around his testicles had lifted him up almost off the ground. And in a little while he stopped struggling and started to cry, as she had done, yet different, too, because the pain was different. He had words and no music, and no tears either, just a rhythm of breath and a contorted mouth, and she stood staring at him, trying to understand him, her quiet face so close to him, her tears dry. How could she understand? She made a quick movement, and his knife fell to the stones. She let go of his wrist and joined her hands together on his sex, hoisting him up still farther. And when he hung limp from her hands, she dropped him to the dirt, and he curled up like a baby, his shoulders shaking, his face turned to the ground.

Then she danced for them as they had asked, for them and for me, too, on the mountainside, in the white, fragile grass, by the dying fire. It was the darkest part of the night. It had gotten cold. The man had curled himself around her feet, and she stepped free of him. Turning her back, she walked a few steps away, and I could see her tiredness in the way she walked. She walked to where the bucket stood, and she stooped to wash her face in it, to wash her arms. She stood up, her back still towards us, and with a simple, awkward movement she let her shirt slip from her shoulders. I could see the firelight on her body, the muscles, the flesh. She pulled her hair back and held it in a knot behind her neck. Then she released it and squatted down again over the bucket, washing herself, scooping up the water and pouring it over her, rubbing her arms. She was using a language of movement that belongs to little girls. The water was cold, I could tell. And I could see it dripping down her back, catching the light, dripping from her legs, scattering in circles when she shook her head. The black night was all around us, and I could feel something opening in my body like an empty hand. I sat cross-legged by the fire. I had taken the gun. The fat man had not moved. At one point he had seemed eager to speak, until I pointed the gun's long barrel at him through my knees and put my finger to my lips. The other had huddled himself together and sat nursing himself, his head bowed, his lips wet. He was watching my sister with pale eyes, so that it was by looking at him and listening to his breathing suddenly change that I first saw a new difference in the language of her body. She was dancing.

Death is the dark mountain where the snow never breaks beneath your feet. To believe in something else, to believe in something after death, that is a savage temptation, and only savages succumb to it. Myself, I would never want to live in a world that had not contained that moment: I watched her a long time. I watched her until she was weak and near collapse. For a long time she kept her back to us, and when she turned around I could see she had been wounded in the side – not much blood now, but I could see the wound was deep. I noticed that among the other things, her breasts, her tangled hair, her beauty, the light painting her body. And the way language vanished from her arms when she saw me – her eyes were partly closed; she opened them and let her head fall forward. And I was overcome with tenderness. I stood up and stepped towards her. She was close to falling, and I stretched out my hand. She came unsteadily, like a drunk, accepting my arm around her like a drunk. This was the first time that I touched her. She was shivering with cold.

Their clothes were too small for us, but we took their riding capes, and in one saddlebag I found larger stuff: a loose red shirt – velvet embroidered with silver thread – and heavy pants. My sister put them on. The rest we left, and left them their lives, too, because they seemed to value them. They squatted near the fire as if numbed by a narcotic, making no movement even when we turned our backs.

It was late when we rode away, near the red dawn. The stars were already dim, covered in a silky haze. My sister was tired, nodding to sleep in the saddle as we came in under the belltower, down through the heavy gateway of our town. She had not spoken once. I dismounted and went to help her, but I had hoped too much – she kicked my hand away and slid down to the ground, standing with her neck bent, her hair over her face, holding on to the horse's mane to keep from falling. But in a little while she gathered her strength and set off across the open stones without looking back. Later, when I came into the hall looking for food, tired after loosing the horses and rubbing them down, she was already asleep in her tangled bed, still in her clothes.

Inside it was still dark, in the entranceway among the beds. Farther on, in the hearth, I could see a pale fire and hear music. Around me people were asleep. I walked among them down the length of the hall. In winter they had never slept so long. They would have been outside by then, trampling the snow, running with the dogs, but in this strange red thaw it was as if the air was starving us. I walked down through the aisles of beds, hearing some flute music from somewhere, a song called 'I don't know'. But it did nothing to ease my mind, for I could see the bodies of some children stretched out on the stones in front of the hearth, their faces mutilated in a way I had already seen. I hated that mark. The barbarians had cut a double line across their brows and a hole through their cheeks, as if they were trying to pollute the emptiness of death with meaning. I hated it; I was unhappy and ashamed to admit it even to myself, for unhappiness, too, is a barbarian ritual. It is the enemy of freedom, and to console myself I thought: things happen by chance. But chance had not killed these children and marked their faces. My lords, you must think we were fools. Now, tonight, it seems so clear – the barbarians had sent soldiers to destroy us. Your bishop had sent soldiers. And even then I knew we were in danger. But we are not easily roused, you can imagine. So I did nothing, thinking that what was clear to me was clear to all. Only I had brought the barbarians' guns, long rifles and belts of ammunition. I threw them down on the stone steps below the stage and turned to go to bed.

I awoke to gunshots. I opened my eyes in stuffy darkness, and for a while I just lay there, listening to the sounds, gunshots and people yelling. I lay there, and in a little while I could see around me and see my sister in the next bed. The night before, she had taken a silver bracelet from a bag of barbarian jewelry. It had been fashioned into a pattern of fighting beasts; now she held her arm above her head, moving her wrist from side to side, examining the effect, not altogether happy. 'They mean to kill us,' she said, in a voice heavy with sleep. This was something she knew, something she had been told; doubtless the barbarian soldiers had told her, for even in a few notes I knew the mode, and I could hear no self, no speculation in it. I understood she was repeating something she had heard the night before. She continued: 'They have a prince . . . a priest . . . a parson, who tells them what to do.'

These words meant nothing to her, I could tell. And I

lost interest. I was more interested in the gunshots, the bracelet, her white wrist. I sat up, rubbing my eyes and saying, 'Why?' to make her talk again. But that was all she knew. She made an answer, but I could hear a part of her own music in it. She was expressing an opinion, and so I listened only to the sound. I loved the sound of her. Some of her melodies I can no longer live without. They have become a part of my own music, part of myself, my own heart's song. My lords, why am I telling you this? It is not the place. And if, then, it was part of my thoughts, it was only a small part. For I was listening to the gunshots. I thought, I will never see her again. And so my image of her then is a special burden: reclining in the half-light in a pile of dirty blankets, her red clothes already rumpled, studying the bracelet on her wrist, her skin the color of honey, her yellow hair, her yellow eyes. Her dark eyebrows – there was no delicacy in her face, no art.

Death is the dark mountain where the snow never breaks beneath your feet. Yet something in the way she looked made it hard to bear the thought of dying. And I cursed my weakness, for a free man comes to love death as a drunkard loves his bottle. It is painful to have reasons to live. And so I turned away from her, and in a little while I got to my feet and wandered outside into the sunlight.

I wandered towards the gate. Barbarians were there. You could hear them trying to break in, the rhythm of their hammers on the wooden beams, the lash of the whip, the beat of the cursed drum. I closed my eyes and blocked my ears, but even then I could feel the slavish rhythm in my heart and in my pulse, so deep within us runs that barbarian music. Our bodies are not made for the life we want to lead, for freedom, for emptiness – I saw that, I felt it in my body. That drumbeat can't be stopped. Knowing that, it was as if something broke in me, something surrendered. I looked up at my brothers and sisters, perched on the walls and on the roofs of buildings, clutching their weapons and their instruments, watching the soldiers break down the door.

Over me above the gate rose up the ruins of a tower, squat, round, broken, hollow. There was a way of climbing to the top. I had discovered it when I was still a child, a way of scaling the stairless stones up to the remnants of a belfry high up above the town. Belfry, I say – once wooden scaffolding had supported a great bell, silent in my memory, except for when the beams had broken and the bell had fallen with a singing clash, as if waiting for the moment when a man was riding out into the snow, out through the double gate with all the world in front of him. Horse and rider died. Biters had taken days to clear away the wreck, for the bell cut deeply into the frozen ground. I remembered as I climbed the tower, the mass of fallen masonry and metal, the broken horse and man.

As I reached the top, my body full of breath, blood in my head, I could hear music around me. At first it had been part of the air, a low woodwind speaking music as a kind of farewell, and I knew that when I put my head up through the opening, I would be struck full in the face by what the musician saw, the beauty of the sun, the sun glinting on the hills. I heard, without listening, the melodies for all these things – red light on stone, on snow, the blood-red light, light struggling with darkness. I pulled myself up into the belfry and saw my brother lying in the shelter of the broken wall, safe from gunfire, playing his pipe. He had worked his song around the hammering under our feet, using it as rhythm. He did it without thinking, I suppose, out of instinct for the sounds around him. There was no reason why the swing of that barbarian cadence should mean the same to him as to me. Why should he want to stop it? He was right to lie there with his music. There was nothing to be done. But I stepped over his body to the lip of the wall, and far below I could see the soldiers slaving at the gate, hairy men in black uniforms. I kicked the stones along the parapet, testing them for falseness. They did not move, but I grabbed up a loose one, the size of a man's head, and threw it down and watched it fall. There was no effect. I kicked the hunks of masonry, searching for a flaw, but I was not strong enough to break the stones apart, not by myself. I worked at it until my face was hot, and still my brother lay there. I cried out for him to help me, and the music changed a little. I tried to find the words that would make him help me, but there were none; he was still free. But his song was changing, there was pride in it, and hatred, and a shadow of laughter. So I bent down to snatch the instrument out of his mouth, and tried to break it on my knee. A pipe made out of black wood strapped with barbarian silver – it would not break. So I battered it against the rocks until it cracked, and the reed snapped off. Then I threw it back at him as he sat up astonished, his mouth looking for words. He grabbed at me, and I stepped out of reach, up on to the parapet.

For an instant I stood, balanced on the narrow battlement, in full view, with the mountains and the sunlight and the open air around me. It was so beautiful and still. The swing of hammers down below had stopped, the drumbeats scattering into silence. And my brother jumped up to stand beside me, violence in his mind, perhaps, but he did nothing. We just stood there, together in the silence and the shining hills, until there came up from the soldiers below us the sound of a single gunshot. And as I jumped down to safety, I saw him press his hand against his ribs, and saw the blood leak out between his fingers, saw the sudden terror in his face, the thought solidifying there that he was going to die not just soon, but then, right then. I could see the pump of his lungs, hear the low music in his throat, and then he stepped backward into the red, quiet air. Leaning over, I was in time to see him dropping like a stone into that mass of slaves.

A boy falling out of the sky – the image seemed to mean something to them, for down below the soldiers left off their work to gather round his body. They were doing something to him, pulling at him, arranging his limbs in some way. I was too far away to tell. A priest in red robes knelt to cut that mark into his cheeks, but I wasn't paying much attention. I was watching my brothers and my sisters on the walls and rooftops, because the image of the falling boy had captured their minds too, had seized and shaken them, so that they had put their instruments aside. I heard a shout, chaotic and unmusical, and they began to open fire on the soldiers with the guns that I had brought down from the mountain, with bricks and rocks, with a drizzle of arrows. We are a peaceful race, and it amazed me to see the soldiers below scuttle back like insects, out of range. One was wounded, and I heard him yell, a high-pitched screaming, full of unconscious music. He expected to be left behind. But another soldier came running back. Above, the sky was cloudless with no wind, and on the tower top I tried to clear my mind. But I was distracted by the noise outside the gate – the wounded soldier and his friend, one kicking and crying, one scurrying around him in a kind of dance. The man bent down to take his hurt companion on his back. They made slow progress, and I watched them a long time as they labored out of range.

One we captured alive. A boy had opened up the gate to go out scavenging for weapons, and just outside, in a litter of sledgehammers and iron bars, we found a man. At first I thought he had been wounded in the stomach, because he was curled up like a baby. He would not look us in the face. And he was praying with fanatic speed; he would not stop, even when my brother lost patience and tried to pull him to his feet. 'Holy beloved, deliver me. I have done no harm, by the hair of your head, deliver me, by the power of your thighs, by the strength of your love. Hold me in your arms, so that I may say, "Sweeter than sugar is your taste in my mouth, sweeter than sugar is the taste of your ministers . . ." ' He went on and on. He wouldn't shut up. So we dragged him up into the town by his shirt, up to the dancing hall, and left him outside, where he lay in a heap.

My brothers and my sisters had no interest in him, for the barbarians did not come back that day. But I was interested. He pulled himself upright, and in a little while I saw him sitting upright, supported in the angle of a wall, crooning to himself, his eyes closed whenever I looked at him, open when I didn't.

In the evening I brought him food, a mush of corn in a bowl, and for a while I stood without knowing what to say as he rocked and prayed, one hand clamped on his genitals, the other on an amulet around his neck. It was unusual just to watch someone so closely. Barbarians took no offense. This one sat cross-legged, rocking. He was an old man, his skin pale and spotted, loose and shrunken at the same time. His hair was gray, streaked with white, tied in a black rag at the nape of his neck. It hung long down his back. He had no beard, and I could see his skinny face. There was no meat on it, or on his bone-white arms. His belly was soft and fat.

I didn't know how to talk to him. Old man? Barbarian? Coward dwarf? But he didn't look afraid any more; he seemed happy, in fact, smiling at intervals, as if at inner jokes. He showed his teeth; they were dirty, but looked strong. 'Old man,' I said.

He started, and his eyes flickered open, as if I had just woken him. And when he turned to me, I saw in his face and in his eyes an expression I had not looked for, something you see in the faces of small children, a mixture of delight and fear. He put his hand out towards me, and I could see the amulet around his neck. It was molded from heavy plastic in the shape of a man's genitals.

'Old man,' I said, holding out the bowl I had brought. 'Here is food for pigs.'

He smiled up at me, looking into my face but not my eyes. 'Is it . . . flesh?' he asked, almost reverently. 'I cannot eat . . . flesh.'

'It is not,' I said. He looked both disappointed and relieved, but he made no motion, and so I squatted down and pushed the bowl into his face.

'Thank you,' he said, words I'd never heard, and the tone made me think he was refusing. But when I tried to pull my hand away, he grabbed the bowl and held it in his lap without looking at it.

'Who are you?' I asked.

'I am God's soldier. And I am happy here. Happy to be here.' He looked around. 'Very glad to have seen it, at the end of my life.'

The sun was down, the sky darkening. Someone had started to play music in the hall behind us. Children came to stand in the bright doorway. One raised his hands and twirled a child's pirouette. 'Listen,' said the soldier, as if I had no ears. 'How beautiful!' I squatted down beside him. I could hear the sound of a wooden flute, played in a difficult and obscure key called 'waterbird'. In that particular tempo you could see a bird rising from the surface of a pool, fanning the water into ripples with its wings. Usually the bird is small and white, with a long straight bill; the pool is crisp on a bright day, but tonight the musician – a very young girl, I knew her tone – had chosen the luminous dark of early evening, a great bird of prey, its wings outstretched, the feathers of its wingtips stretching wide like fingers, circling exhausted over an endless sea. In the alien water it will sink without a trace. The music changed, the bird disappeared into the dark, and you could see the stars coming out one by one, a song we called 'first stars'.

The soldier spoke again. He said, 'We only have tonight to listen. My prince is camped under the hill. Cosro Starbridge. Tomorrow he will burn the town. He's sworn an oath to level every stone. The parson has already blessed the gallows. He's going to kill you all. And me, too.' His voice was dreamy, and I was surprised by how much he seemed to understand. Not the bird, not the water, not the stars. That was part of a language only we could hear, the images summoned out of forms and choices meaningless to a stranger. Yet he was responding to the music's other part, the melody, the song of the artist, as sad as she could make it at so young an age. She was afraid of death. Death sang in every note. Like me, she was afraid.

'Why?' I asked.

He smiled as if he were smarter than I. A dog was slinking past the porch, his head down. 'He knows,' said the soldier, pointing. 'Ask him.'

This meant nothing to me. Then, I knew nothing of barbarian heresy, or adventism, or the prophecies that foretold their god's rebirth in the first days of spring. I would have had no patience for it. This soldier was an adventist, I know now. He was a rebel against his own kind. Here in this dark city there are armies of them, waiting for their king, their savior. The jails are full of them. They swing from every public scaffold. In those days they had a prophecy that god would be born out of my people. Without understanding freedom, they worshipped it.

I knew nothing of all this. I made no distinction between barbarian creeds. But I was interested in the soldier. He was listening to the music, which was changing, and I wondered whether he could sense its change. His eyes were full of tears. 'I am so happy to be here,' he repeated. 'Here at the end of all things.'

His food still lay untasted in his lap. And in a little while he spoke again: 'So happy just to listen. I have heard so much about your music. In midwinter, when I was young, in the ninth phase, the bishop would have whipped a man for whistling in the streets. Already then they were afraid. Already they had begun to lose control. Now they are a hundred times more desperate. They want to kill you all.'

'Tell me,' I said.

He smiled. He brought his hand up to his mouth. 'This is the last night,' he said, pointing towards Paradise, just rising. 'It won't be visible again, not in my lifetime. But look, you can see the mountain where I used to live, that black spot. Look.' He sniffed. 'It has been warm here. Tonight it will snow. And tomorrow morning, that will be the end. I think the sun will never rise again. And look.' He motioned to the stone table not far away, the statue lying on its back. 'The idols are broken. Tomorrow we shall see. False priests and false governors. At the hour of seven-times-ten they shall be overthrown.' He was a fanatic. He told me of a plot to murder his commander. His eyes stretched wide. But in a little while he spoke more softly, and then he turned to me. 'Our general pretends to take advantage of the thaw. He pretends he is hunting atheists and cannibals, and clearing out these hills for good and all. But it is more than that. He is afraid. He is searching for the One. The risen One. The risen Angkhdt.'

I looked around at the gathering dark. Music had started again, one of the many kinds of fire music, boastful, proud, and you could see fire flashing from the empty doorway of the hall. The soldier sat with his own thoughts, rocking and humming, and fingering his amulet. So I settled back to listen, and I watched the stars gather and combine as darkness fell, solitary at first, the brightest, one or two in all the sky. As I watched there were always more, filling up that aching space with light, with stars and patterns, numberless, nameless.

Some children came down through the bright doorway, running and laughing, and carrying torches. You could see their faces in the torchlight, dirty, thin, and full of joy. One threw her torch high up into the air, meaning to catch it as it came down; she missed, and it exploded in a shower of sparks. And then they all ran down together across the open stones towards the tower gate, their bodies disappearing in the dark, until below us all that remained were their high, wordless voices and the flickering lights, chasing and spinning, part formless dance, part ruleless game.

The soldier, too, was covered up in darkness. His body had retreated from my sight, and in the long silence I would have let his image go as well, until I remembered nothing. I would have cleared my mind, opened up my hand, and like a timid animal he might have stayed for a while, trembling on my palm until I prodded him away. In the end he would have gone, just as if he had been eager to escape. I would have forgotten him and everything. For that night I was in love. It filled me like a brimming flood, too deep, too painful for joy. I felt it around me as if for the last time. In the cooling dark, I could hear it in the music, in the scattering voices, see it in the children's restless torches, mocked from above by an eternity of stars.

But in time the soldier spoke again. I was surprised to hear the sadness in his voice, for without thinking I had thought that my new ecstasy was filling all the world. 'The stars will shine like day,' he said. 'And in the new light, the earth will blossom like a flower in springtime, and it will need no tending. Stones will move, and fish will speak. Birds will speak. The earth will bring forth all good things, and all men will be free. And Angkhdt will wipe the dirt from our faces, and He will stand up like a giant in the farthest north, and He will say, "Bring to me all tyrants and false priests, all kings and Starbridges . . ." ' The old man's voice sounded so sad. 'I shall not live to see it,' he said, turning towards me, and I could see the outline of his face. 'I have come to prepare the way . . . I had hoped to see Him,' he continued, his voice breaking. 'No matter. In the new starlight He will come, born of this music.'

His breath stank. I reached out to grab the string around his neck, to twist it in my hand until the slack was taken up. I held him at arm's length and shook him once, gently. He went quiet, and I looked up at the stars. 'Please,' he said, his voice full of fear. 'You don't really . . . eat flesh? You are not cannibals . . . as they say?'

I released him and stood up. It was too cold to sit. He followed me into the doorway and grabbed me by the arm. Inside the hall, my brothers and my sisters had slaved in from somewhere the corpse of a horse. Some were stripping the skin away from the flesh, pouring off the blood into wooden buckets; some were sawing through the bones, breaking the joints apart; some were building up the fire. It was like a drug, the smell of fresh-cut meat. For me and for the barbarian too: he looked past me into the uncertain light, and at first he didn't understand what they were doing. When he did, the strength of his body failed. He leaned against the doorpost, panting heavily, his eyes wide with fear, and there were tears in his eyes, and his shoulders and his neck fell forward. He raised his hand up to his face, and with infinite effort dropped his forehead to his palm, and then ducked it to his armpits, once to each side, and murmured a little prayer.

I left him and walked down into the hall, looking for someone. The music was saying something to me. It was in a form called 'no regret', played with wavering purity on the long horn, a large, difficult, metal instrument, which someone had left behind when all the rest of us were left behind. The boy who had picked it up to make it his still did not possess the lungs for any but the easiest modes. This one, 'no regret', he played tentatively, using a melody plainer and sweeter than usual. He knelt wheezing on his bed in the hot firelight, and others squatted near him, listening. And the music told me something too. I thought, if I am going to die tomorrow, I don't have time to cleanse myself of my desire. I may have time to satisfy it.

My brothers and my sisters were moving towards the center of the feast, to where the butchered horse was thrown on to the fire. Their desires were of the simplest kind. But mine was different. I had no interest in the food, though I was hungry. Instead, I turned aside and walked away under the shadows of the wooden arches, to my own bed and the bed beside it. She was lying on her side, with one arm stretched out. She was still asleep, or asleep again, for she had stripped off some of her red clothes and lay part-naked under dirty blankets.

I sat down on my bed. The song told me not to be afraid. I wanted to touch her, to make some mark on her before time closed its hand. I reached out to touch her on the arm. I touched her with my entire hand, and felt her blood, her bone, her muscle, everything. I ran my thumb along the bare, sleeping flesh, listening to the music. I ran my fingers all along her arm, from her shoulder to her palm, and yes, it was a beautiful arm, though in places it was cut and torn – rounded and strong, the hair golden and fine along her wrist. I could have done anything to her as she slept, I don't know, I barely knew what was involved – touched her where I wanted, yes, her sleep seemed deep enough, untroubled by noise, untroubled by the boy's long horn. She had no regret. My brothers and sisters were clanging bells and shouting, and behind that rose the sounds of eager activity around the fire – all that had not sufficed to wake her. Yet I myself was painfully aware of everything, every noise, every motion.

I sat cross-legged, and she lay beside me with her face pressed against the outside of my thigh, her elbow in my lap. She lay soft and responsive, so I touched her with more force, to press some hardness back into the long muscles of her arm. And as her body came alive under my hand, her spirit coming back from wherever it had been, I thought of all the times I had seen her, every image, every song. So we woke to each other, my fingers suddenly sensitized by memory, her fingers opening under mine, responsive at first, then tight and hard as she woke up. That was the moment. I will remember it. And since then I have dreamed of loving, and all my dreams have been like that, trying to recapture the brittle tension not even of her kisses, but of that one moment, that moment when I held her by the wrist, reawakening to her as if from sleep while she pulled sleepily away. She tried to pull away, and I clamped my hand down on her wrist.

She let me hold her. Without relaxing in the slightest degree, she raised herself up on her other arm and looked around.

Around us, the fire was burning brighter. On a table in the center of the hall, my brothers and sisters had piled roasted joints of horsemeat, high up to keep them from the dogs. A little girl had jumped up on the table's back, straddling the carcass like a rider; with a stick she beat away their snapping mouths, until my brother reached up for the horse's head, bigger than his own. Holding it up between his hands, he did a dance, grinning from behind its cruel, empty beak. And then he threw it far away into a corner where it rolled along the floor, the dogs skidding and sliding after it, biting at each other. And to the other side he flung the neck, a bucketful of entrails, its feet and claws, and even a great haunch of meat, so drunk he was

61

with generosity. My sister hit him with her stick. But I could see there was enough for all, because the pony was a fat one, a barbarian beast, shot in the white grass, and not one of our starving nags.

I squeezed my sister's hand, and she squeezed mine. I turned to look at her, and she looked away and lay back in the shadow of the wall. But even so I could see her naked shoulders and her arms, and her golden hair around her face. I could see her frowning, biting her lips. The shadow cut across her face. I kept staring at her, trying to memorize her beauty. And she would glance at me and glance away, holding my hand so tightly she was hurting me. I reached out and took hold of her jaw, and pulled her towards me, and when I kissed her I could feel her tense, hard lips, and feel her teeth clenched tight beneath them. She let me kiss her on the mouth.

I was with her the whole night. When it was almost morning, we walked outside into a snowstorm, to watch the snow falling out of a clear sky, the stars like chips of ice, and Paradise small behind the mountains, circled by a ring of ice. The thaw was over; it was the first night of spring, and the snow was coming back. Some little girls were throwing snowballs. I heard some music from the rooftops, fragile and sweet, a song called 'children playing', and when they heard it, the girls stopped and looked at each other as if confused, their arms at their sides. And one held up her wrist and stared at it, and turned it, and turned each finger in a movement so delicate, so expressive of the music, that it was as if another instrument had joined in, playing in a kind of harmony.

2

Among Strangers

Morning was making its first suggestions as the voice of the antinomial flickered and went out. Not a moment too soon, thought Doctor Thanakar, stretching his crippled leg out on the carpet, relaxing for the first time in many hours. The man's story had seemed to require physical discomfort to understand, for whenever the doctor had relaxed his body he had lost the sense, so he had spent the night cross-legged, his back and shoulders stiffly hunched, his hands held out in front of him. It was as if sorting the narrative out from all the vagaries of music had involved tedious manual labor that could only be performed in that position.

For at times while speaking, the antinomial would play on different instruments – gentle, interminable melodies without repetition or variety. Sometimes he would chant the words, or clap his hands between them, or space them so irregularly that it was hard to make the jumps. Sometimes he would sing, or talk in a dreary inaudible monotone, and the doctor would have to strain to understand. In the dark warehouse, it seemed to him the voice illuminated the story as badly as a flickering candle would a book. Intermittently, though, the man had played a flute, and that had been enough to compensate. For then it had been restful to listen, when music was the end and not the means.

Morning came in through narrow windows high up along the walls, and the doctor looked around. He and the prince had come there in the dark for entertainment, and at first, while the antinomial was singing, a girl had heated wine for them. She had burned a dirty fire, and he had seen her

63

face and shadows in the empty space around them. Even when the prince was drunk, she had fed it for a while longer with handfuls of dung. But then she had gotten up and gone, the fire had burned out, and Thanakar had sat for hours, listening to stories in the black dark. Now, with the windows turning pink, and pink light playing on the walls, he was surprised to see the warehouse was full of people. Antinomials were wandering between the rows of mattresses, or sitting among piles of broken bottles, or lying wrapped in rags. He was surprised that they had made no noise, required no light. And he was anxious to see them there at all, though none paid any attention. None had yet approached the remote corner where he and the prince sat on a shred of carpet.

The girl, though, had returned sometime in the night, and was standing motionless quite close to him. She was dressed in a coarse shirt of unalleviated white, rolled up to the elbows and open in the front, so that he could see the hairless skin between her breasts. Her legs and feet were bare. It was a pose too frankly immodest to be stimulating. He had friends who came down nightly to this section of the docks, looking for antinomials, addicted to their powerful bodies and cheap fees. The doctor found it unimaginable, even if he had been able to imagine, in principle, paying for a woman's body with a bucketful of entrails or a yard of cloth. To him the antinomial women were intimidating and unfeminine. This one was over six feet tall. And while he might admire her lithe bulk, her long legs, her unmarked face, her short, simple hair, she looked too alien to be beautiful. In the quiet air, she was humming a quiet, tuneless song. Perhaps, he thought, if he had been able, he could have heard in it the expression which her features lacked. What was it? Sadness without experience, perhaps.

The storyteller was asleep. And the prince slept too, cross-legged, his head bobbing up and down, his sweet, lunatic face uneasy even in slumber. Though that was no surprise, thought Doctor Thanakar. It was a sign of madness that he could sleep at all in that position. For the warehouse was worse than unfurnished – mattresses and couches strewn with animal products. He had not wanted to stay, but the prince had barely seemed to notice, and had sunk to the floor with a contempt for his own dignity that had touched the doctor's heart. The girl had brought them wine, and Abu had taken the cup out of her hands with childlike unconcern – a dozen cups, and now he slept. The doctor envied him. Prince Abu's drunkenness was the aspect of his condition that the doctor had most wished to share, yet each time the girl had offered him the cup he had refused. She had offered it with passable politeness, but each time his own fastidiousness had shamed him into thinking she was mocking him, that their host was mocking him by squatting happily upon his hams the whole gigantic night, leaving the leather couch unoccupied as if in deference to his guests. Eighty months, eight thousand days had passed since the antinomials had fled that savage life up in the snow, the one they now described with such nostalgia. They had left in the last phase of winter, and it was now midspring. A whole new generation had grown up. But still the antinomials had not learned the value of other people's comfort. 'My lords,' the man had sung, in such a gentle tone. Yet so much of his story had seemed calculated to offend them. It was true, his people had been brutally misused. But it was partly their own fault. A cousin of the doctor's had given a party, and had hired a troupe of antinomial musicians. But when the food was served, they had come down from the platform to mix with the guests. They had put their hands into the food, and everything had to be thrown away.

The prince was talking in his sleep, guttural languages known only to himself. Thanakar looked at him with mingled irritation and concern. And when he turned away again, he found the girl was staring at him. In a sense, even that was peculiar and exciting, even though her expression was one of fierce indifference, for women rarely looked him in the face. Occasionally a servant would meet his eyes, a female of his household or one toiling on the road, and he would always turn his head, humiliated and embarrassed. But there was nothing envious or curious about this girl's stare. It rested lightly on his face. As his host had said, the antinomials had no personalities, not in the way he knew. She was singing a small tune and then she stopped, and for the first time there was some content in her face, a smile, a reaction. She smiled. A cat had jumped on to the carpet from behind a pillar, a huge and golden cat. It was followed by a second, and then a third, of the same unusual size, the same splendid color. Golden sunlight was coming in through the windows; these cats were like sunlight made animate. They furnished space in the same way.

Smiling, the girl sat down and stretched out her legs. A cat walked round her once, twice, stepping over her legs with exaggerated care.

The cats paced and turned, rousing the sleepers. Prince Abu woke up shivering, for as always, his sleep had been a thin and insubstantial cover. As always, he looked around him with a kind of fear, and Thanaker could tell he had forgotten where he was. His dreams took him on such hard journeys, he woke up miles from where he went to sleep. The doctor would hear about it presently. In the meantime, he leaned forward to touch his cousin's knee, to catch his eye, and it cheered him to see some reassurance come into that tired face.

Abu and the doctor were the same age. They had been born within two months of each other, at the end of winter. Now they had reached the burning middle of man's life.

Apart from that, and friendship, they shared little. Winter babies are alike, people said, gloomy and fat. It was absurd. True, he was morose, the prince was overweight, but there resemblance ended. Abu was prematurely old. Not withered or bent – his skin was young and smooth. But his eyes were old, his cheeks yellow and puffy with drink, and he was losing his hair. Yet in a way, also, his face had retained some of the best of childishness: his frank, pure expression, his childish delight in little things, the sudden sweetness in his eyes when they had focused on the cats moving back and forth, back and forth across the carpet. It was a look that made it easy to forget his defects, the small futility of his hands as they fluttered near his throat, pulling at the buttons of his uniform. He had worn an overcoat and had worn gloves over his golden tattoos. The doctor had insisted on that much of a disguise at least. But in the fever of drinking he had stripped them off, and now he sat smiling and nodding, his useless body gorgeous in white silk and gold embroidery, his palms marked with the symbol of the sun, his fingers decorated with lists of privileges. In the worst slum of the city, he feared nothing. Among people who had every reason to hate him, he was as trusting as a child.

Prince Abu laughed and clapped his hands. Their host, the antinomial musician, had risen to his feet, had stood up straight to his enormous height. Thanakar looked at him in good light for the first time. He had heavy lips and a hard jaw, a cruel face, but the unusual thing was the way it mixed black with white: black hair with a peculiar streak of white along the parting; a livid scar running down from outside of one eye along his dark cheek; black eyes, with a milky circle at their center like a cataract.

Unlike the girl's, his face was full of motion – nervous now, unsure, and perhaps a little angry. The doctor thought that such a struggling mixture did not suit his features. It was as if he were spoiling with thought a face intended to express feelings only – simple pleasure, simple pain. The man reached down for his guitar. It looked too fragile for his massive hands.

'It is enough,' he said. 'More than enough. I didn't want to fall asleep.'

'Please don't apologize,' said Doctor Thanakar politely. 'It was only a few minutes. We were quite comfortable.'

The antinomial looked puzzled. He ran his finger along a steel string, making a little noise. 'You don't understand,' he said. 'No apology was intended. I mean that you have stayed here long enough. Too long.'

He would have claimed, thought Thanakar, that there was music in his words. But as usual, it was irritating and presumptuous. Thanakar tried to rise, but the prince had grabbed him by the sleeve. 'No offense, Cousin,' he cried in his high, gentle voice. He was still drunk. He stammered something, closed his eyes and partly opened them in a way that was habitual with him, showing only the whites, his lashes trembling as if with the effort of speech. 'No . . . No offense taken. He is right. It is late.'

Thanakar shook himself loose and rose painfully to his feet. But already he felt a little foolish. His anger had come quickly and was just as quickly overwhelmed. At his full height, the top of his head was on a level with the antinomial's armpit. 'My cousin is Prince Abu Starbridge,' he said sulkily. 'You cannot understand the honor we do you just to come here.'

'No doubt,' replied the antinomial. 'But this I do understand. I played my flute, and gave you drink, and told you the story closest to my heart, and it was not for my own happiness, my lords.'

The cats walked back and forth. 'I'm not sure what you mean,' stammered the prince.

There was a silence. And then the girl spoke from where

she sat, smiling and looking at the cats. 'He is asking to be paid,' she said. 'It's a form of begging. Surely it's a tune you know.'

Thanakar frowned. They had paid already, a price already agreed on, and they had been generous. They had brought down baskets of food, real vegetables and valuable fruits, and loaves of bread, and chocolate, enough for several men for several days. They had carried them with their own hands. He turned angrily away, for the price had been agreed, but from the floor Prince Abu blinked and stammered. 'Oh,' he said, 'of course. How stupid. I forgot. I brought him a gift. He told me what to bring. It slipped my mind, I'm sorry. Let me see . . .' He fumbled with his overcoat and drew from an inside pocket a bulky package wrapped in linen. 'It's not quite what you wanted.' He undid the strings to reveal a wooden case. Inside lay a pair of silver dueling pistols in a nest of velvet.

'I know you were expecting something more practical,' continued the prince apologetically. 'But I don't have much access to firearms.'

The antinomial made a little noise on his guitar. 'Single shot?' he asked.

'Yes, I'm sorry.'

'Ammunition?'

'N-no.'

'Are they . . . valuable?'

'I suppose so. Fairly.'

The antinomial put down his guitar and knelt beside the prince. Reaching for the box, he ran his finger down the long, intricate barrel, the carved stock. 'It doesn't matter,' he said grudgingly. 'Perhaps I can exchange them. But next time I want something I can use.'

'Abu, are you crazy?' exclaimed Doctor Thanakar. 'You promised this man guns?'

'Yes, and what of it? What's it to you? I don't see why

not. He could have bought a cannon for all the wine I've drunk. You are all extremely rude. I've got such a headache.'

Impatient, Thanakar turned back to the antinomial. 'What do you mean by this?' he demanded. 'What do you mean to do?' But the question was a useless one. The man raised his head and gave him a long stare, and then gave it sudden cruelty by squinting slightly, although the light hadn't changed. The girl behind them was still humming, playing with the cats.

'For God's sake, don't bite him,' warned the prince. 'That's all we need. He needs them to defend himself. You are always telling me how badly they are persecuted.' And to the antinomial he said, 'My cousin was at the battle that you spoke of. When he was very young.'

The man squinted as before. 'It was no battle,' he said after a pause. 'I was not there,' he continued grimly. 'I ran away over the snow.'

Embarrassed, the doctor turned his head. Some antinomials had gathered near to listen, and a boy was standing in the shadow of a metal pillar, one of a long row that ran down the center of the warehouse. He was wrapped in a leather cloak, and he held a kitten to his chest. As he stood, the other cats came to him, to rub against his legs. 'You were at Rangriver?' he asked Thanakar in a rich, low voice.

'No,' explained the doctor hastily. 'I was just a child. I came later, with my father. My father wanted me to see . . . the . . .' He felt acutely nervous, aware of people gathering around him, huge men and women, with cruel empty faces. The boy was not like them. When he spoke, it was as if he were alone with the doctor in the immense hall, and there was nothing to fear. He spoke softly, and the hand that caressed the kitten seemed to soothe the air.

'That's interesting,' he said. 'Is that where you received

your wound?' He nodded towards the doctor's crippled leg.

Thanakar scanned his face for traces of laughter; there were none. 'No,' he replied. 'I fell when I was small. I was dropped.'

'But still, you were there.'

'Yes.' He had been there, limping shamefaced at his father's side, standing in the snow. At night they had camped back with the baggage, but in the afternoon, after the fighting, his father had taken him down to see the executions. The soldiers were in a brutal frame of mind, for many had been killed in the fighting. Though starved and defenseless, the antinomials were inhumanly strong, and though unorganized, they had fought with bitter, happy courage, shouting and singing. But by afternoon it was over. Only a few hours, really. The red sun had glowered from the horizon all day, but still the time had seemed intolerably long, and he had stood with his father as the soldiers built a gallows twenty feet high, and he had stood and watched as they had mutilated children his own age and younger, and cut the mark of absolution into their faces, and strung them up. Behind him on the dais, the priests had sat in scarlet robes, old, blind, obese, whispering to each other in their castrate voices. It had been very, very cold, the end of winter, the beginning of spring, and the sun had barely risen. It had snowed all day. They had hung a boy of his own age, and he had started to cry. His father had cuffed him on the ear and knocked him down, to remind him of his duties.

'Yes,' he repeated, 'I was there. I am ashamed to say it.'

The boy eyed him curiously. 'Don't be ashamed,' he said. 'I want to be there. Have been. That's not right. What do you say?'

'I would have liked to have been there.'

'I would like . . .' He laughed again. 'I was born here in

this room. I have no memories of freedom.' He sighed and raised the kitten to his ear. 'Enough,' he said. 'My brother wants you to go, though he is too polite to say.'

Prince Abu pulled Thanakar by the trouser cuff, and reflexively the doctor reached down to hoist him to his feet. The prince got up. 'Can you come with us?' he asked.

The boy laughed. 'Dressed like this? The bishop's purge would shoot me in the street. No, I am going to bed. We are nocturnal, mostly, nowadays. But you will see me again. You will come to watch me dance.'

'When?' asked Abu.

'I'm not sure. Paradise is rising. When?'

'In fifteen days.'

'In fifteen days, then. On the first night of the festival, at midnight. I am dancing here, on the docks. Pier . . . I don't know. Follow the crowds. It's a sight not to be missed.'

'We will certainly come,' promised the prince, but the boy was already walking away, the cats following. Abu called after him. 'I'll bring you gifts. What gifts will I bring?'

The boy stopped and turned. 'Just yourselves,' he said. 'I am not like my brother. I have an audience of my own people. I am not a slave to hate. Not yet. Just come yourselves.'

'No. I want to bring something.'

The boy laughed and walked on, down along the row of pillars, among the mattresses, leaving them standing on the carpet, leaving his brother squatting, and fingering the silver pistols, and squinting after him, white circles in the middle of his black eyes. The girl had disappeared.

Huddled in their overcoats under the spring sun, the doctor and the prince picked through miserable streets.

The antinomials had made their homes in a row of abandoned warehouses by the river, left over from the days before the war, when the city had been a busy port. The one where they had spent the night was built out over the mud on a wooden dock; walking back among the rows of silent antinomials, half a dozen times they paused on the lips of ragged holes in the flooring, the dirty water a few feet away. At the entrance they passed over a barricade of metal beams, barbed wire, concrete blocks, piles of broken plaster, broken glass. There the prince wanted to rest and talk, but Thanakar signaled silence. The streets here were crowded, and he was afraid someone might recognize the accents of their caste. So, in silence, they stepped past heaps of garbage and up through filthy alleyways. It was a useless precaution, he realized. Their faces were well known. 'Look, there goes the prince,' cried out a voice, a red-haired prostitute from an upper window. She waved, and Abu waved back. It didn't matter. Few looked at them or if they did, their faces were not hostile. Some smiled, not at him, but at the prince, and the prince smiled at everyone. And Thanakar realized that he had nothing to fear, that his friend protected them with an aura of foolishness big enough for both. Coming to this section of the city in search of drunkenness or vice, people had been robbed and even killed. It was the home of runaways, cannibals, flagellants, Dirty Folk, Brothers of Unrest, arsonists, perverts, addicts, adventists, atheists, and heretics of every kind. People had been murdered in bright day. But this morning, women smiled at them out of starving, gap-toothed faces, and men squatting on doorsteps took no notice. Boys were playing marbles in the gutter. One came running, and soon they were surrounded by a pack of dancing, tattered children. Abu stopped and produced from the voluminous pockets of his overcoat five stone coins and a single sourball, which he proffered with

73

apologetic solemnity. Unsatisfied, the children stood in a circle, screaming, but they seemed harmless, and in a little while they ran away. Thanakar noticed that one was imitating his limp, and another was laughing.

'You have a lot of friends,' he remarked.

Abu shrugged. 'I've come here many times. I told you these coats were stupid.' He flapped his arms. 'I should have worn a mask.'

'Never mind. We're almost to the car.'

'How far? Can we rest now? Please don't punish me. I can't walk as fast as you. I realize that you're angry at me for telling them you were there at the last battle – you know – the antinomial crusade. Rangriver. I thought it was interesting.'

'That's all right. They could have killed me, that's all.'

'I don't think so. I don't know how to explain it. I feel safe there. I know they're dangerous, but I can't feel it.'

'It doesn't matter. Let's go.'

They were standing in the gutter of a narrow street, next to a barricade of sawhorses. 'No wait,' protested the prince. 'I've got such a headache. It's your fault. You said you were going to help me with the wine. I had to drink it all myself.'

'Believe me, I would have liked to,' said Thanakar. 'Anything to get me through that awful music. But I couldn't stand the idea of her touching the cup. It seems stupid now.'

'Why? It was silver. I brought it from home the first time I went.'

'No. I don't care about that so much.'

'What then? You told me yourself that the pollution laws are nonsense, an idea made up by priests to keep people apart.'

'Yes,' said Thanakar. 'I know. But there is a difference between being medically sure and . . . absolutely sure. Besides, her hands were probably filthy.'

74

'Well anyway, did you enjoy yourself?' asked Abu. 'I think it is my favorite place. I could listen to him talk forever. It's such a beautiful way of talking.'

'I found it irritating.'

Prince Abu laughed. 'You should have had something to drink. I can picture you trying to understand each word. What did you think about the boy? Wasn't he incredible?'

'What boy?'

'The boy this morning. With the cats. I'd love to see him dance.'

'I didn't like what he was wearing,' said Thanakar.

'What was he wearing?'

'You didn't notice? It was skin. Leather.'

'I noticed what was on the bed. You could smell it.' Abu shivered. 'It's disgusting, the way they treat animals. He was dressed in leather?'

'Yes.'

'What kind?'

'I'm scarcely a judge.'

'It's disgusting, the way they treat animals,' repeated Abu after a pause. Then he brightened. 'But he was incredibly handsome. Not so big as the others. He was probably a half-caste. The pure bloods don't breed much anymore. It's sad.'

They had started walking again, and had come out of the slums into neighborhoods that were simply poor, rows of wooden houses, put up for common laborers by the episcopal authorities. In an alleyway, they found the doctor's motorcar. The driver woke when Thanakar rapped on the glass, and staggered out half-dressed to unlock the cramped luxury of the back seat. Inside, the prince unbuttoned his overcoat. And as the car wheeled clumsily out into the road, he picked the conversation up in the same place.

'He was incredible.'

'I didn't notice.'

'How can you not have noticed? He was incredible.'

'So I understand. Describe him.' This was a game they played at lucklessly during their professional consultations.

'Yes, doctor. He was very, very . . . handsome.'

'That's a judgement, not a description.'

'It's both. Handsome people always look alike, just as good people always do the same things.'

'How philosophical.'

'Well, so what if it is?' complained the prince. 'You're like my brother-in-law. Just because I'm fit for nothing doesn't mean I'm a fool. Necessarily. I try my best. It's not easy, being a prince. You should be glad that fellow dropped you.'

Bored, the doctor stared out of the window. They had passed into a jam of vehicles leading up to the city gates: old men pulling handcarts of what looked like garbage, a huge wagon pulled by six young men in harness. Occasionally an episcopal truck, honking impatiently, in from the factories and food collectives far beyond the city. A few Starbridge motorcars, like his own. People lined the streets, dressed in yellow clothes, the urine-colored uniforms of poverty and work. When they saw the doctor's motorcar, they stood still and made the obligatory gestures of respect. The doctor yawned unhappily.

'He had beautiful hair,' said Abu.

'What color?'

'Brown. But very thick.'

'What color eyes?'

'Blue.'

The doctor picked his beard. 'You find that beautiful? It's illegal. He should be in prison.'

'The law can't touch him where he is.'

'Don't be too sure.'

'But I am sure,' exclaimed Abu. 'Things are changing.

Two thousand days ago, the purge cleaned out that area every month. They can't do it anymore.'

'It's the manpower they lack, not the will. Who will stop them, when the army comes back? You'd better pray the war lasts forever.'

'I pray for our defeat.'

They had reached the gate. Outside, traffic halted at the checkpoint, and a guard came round among the vehicles, examining papers and consignments. He peered at them through the window with feigned suspicion, while they held up their tattooed palms. Beyond them, through the massive doors, waited the ancient city of Charn, capital of the diocese, holy city, with its seven thousand pagodas and its countless shrines lining the open gutters: shrines to Angkhdt the Preserver, Angkhdt the God of Children, Angkhdt the Charioteer, warlike Angkhdt with seven heads. Now, in the early morning, each shrine was surrounded by worshipers, bending low into the opening to smear the image with blue kaya gum, chewing it into a reverent and narcotic paste, dribbling it out into their palms, bending down to smear the idol, in most cases invisible under years of blobby worship. The squatting attendant beat a drum and struck a match, and the idol would burn for a short time while the devotee stood back, hands to his chest, reciting one of the forty-seven sacred lists of obligations.

The gatekeeper saluted. Behind him waited princely Charn, with its deep, wooden, crooked, narrow streets, and at every crossroads brass statues of Starbridges on horseback – judges, generals, priests – in this season speckled with the dung of countless small green birds. Desolate Charn, with no grass or vegetation anywhere, not a living tree or flower. Summer would see them come in desperate profusion, after the sugar rain. Then the growth would rot the wooden houses with their high galleries and steep snow roofs, and send them crashing to the ground.

At the gate, the crowd around the front of the motorcar loosened and dispersed. In the gap, Thanakar could see his destination, rising over roofs and towers, still miles away, the grim Mountain of Redemption, a city in itself: circle upon circle of ramparts and black rock. It had no top. The traditions of the Prophet Angkhdt had required God's temple to be built supported on a prison of one million souls. The text was vague, the translation unsure; as always, the controversy had been bloody. But the nineteenth bishop had resolved its literal meaning. He had discovered ancient plans and diagrams, blueprints, and memoranda dictated by Angkhdt himself, but ten lifetimes later the work was still unfinished, though there was no lack of inmates. The Temple of the Holy Song had had to be constructed on a steel scaffolding arching from the mountaintop, while far beneath it, stonemasons slaved to fill the gap. The temple was invisible, uninhabitable, swayed in every breath of wind. Four thousand feet below, the Starbridge palaces ringed the prison's base – temporary housing already crumbling with age. When the building was completed, the Starbridges would live on top.

In the motorcar, the doctor thought: without hope, fear can never be maintained. Without the temple, people would never tolerate the prison. They would rise up. For this reason, the base of each strand of the temple's web is guarded from sabotage by a troop of soldiers.

The most powerful priest in Charn was not the bishop, but the bishop's secretary, Chrism Demiurge, and he was waiting for the doctor when he got home. Thanakar's housekeeper met him in the hall to warn him. 'He's in your parents' bedroom, sir. Please God be careful what you say.' Thanakar smiled. She loved him. She had been his nurse.

It touched his heart to see the terror in her fat, kind face – she was afraid for his sake, she didn't know why. He knew. For more than a hundred days he had experimented on his parents' sleeping corpses, trying to rouse them, to break the mystery of the sleeping drug before they started to decay. Not because he missed them, or wanted them back, but in the interests of pure science, perhaps. Prince and Princess Thanakar Starbridge – perhaps if they had loved him more, he might have shown them more respect. He hoped his injections had left no trace.

'Did you give him something to eat?'

'They don't need more to eat, that lot,' said Mrs Cassimer. 'They'd eat you out of house and home. Please God be careful, sir.'

'I'll be careful.'

At the doorway to the bedroom, he paused. The room was dark, the curtains thick. He had been an adolescent when the priests had put his parents to sleep; it had been almost five thousand days. Yet still they were in the first stage of their journey back to Paradise – they were getting younger. The drug had smoothed their faces and their skin, blackened their hair, so that they lay like a new bride and bridegroom in their wedding bed. Their bodies smelled of incense. In time, the smell would sweeten. Already, a week before, he had noticed an unhealthy flush of yellow on his father's fingertips; it was the first sign, and the second would be the incense sweetening as their spirits drew back along their drying limbs. The process, once started, would be swift, the soul's flight to Paradise, but their bodies would be carrion, and as if to emphasize that part, the bishop's secretary stood hunched over the bedstead, plucking at them with his long fingers like a scavenger bird. The doctor's father groaned and pulled away.

The secretary was an old man with a long neck and a

withered, sharp face. Thanakar's shadow in the doorway caused him to look up and turn his luminous blind eyes.

'Good morning, Monsignor.'

'Ah, Thanakar,' said the old man. 'Come in.'

He spoke as if the house was his. And in a sense it was. All things belonged to God, and he was God's chief minister. The doctor moved his tongue around the inside of his mouth. The presumption made him angry. He came down into the room and limped across to yank open the curtains.

'Can I offer you a cup of water, Monsignor?'

The old man blinked in the sudden light and turned slowly towards the windows. 'No, thank you. No water, thank you. I'm not thirsty. I just stopped in for a minute.' He paused, perfectly comfortable with silence. His eyes drifted around the room.

'Well, can I offer you anything?'

Again, the old man waited before replying. 'I don't think so, thank you. I would have taken anything I wanted. No, there is one thing. You can offer me advice, my son.'

'Whatever I have is yours,' responded Thanakar between his teeth.

'I know that, my son. I know that.' The old man sighed. Pulling his scarlet robes around him and stretching out his hand for guidance, he walked around the bed. Accurately, deliberately, slowly, he picked the princess's wrist up from beneath her gauze sheet, and with the fingers of his other hand he opened wide the eyelids of his right eye, until it seemed to bulge out of its socket. Then turning towards the light and bending low, he raised her wrist up to his eye, until it was an inch away.

'What are these marks?' he asked.

'What marks?'

'These marks.'

At the window, the doctor screwed his face into a

priestlike grimace. Crouching, he twisted his body into a mimic of the old man's. 'Injections, Monsignor,' he replied, and without meaning to, he allowed a parody of castrate gentleness to creep into his voice, so that the old man turned towards him curiously.

'Injections, my son? What for?'

'Vitamins. There aren't enough in their regular diet. Not to keep them . . . healthy.'

The secretary stared at him, and under the fixed scrutiny of his blind eyes, Thanakar relaxed and stood upright.

'That is not your concern,' said the old man after a pause. 'What vitamins?'

'B.'

'Vitamin B.' The secretary turned back to the princess's wrist and rubbed it between his fingers before putting it carefully back down. 'You are not,' he continued, 'a religious man.' The words were phrased midway between a question and a statement.

Thanakar said nothing. 'My son,' said the old man gently. 'My son. This is not a . . . social call. Not completely. I have heard rumors about you that disturb me, for I knew your father well.'

Thanakar said nothing. His mother turned over on her side. She was naked under the gauze sheet. It pulled away to show her naked back.

'Lately you have gone up more than once into my prisons. Why?'

'I am doing a study, Monsignor.'

'What kind?'

'I am studying the long-term effects of untreated illnesses.'

'Yet you have been observed carrying medicines and painkillers up into the wards,' pursued the secretary gently. 'Surely that would . . . invalidate your results?'

The doctor combed his long black hair back from his

forehead with the fingers of one hand. 'I have no apology to make,' he said finally.

'I ask for none. You will not go there again.' The secretary's voice was pitched, once again, midway between a question and a command.

'I go where I want. It is my birthright. You can't take that away.' Thanakar opened his palm to show the golden key tattooed under his wrist, the mark that opened all doors.

The old man sighed. 'You think you have been badly treated. And truthfully, I understand it. I understand. There is a reason for it. You are a cripple. It is . . . unfortunate. Very unfortunate.'

This remark was also a key that opened doors. 'Unfortunate!' cried the doctor. 'Unfortunate! You did it deliberately. You know you did. You dropped me. It was the only way that you could get your hands on my father's property.'

'You are wrong. The wealth of the earth belongs to God, and to the ministers of His temple. We lend them generously to some families. Your father has no sons capable of inheriting his name. It is unfortunate. Simply that.'

'Bastard! Eunuch!' shouted Thanakar, stung to rage. 'My father always hated you,' and the figure on the bed stirred and groaned, half-awakened by his son's voice.

There was a long pause before the secretary spoke. 'You are talking foolishly, my son. Very foolishly. But believe me, I understand. Sometimes when I go up to the mountain, the human suffering there is too much to bear. But remember, they are God's prisoners, not ours. He is punishing them for crimes they committed before they were even born, not on this planet, but in Paradise. As you know. You and I, we are only His instruments.'

'That makes you feel better, does it?'

The secretary eyed him thoughtfully. 'You are not a religious man,' he said again.

'There are many kinds of religion.'

'You're wrong. There is one kind. But there are many kinds of criminals. Tell me, when you go down among the atheists with Abu Starbridge, do you drink with him?'

Thanakar stiffened. 'Prince Starbridge is my patient,' he said stiffly.

'Yes, it is unfortunate. Yours is not a healthy influence, my son. And I'm sorry for his family's sake. His malady is an obscure one. Self-destructive, is he not? I think I know. Abu Starbridge has lost his faith. No wonder he is so unhappy. The world's too grim to live in without faith.'

'No, damn you. You're a liar. It's faith that's made the world the way it is.'

Chrism Demiurge was silent for a moment. When he spoke again, his voice was gentler, higher, more compelling. 'I'm sorry to hear you say that,' he said. 'Very . . . sorry. It pains me to hear you because, don't you see, we must stand together, you and I. As a class. The Starbridges must stand together. Our system has its flaws. None knows that better than I. But it has stood the test of seasons. Do you think a weaker system would have kept this city fed? All winter and now spring – more than a lifetime with no food worth the name. You have no conception of the work involved. You are too young to remember, but don't you see – the rigors of the climate here require strong government. How long do you think we could survive without it? Maybe in your lifetime, maybe you will live to see some loosening of the rope. When the weather changes. But I am an old man.'

Once, a barber from the middle class, an adventist or a rebel angel, had thrown a bomb at Marson Starbridge in his carriage. That had been when Thanakar's father was still awake, and he had taken Thanakar to watch the execution. The barber had been crucified, bolted to a steel cross through the holes drilled in his wrists, ankles, and chest. He was a large man, with coarse hair and a red beard, and on the cross he had spat, and jeered at his executioners, and sung songs of insurrection. The man was a hero; in comparison, Thanakar was nothing. He was not likely to be crucified. But still, the image was in his mind all day, after the bishop's secretary had left. He had tried to read, and study in his workroom, but his mind wouldn't follow his directions, and he had ended up pacing nervously through his apartments, staring out the windows. Later, he went to see the prince.

The Starbridges of Charn lived in a seething warren of towers and courtyards, all parts of the same enormous building, clutched to the first ramparts of the Mountain of Redemption. To get to a point directly opposite, you took an electric car more than a mile through the solid rock, but for shorter distances there were elevators, and airless stairways, and mirrored passages bright with chandeliers. The apartments of the rich lay behind gaudy doorways; at one of the most impressive, a silver door set with the gilt image of the sun, Thanakar stopped and entered without knocking. The prince was still asleep. His housemaid curtsied. She was a foreign girl, with a wide, flat face. It didn't matter, said Thanakar; he would write a note. Don't wake him. And so he sat down at a desk in the hall and took out the notepad that he always carried, but there was no message in his mind. Instead, he drew caricatures in furious, thick lines – the balding prince, grinning queasily. And then, catching a glimpse of himself in a mirror opposite, Thanakar sketched himself, taking no pity on his high forehead and long nose. The housemaid was back, curtseying, with a cup of unrequested tea.

'The commissar would like to see you, sir.'

He took the tea and let it grow cold at the corner of the desk while from memory, he sketched the commissar,

Micum Starbridge, Abu's brother-in-law. His pencil ripped through the paper. The commissar had a big chest, short neck, bristle hair, and a face, at least in caricature, like an old pig.

It was not a fair portrait. Micum Starbridge was a sad, kind man, who had fought his whole life in the eternal war. Now too old for active service, he worked in the Department of Secular Police. Though born in the twelfth phase of winter, he was still vigorous, his face soldierly, brisk, and piglike, except for his eyes. They were large, liquid, and immensely sad, qualities missing from Thanakar's sketch. They saved his face from ugliness.

When Thanakar entered the commissar's study, the old man was staring out over the city from the window. Far below, it stretched out to a line of hills, stretched to the horizon in radiating circles of prosperity. New civic ordinances required men to paint the tiles of their rooftops in the colors of their caste. New laws like that exhausted and depressed the commissar, but however much he might have been opposed in principle, he had to admit that the effect was beautiful in practice, at least to the inhabitants of high towers. Below him, the clergy and nobility lived in a speckled bull's eye of red and gold, and from there, rough concentric circles of magenta, purple, violet, cobalt blue, stretched out to the slums and suburbs, where drab gray and urine yellow mixed well with dust and distance. Sprinkled throughout were mixtures of irregularities – white hospitals, black barracks, red commercial buildings, and the brass belltowers of countless temples. As he watched, one chimed and others joined in, a signal to certain types of workers that their day was over – time to return home.

He turned when the doctor came in, and held out his hands. To Thanakar he seemed, as always, unnecessarily cordial. It irritated him the way the commissar caressed his

85

hands, as if he were trying to impress the fact that though others might reject him for his leg's sake, Micum Starbridge never would.

'Come in, my boy; come in,' said the commissar. 'Why do I never see you? You know you're always welcome. I knew your father well. My God, but you look just like him when he was a young soldier! Put you in uniform . . . You know you're always welcome here,' he repeated, and looked at him out of his melancholy eyes. 'Why do I never see you?'

'Perhaps because you never look.' Thanakar had made up his mind to try to be offensive, and it irritated him to see that the commissar didn't seem to mind. There was no pause, no flicker in his face. It was as if he thought that Thanakar had ample reason to be abrasive, poor boy.

'Ah, well, to tell the truth, we're not doing so much entertaining these days,' admitted the commissar vaguely. 'My brother-in-law, you know. It makes things very difficult, and my wife is also sick.'

Thanakar remembered Abu's sister from before her marriage, a pretty girl, and at the time it had angered him that she had married someone so much older. He hadn't seen her since; nor had anyone else.

'I'm sorry to hear it,' he said.

'Yes. That's why I wanted to see you. Tell me, how is the prince?'

'Better.'

The commissar seemed to expect a larger response. When none came, he said, 'That's excellent. I had noticed it too. And his drinking?'

Thanakar shrugged.

'Well,' exclaimed the commissar with sad heartiness, 'I didn't mind a drink myself when I was young. When I could get it. Tell me,' he said. 'Where does he get it?'

'No one you know.'

'I'll bet. I'll bet. Yes, well, I suppose it's better not to know. It's for the best.' He paused and looked around the room. 'But no. Listen. I want to talk to you about my wife.'

'Have you seen a doctor?'

'No.' The commissar sighed. 'No. It's not that easy. You're not married, are you, Thanakar?'

The doctor felt the blood in his cheeks. 'You know I'm not.'

'No. Of course, how could you be? Well, in some ways you're lucky. It's very complicated. All these regulations. I don't give a damn about them myself,' said the commissar, and unconsciously he touched the tattoo of legal immunity on the thumb of his right hand, 'But in a way, it's a question of duty. And some of them are for the best. I can see the sense in some of them. But when something like this happens, it's not . . . convenient. I should be able to send her to a doctor. But there aren't any women doctors anymore, except for midwives, and that's not the problem. I wish it were. So I thought you wouldn't mind having a look at her yourself. I mean, I could describe the symptoms, but it's not the same.'

'It's against the law. A married woman.'

'Yes, I know. I'll understand if you refuse. But I thought, well, you're practically a member of the family. And you've been so good for Abu. So discreet.'

Thanakar said nothing.

'I'm sorry to put you in this position, my boy, but I've been worried.'

'It's serious?'

'No. Well, I don't know. It's . . . peculiar.'

Thanakar looked down at his boots. Then he nodded.

'You'll do it?'

'Yes. For a fee.'

The commissar looked surprised. 'Well, yes, of course. I suppose so. Anything you say.'

'Not like that. I want your help.' And Thanakar described his conversation with the bishop's secretary. 'I need your protection,' he said.

The commissar waited before replying. 'Sit down,' he said, and then he moved over to his desk and stood by the window looking out. When he spoke, it was to change the subject. 'The war's not going well,' he said. 'Did you know that?'

'I had heard rumors.'

'Yes. It's hard to hide so many deaths. Do you know why we're fighting?' he asked, standing with his hands behind his back, his back to Thanakar. 'I mean, not the history, of course. The cause?'

'I suppose it's a religious controversy. The kings of Caladon are heretics.'

The commissar sighed. 'They are all religious controversies. In my lifetime we have fought a dozen heresies and crushed them all. We had limited objectives, always. At Rangriver, we couldn't spare the troops to get bogged down. We needed them for other wars – this war with Caladon was already old when I was a child. To tell the truth, we cannot win. Yet it, too, started as a war of conscience, more than a year ago, a heresy peculiar to that winter. Argon Starbridge – not the present king, you understand. His great-great uncle shared the same name. They are all named Argon, the kings of Caladon, but this one was not as foolish as the rest. He was a mystic. He taught that men, ordinary men, you know, can . . . what? Effect their own salvation? Themselves. It's a dangerous belief. I'm not saying it's not dangerous. Dangerous and wrong. But I don't mean that. I mean, how did it start?'

'I don't know. It seems a natural thing to believe.'

'Yes. Perfectly natural. It's strange. When I was young, everyone knew this story. It doesn't matter. I'll tell you.'

The commissar paused, then continued. 'King Argon Starbridge, the first King Argon, had no son until he was an old man. Late in life, past the time when women, generally speaking, have children . . . amid much public rejoicing, I imagine. But the difficulty was the boy was marked – physically perfect, you understand, but with one blue eye. The queen refused food and locked herself into her room. It must have been something from her family, and the shame, well, you can imagine. But some people thought that in this case, the old king's only son, some exception might be made. At least the king thought so. Especially since the bishop there in Caladon was his own brother. Barred from succession; leave it at that, they said. But the bishop, maybe because he was the king's brother and wanted to show himself impartial, I don't know – whatever the reason, it was a terrible mistake. When the baby was presented, he announced the child was cursed, a great criminal, enemy of God, marked for damnation, everything. I don't know, perhaps he was. But the bishop condemned him on the spot to life imprisonment, and the king was broken-hearted. When the boy was taken away, he collapsed on the floor because, of course, nobody survives that kind of treatment, especially not a child, and in fact the boy died . . . soon. The king neglected his duties and brooded by himself. And when the news came that the boy was dead, he insisted on giving him a royal funeral, against all custom. He wasn't going to see him burnt like a criminal. He carried the body in his own hands. The bishop was outraged, but when he moved to act, the king had him arrested, him and all his priests. There was bitter fighting, but in the end the king crucified his brother and hanged the rest. That was the start of it – in my great-grandfather's time. Clarion Starbridge mobilized our army and marched north. We've been at war since then. In my childhood, the front line was more than two hundred miles north of the city, way on the other side of the Caladon frontier. Now, of course, it's very close.'

There was a long pause. The commissar had moved around the room as he spoke, gesturing with short, brisk movements of his fists. As he concluded, he stood up straight and again clasped his hands behind his back.

Thanakar sat, confused. If there was a connection between this story and his own, he couldn't see it. But he believed there must be, for the stories seemed to resonate together without touching at any point. 'Why are you telling me this?' he asked.

The commissar frowned. 'Well I would have thought it was obvious. The war's not going well. The bishop is afraid of people who don't seem quite resigned to their fate. Young men with grievances . . . of that kind.'

Again Thanakar felt a flush of confusion in his cheeks. 'The circumstances are not the same,' he said.

'Aren't they? You believe they're not. It was an accident, you know. What happened to you.'

'He dropped me. Everyone knows it. He threw me down deliberately. Down the steps.'

'It was an accident,' repeated the commissar. 'Otherwise they wouldn't have done it like that – not if they were punishing your father, or stealing from him. Not at your final presentation, after you had already gotten your names and your tattoos. They would have done it at your birth, like young Prince Argon. Not, of course, that they weren't right. One blue eye. Bad business. You were just unlucky.'

Thanakar said nothing.

'Anyway,' continued the commissar, 'You can rely on me. Nothing to fear. I won't let them touch you. You're like a son to me.'

'Thank you.'

'Not to say that you shouldn't give it up. Visiting the prisons. The painkillers, I mean. The medication. You can't do much good that way. The real problem's something else.'

Thanakar stood up. 'Thank you.'

The commissar looked at him anxiously. 'Sometimes I express things badly,' he admitted. 'You forgive me?'

'There is nothing to forgive.'

'Then why don't you stay to dinner? My wife will join us. The four of us. Quite a . . . jolly party.'

These conversations transpired on July 92nd of the eighth phase of spring 00016, in the holy city-state of Charn, in the northwest corner of the possessions of the emperor, in the hundredth month of his interminable reign. That year it was an old-fashioned city of twisting alleyways and wooden houses, a trading center for the region. Formerly most shipping had run by sea, but in those bitter days the gulf was choked with warfare, and so the priests shipped their goods by rail, overland, down through the infant deserts to the great manufacturing centers of the South – in summer, oil of roses, prayer birds, sandalwood, rubber, black ivory, and orchids; in autumn, lumber; in winter, quarried glass; and in springtime nothing at all, for there was nothing. The war was very bad.

That year, Paradise was visible for one hundred and eighty-four days at the beginning of spring, at the time of the solstice thaw and the last antinomial crusade. The next time Paradise was visible, more than eight thousand days later, it rose on the night of August 7th, in the eighth phase of spring. That night there was a great festival in Charn, and all the temples of the city were full of candlelight and incense and the urgent, huddled faithful, filling the vaults with old-fashioned chanting – the forty-eight names of self-denial, the seventeen obligations of parenthood, the nine kinds of love. In celebration, the bishop's council had

91

arranged a truce in the eternal war and exchanged prisoners with Argon Starbridge. There were numerous misunderstandings and delays, but in the end the first trucks arrived after sunset of the first day, and unloaded in the packing yards outside the city gates. There was a big crowd to welcome them, and a complicated official reception, but in spite of that it was the dreariest, most dismal spectacle that anyone had ever seen: more than twenty thousand broken-down old men, veterans of forgotten campaigns, men whose whole lives had been spent as prisoners of war. And even though the worst had been culled out at the border, and the rest washed and fed and issued new uniforms, nothing could disguise the fact that few knew even where they were, and few could recognize the families and friends who had been rounded up to greet them.

One of the oldest, however, was still cogent, and had been asked to address the crowd. He was a small, wrinkled, obsolete old soldier, wearing his white hair in the style of a previous generation – long down his back and fastened with an iron ring. But his eyes were still bright, and he reached the top of the dais without assistance, and in fact he began beautifully, describing the conditions of his captivity – the snow, the stink, the grinding work – in words too weathered and old-fashioned to offend. He was making an excellent impression, and the curates in the bleachers behind him were whispering and smiling, the captain of the purge nodding benignly, the canon expanding with relief, until the soldier paused and swallowed, and started again.

'Sweet friends,' he said, in his old, quavering voice, but the effect was like a needle or a shock, because the canon and the clergy sat bolt upright at the sound and looked towards the speaker with expressions of horror and disbelief. The greeting 'sweet friends' was strictly adventist. The

old soldier was a heretic. 'In all this suffering,' he said, 'it was easy to submit. Thousands did, died in their sleep, or with their shovels in their hands, or in attempts to escape that never could have succeeded. The men you see here around you are just one sad fragment of the proud regiments that marched out so long ago, flags flying, chanting the names of victory. Some died in battle, some were captured, and some came home to die in bed. The ones who survived, it is because they made a purpose out of living. For once I lay down with a defeated heart, I prayed for death in my little cell, sweet friends, I prayed for death to take me as I slept. I curled up on the floor of my cell, and in the middle of the night I dreamt that I woke up to someone shaking me, and a voice calling me by my name. "Wake up," it said, "Wake up, Liston Bombadier," the purest voice, it was a light in that dark room, it was like a light glowing all around me. I staggered up awake – "Lord, Lord," I cried, "Where are you? Why can't I see you?" "But I am with you after all, Liston Bombadier. I am with you every day." "Lord," I said, with tears in my eyes, "Why can't I see you?" And the voice said, "Listen to me. What you hear and feel around you now is just a dream. It has no substance but to reassure you. And to promise you that you will not feel death until you see me face to face, standing in my flesh. In my flesh. And on that day . . ." '
Up to then, the canon had seemed to hope the man would keep his talking within the bounds of orthodoxy, or perhaps he was too stupefied to speak, but at that point there was a hissing stream of bad language from the captain at his side, more furious for being whispered, as if it were escaping from under pressure. 'Sweet balls of Beloved Angkhdt,' swore the captain. 'Whose idea was this?' and all the curates looked at one another.

'What's to be done?' whispered the canon, and in fact there was nothing; the effect of arresting the man, or dragging him away from the podium, was unthinkable. The crowd around was staring at him with open mouths.

' "And on that day," ' continued the soldier, ' "I will wash all the pain of living from your body, and all the memory of suffering from your mind. On that day, the earth will bring forth her fruit without tending, fish will fly, and animals will talk. And it will never be winter any more, never any more. The powers of earth will be overthrown, and no man will be hungry, and all men will be free . . ." '

'That's enough,' whispered the captain, and a few curates scuttled away to pull the power on the microphone. But whether they were confused by urgency, or whether there were some jokers among them, after a few moments' fumbling all the lights went out in the arena, and the soldier's voice boomed out, unimpeded in the sudden dark, seeming louder than ever: ' "On that day I will gather up into my hands all the oppressed. But all the rich men and the priests, the Starbridges and torturers, they will wish they never had been born – " ' And then the power was cut, and there was silence.

Thanakar and Abu Starbridge were wandering through the crowd. They had stood among the people, listening awestruck to the soldier's speech. The lights went out, and then the soldier's voice, extinguished as a plug was pulled. But around them, the crowd of people seethed and whispered in the dark, as if the broken current had been transferred to them. Vague shadows moved and blundered, and from the direction of the dais came the sound of muffled banging and soft yells. The people shouted angrily and stamped their feet, but it was dark and there was no direction for their anger. In the dark, the doctor put his hand out and took his cousin by the arm.

And then, as perfectly as if it had been rehearsed, a man cried out, and then another, and then the whole mass of people were crying and groaning with wonder as the white

94

rim of Paradise showed among the hills of the eastern horizon, hours before it was predicted. As it rose, white and mystical, seeming to take up half the sky, the noise around the cousins loudened and then died away. And in the new, stark light, they could see men and women falling to their knees, their lips trembling in prayer, and some, more miserable than the rest, perhaps, shook their fists and whispered curses, tears standing in their eyes. From somewhere near, a temple bell tolled deeply, and then another and another, all over the city, searching for unison, until finally they all swung together in a dolorous harmony. All stopped at once, and there was quiet for the obligatory count of twelve, and then from every mouth in the vast crowd, and from the festival grounds close by, and from all the people in the streets and slums around them, spilled out in unison the first words of the great psalm of despair: 'Break me, oh God, break my hard body into dust, for I have forgotten every lesson from Your lips. Poison every cup, every dream, every attempt. No rest, no peace, no happiness, no. Never, never, never,' and on these words the temple bells swung again – 'Never, never, never. But.'

Thanakar and Abu looked around them at the different faces. Defeated old women sat back on their heels and whispered it, defiant young men spat it out as if they hated every word. But they did recite it, all of them, whether with anger and disgust, whether with tears and broken hearts, whether they mouthed the words only or spoke them from their souls. It was proof of the enduring power of the myth, of its effect on every life, the power of the risen Paradise, the planet that could melt the snow and pull the tides three hundred feet in a single night. People knelt with outstretched hands, praying to its bright surface, as if in its shadows and its mountains they could see the palaces and the bright castles of the blessed, perhaps even the windows where they once had lived, the faces of the loving friends that they had left behind when they were born.

'Never. Never. Never. But. But oh my God, accept my life as payment towards the debt I owe, and help me to bear what is to come.' The psalm ended. Under the bleak light, Abu and Thanakar looked towards the deserted dais, the empty arena, the black uniforms of the bishop's purge, hundreds of them, materialized from nowhere: stiff black uniforms and the silver dog's head insignia; in those days their mere presence was enough to disperse the thickest crowd. They weren't even armed, but already people were getting to their feet, dazed, their wits scattered, clearing away down side streets and through the mass of trucks. In those days it was enough for the spiritual police just to stand there, relaxed and even smiling, and in a little while the packing yards were empty, the war veterans hastily paraded away somewhere, down to the festival grounds.

The cousins barely noticed their departure. They stood alone in an empty, widening circle, in the middle of the draining crowd, looking upward, entranced, for they were Starbridges, and the purge meant nothing to them, and at that moment the festival had begun, in a frenzy of fireworks and light. First the guns on the Mountain of Redemption fired an evil, sulphurous salute, and laid down a pall of smoke over the whole city. It extinguished the sky, the face of Paradise, and people put their hands over their ears. Then there was quiet, and as the smoke thinned away, people could see emerging out of it the lights of the Temple of the Holy Song, far away above the mountaintop, glistening among the delicate threads of steel like drops of water in a spider's web.

The silence was broken from the other side, beyond the eastern gate, by a single muffled report, and the first rockets burst over the fairgrounds in a tangled spray of silver and lime green. With interruptions, the fireworks would continue the entire night. The separate provinces of the empire were holding a competition, and a man could see the different character of different areas in their choice of colors and forms. Squat, stone-headed Southerners preferred only noise, huge rhythmic spatterings of explosions. Pallid, angular Gharians had developed projectiles made up of whistles and singing bells. Complicated urbanites from the immense, remote fire-cities of the Far West made lingering patterns in the sky, shimmering dragons and exploding birds with long red tails and exploding eyes. Sibilant weavers from the lakes of Banaree, where in springtime it was always milky morning, preferred calm and sparsity and empty spaces. Their rockets rose slowly: a small light would ascend, drawing a straight stalk behind it, and then petals of color would open noiselessly against the sky – gentle, silent blossoms of amber, lavender, and a hundred shades of blue, sent up separately into the expectant sky. There were spaces of darkness in between each bloom.

Abu and Thanakar were in the crowd once more. They had passed beyond the city into a great promenade of stalls and booths and garish lights, sweetshops, wheels of chance, bumper cars, barkers, soothsayers, and drunks, dressed in all the colors of the spectrum, because for the three nights of the festival, obligations of class were forgotten and people mixed freely. Still, there were few Starbridges in the fairgrounds, so the two cousins found themselves moving in a circle of eager familiarity. They loitered, and ate ice cream, and watched the fireworks burst above their heads. An old palmist with an old beard and yellow teeth grabbed Abu by the hand, to croon over his lines. Abu laughed. 'Go on,' he cried over the pressing din. 'Tell me the girl I've got to marry. Tall and thin? Short and horrible?' He was partly drunk, and held a plastic bottle of wine in his other hand.

The old man peered, and frowned, and shook his head. 'Abu Starbridge,' he said slowly, as if he could read it in the lines. 'Marry? No. You will not marry. I don't think so. No.' He rubbed the prince's palm. 'No, see. Look here. Death by fire. Not far away.' He brought his own hand up and peered at it. 'I have the same mark.' He traced along his own lifeline with a withered finger. 'Here. Death by fire.'

The crowd had quieted down. People stood around them in a circle. Some squatted on the ground. 'See?' the old man continued. 'All in the same place. My grandson has it too. One man out of six. I've counted.' He gestured vaguely around the circle of faces and looked up, his eyes puzzled and worried. 'What does it mean? Death by fire. So many of us, all at the same time.'

'It can't come soon enough for me,' said Abu, and he put his bottle to his lips. But before drinking he paused, because the old man was still staring at him with the same puzzled expression, and all around the small circle, people shuffled and looked down.

'That was tactless,' muttered the doctor.

'I don't understand. Why are they looking at me like that?' whispered Abu.

'You think everyone is like you. You have nothing to fear from death. A Starbridge prince. You'll go straight to Paradise. But these people fear it. However miserable their lives are now, their next ones will be worse, which-ever horrible planet they're condemned to.'

'Nobody still believes that.'

'Everyone believes it. And even if they only half believe it, isn't it enough to make them miserable?'

'Drink up,' said a thin man at the edge of the circle. 'Starbridge. What do you care?' He motioned towards Paradise with his head. 'What do you care about us? Two

98

weeks ago my brother died. The priests marked him down for the sixth planet. He was twice the man you are.'

Abu blinked. 'I'm sorry,' he said. 'My cousin could have saved him. He is a great doctor.'

The man snorted angrily, and Thanakar said, 'Stop it, Abu. Pay attention. Look at his clothes. Listen to him – he's not permitted medicine. None of these people are.'

'Yes, listen to me,' interrupted the thin man. 'I took my brother to the hospital. They threw him out; not even a painkiller, they said. Nothing that might dilute the punishment of God, they said. Punishment for his sins. Listen to me – he'd never done anything. God help him, he'd even believed in your religion. It was punishment for being poor, that's all. Punishment for having had to work all his life. Bastards! Drunken pig! Do you know what it's like, the sixth planet? It has no air.'

Above them, a firework fish broke noisily against the sky, its scarlet tentacles drifting and unwinding in the idle wind. Thanakar took his cousin by the elbow. 'Let's go,' he said, but Abu wouldn't move.

'Why do you hate me?' he asked the thin man. 'I've done you no harm.'

'No, not you,' answered the man savagely. 'Never you. Just robbed me ever since you were born. Just grown fat while I starved.' The crowd was moving angrily, and Thanakar pulled the prince away. A ragged woman reached to restrain them. If she had grabbed his arm, the doctor would have pushed her back. But the tentative fumbling of her fingers, as if she feared polluting him, made her hold a strong one. She hesitated to touch his sacred flesh, and her hesitation made the doctor stop, ashamed. She would not look at them. She ran her tongue around her teeth, stained blue with kaya gum, and then she whispered in a voice as fumbling as her hands: 'Sir. Doctor. Forgive me . . .' and her words scattered away.

'What is it?' he answered. The woman was kneeling in front of him, in a posture of abasement that he hadn't seen in a long time.

'You are a doctor?'

'Yes,' he said, making himself smile.

'Please. My little girl is very sick. I'm afraid she's going to die. She has the fever.'

In the silence that followed, it seemed to Thanakar as if the circle of faces around them had tightened suddenly, closing off escape. People stared at him with differing expressions, some hostile, some smiling obscurely. Trapped! Damn! he thought.

"It's illegal,' he said guiltily, and around the circle he could see in people's faces the hardening of their thoughts. So many expressions, but not a single sympathetic one. It made him angry that they had already judged him in their minds. They thought he had no heart, like all his kind.

'Please, sir,' mumbled the woman. 'For the festival.'

'Where do you live?' he asked, because he wanted to see some change, some loosening in the circle around him. But once the question was out, he realized that he had trapped himself, because Abu touched him on the shoulder and whispered, 'Good for you,' and because the woman raised her head and looked at him with such an expression of gratitude, it was as if he had already saved the child's life.

'Not far,' she said.

This was inexact. After the decision was made to go, they stood around waiting, for unclear and shifting reasons. People jabbered to each other in languages the doctor didn't know. There seemed to be two opinions about where the child was. A message was sent, a reply expected. It never came, but in the meantime people argued about how to go and what to bring. They would need electric torches. None were available. Someone's brother had one. And then suddenly they all started in a crowd, turning away from the fairgrounds into a filthy labyrinth of streets.

Thanakar had waited with a sense of anticlimax. But as he and Abu marched along, the street illuminated by fireworks and the fitful torch, picking through gutters filled with garbage and stinking excrement, Thanakar was overwhelmed by nervousness. The woman who had originally accosted them had vanished, and instead the whole crowd was accompanying them, twenty people at least. More joined them at every twist of the narrow street, and often they had to stop while a whole jabbering conversation flowed around them. But finally, after more than half an hour, they stopped outside a house as wretched-looking as any Thanakar had ever seen, a wooden shack with boarded windows, guarded by a bony dog. It rushed to meet them, snarling and showing its teeth, but someone threw a stone and it whimpered away.

The prince and the doctor stood apalled. But they had come too far to turn back, so they stepped in through the littered yard and up the steps, to where one man was swinging the electric torch. By its light he showed them a crude placard next to the doorway: CONFESSIONAL. SIN EATING. 'Dirty place,' he confided. 'Very bad. Not a good place.' He grinned and stepped aside to let them enter.

The house was divided into two rooms. In front, through a glass doorway, they could see the sin eater, sitting with a client, but they had no time to look, for the crowd propelled them past, to where a woman knelt next to a broken armchair. It was the woman who had stopped them at the fair. She had changed her clothes; unnecessarily, thought Thanakar, for her new dress was just as dirty, just as torn as the old. He looked around. Light came from a kerosene candle. It reflected dully off a wall decorated with pictures of animals clipped from magazines. On a bed nearby, under the woman's hand, in a nest of dark sheets, lay a sleeping child.

No one followed him into the room. Thanakar had an impression of the doorframe behind him rimmed with faces, from the lintel to the sill. It was very quiet, and Thanakar could hear the sounds of the confession from the other room. The prince stood near, frowning and grinning. He took a drink from his plastic bottle.

The child was a girl, perhaps two thousand days old. The doctor approached her warily. Under her hair he could see the circle of her scalp; it looked so small and fragile, yellow in the yellow light. The light glinted in the hair along her arm. He said, 'Is this she?' At the noise of his voice, the child turned her head, and he could see her puckered face.

'She's lovely,' said the prince behind him.

'Yes,' murmured the woman softly. It was as if the presence of her child had given her strength. In her own home, her fumbling servility had disappeared. She didn't rise, or look at them, or ask them to sit down. There was no place to sit.

The doctor cleared his throat. 'You understand,' he said, 'I have no medicine with me. No equipment.'

'I have faith in you, sir,' said the woman simply.

The doctor cursed under his breath and exchanged glances with Abu. He rubbed his hands together as if washing them. 'What's that smell?' he asked.

'Smell, sir?'

On the floor by the girl's head lay a bowl full of vomit and wet feces. 'This room is very dirty,' he said.

'Dirty, sir?'

'That's what I said. Do you have any clean bedsheets?'

The woman looked up and shook her head. There was a hint of panic in her eyes.

'Never mind,' said the doctor hurriedly. He sat down on the bedside and ran his fingers over the child's fine, almost

102

transparent brown hair, not quite touching her. Even so, he could feel the fever in her head. Sweat glistened on the hairs of her upper lip. 'How do you feel?' he asked.

The child said nothing, and turned away her face. Under her ear he could see a place where some cosmetic cream had dried in a thick crust, and he picked at it idly with his fingernail. It flaked away, and under it he saw a red birthmark, one of the many signs of the unclean. God had marked her. Thanakar put his finger on the mark. 'How long has she been like this?' he asked.

'She was born with it. Sir.' There was a note of bitterness in the woman's voice.

'That's not what I meant,' he said. 'I meant the fever.' But he kept his finger where it was. 'You are runaways?'

'Yes. They wanted to put her in prison. They said she was a witch.'

'It doesn't matter. I am not the purge. But I'm surprised you let me see her. You must be careful.'

The woman seemed close to tears. 'Oh sir,' she said, 'I thought she was going to die. Her fever just goes up and up . . .'

'She'll be all right. How long has she been like this?'

'Four days. What more can they do to us . . .?'

'She'll be all right. Tomorrow I'll send something to take the fever down. In the meantime, you must try to keep her clean. I'll show you. Bring me a bucket of warm water, soap, and towels.'

The woman started to cry, and one of the men in the doorway said, 'There is no hot water, sir. No towels.'

'Cold water, then. And soap.'

'Soap, sir?' said the woman in despair.

'Yes. Soap. Is that so difficult to understand?'

'Don't bully her, Cousin,' came the prince's gentle voice.

Thanakar pulled the sheets away from the girl's body. She turned her face back towards him and opened wide her eyes, staring at him without speaking as he moved his fingers down her body and unwrapped a grimy bandage around her knee.

'Why do you want soap, sir?' asked the woman.

The doctor bit his lips. 'I want to wash her.' Under the bandage was a deep infected sore. Her whole knee was covered in a leaking crust of scabs.

The woman got to her feet and said some words in a strange language. One of the faces in the doorway disappeared.

The girl's feet were encased in plastic shoes. As Thanakar removed them, she cried out. Underneath, her feet were covered with dirt and blisters. The shoes were several sizes too small. He took them off and laid them by the chamberpot. 'She shouldn't wear these,' he said quietly.

'No shoes, sir?' the woman asked, her voice tearful. 'But shoes are good. Aren't they?'

'Not these shoes. Look what they are doing to her feet. It's a wonder she can walk.'

'She can't walk, sir.'

The girl lay on her back. She was dressed in a ragged nylon smock, with buttons running down her chest. Thanakar unfastened several, and as he did so, he felt the air in the room change. The girl's eyes widened and filled with fright. And behind him, the men who had been standing in the doorway came in and stood or squatted all around, staring at his hands. There was no hostility in their faces, only total absorption in his smallest movements, as if instead of simply peeling the smock back from her narrow ribcage, he were making an incision and peeling back the skin. A man came in with a bucket of water and half a bar of soap. Taking them from him, Thanakar started to wash her, with clever movements of his elegant white hands.

For Prince Abu, the tension in the room was hard to bear. With an unclear idea of stepping out into the street and waiting there, he wandered through the doorway. But as he passed the entrance to the other room, he stopped. Someone had pulled a curtain over the glass, but the door was partly open, and he looked inside.

It was something he had read about. In popular mythology, a man died only after he had made a total of 400 mortal errors. It was an idea that had grown out of the commentary on the 1,019th verse of the Song of the Beloved Angkhdt: 'Sweet friend, how long have I known you? How many days have I sensed you near me, sleeping, waking, your body within reach. Without you, I would have made myself a hell long ago and furnished it with lies, and memories of four hundred women left unsatisfied. Dear love, you have taken these things into yourself. Love, you have saved me . . .' The text was obscure, but it had led to this, that blameless men with nothing left to sell would sell their blamelessness. A sick man would come in, afraid of death and damnation, the weight of his mistakes suddenly intolerable. And the confessor would take them on himself, one by one, a few at a time, into his own body, according to a simple ritual. The sick man would sit down and try to capture in his mind all the particulars of the sin that he wanted to expunge. On his lap he held a box of colored powders – black for bitter thoughts, red for evil actions, green for harmful words. He would make a selection, and holding some powder in the pouch of his lip, he would begin to talk about his sin, every aspect of it, germination and result, everything that weighed upon his conscience. Besides its foul taste, the drug was a powerful expectorant, and by the time the man had finished talking, he would have filled a stone basin with colored spit. Then he would rinse his mouth out with sweet water, and his confessor, after prayers and exhortations, would drink down the contents of the basin. And at the end, the sick man would have stepped back from the grave, and the healthy man would have taken one step towards it.

Abu had read about this ritual, but he had never seen it. There in the dark room, by the light of a single candle, he saw a fleshless, toothless, bald old man and a pale young one. They sat opposite each other on wooden chairs, leaning over a stone pot set on the floor between them. Both were too absorbed in what they were doing to notice the prince standing in the doorway.

The old man had almost filled the basin with black juice. 'It was wrong, I know,' he mumbled. 'But it wasn't my fault. My wife hired her when I was gone from home. I wouldn't have objected, not that, but still, there was something unnatural about her. Something wicked in the way she disturbed my sleep. I couldn't sleep. I thought about her constantly. I neglected my business. It wasn't natural, not for a girl like her. A serving girl, from the lowest family . . .' He spat a jet of juice into the bowl and then continued more distinctly. 'She wasn't good-looking. It wasn't that. She looked . . . vulnerable. Weak. It maddened me. She was a witch, I tell you. It wasn't my fault.' The juice ran down his chin.

'No excuses,' said the young man.

'No. Of course not. That's not what I mean. I was bewitched, yes. I thought about her. Nothing dirty. I thought about her.' He emptied his mouth again.

'Don't lie,' said the young man. The old man sighed, rubbing his hands together in his lap, hunched over the basin, and when he continued, he was almost inaudible.

'I used to imagine her naked,' he confessed. 'At night I used to lie in my bed and imagine her . . . breasts.' His voice trailed away.

'Her breasts.'

'Her breasts, yes,' the old man repeated loudly. He sighed. 'I used to imagine touching them.'

'How many times?'

'I don't know. It doesn't matter. I didn't do anything. At least, not like that. I used to . . .' His voice died down to nothing, and he emptied his mouth into the bowl.

'Tell me.'

'I used to beat her. I would find fault with her work.'

'Stop,' commanded the young man. He held out the box of powder and motioned towards the red compartment. Sighing wearily, the other took a pinch of red and put it in his lip. Then suddenly he pitched forward and clapped his skinny hands to his mouth.

'Keep it in,' commanded the young man. 'Don't spit it out.'

The old man's eyes and nose were streaming water. 'God, it burns,' he cried when he had recovered his speech.

'Yes, it burns,' agreed the young man softly. He held out the box again.

'Ah, God, no more. Not again. Have pity.'

'Take it.'

Moaning and weeping, the old man took another pinch.

'Now, tell me. What did you do?'

'I . . . I beat her.'

'Louder. Stop mumbling.'

'I beat her.'

'How many times?'

'I . . . I don't know.' The man was weeping and wringing his hands. 'I can't remember.'

'Think. Visualize each time.'

There was a pause. And then: 'I beat her seven times.'

'How hard?'

'Not hard. I swear to God not hard.' The old man smiled pathetically. 'I'm not strong. She was a healthy girl. At least . . .' He spat red drool into the pot. Abu could see it clearly, floating on a puddle of black. Action floating on the surface of the mind, he thought. He raised the bottle to his

107

lips, but the movement changed the shadows on the floor. The old man looked up and sat back in his chair. 'Who are you?' he cried, red drool running down his chin. 'What are you doing here?'

Prince Abu moved out of the doorway to let the light fall on his uniform. The old man stared at him, astonished. The juice made strings of liquid down his clothes.

'I'm sorry,' said the prince. 'I'm sorry to disturb you.' But the two men sat there staring without moving. 'My cousin is a doctor,' he explained to the sin eater. 'We came to see your daughter.'

Still the men said nothing, and then slowly, as if unwillingly, they got to their feet to make the compulsory gestures of respect, knuckles to their foreheads, hiding their eyes.

'No, please,' stammered the prince. 'Never mind that. We came for the carnival. I'm sorry. I didn't mean to disturb you. Please continue with your . . .' He broke off, embarrassed, and stepped back through the doorway and out into the passage. From the other room there came a yell of pain, and he could see Thanakar rising from the bed, holding his finger.

'Ah,' he cried. 'She bit me. Like a wild animal.' And then he smiled.

'They hate us,' remarked Abu sadly, later, as they walked down to the docks.

'They have their reasons.'

'But we are good men, aren't we? We do our best. We treat them kindly.'

'And if we were bad men and treated them cruelly, what defense could they have? That's the point. What law restrains us? I have seen my own father knock a servant's teeth out with his fist.'

'He must have been provoked.'

108

'He was not provoked at all,' exclaimed Thanakar, irritated by his friend's lack of imagination. 'He was a cruel man. Maybe not always, but after a lifetime in the army. It's the life we lead. You know that for every two like us there are twenty like him. They think God himself gave them their tattoos.'

'Then I'm thankful to be unfit for military service. You should be too.'

'I should be. Do you know where we're going?'

'I'm following you.'

They were walking arm in arm, because they had walked too far for the doctor's bad leg. He stopped for a moment under a streetlamp in the small deserted street, to take his weight off it, to lean on Abu's shoulder. Looking up into his face, he thought he saw some resemblance there to the prince's sister. Seeing her fifteen days before, at the commissar's dinner, he was surprised that brother and sister could be so unalike. Under the streetlamp, he took pleasure in reconstructing the memory of her features from her brother's face. Prince Abu was balding, fat, sweet, ineffectual, sweating heavily even in the cold night, his eyes bright and rebellious under folds of unhealthy skin, as if they were held prisoner in his face. Again, his lips were fat, but under them his teeth were white and delicate, like pearls hidden in a flapping purse.

In his sister, it was as if the barriers of flesh were stripped away, and Thanakar could imagine that their skulls would look the same. Their teeth, their eyes were similar.

'Why are you looking at me?' asked Abu, smiling.

'Do you mind if we wait here for a minute?'

'If you like.'

In a way, her eyes were like her husband's too. Perhaps that's what bound the three of them together in that strange house, the lack of harmony between their faces and their eyes. She was a perfect example of her class, docile and submissive. It was part of the obligation of her name always to speak pleasantly. But even though by law and custom she was forbidden ever to make any bitter judgement or any harsh remark, yet her eyes complained. The brightness, the bitterness in them combined with the perfection of her manners to make a tension that seemed sexual.

'What are you thinking about?' asked Abu.

'Your sister.'

'Did you like her?'

'In a way.'

'I wish you could have married he. She is just your age.'

Since meeting her at dinner, Thanakar, too, had speculated what it would have been like if she had married him and not the old commissar. Their families were connected; it would have been a likely match, if not for his leg. He would have been a prince and married her, and his children would have inherited his house and income. He would have broken down the barriers of the courtesy that she had learned in school, and in time she would have become a free woman, capable of loving. It was a stupid fantasy, without detail in his mind, because as always his leg wouldn't permit him to limp over the first if. His child would never wear his clothes. For this reason, he thought, it was too much to expect him to forget what small privileges he had. Abu could shake beggars by the hand, drink from polluted cups. What did he care?

Abu laughed. 'How stern you look.'

'Shall we go?'

They walked away into the dark beyond the streetlamp, and at the end of a long alleyway they found a makeshift barricade of garbage and concrete, lined at the top with barbed wire and sheets of corrugated iron. They walked along it till it joined another, higher wall, and at the gate a wide, vacant face, shiny in the light of an acetylene lantern on a pole, looked out at them through a hole punched in the wall. It looked a long time out of bulging, expression-less eyes, motionless, unresponsive to inquiry, entreaty, threats, silence. Framed in the square hole, it seemed less a human face than a picture on a wall. It seemed deaf and blind. But Abu laughed, and at once the face changed, its lips twisting into a silent grin, revealing long antinomial teeth. That was all; there was no more movement, but from behind the wall came a shuffling and a banging, and the gate swung open on wire hinges. A man stood in the gap, gigantic and muscular, dressed only in a pair of cotton breeches, roughened to look like leather. Unlike the gatekeeper's, his face was animate. And he spoke, too. Sound bubbled on his lips, nonsense syllables set to a frothy tune, as if he were laughing to music. With his palms, he beat a loud, complicated rhythm on his thighs and his chest, finishing with a roll across his belly, which he distended for the purpose. 'In!' he shouted, in rhythm with the slaps. 'In! In! In! In! In!' He stepped aside.

Summoning courage, the cousins stepped over the con-crete threshold on to a kind of platform set into the top of the barricade. A number of men and women were standing around or sitting, wild, savage-looking, scantily dressed. But as usual with antinomials, there was no sense of menace about them as a group. Thanakar, as he entered, felt that he had interrupted nothing. The chairs were not set in any kind of order, nor was there any focus of activity – no cards, tables, bottles, food, fire, conversation, nothing to make a newcomer feel either uncomfortable or welcome. One woman with tangled hair and a long gaunt face was singing to herself, music with no words, only inarticulate combinations of vowels. Nobody seemed to listen. Each one seemed imprisoned in a separate world. Thanakar noticed with no particular sensation of alarm that they all carried weapons, cruel knives, or quivers full of arrows. One man was fixing an old gun. Thanakar thought: that they even have a wall and a barricade, that they even think to protect themselves, shows how they have changed. The way they sit together shows how they have not.

No one took any notice. The antinomials seemed lost in their own occupations, whether it was stamping on the floor, or staring at nothing, or making a single repetitive motion of their hand and wrist. Still, Abu and Thanakar passed through them warily, as if through a ward of prisoners. There was no reason to fear them. These people were not slaves to passion, or violence, or even comprehension. Yet physically, they were powerful and gigantic; the light shone along their shoulders and the long muscles of their backs. And though some looked ill and hungry, none looked weak. Besides, they had rejected reason, and there was no telling when one might reach out his long arm. It didn't happen. Abu and Thanakar walked through, and though some looked up and stared at them, most never raised their heads.

The prince had been there once before, drunk. He scarcely remembered. But still, it was easy to find the way without asking questions, because the platform shelved into the open air, out from under a crude canopy. Standing on the edge, they looked from a great height over an abandoned railway yard, left from the days when freight trains used to run down to the docks through webs of tunnels under the city. People lived in there, a whole subterranean world. And here too: in abandoned boxcars and among rusted sidings, the antinomials had made their homes, though most preferred possessionless lives in the huge, ramshackle warehouses that fingered the yard – urban resonances of the cold communal halls they had left so long ago.

A spidery ladder led from the platform down into the yard. There was a spring wind off the river, smelling of

112

mud and dirty water. It made the ladder tremble. Thanakar's feet rang each steel step. It was very dark. Paradise was sunk into some clouds. And from down below, there were no strong sources of light, only glimmering lanterns and small fires. They climbed down past the mouth of one of the railway tunnels, 100 feet from upper lip to lower. Far inside, they saw a red glow, and shadows leaping on the walls. Some long-forgotten civic pride, left over from another season, had decorated the tunnel's mouth with colossal seated statues of Angkhdt the God of Industry, one on either side. The brick was crumbling away, but you could still recognize the outlines of the great dogs' heads, their snouts ten feet long. The ladder wound down between them.

At the ladder's end, Abu and Thanakar stood in the dark between the railway tracks. 'What are we doing here?' asked the doctor.

'No biting,' answered Abu. 'Still I wish we had a flashlight . . . if I were a slave to wishing, that is.'

They both laughed, and Abu uncorked his bottle. 'Give me some,' demanded Thanakar.

'Just a taste. It's very strong if you're not used to it. Even if you are.'

'Just a taste.' The doctor held out his hand, and Abu passed the bottle. 'Don't get drunk,' he cautioned. 'I can't carry you back up.'

The doctor drank, gurgled and coughed. 'My God, that's horrible,' he said, as soon as he could speak. 'What's in it?'

The prince took the bottle back and drank a long, meditative swallow. He held the liquor in his mouth, as if trying to analyze the taste. 'I want to walk,' he said, taking the doctor's arm. He shook the bottle in his other hand, to hear how much was left.

They walked down towards the river, stumbling in silence between the railroad tracks. When Abu spoke, his voice was soft and serious. 'I've often asked myself. I think it must be distilled from a mixture of the illusions it creates. It doesn't remind you of anything else, and it leaves no aftertaste. That is because it takes away your judgement and your memory. It's very thick, and so it makes your mind unclear. And it burns your throat. Sometimes, when you've drunk too much, it's as if there were a fire all around you. You can feel it underneath your skin. I don't know. They say it's made from blood.'

'Blood?'

'But I don't believe it. If it were, how could I drink it?'

They had reached a line of boxcars pulled up on an old siding. In the doorway of each one burned a small lantern. People squatted, talking. As they passed, one stood up and shouted to them in a harsh voice.

'Biters,' whispered Abu. 'Wine sellers and pimps. Take no notice.'

'Come!' shouted the biter.

'Ssh, take no notice,' repeated Abu. And then, 'What a snob I am,' he said, laughing. Possessed of a sudden impulse, he walked over to the car. It was arranged as a kind of store, disorganized, but clean: bins of vegetables, tools, clothes. Bottles of liquor. The man who had called to them stood in the doorway, scowling down at them. The atheist's cross and circle was branded on his forehead, and on his cheek, too, the scars persisted where he had been cut. He had been arrested more than once.

'Yes?' asked Abu. 'What do you want?'

The man glared at him. Then, with a jerky dismissive motion, as if he hated them, he gestured towards the wares in his shop. The gesture included a ferocious young woman sitting on a packing crate.

'What is this?' asked Abu, pointing to one of the liquor bottles.

The man's scowl deepened. 'Wine,' he said sulkily.

'What's it made out of?'

The man stared at him. 'Wine!' he shouted. 'Wine!' He kicked the bottle with his toe.

'But what's it made out of?' asked Thanakar, smiling. 'You made it yourself, didn't you?'

The biter pulled his lips back to show his teeth, heavy and carnivorous, and gleaming white. He pressed his fists to both sides of his forehead and squatted down in the boxcar door until his face was level with theirs. They could hear a rumble of anger, deep in his huge chest. 'Wine,' he said, carefully and slowly. 'It's made from wine.'

Abu pulled the doctor by the elbow, and they backed away into the dark. 'I hope you'll be satisfied with that,' the prince remarked as they turned away. 'I don't think you'll get a better answer.' From the boxcar behind them came a roar of rage, and then a bottle hurtled past their heads, missing them narrowly, crashing up ahead.

'Wine,' remarked Abu.

'Unpredictable fellow,' commented Thanakar, taking the prince's arm.

'Yes. It's not fair. The biters have a hard life. The others hate them because they have no pride. Yet without biters, the rest would starve.'

The cousins walked on, reaching an area of the yard where there was more light. They saw antinomials hurrying and ambling in the same direction, down towards the river where a crowd was forming on the bank. Upstream, the monstrous skeleton of the harbor bridge stretched into the darkness, for the suburbs on the other bank were all abandoned. Nearer, a row of docks stuck out into the mud. Because of the Paradise tides, the river had completely disappeared. Where it had been, the mud was dozens of feet thick.

Where the crowd was, the embankment overlooked a platform slung on steel wires between two docks. In normal times it must have floated on the surface of the water, but now it hung suspended, fifteen feet above the mud. A bonfire burned on it, but besides that it was empty, though crowds of people sat and stood on the concrete embankment and on the docks on either side.

'We're early,' said Abu. 'I thought we'd be too late.' They reached the embankment, and he sat down happily and kicked his feet over the edge.

'I wish we had brought something to sit on,' said Thanakar, looking dubiously at the dirty ground.

'Oh well.'

A ladder hung from the underside of the platform down to someplace hidden in the mud, and as Thanakar sat down, some people climbed up from below and sat down by the fire. Abu scanned their faces, but they were far away and hard to recognize, until a huge golden cat leapt from the lap of one and sauntered carelessly across the stage to where a man was fiddling with the fire.

Thanakar looked around. The antinomials were completely silent, standing or sitting cross-legged, or hugging their knees. No one seemed part of any group. Again, there were no conversations, though some people hummed lazily to themselves. Yet they must have lived together their whole lives. Suffering and war, hunger and despair still had not given them a thing in common. In a crowd, their coldness and their isolation seemed uncanny.

A man stood on the platform and raised his hands. As a request for silence, it was unnecessary, yet even so it seemed to signal the beginning of something. He climbed back down the ladder into the mud, and after a while another man stood up and stepped into the center of the stage. In the glare of the bonfire, he seemed unnaturally tall and thin, and he carried a silver trumpet in his hands. He stood polishing it and smiling, and Thanakar could see the gleam of his teeth. Then he put it to his lips and blew a silver note. It lingered, and when it died away, he blew another, piercingly high. It seemed impossible for a man to have lungs that big, or else it was as if he had found a way of releasing the sound into the air without having to press it with his breath, as if in the metal of the warehouses and the great, gray bridge he had found a resonance, for the sound echoed all around them. Another note, low and deep. Thanakar was reminded of the Banaree fireworks above the fairgrounds, sending single, unmixed colors up to wash the sky.

Another note, pure and high, aching and limitless. At the end, the slightest modulation, just a tightening of the tone.

After that, he was silent for at least a minute while he inspected the bell of the instrument and smiled into the crowd. Then he played again, quiet and tentative, wisps of notes and melodies that went off nowhere. But out of each he collected something that he seemed to like, as if he were gathering threads into his hand, combing them out, rejecting some, twisting the rest together. For out of single notes and phrases the music acquired bulk, direction, tension. It stretched on and on.

Finally the trumpeter paused, his cheeks distended and sweaty. Bending back, he raised his trumpet to the sky and blew out a dirty spray of notes, full of double tones and squeaks. Then he was finished. Turning his back on the silent audience, he returned to his place and sat down, pulling his cloak around him, hiding his face in his hands.

'I've heard him before,' remarked the prince. 'That last part is his signature. The song of himself. I remember it.'

'Clearly a neurotic type. Pass the wine.'

Abu gave the doctor a curious look, but said nothing. Thanakar didn't care. He wanted to feel the liquor's kick. He wanted to feel as if a hole had been drilled in the top of his head and the liquor dribbled in, soaking some parts and not others. He wanted to feel it.

Musicians played, women and men. When they were finished, they wandered around the stage or climbed back down the ladder out of sight. After a long time, the platform was empty, save for two seated figures, one on either side, and the huge, pacing, golden cat. One rose to his feet and stalked to the center of the stage. He raised his arms, and his cloak slid away from his shoulders. He was naked underneath. He raised his hands in a lazy gesture, to scratch behind his neck, to pull the hair back from his face.

Thanakar recognized the boy that they had come to see. He stood casually, legs spread apart, hands on his hips. As Abu said, he was handsome, with clean hard limbs and a delicate face, neither brutal nor empty like most in that crowd. Thanakar saw the first flickers of drunkenness in the color of the boy's skin. It seemed ruddy and alive. And perhaps there was more to it than illusion, because for the first time the crowd seemed to be reacting, too, though the boy had done nothing yet. But people around them had lumbered to their feet, and some called out. They were staring at the dancer intently, as men might look into a fire, which has motion and energy even in stasis. For Thanakar, the drug had lit a fire under the dancer's skin, so that when he started, with a lazy swirl of arms around his head, it seemed even after his arm had passed that Thanakar could see a burning trail behind it.

Thanakar stretched out his leg and looked around. Things had not changed since he was a child. Still he sat while others danced, his bad leg aching. He swallowed some drink and looked over at the prince's face, as he stared at the stage with childlike absorption. It seemed unfair to envy him. Yet Thanakar could see why the prince was more at ease here than in any other part of the city.

He resembled these people; he stared as they did, part of what they saw.

Thanakar took another sip to help him concentrate, because again he had lost himself, his thoughts vanishing to nothing. Why couldn't he stare like that? The dancer somersaulted through the air, surrounded by a wheel of light, and the crowd moved and stamped. People cried out. The dancer was standing on his hands, his legs bent over almost to his head, tendrils of light coiling around him; it was incredible. Thanakar looked up at the sky, pursuing fantasies of loneliness. He felt there was a secret to loneliness, an attraction that only he out of all that crowd had failed to understand.

But he looked back when the second figure on the stage shrugged his cloak away and rose. He walked to the far edge of the platform, to where the bonfire had burned down, and pulled his hair back with the same gesture as his brother. And then he stood and raised his arms, but there was no accompanying flame. Instead, a small current of sound seemed to form around the motion, fast when the boy moved faster, stopping when he stopped. The doctor looked around to see if he could find the source. But it was not exactly music, or at least it didn't remind him of the sound of any instrument or combination of instruments. It was more like singing, only more supple, more responsive to the slightest twist of fingers than a voice could ever be.

The second dancer made a rapid circle around his brother, the sound accompanying him, sinuous and clean. The crowd was silent, and the doctor wondered whether they could hear it too. 'Do you hear it?' he whispered to his cousin. Abu turned towards him, smiling patiently, but as the doctor looked at him he saw his brows contract, and at the same moment he heard gunfire, so that his first impression when the shooting started was that his cousin, too, could make sound out of movement. He had confused cause and effect. Abu pointed to a stream of light.

It flowed over the bridge from the dark shore opposite – men with torches, shooting as they came. Over there, the city was disused and boarded up, but people lived ratlike in the cellars. The road from the bridge led down to the municipal gallows at the city limits. The stream of torches came from there.

Now Thanakar could hear singing too, religious anthems, bigoted old war songs from the antinomial crusades, and Abu and Thanakar struggled to their feet. Around them, the crowd barely reacted. Some sat glumly, sucking their knees, others turned contemptuous backs. But the dancers had stopped, and stood motionless on stage. And in a little while the crowd started to disperse in different directions. People stalked away to get their weapons or their musical instruments. Thanakar grabbed Abu by the shoulder. 'Let's get out of here!' he shouted. Men with torches were streaming down the access ramps, not far away, and occasionally a bullet whined close.

The cousins turned away and hurried back the way they had come. The doctor found it hard to run. He tripped and fell full length, hurting his shin. Abu crouched by him, and they rested in the shadow of a boxcar to let an armed party of antinomials run past the opposite way. The prince was out of breath. He sank down wearily to the ground and put his face into his hands. Thanakar stood up and leaned his back against the boxcar. He could see the bridge ablaze with light, and new fire burning by the docks. Where they were, it was dark and strangely quiet.

Abu whimpered at his feet. Under stress, sometimes the prince's thoughts became disjointed, a running mix of questions and answers. 'Oh God,' he said, 'Why is it like this? How can it be like this? How can I do . . . Think. Think of what to do. What are the obligations of your

120

name? One: courage. Two: duty to your . . . class. Three: courage. Four, four – how can they do it, every time? How can they ruin it?' He sat back against the doctor's leg, and Thanakar reached down to touch his hair.

'Hush,' he said. 'It'll be all right.'

'Who are they?'

'The purge, I guess. I don't know. There was a hanging tonight. Forty heretics, in honor of the festival. Didn't you get an invitation? It must have gotten out of hand.'

'The purge. The purge, the purge, the purge, the purge. How can they? It is not my will.'

'I don't think so,' said a voice near to hand. An enormous shadow stepped out of the dark between two cars, and then a man came out of it, walking towards them. He stooped to pick up Abu's bottle from where he had dropped it, and he threw it into the prince's lap with a contemptuous snap of his wrist. Thanakar recognized the voice and then the man, his cruel face, his heavy lips, the white centers to his eyes. He had exchanged Abu's silver pistols for something more murderous, a machine revolver stuck into his belt. He carried a wooden flute.

'I don't think so,' he repeated. 'Not the purge. Just a few barbarians, like you. Don't be afraid. It's common enough. There's hardly a month without something like this.'

'Barbarians,' groaned Abu. 'Barbarians.' He uncorked his bottle.

It was quiet where they were, though in the distance they could hear shouting and gunfire. The antinomial lifted his flute and played a little tune. He stopped to listen, and Thanakar could hear a response, a flute playing from elsewhere in the yard, and then it stopped. The antinomial played again, just five notes. Again came the response, and then Thanakar could see a lantern swinging towards them from across the yard, a man in its circle. He came close, an older man, with curly white hair and a machete in his belt.

'Good hunting,' he said. And then the two of them conversed together unintelligibly, in a mixture of words and sound. The older man pointed up above them to where the barricade loomed past, where Abu and Thanakar had crossed earlier that night. It was quiet there, a black wall against the darker black. Not far away, the railway tunnel opened its throat, guarded by its crumbling sentinels.

The older antinomial squatted down and held the lantern up, to peer into the prince's face. Abu's cheeks were wet. He had been crying, and the antinomial stretched out one finger to touch his cheek and then brought it back to look at it. 'Water,' he said softly. 'Wet,' and then he added something, a musical phrase that sounded like a question.

A flare burst above the barricade, lighting up the sky. The man with the cruel face looked up, squinting. Above them, the wall erupted into noise, a clattering of gunfire. As they watched, flames showed in several places along the top.

'Barbarians,' said the man. He spat.

The older antinomial looked up from where he squatted near the prince, his face more puzzled than concerned. 'A bad one,' he said. 'Both sides at once.'

The other nodded. He pulled his pistol from his belt and pointed it at Abu's head, and squinted down the barrel, his lips tight for a moment, and then he put up his arm. 'No,' he murmured, in a tone of infinite regret. 'Not fair. Not fair.' He stood looking at them, and then he motioned with his gun up towards the barricade, towards a section that was still dark. 'Go,' he said. 'Don't come back here. Leave me alone. Leave us alone.' He turned and walked away, down towards the battle at the bridge. A flare lit up the sky. Thanakar could see him throw his flute away and start to run.

'Come,' he said, reaching down again to touch the prince's hair. 'Let's go. It's not safe here.'

122

Abu was looking down where the man had run. 'He never saw her again,' he said. 'That girl with yellow hair. You know that, don't you?'

'Hush now. Don't be afraid.'

'I'm not afraid. It's just that it's so sad. I mean the girl that he loved. Woman, now. Isn't that sad? He never saw her again after that night. In the snow. He doesn't know if she's alive or dead.'

'Hush, now. Enough. Let's go.' Thanakar bent down to caress the back of his neck.

'No,' said the prince, speaking without stammering or whimpers. He sat up straight, and his face put on a small defiant smile. When the man was threatening him with the gun, he had started to feel stronger. He feared so many things, but death wasn't one of them.

'No,' he said again. 'I don't want to. I want to stay.'

Abu's hair was thin on top, long in the back. Thanakar reached down to take a handful of it underneath his collar. 'Come,' he said. 'You can make it. I'll help you.'

Abu tried to pull way. 'Cousin, you're hurting me,' he said. 'I can stay if I want.'

'No you can't. It's not safe here.'

'I am not afraid,' said the prince. And then pleading: 'Don't you see, if I go now, they'll never let me come back. It's like choosing sides. Believe me, I'll be safer here. They won't hurt me.'

The white-haired antinomial had listened to this conversation without seeming to understand it. Now he reached his finger out again to touch the prince's cheek. Abu pulled away.

'Don't touch me,' he complained. 'Why does everyone keep touching me? Just go. Go get the police. Find my brother-in-law. Tell him I'm in danger here.'

They listened to the rattle of the guns. 'He won't come,' said the doctor. 'He won't do anything. What can he do?'

The antinomial had not withdrawn his hand. 'Micum Starbridge,' he said.

'Yes,' said Abu. 'He's my brother-in-law. He'll come stop this. I know he will. Please, Cousin. Please go.'

'I can't leave you here. You know that.'

'Yes you can. Please, Cousin, it is my w-w-w-wish. I'm sorry, but it is. It is my wish.' He held up his palm and spread his fingers out apologetically, so that Thanakar could see the golden sun tattoo.

The doctor stepped back, and his head snapped back as if he had been slapped. 'Yes, sir,' he said.

'Oh Thanakar, not like that. I'm sorry. Just go, please. I'll be all right. I'm not afraid.' He smiled ruefully. 'Courage is an obligation of our class.'

When the doctor went, the antinomial went with him with the lantern, lighting his way. Abu sat alone, leaning back against the boxcar, drinking, watching the fire along the barricade. In the center of the railway yard, the night held him in its empty cup. For a long time he sat. He had hardly dared hope that he could be alone; just a few of the right words and everybody had left, and he was free to drink a little in the dark. Others could run away when they wanted to be alone, but he was fat and weak, and it was hard for him to run. Instead, so often, events seemed to combine around him in a spinning circle, and it was a relief to know that there was always something you could say to make the circle widen and recede out of sight. He watched the line of flames, and then behind him, the fire at the bridge. So often, it was enough just to raise your hand, he thought. It was the first time he had used that power on his cousin, however, and it made him sad, for Thanakar would take it to heart. He would take it so to heart, and the more bitterly because he didn't believe, intellectually, in the power of the tattoo. But physically he was helpless

124

to resist, slave to . . . what? The mythology that had sunk so deep inside their bones that minds and opinions could mean nothing.

The prince's tattoos were unique in Charn. The priests had been excited at his birth. Some happy confluence of stars, some strident crying in the language of the newborn had convinced them that he had been a king in Paradise, in another lifetime. Abu looked up. The planet's silver rim showed beneath some clouds. It could not be true, for Angkhdt had said that all were free in Paradise, free as birds, men and women free and equal, spirits of pure light. There were no kings there. And even if there were, surely a king who had fallen down so far, so heavy with his own sins and misery, should be reborn lower than a farmhand. But the priests had loaded him with obligations and a horoscope that he had carried like a cannonball throughout his childhood – a great general, judge of men, scourge of heresy. If so, he had thought, and not just he alone, why had God given him so few gifts to accomplish such great aims? Unathletic, nearsighted, undisciplined, asthmatic: these flaws seemed like sins in a child with such a brilliant future. But eventually he had given up, stopped wondering, and after a while the priests and the parsons also had stopped, admitting their mistake, though the tattoos and the power remained, an embarrassment to them all.

Yet sometimes on clear nights Abu still thought that greatness and strength might descend on him from the sky. At such times he wanted to be alone. He swallowed some of the harsh wine, almost the last. Even the miserable and the cowardly might find a cause to fight for, he thought, and you didn't have to have a hope of victory to try. That night, watching dancing among these outlaws that he had come to love, not knowing why, he had thought for the first time that he had power he could use to help them.

Paradise was showing now, beautiful and full, silver fruit

hanging in a tree of darkness. Abu drank the last of the wine and staggered to his feet. The world heaved and bucked. And as he walked down towards the bridge, and the darkness gave to light, and the quiet gave to screaming noise, and the solitude to angry and demented faces, the wine he had drunk comforted him and made the people dance around him, made the bloodshed and the bullets and the heat seem like hallucinations. In his uniform he felt as invulnerable as a god, because these barbarian rioters were just the men to respect it.

At the bridge, the antinomials had fought among the access ramps, but they had been driven back. The rioters – small men but very numerous, dressed in the yellow clothes of poverty, their faces gutted by the fires of poverty – had pushed them back. Abu Starbridge staggered to the top of a heap of sandbags. He stood there, splendid in his uniform of white and gold, and raised his hand above the throng, his palm shining in the firelight, etched with the golden sun in splendor, the symbol of his inexorable will. Some of the little men stared at him, amazed, some sank to their knees, and some took no notice. His voice, shouting, 'Stop! Please stop!' was drowned out in the din.

Thanakar got stuck in a parade. As he hurried through the city gates, up towards the Temple of Enforcement, the streets had been stiffening with people. Exhausted, he had pushed forward without thinking, struggling through the crowd. People gave way, making the gestures of respect. Now he wished they had stood firm, because behind him they had packed so tightly that there was no way back, and in front the procession stretched for miles along the Street of Seven Sins.

He stood sweating in a crowd of seminarians. They had the places of honor by the roadside, and Thanakar had a good view too, because they were young and small, and he could see above their heads. There must have been a hundred of them, with red robes and high voices and shaved heads. Thanakar cursed, but in a way it was good just to stand there resting, because he had come such a long way and his leg was tired.

The road was lined with torches and with men who stood with gas lamps balanced on their heads and on their shoulders: small tanks, like bags of roots, and then the candelabra branched from them, like little trees lit with fiery blossoms. In the road, muscular young men tumbled through the air, leaping, and twisting, and slipping in hot rivers of elephant piss. Then came men cracking whips, and firedancers of various kinds. Men danced with torches in their teeth. Others tossed huge wheels of fire above their heads. Others had attached one end of a long rope to their hair, the other to a burning lamp. Wiggling their necks, they swung the lamp around them in wide circles while they clapped their hands and danced. They got down and rolled along the ground, the lamp skimming in a circle just above the tar.

Then came some elephants, painted in gay colors. In summer, they flourished in the summer jungles near the city, but these had been imported for the festival, brought up from the South in railway cars. The cold had made them sick. Their eyes shone feverishly in the torchlight, and some had a peculiar gummy liquid hanging from their tusks. They bellowed mournfully, but the sound was covered up with drumming. Drummers marched behind them, bare-chested, with white turbans and white baggy trousers fastened tightly at the ankle. They tied their drums across their waists, and beat on the ends as if to break them. In all processions there were hundreds of them, and in this one there were thousands, jumping, swaying, leaping in unison, their complex rhythms rolling up and down the line.

They leapt and turned in front of him, leapt and turned, back and forth, back and forth, banging on their drums with blistering palms. And as they passed, he could feel the rhythms in his body, as if a drummer had gotten loose in there and was drumming on his heart as if to break it, because he knew what came next. These parades were all the same. Elephants and skeleton dancers, shaking rattles to imitate the chattering of bones. Elephants; and then he could see them too, the flagellants, and hear the singing of their whips, and then his heart was breaking, as it always did, and he could feel tears closing his throat. They passed in front of him, the flagellants, his private symbol for what the Starbridges had made out of the world.

They were naked to the waist, their hair and beards were long, their faces stony hard. Their whips were knotted with nails and fragments of shell, and the blood ran down their backs. They scourged themselves to a rhythm of stamping, over their shoulders, alternating sides, the thongs licking their armpits and the tender flesh under their arms. With every breath they struck, and with ever exhalation they stamped another metal step, their ankles chained together. In the interstices between the rhythmic crash and stamp rose up the voices of a boys' choir, like wild reeds growing through an iron grate; they walked between the men, dressed in white surplices, nursing candles, singing hymns, their sweet wild voices poking up high.

The doctor turned away. Coming up from the railway yard, he had already seen horrible sights. After they had left the prince, he and the antinomial had climbed the barricade and walked along it looking for a place to cross. In the mouths of narrow streets above the yard, crowds had gathered, throwing stones and firebombs. Here and there, groups of soldiers made more organized assaults. For a while, they had got nowhere, for the antinomials had blocked them, fighting like lunatics with no discipline or order. For a while, strength and courage had prevailed against numbers. The crowd fell back before a single furious giant wielding a length of four-by-eight, batting gasoline bombs out of the air so that they burst around him in a burning rain. Other antinomials stood around or squatted, watching, until for no apparent reason they too found themselves filled up with the same spasmodic rage and would leap down from the barricade, screaming like demons, throwing huge chunks of masonry down into the crowd. Flailing two machetes, a woman jumped down twenty feet into a mass of soldiers.

Watching from a protected spot, Thanakar had put his hands up to his face. The antinomials were magnificent – their pride, their power like a force of nature. One man was storming through the mob, his head and chest and shoulders looming far above their heads, smashing them down with a hammer in each hand. Another lifted a soldier up above his head, one hand in his crotch and the other round his neck, bending the backbone like a bow until it snapped.

It couldn't last. Thanakar saw some soldiers of the purge, in black and silver uniforms, hanging back to organize their fire. One carried a sharpshooter's rifle; he lifted it, and an antinomial fell to her knees, stumbling and roaring, shot through the eye. And then, one by one, the rest went down and sank into a surge of bodies. The crowd broke through.

From their place of safety on a deserted stretch of wall, Thanakar's antinomial had watched with expressionless eyes. He turned and pointed down a quiet slope of refuse and barbed wire. 'That way,' he said, and handed Thanakar the lantern.

'Thank you. You're not coming?'

'No.' The man undid his cloak, stepped out of it, and tossed it on to the wire fence, where it caught and hung like a ghost. Old and white-haired, he was still muscular, his body hard and strong. He unbuckled his machete from his belt and tested the heavy edge along his palm. 'No,' he repeated gently. 'This is far enough. Far enough, I think. Far enough for me. No, I am with my family. Brothers and sisters.' He swung the blade slowly around his head, a last salute from someone who never in his life had said goodbye. There seemed something else he wanted to say, but whatever it was, he didn't say it. He turned and walked back towards the hopeless fighting, whistling a little song.

In the parade, in the din of the drumming and the stamping flagellants and the high pure voices of the boys, Thanakar tried to recollect that little song. It had sounded so unsure. If there was language in it, it was almost meaningless, just a little stuttering at the end of a sad life. One kind of music, he thought. And this is ours, the rhythm and the whips. Men lashing themselves bloody for no reason. Some of the seminarians around him hid their faces, blocked their ears.

'Thanakar! Thanakar!' Someone was shouting to him. An enormous palanquin, yoked back and front to braces of elephants, was loaded with Starbridges. They waved to him, and he pushed through the crowd and stepped down into the road. In a few steps he reached them. The palanquin was slung low, so that his head was almost at a level with the head of Cargill Starbridge, a young man in military uniform, a relative of his.

'Intolerable noise,' the man shouted, smiling, indicating the flagellants up ahead.

'I'm surprised you can stand it,' the doctor shouted back.

'Bah. Lunatics,' Cargill Starbridge tapped his head confidentially and lowered his voice to a soft roar. 'Completely gone.'

The elephants walked slowly, and Thanakar had no

trouble keeping up, his hand resting on the litter's golden rail. 'Listen,' he shouted. 'There's a riot down at the railway yard. At the waterfront.'

Cargill Starbridge winked one eye. 'I know,' he replied. 'Bishop's idea. Bishop's secretary. Not bad, really, using civilians. Teach those cannibals a lesson. No way to do it properly, of course. No men. You'd need a regiment.'

'Prince Abu is a prisoner down there,' bawled Thanakar, but the drumbeats knocked the sound away.

'You know about the adventist? Returned prisoner. Gave a speech. Completely mad.'

'I was there.'

'Lucky dog. I missed it. I was at the hanging. Secretary made a speech. Counter example: spontaneous outrage of the people. Death to all heretics. You know the kind of thing. Then he passed out weapons. That started them off. You should have seen them. Madmen.'

'Abu's a prisoner down there,' but the man had already turned away, was yelling something to a woman at his side. 'I've got to find the commissar,' shouted Thanakar.

The man turned back. 'He's right behind you.'

'Where?' But then Thanakar saw him, unrecognizable in his festival clothes and a demented turban of pink silk, waving down at them from the back of an elephant not far behind.

Thanakar let the palanquin go by, and as the elephant came up, he jumped for the rope ladder hanging down its side and climbed up to the howdah on its back.

'Smoothly done,' said the commissar. 'Your leg all right?' It was quieter here, up above the level of the crowd.

'I hate this parade,' he continued after a pause. He reached down to stroke the elephant's neck, and when he brought his hand back it was wet with sweat and a peculiar white scum. 'Look at this. It's murder. Poor brute. Where's the prince?'

131

'At the waterfront. He's a prisoner.'

The commissar sighed. 'I was afraid of that,' he said after a pause.

'That's all you have to say?'

'Too late now. The operation's over.' He looked at his watch. 'Limited objectives, the swine. Why didn't he come back with you?'

'He preferred to stay.'

'Then it's his own damn fault. Prisoner. He should be ashamed.'

'He might get hurt,' said Thanakar.

'I doubt it. I can't see them shooting prisoners. That's more our style, these days. Did you hear? There was a hanging at the city gallows, a big crowd. The bishop's secretary promised them a month's remission for every atheist they kill before five o'clock. Lying pig. As if it were that simple.' The commissar frowned. 'Abu will be all right. They might knock him around some. Might knock some sense into him.' He was staring down into the flagellants, and as usual his eyes were very sad.

For a while Abu had done some good. The rioters had hung back, confused. They had held their fire, afraid of hitting him. But he was on one single rampway; there were others, and around him the antinomials were being pushed back, overwhelmed by numbers and the force of hate. The rioters were desperate for blood. They had been offered some remission for their sins, the chance of a better lifetime in whatever hell was waiting for them in the sky after their deaths, if they could only just kill one, just one, even a little one. And finally, as the minutes ticked towards five o'clock, Abu found that he could no longer hold them back, though maybe if he had been someone else, stronger, braver, smarter, better, sober . . . But the crowd no longer cared. They drove him back, pelting him with rocks and curses. In the hope of murder, they were delirious, and he would have been trampled if a woman hadn't grabbed him by the collar and pulled him away.

She pulled him back into the dark and up a small dark slope. At the top stood a line of railway cars, and one had fallen on its side. Climbing on the wheels, the woman undid the clasp and pulled the door back along its sliding track. It revealed a hole leading down into the hillside. The woman grabbed him by the arm and pitched him in over the side. He climbed down obediently. As she stood on the door above him, preparing to descend, trying to light an electric torch with inefficiently large fingers, Abu realized she was hurt. A stone had opened up a deep cut over one eye, and there was blood crusted around her lips. She had broken some teeth, and she was crying and slobbering and wheezing music through the ragged gaps. Tears flowed down her cheeks. This sign of weakness made her seem somehow even more violent and intimidating; standing below her, Abu thought he understood some of the animosity that ordinary people felt for the antinomial women. It came from fear. At hangings, the spectators wailed with delight and shouted obscenities. In prison, gangs of jailers raped them.

Sniffing and wheezing blood, the woman fumbled with the torch. The prince reached up to help her, but she hit him across the face with the back of her hand, a careless slap, so that he staggered and fell down. She pushed back her hair and shook the flashlight furiously. Nothing happened, and so she threw it against the side of a nearby car, laughing when it shattered.

The hole led down into a tunnel in the earth, barely big enough to crawl through. The woman pushed Abu along it in the dark; he was on his hands and knees, and she pushed him from behind. Then, after a long while, the walls and ceiling seemed to open out, and she stopped pushing him;

he sat down on a pile of stones while the woman muttered in the darkness, and groped around him, and found a lamp, and lit it. She squatted near him and ran her fingers experimentally over her face. The tune she hummed had changed. The frustration had gone out of it, and it seemed more methodical, more regular. She rose and went out of the circle of the lamp into the dark, and returned with a bucket of water which she put down on the floor and sat cross-legged around it, washing her face and rinsing her mouth. Then, to Abu's surprise, she took a mirror and a comb out from a pocket in her shirt. The humming changed again as she examined her reflection – an intake of breath mixed with the melody, and Abu seemed to hear some humor in it too, when she smiled and displayed her broken teeth. She started to comb her hair.

'Where are we?' asked the prince.

The woman looked at him and frowned, a puzzled expression on her face, as if she had forgotten who he was.

'Why did you bring me here? Please tell me . . .'

She said nothing and resumed combing her hair.

'Where am I?' repeated the prince miserably. He felt sick. His clothes were filthy and he was very tired.

'You are free to go,' she said, motioning away into the dark.

'No. I don't know where I am. Do I sound ungrateful? I guess you saved my life. Back there it was so . . .'

'Stop that,' she interrupted, pouting into the mirror. 'There is a tune called "I forget". '

'I can't forget. It just happened.'

'It is a hopeful tune.'

'I'm afraid I don't understand.'

'You're safe here. There's no need to be afraid.'

'That's not what I meant. I mean I don't . . .'

'Stop talking!' she said. 'You are like a baby. I try to help, but you can only remember the last time you were

134

fed and look forward to the next time. Why should you understand?'

'Thank you,' muttered the prince. 'Thank you for explaining so well. You people can be very irritating sometimes.' He leaned back against the pile of stones and closed his eyes.

'You also,' said the woman softly, examining her teeth.

'You're awake,' said someone close to his ear.

'Yes.'

There was the sound of a match being struck, two sparks, and then a sudden light. The boy held a matchstick between his fingers. With his other hand, he stroked the cat in his lap. Before the match burned out, Abu could see other people around them, sitting, standing, nursing wounds, lying full length. The woman who had brought him there was lying down asleep.

'Where are we?' asked Abu in the dark.

Again the boy lit a match. It burned out, and he dropped it. When it was dark again, he said, 'Picture it.'

'What do you mean?'

'Fighting.'

Once again, Abu didn't understand. It was as if two different languages shared the same vocabulary. He sat up in the dark and caressed his forehead with his fingertips.

'Picture it,' commanded the boy impatiently. He struck a third match, and Abu could see his imperious blue eyes, a man drinking from a bucket, other people looking at him.

'I don't understand,' he said when the light was out.

'That's right,' said the boy's voice approvingly. 'Confusion. Violence. Danger. Death. Picture death.'

'I can't.'

'Neither can I. Neither can anyone.'

'I don't understand.'

135

'We are slaves to circumstances beyond our control,' said the boy's voice in the dark.

'Can't you make a light?'

'Of course.' The boy lit a fourth match. 'My sister saved your life,' he said when it was dark again.

'I'm very grateful.'

'Picture now. Sunrise. The barbarians go away.'

'Look,' said Abu. 'Couldn't you please light some kind of lamp? Please?'

'No. The picture is unpleasant.'

'It's hard for me to concentrate in the dark,' complained the prince.

'No light. I prefer it. We prefer it. Someone would have lit one otherwise. There is a lamp.'

'I know.'

'But this is not a happy time for us. Not a proud time. Some of us are hurt. Tell me: why did you come here?'

'I came to watch you dance. You invited me.'

'Yes. I danced for you. You promised me a gift, and I refused. Now I want something.'

'I brought you something.' Abu fumbled in his pockets as the boy struck a light. He had brought a purse filled with gold dollars, each one stamped with the head of the Beloved Angkhdt.

The light went out, and Abu felt the boy take one of the coins out of his palm. 'What good is this?' he asked.

'It is more useful than guns.'

'For a biter. I don't know how to use it. I have a simple mind. No, I want something. Not this. Don't make me say it. Guess.'

'I'm afraid I can't.'

'Don't be afraid.'

'I mean I can't guess.'

'Then I'll tell you,' said the boy. 'I want to understand

136

my life. Is that shameful? You can see why I don't want a light.'

'I don't understand.'

'Don't say that anymore! I mean, why do men attack us in the night? Why do we have to live like this? What is the power in this horrible place? Where does it come from? How does it work? I've lived here all my life and I don't know.'

'I'm not sure . . .'

'Don't you understand? I live without history or knowledge. When we were free, that kept us free. Now we are slaves, it keeps us slaves.'

There was a long silence, broken by the sound of splashing water. Finally Prince Abu cleared his throat. 'They hate you,' he began, 'because you are heretics. Atheists.'

'I don't know what that means.'

'Because you eat meat.'

'I don't eat meat. I can remember every time I've tasted meat in my life. Nine times. We have nothing.'

'Then they are told to hate you.'

'Who tells them?'

Prince Abu tried again. 'Have you ever heard,' he asked, 'of Nicobar Starbridge?'

'Speak louder,' said a woman's voice.

'Nicobar Starbridge,' Abu continued, 'was the founder of your . . . sect. A great heretic. This was . . . eight seasons, almost two full years ago.'

'I don't understand,' said the boy's voice from close by. 'Nicobar Starbridge. A barbarian.'

Abu smiled. 'Yes, a barbarian. Did you think you were a different species? There are men in Banaree who look just like you.'

There was silence in the cave. The sensation of gathered human presence vanished suddenly, as if the space had emptied out and he were left alone, talking to the empty dark. 'This was not so very long ago,' he said loudly. 'Eight seasons, almost. Seven generations. Your father's grandfather's great-great-grandfather. I can't believe you've never even heard of him. It was in summertime.'

And then he told them, in the simplest language that he knew, their own story: how Nicobar Starbridge had been born a priest; how he had lived and studied in the capital, in the Twilight Temple. Even as a young man he had been famous as a conjurer and theologian, but he had run away before his first irrevocable vows, the night before he was to offer up his manhood on the altar. A temple servant had unlocked his cell, a woman, a seductress, and he had run away, taking some volumes from the library.

He told them how the fugitive had lived like a beggar on the roads, dressed as the lowest kind of laborer, his tattoos covered with dirt. He had labored in the mines, in the quarries, in the lumberyards, among the poorest of the poor. And about how he had resurfaced in the company of another woman, a Starbridge from Banaree. She had left her husband and her children to join him, and had cut the chains of matrimony to join him on the road and bring him money so that he could print the first of his books – a reinterpretation of the Song of the Beloved Angkhdt, and a new translation.

Abu summarized the arguments of the book: how Nicobar Starbridge had claimed that the bishops and the archbishops had founded their authority on mistranslations. He claimed that the prophet's great description of his soul's journey through the universe, through Paradise and the planets of the nine hells, had never been intended allegorically. It was a simple travel diary in verse, telling of real places a real man had been; some he liked, some he hated. The prophet's description of the perfect love that chains the universe and all mankind was, according to the new translation, part of a long erotic poem.

Abu told them how, later, the priests had woven the erotic language of the Song of the Beloved Angkhdt back into allegory, so that later it had come to be accepted and become part of the myth. But in those days even to suggest that the song had a pornographic part was blackest heresy: Nicobar Starbridge and his mistress were hunted up and down the country, and the book was burned.

Abu stopped talking. 'I'm sorry,' he said. 'I'm telling this badly. Am I making any sense?' How could they possibly have understood a word? And in fact nobody answered him, so he stopped to catch his breath. In a way, the darkness and the silence helped him to concentrate, and when he continued, it was as if he were explaining a series of pictures he never could have seen so clearly in the light. Some were real, some imaginary; the real ones better drawn but less well colored. Dark browns and grays, pictures from his nursery walls: Nicobar Starbridge sitting at a table in his monk's cell, an ugly, pale boy, surrounded by books and all the hardware of conjuring and priestcraft, grinning devilishly at his image in a mirror. Nicobar Starbridge in yellow rags, preaching to the multitude, while to one side a naked woman is molested by monkeys and wild dogs, and in the window of a nearby house an old man is playing drunkenly upon a harpsichord. The riot at the bishop's market and the destruction of the tea exchange, the crucifixion of the merchant princes, with Nicobar Starbridge in the foreground, a demonic figure in mock judicial robes, ripping pages out of a book held by two angels. And finally, the destruction of the rebel armies – October 51st, third phase of summer 00014: Borgo Starbridge, the bishop's general, seated on a hill, poring over a military map, while on another hill stood the rebel city in the shape of a great chamber pot, and all around, the plain was covered with struggling black and yellow figures, soldiers and rebels, painted in exquisite detail. And in the background, the canvas is lit by a row of funeral pyres tended by skeletons and happy patriots, a picture in itself, the burning of ten thousand heretics, for the fires burned for months that summer, and on the horizon whole forests are cut down to feed the pyres, and men are building a pile of wood up higher than a hill to burn the temptress, the seductress, Nicobar Starbridge's mistress and companion, devilishly beautiful, with burning hair, while from the clouds above her, dog-faced Angkhdt scowls down.

In the dark, a voice said, 'Tell me. Don't stop.'

So Abu told the story of the pictures, and told how Nicobar Starbridge was a traveling preacher in Banaree, preaching revolution in the simplest language, among the desperate and the starving, the homeless and the meek. He preached that God gave Earth to men as a free gift, to live in as they chose. He preached a new society where men and women would be free and equal. And finally, he preached violence, the destruction of property, factories, homes, the murder of the rich. He attracted a great army of disciples, men and women, who called themselves Children of Paradise and roved the countryside in marauding bands. Some ran naked, some clothed, and if anyone was found with any money or possessions, he was whipped out of the group.

Abu told them how the Children of Paradise had captured a small town and renamed it the City of the Pure in Heart, and how they lived there in an ecstasy of dirt, and hunger, and drunkenness, and lust. And how, living with his mistress in a high tower while his followers rioted and drank, Nicobar Starbridge had written his last great book, and in it he rejected all knowledge and learning, and dreamed of a new language with no words to describe the illusions of past and future, for of all the lies that gave men power over their brothers, these were the worst.

Abu said, 'It was his last work, because soon after, the bishop's army took the city and burned it, and burned all his followers alive in a terrible purge. Nicobar Starbridge was captured, and he was taken in a cage to the palace of the emperor, who kept a kind of zoo for famous heretics. He put them in cages, and in the evenings he liked to walk in the gardens and discuss philosophy and theology with them. I've seen a portrait from that time. The emperor has dressed him up in scarlet robes, and has given him a scepter like a bishop or a prince of the church, as if he had never turned away. With his other hand, he is grasping one bar of his cage, and even in the painting you can see the whitening of his knuckles as he squeezes it. He is very ugly. He is wall-eyed, and his hair and beard are very long. He lived in a cage in the emperor's garden until he was very old.

'And that was all. In most places, the revolt died out. But in Banaree, a group of men and women made a ritual of cleansing and rebirth – fire and water, I'm not sure of the details. They purged themselves of all possessions and desires. They took to the woods before the soldiers came, to the great summer forests of that year. At that time it was all untamed, stretching up without a break to the far north.'

There was silence, and then a woman's voice came out of the dark. 'I don't understand,' she said. 'Why are you telling us this story? Who are these people?'

'You. Your ancestors.'

'But that is a long time ago.' Her tone was near despair. 'I am not old.'

'I'm sorry. I'm explaining so badly. I'm trying to explain why those people were attacking you tonight. Why the people hate you.'

'Why do they hate us?' asked the woman.

141

'Because you are different. And . . . other reasons too. Let me tell you another story, this one from not so long ago. Maybe some of you were there.' Abu paused and let the dark illuminate for him another set of pictures, the lines and colors crude and childish, for he had been a child at the time. Antinomials attack the mail. Portraits of atheists: children. Portraits of atheists: mother. Riders in the snow. The cannibal's dance. And he told them how in the last phase of winter, when he was just a schoolboy, an armed band of antinomials, led by a tall man with only one hand, had come down from the far north to loot the farmers in that district. They had stolen horses and murdered livestock, and for more than a month they had terrorized the people there, killing policemen, taking prisoners, burning farms, and stealing food. The bishop sent an army, which chased them to a mountain north of Gaur. They had a fortress there and made a desperate defense, but the general was in no hurry. He surrounded them and starved them out, but hundreds of days later when the walls were down and they were overwhelmed, he found that they had kept themselves alive by eating the bodies of their prisoners, and their brothers and sisters who had died fighting.

There was silence again, and out of the dark came the same woman's voice, desolate and low. 'I think there is no hope for me but death. I cannot understand these stories. I never . . . heard them before. What are antinomials?'

Prince Abu sighed. 'You,' he said. 'People without names. Atheists. Cannibals. You have no God.'

'And what is . . . what is God?'

'Sweet God,' prayed the bishop. At six o'clock the sun rose, white and heavy on the white horizon. The bishop had been up all night. ' "Sweet love," ' she quoted happily. ' "How sweet it is to watch you sleep, your body like an unstrung bow, unstrung by loving hands." ' The festival

142

had exhausted her, but the worst was over, and she had been left alone in the aromatic gardens of the temple to watch the sun rise over the rooftops of her city. Around her, sparkwood, dogwood, black magnolias, suntrumpets shot their seed over the careful borders of the lawn; as she sat on the grass next to the fountain, streamers of flowers fell around her. It was the only garden for 300 miles, the only grass, the only flowers, the only living trees.

'Sweet God,' she thought, and she turned her head and listened for His footsteps in the garden, where Angkhdt himself had lived and worked, and tropical flowers grew miraculously in the open air, no matter what the season. She had seen an orchid open to the snow. 'Sweet God,' she thought, 'Are you still with me?' because inevitably ceremonies and festivals – candles, solemn fat old men, the clustered spirit of a million true believers – would pack into a mass so ponderous that it could crush a stronger thing than God. At night the bells, the chanting, the suffocating ritual would frighten Him away, and she was never sure He would return. Every morning she sat alone, waiting in the garden for His timid step.

Her metal headdress lay beside her. Carefully, so as not to prick herself, she began to get out of her clothes, recalcitrant wire and layers of spun steel, pulling the steel cloth down her arms and down her legs until it lay like peeled snakeskin in the grass next to her boots. She let down her hair, pulling out the pins, shaking it loose over her shoulders. And, dipping her steel skullcap into the pool, using it as a basin, she washed the makeup from her face, rubbing the white pigment into milk, so that it ran down between her breasts.

She rinsed her face, and stood, and yawned, and walked sleepily across the lawn.

She left her clothes where they lay; they were uncomfortable, and she was glad she wouldn't have to put them

on again. The bishop had more then eighty thousand suits
of clothes, one for every day of the interminable year. Most
she would never live to see. Some of the more delicate
ones, she knew, rotted and were remade several times
between wearings. It was foolishness, something for the fat
old men to do, while underneath she always wore the same
white slip. Blind, crippled, castrated, how could they
understand? She was the bishop, and in her heart she kept
the heart of love, inviolate, unsuspected, the crystal spark
of the world's faith. There was no reason to wear anything
at all.

She laughed and ran up the steps into the cloister, into
the sanctuary on the way to her own room. She stopped,
reflexively, though she was eager to go on, eager to pull
the curtains and lie down in her own bed. Yet she was
unwilling ever to waste a moment in the sanctuary, walking
through it as if it were just a place between two places. So
she hesitated by the marble columns at the entrance of the
shrine, a cave where Angkhdt had lived for one full month
of his great journey, sleeping here with the so-called 'black
woman' ('. . . arms like night, midnight, three o'clock,
dawn . . .'). Here he had written verses seventy-one
through one hundred and sixteen.

Nothing remained from that time. But at the end of the
altar, next to an oil lamp, sat a statue of the prophet. The
marble gleamed in the light, heavy and yellow, the hard
heavy shoulders, heavy thighs. The sculptor had gestured
gently towards the old myth, elongating his jaw a little,
putting hints of hair along his forehead and his cheeks, just
a roughening of the stone. His eyes were simple slits, but
beside that his face was human, and the small marks of
deformity only emphasized his human parts, his wide
straight nose, his marble lips.

He held out his stone hands, empty most of the year,
but today they carried the holiest relic in the world, the

skull of Angkhdt himself. It was broken in places and the jaw was gone, but all the cracks and joints were filled with silver, the jaw rebuilt with silver. The skull was tilted in the statue's hands, and the stone eyes looked down into the empty sockets of bare bone as if scanning them for movement, like a dog.

'Please,' asked Abu, 'can I have a drink of water?'

'There is water,' said the boy's voice.

'Can't you light a light? I'm sick of this darkness. I feel as if I had been swallowed. There's no air in here.'

'Light can't help that.'

'No. I don't suppose any of you have a drink,' continued Abu petulantly.

'Suppose.'

'Oh, never mind. Water will do fine.'

The boy lit a match. It shone on tired faces, or people curled up sleeping. Nobody moved, and it burned out.

'Well?' demanded the prince.

'I don't understand,' said the boy. 'You want water. There is water. Are you lying to me?'

'I want someone to get it. Please, will someone get it for me?'

'I don't understand,' said the boy again after a pause. 'Are you hurt?'

'No, I'm tired. I want someone to get it. Or I won't tell you any more stories.'

Abu felt a cup pushed into his hands. He took it and drank.

'You have no pride,' observed the boy.

Abu took another drink. 'You don't understand at all,' he said. 'You never will. Why you stay here is a mystery to me. Why you don't go home.'

'I was born here. This is my home.'

145

'Yes, but there is nothing for you here. Why not go back?'

'I know the songs,' replied the boy. 'No one can live there. There's nothing to eat. There's nothing but snow.'

'But . . . hasn't it gotten warmer here since you were a child? It's spring there too. Up by Rangriver, it's nothing but green grass. No large animals yet, but plenty of rabbits. The trees won't grow back for another generation. But God knows it's a better life than here.'

He heard movement in the little cave, exclamations, and a hand closed painfully around his knee. 'You're lying,' said the boy. 'Don't lie.'

'Why should I lie? Don't you know? Hasn't anybody ever left here to go back?'

'Yes,' said the boy. 'They are alive or dead. We are not like you. We can't see it through their eyes.'

'Then let me tell you.'

'No. You see, but you don't understand. I don't want to see that way. Now there is grass. What color?'

'Green and gold.'

'Long or short?'

'Waist high.'

'Snow on the mountains?'

'Yes. Near the peaks.'

'Birds?'

'I don't know,' admitted Abu.

'Yes,' said the boy. 'You see, I do know. There are birds of prey. Hawks and harriers.'

There was a long silence, and then Prince Abu broke it. 'Let me finish my story,' he said. 'About the cannibals. I haven't finished.'

'No,' said the boy. 'I know what you will say. They wanted to kill us after we ate them. So they sent an army when the weather changed. The Paradise thaw. They burned our town. Your cousin was there.'

146

'You're right,' said Abu, surprised.

'You think I'm stupid. But I was born here. I know how to talk, how to think. I learned everything I could. I am young, and I can't live in a past I never knew, like my fathers and my mothers. Always in the past. The eternal present, always in the past. But I can't live that way, because I want compensations for slavery. I want comfort . . . in my mind. I want to want things, to believe things.'

There was a pause. Abu broke it dubiously. 'Well . . .'

'Tell me about God,' said the woman's voice.

Abu sighed and cleared his throat.

'The truth,' demanded the boy fiercely. 'No lies. Not even one.'

'I don't think you know when you're well off,' muttered Abu.

Then he spoke aloud. He told them about the power of the priests of Charn, how they owned every bird, every fish, every dollar, every stone. He told them about the episcopal factories, and the million-acre slave farms, and the towns of slaves clustered around a single temple, making umbrellas, silk, forks, olive oil, a different product from each town. He told them about the parsons coming to visit newborn children, casting horoscopes, checking for imperfections, listening to them cry. He said, 'They believe that when a baby cries, it is saying something. It tells the story of another lifetime. It mourns its sins. And the priest listens, and in a few minutes he has given it a future and a penance. He names it. He engraves its future on its skin: education to such-and-such a level; work; address; permission to marry; name of wife; permission to breed; permissible food; permissible clothes; everything.'

'But you are different,' said a voice.

'Yes. I am a Starbridge.' He told them about the Starbridges, that enormous family from which all priests and rich men came, all generals and kings. 'The laws aren't

147

meant for us; we have our own. And at one time we could be born from any family. But the fourteenth bishop argued that God punished sinners by placing them in poor families, and rewarded the virtuous by making them born rich. It's a theory called predetermination.'

There was a silence, and then the woman's voice said, 'You're not telling me what I want to know. There is a reason for all this. Some kind of . . . love. Tell me about that.'

'It's the way things are.'

'No. I don't believe that. There is a man – was – long ago. Someone. A reason why you live like this.'

'We have a story,' said the prince. He told them the travels of the prophet Angkhdt. He described for them the painting on the door of every temple – Angkhdt turning the planets back towards the sun with his bare hands; Angkhdt making an end to winter; Angkhdt bringing the rain.

He told them about Paradise and the nine planets of hell. 'This is the first of the nine planets, the most beautiful of all. But there is something here, some smell of failure or decay that ruins everything. Some touch of death that ruins everything.

'And when it sinks from Paradise the soul comes here. And this is just the first of the nine planets. It takes a long time for a man's flesh to burn away. It's a chemical process. Am I making sense? It's a long, long journey back to Paradise. A long journey through the stars. It takes a long time to come to Paradise again with all your human flesh consumed away.'

'But you. You are different.'

'Yes,' sighed Abu, depressed by this unlooked-for understanding. 'I am a Starbridge. The world was put into my family's hands to keep this system working. And I won't die, unless I die by violence. I'll be given drugs and put to sleep. And when I am asleep, I'll dream. And out of every dream will grow another dream, and it will be like walking through a sequence of rooms until I open the last door, and I'll be home in Paradise again.'

He took another drink of water.

'That's the truth?' asked the boy's voice, finally.

'That's what millions believe.'

'Everywhere.'

'No. The world is big. I'm talking about this empire, these dioceses. Elsewhere . . .'

'Well?'

'Elsewhere there are other legends.'

'Legends!' Abu felt the boy's hand grab his knee again, fingers pressing into his skin. 'Barbarian! Do you think I care about your legends? Do you think I'm like you? I live in the world. Bricks and stone, no power on earth can change it. Barbarian! This is what we ran away from. My father's father's father's . . . When he migrated into the physical world. Do you think I want to understand your theories?'

'Please,' said Abu. 'You're hurting me. I'm sorry. It's . . . difficult.'

'Difficult!' The boy did not relax his grip. 'Do you believe it?'

'I believe . . . something.'

'Something!'

'Life isn't perfect. There's a reason why life isn't perfect. I believe that. Please. You're hurting me.'

'But you live as if you believed it all, don't you? Starbridge!'

'Yes. I suppose I do.'

'But how can you? Don't you understand – if it is not true, every part of it, then it is a vicious lie, every part of it.'

Abu said nothing, and the boy continued. 'You don't

149

care whether it's true or not. What do you care? You have your money.' He let go of Abu's leg to grab the purse out of his lap, and the prince wondered how he could see so clearly in the dark. Abu heard the purse rip open, the coins flung away.

'You don't care whether it's a lie or not,' repeated the boy, softer now. 'But I have nothing. Nothing to lose. Listen to me. Your power hangs like a stone in a web of lies. Who is the spider? Who reknits the threads when they snap in every wind?'

'What do you mean? There are thousands of priests.'

'Yes. Who is the spider?'

'There's the bishop.'

'Yes. The bishop. I have heard of the bishop. This legend is a lie.'

'There are parts of it no one believes,' admitted Abu.

'How can you say it so calmly? You sit and grow rich in your palace. How can you do it? Are you happy?'

'No.'

'Nor I. But I have a plan for happiness. I have heard of the bishop. These soldiers who attack us, they're called the Bishop's Purge. They follow orders from the bishop, is that true?'

'Yes, I suppose so. Ultimately.'

'Then I will kill this bishop. And the stone in the web will fall.'

3

Thanakar in Love

Spring is the bitterest season of the year. A man in autumn, looking back on the bloodshed and the frenzied cruelty of these seasons long before his birth, is terrified by visions of the future. Perhaps from a high window he can see men and women working in the endless afternoon, free in their own fields. They are happy, for they were born and grew up in the sunlight, in summer and in autumn, amid the birth and rebirth of new ideas, new technologies, new freedoms, new pursuits. The grip of tyranny has loosened from their lives.

But civilization is bound to a wheel among the stars, and already in autumn the nights are getting cold. The snow will come, the world will start to die as men, caught up in the process of their own survival, will abandon all they love, let it recede into the past, a memory of Paradise. New sciences, new art, all the new ways of making, the new freedoms will be lost under the snow. And all that time the priests will wait, blind and quiet in their temples as the world dies around them and new men are born who can't even remember, and then they will take all the strands of power back into their own hands, slowly, patiently, one by one.

Spring is the starving time in Charn, eight thousand days from Paradise thaw until the sugar rain, and nothing grows until the rain comes. But a few things reawaken, and when the ashes of the waterfront were still heaped up in lingering piles, Doctor Thanakar experienced a new sensation – happiness. He could feel it inside him like a seed as he limped along the palace galleries between his laboratory and his apartments, between the apartments of his patients.

Prince Abu had not come home for days, but finally the commissar had found him living in a cave, an antinomial bolt-hole where he had waited out the danger, dazed and weak in everything but will. He had not wanted to return, so the commissar had waited till he slept, and then had him bound and drugged and carried home. He had woken in his own bed, in an uncharacteristic rage, and since then no one had seen him, for he had locked his door. For a few days the doctor had sent messages, and pounded on the door and waited outside, and sketched frustrated caricatures of his friend, emphasizing his baldness and his fat. The door was shut, and Thanakar pretended that he didn't mind, pretended he was still angry at the way the prince had ordered him away the night of the riots. He was used to his friend. Abu was a man without the strength to resist. Fragile, clumsy, apologetic, he swallowed grievances until they choked him, and then spit them back in fits of petulance, forgettable and soon forgotten.

So even as he sat scribbling outside the prince's door, Thanakar was happy. He sent messages and funny notes, which were delivered with the prince's food. He drew cartoons of mutual acquaintances and patients – Starbridge officers whose hopeless faces and pitiable wounds he could make grotesque with a few deft slashes of his pencil; widows and spinsters past the legal age of childbirth, scared to death of dying, trying to delay with makeup and vitamins the moment when the bishop would send apothecaries to put them all to sleep; and a whole vicious series featuring Charity Starbridge, the prince's sister, the commissar's wife. These drawings were as cruel as he could make them, because his new happiness was half on her account.

Long before, Prince Abu had tried to kill himself, or tried to try. Even that, for ordinary people, was a desperate crime, the spiritual equivalent of breaking jail. In a Starbridge it was considered madness, cowardice, dereliction of duty. Thanakar thought that perhaps he should fear a second attempt, but he didn't. It was part of his new optimism. He thought that eventually, if he sat outside long enough, the door would open and Abu would stumble out, vague, apologetic, and very thirsty. In the meantime, after he had folded up his drawings and slipped them under the door, Thanakar would limp down the hallway almost every day to visit Charity Starbridge. She was afflicted with a kind of melancholia common among young women of her class – a combination of idleness, loneliness, and drugs. The personality relaxers prescribed for married women by the bishop's council had certain side effects. She complained of stiffness in her neck. She was still too shy to look Thanakar in the face, so he would stand behind her chair to talk to her. She would loosen the strings of her bodice and pull the cloth down over the hump of her thin shoulder, and he would stand behind her with his hands around her neck, rubbing and caressing so gently at first, and then harder until he felt her muscles loosen, and her head fell forward of its own weight, and her black hair fell around her face.

In those days, too, he had another patient. At first he had gone secretly. But as time went on he became careless, and visited in plain daylight, and brought his car. It was more convenient, so that he didn't have to carry the gifts he brought – fruits and vegetables, blankets and warm clothes. And always things for the little girl: sweets, dresses, picture books. His father had had a dictum: 'Stroke them and they bite you, whip them and they lick your hand.' As usual, his father had been half right. Her teethmarks still showed on his thumb from the first night he had washed her and changed her bandages, so at first he was careful not to touch her again, but sat and gave directions to her mother. Even so, the first few times, Jenny's little body was stiff and frightened, her eyes full of suspicion when she saw him. But Thanakar was clever enough to be patient. He would dump the presents he had brought her carelessly on to the floor, and the next time they would show signs of her touch. And one day he brought her a doll with a white porcelain head, and she took it gravely from his hands.

Her fever and the pains in her chest yielded to antibiotics, and her infections dried. After two weeks she would smile when he came into the room, and after two weeks more she would wait for him by the window and run to greet him as he limped up the path. Then she would take him by the hand, and they would go for walks, or she would rub her cheek along the sleeve of his coat when they sat together on the bed. He would put his arm around her shoulder, and she would snuggle up against the soft material, sucking her thumb, peering at the picture book that he was holding in his lap.

As he watched the absorption with which she studied the illustrations, he felt a mixture of emotions. He had brought her all his own books, the ones he had loved when he was a child – stories of magic and fantasy, boys turned into eagles, adventures at the bottom of the sea. Some of the margins were marked in his own childish handwriting, and some of the pictures were torn in a way that brought back some urgent, long-forgotten memory. At such times, looking at her serious, pale face, the way her legs dangled without touching the floor, he felt himself transported back to his own miserable childhood, the days of studying those same picture books while the endless winter howled outside. Then, reading, he had not been looking into the past, but to the future, a magic time when he would be a man and all wrongs would be righted, all insults savagely avenged. Now, looking back, he could remember a whole scene – some burning humiliation, and in the end he had run into his room slamming the door, pulling the book violently from the shelf, so that the picture tore just so. Then, kneeling over it, he had put his finger on the tear, studying the picture without seeing it, as he was doing now. And in an instant, the boy raised his face to stare into the future just as Thanakar looked back into the past, their eyes meeting as if through a sequence of mirrors.

He, too, had been an only child, though the bedroom in his father's house was not like this. His own room had been unusually luxurious, as if his parents had tried to expiate through luxury the guilt they felt at hating him for something that was not his fault. No, not hate, surely, but disappointment, and it amounted to the same thing, for he had hated himself loyally for their sakes. He remembered his mother holding her arms out, and he had limped into her arms. And all the way, across acres and acres of polished floor, he was studying her face, convinced that it was only through the most muscular exertions of her will that she was able to keep that mask of love over her face. Later he had come to realize how his own sensitivity was cheating him, but it didn't help, because the cause was real: he really was a cripple, and he was their only child. In those days his limping had been worse. Every phase of winter, every phase of spring had brought with it a new therapy, a new series of operations, something that might show some progress and squeeze some dispensation from the priests. Each one had aggravated his condition, until he could barely walk. And even though he knew instinctively that he couldn't begin to heal until they left him alone, still he submitted to every cure with masochistic glee. He took pleasure in the incompetence of surgeons. He had decided to become a doctor.

Sitting with his arm around the little girl, sometimes he

felt he loved her because of the mark on her cheek. It was a large red mark near her left ear, and a priest would say that God had pinched her underneath the ear before releasing her into the world, to mark her with His curse. They had said something like that about his leg, though her case was much more serious because she was born like that, and because her family was poor. He wondered how she had escaped growing up in prison, but by the time he and Jenny had become close enough to sit like that, side by side, he no longer spoke to her parents much. At first they had been eager to please. They had accepted his gifts with a humility that had made him wonder whether he was doing the right thing. They kept the house clean for his visits. But after Jenny was well and he kept coming, they changed. The woman became surly and uncommunicative, the man increasingly nervous. Gradually the dirt started to come back, as if cleanliness were just a whim of his which they no longer wanted to indulge. Thanakar didn't care. Even though he understood how they were beginning to fear him, to wish their poverty didn't oblige them to accept his gifts, still they did accept them. As long as they did, the doctor felt that he could come when he pleased. Their nervousness and sullenness made him impatient. Surely they could see how clean his motives were. They thought he was trying to steal her. But her poverty was part of what he loved, her stupid parents and her filthy house. But if he didn't feel capable of explaining this to them, it was because in another sense he realized that their fears were justified, that every smile she gave him took her farther away.

He loved the way they loved her. Other parents would have given her up to the judicial system and forgotten her, but these had become outlaws for her sake. He thought about his own parents. For a long time he had felt as if he owed them nothing, because of the pain of those operations on his leg. But yet, how unfair children are. He had been so eager. Perhaps, if he had not been so eager, his parents would have desisted after the first few failures. They could not have been expected to understand that his eagerness was a way of gathering up justifications to use against them in his heart. It was the way he had found to overwhelm his spontaneous feelings for them – the natural love of the miserable for the magnificent. In Jenny's parents he had seen at first some of that same love in the way they had treated him, and now he saw some of the work it took to bury it. They were unfair to him, like children.

'I'm worried about your health,' he told Jenny's father. The man was sitting alone in his consulting room with his head in his hands, his snuffpots around him on the floor. The doctor stood in the doorway, and as he spoke the man raised his face, handsome, with his daughter's pale skin and perfect features. He blinked, as if unable to recognize his guest, and then got wearily to his feet to make the gestures of respect. He was very thin.

'Don't get up,' said Thanakar.

'I would prefer to stand, sir.'

Thanakar shrugged. 'I'm worried about your health,' he said again.

'You're too good, sir.'

Thanakar examined his voice for traces of irony. He found irony mixed with unhappiness in equal parts, but even so it would have been enough to make him give up, angry, if he had not already rehearsed what he was going to say: 'I want you to stop this. This employment. If you continue, you'll die. You'll be dead in a thousand days.'

The man sighed. 'What must I do, sir?'

'I don't know. I didn't think you'd be sorry to give it up.'

'It's my work, sir.'

'Yes, I know,' said Thanakar, irritated. 'What I mean is, I could help you find something better.'

'You are too good.'

'Damn it!' cried the doctor. 'Why do you insist on turning me away? I want to help you. Do you think I come here for myself?'

'Yes, sir.'

'Yes. Yes, of course. If we can't be polite, at least let us be sensible. You're right, of course. But we both have something to offer. Haven't I given you enough money to give this up, to start something new?'

'What, sir?'

'Well, what is your name?'

'Pentecost, sir.'

'Not that name. Your working name.'

'Wood.'

'Were you a lumberman?'

'Carpenter, sir.'

'Skilled?'

'Yes, sir.'

'So why can't you set yourself up somewhere? I'll give you the money. Who's the chaplain of the guild here? I'll talk to him.'

'I have no papers, sir. Surely you must realize that. I ran away from . . . home, when Jenny was born. They were going to put her in prison.'

'I see.'

'I don't think you do, sir. Otherwise you wouldn't leave your car down in the square and walk here in broad daylight. Do you think a man like you isn't noticed? As for my health, I'm grateful for your concern, but I don't have a single client now. God, I wish I'd had the strength to turn you out after the first night, but my wife was begging me, and how was I to know you'd be so . . . careless? I wish I'd had the strength to run away. Now it's too late.'

'Is that what you want?' asked Thanakar, after a pause.

'Don't you understand? My daughter is the only thing I

have. Up until now, there was never a way for me to hope even the smallest hope for her. But you'll be able to do something for her, won't you, sir? You're a powerful man. You'll find some way to protect her. That night you came, she was so sick. And now she's well. Don't you think I'm grateful for that? Sincerely?' He looked sincere, his hands clasped in front of him, his dark eyes.

'You make me feel ashamed,' said Thanakar.

'Oh no, sir. We're nothing without you. You've been so kind. She's happy when she's with you. Don't think I can't see that.'

Because he was ashamed, Thanakar packed his bag and set out for the mountain.

He took an elevator up to the topmost roof of his wing of the palace, and from there the way led up dozens of flights of steep stone steps. It took almost an hour to climb. The way was unguarded; it was never used, for most traffic drove along the roadway and up through the fifteen gates along the other side. Thanakar didn't want to cross that many barriers. Even in his car it would have taken longer, for at each gate they would have found ways to delay him, though in the end they would have had to let him pass. On foot, the path was difficult for him, and he took time to rest whenever the stairs broadened past a deserted blockhouse or abandoned barbican. The bishop no longer had the men to guard all the entrances up into the prison. Even at the top, the gate was unguarded. Out of breath, Thanakar stood under the gigantic arch, letting his gaze pass idly over the inscriptions: justifications for the prison's existence, six-foot letters in a language nobody could read. Behind him, far below, the city stretched away into the hills. Far in the distance, he could see the towers of the bishop's palace, the Temple of Kindness and Repair, glinting in the afternoon sun. The air was rich and quiet. Sparrows quarreled at his feet.

He passed in underneath the arch and stood squinting across a stone parade ground, one of four, almost a mile across. Flies buzzed, and here too the air seemed still and drowsy. The mountain, so big that even from here you could only see a part of it, rising up layer by layer, circle after circle of black battlements, filling the sky, disappearing into the clouds – even the mountain had a drowsy aspect, as if the crimes committed there were so ancient and bulky, so much an indissoluble part of the rock, that they had lost their urgency. They had no voice. The air was perfectly still. The building slouched on its foundations like a bloated old dictator peacefully sleeping in his chair.

A company of soldiers came out through a postern gate on the far side of the parade ground. Their needlelike footsteps, the click of their boots, the officer's sharp cries seemed blunted at first by distance and the heavy atmosphere. The doctor picked up his bag and shuffled towards them, and as he did so, the sounds regained their edge – the steelshod boots, the metallic clash of their weapons – until he came near and they wheeled to face him, saluting in formation, smashing their rifle butts to the stones. Then everything was quiet once again as they waited for him to cross along their front, but it was a different kind of silence, tense with embarrassment and broken by a noise the doctor had not noticed before, the ragged patter of his limp.

Thanakar moved down the line, feeling unusually deformed. But he put his shoulders back and, as was his unhappy custom, examined their faces to see if they were laughing at him. They weren't, but for him the soldiers' earnestness gave them a collective irony that would have been dissipated by a single quivering lip. Thanakar searched eagerly for some sign of mockery, but there was nothing, just pop-eyed boyishness and stiff black uniforms.

160

They were so young. Thanakar passed the officer, a dark clean boy, his face frozen into a rictus of subservience, and the doctor felt his first contemptuous instincts being polluted by a small amount of sadness. There was no reason for young men to be clever if they were going to die so soon. The eternal war in which their fathers and grandfathers had fought was all around them, yet it was easily forgotten. There was no news, not even lies; there never had been. But Thanakar caught wisps of rumors from his cousins in the army. Even they knew nothing. There was fighting near the city now. You could hear the guns sometimes – where? North, east, west – you only saw it indirectly by how many things were missing: how empty the shops seemed, how pitiful the food available to the poor, how few men in a crowd.

The soldiers marched away, and Thanakar crossed the rest of the parade ground. He entered the mountain through a small postern, thirty feet high, carved in the shape of the twenty-first bishop's open mouth. The stairs led up his tongue. Inside, all was submission and subservience, though as he penetrated the dingy corridors, the cell-like offices so small they made you forget where you were, the wardens and the guards seemed increasingly sullen. He was abusing his right. They knew it, and they hated him for it. At the checkpoints, he held his palms up with contemptuous nonchalance, and they were powerless to disobey. They knew better than anyone the penalties for disobedience.

In a windowless cubicle, he stopped before the desk of the subdirector for the ninth day of the week, a middle-aged man with a face full of warts, too ugly for active service, Thanakar supposed. No, the white ribbon of the winter war snaked through his buttonholes, and in his eyes there was a look of – what? Intelligence? Thanakar reminded himself that these men were all criminals, rapists, murderers, toadies. Yet as always, they had human voices.

'I thought we had seen you for the last time, sir,' said the man. His name was Spanion Locke, printed on a card pinned to the front of his uniform.

'You were mistaken.'

Locke stared at him sadly. Then he shrugged. 'Where do you want to go?'

'Heretics.'

'Heretics.' The man sighed. 'Sir, can I . . . may I ask you what you're planning on doing?'

'No.' The doctor had no idea himself.

'Will you open your bag?'

'It's my private property.'

'Sir, you understand it's against the law to bring unauthorized drugs into the wards.'

'That can't apply to me.'

'No, sir. But may I ask you what you're planning to accomplish? We have more than one million inmates here.'

'I know that.'

'Yes, sir. But if you're just trying to prove a point, I thought you might want to know what effect it has on other people.'

'What do you mean?'

'Well, sir, for one thing, if I let you pass, I'll lose my job.'

'My heart bleeds, Lieutenant.'

'Captain, sir.'

'I'm sorry. I guess I anticipate.'

'Very funny, sir. I'm not talking about that. After your last visit, the chaplain made the penalties very clear if you came again. As I say, I am unable to prevent it. But . . .'

'Please, Captain, spare your breath. Any punishment they give you has been earned a hundred times, I'm sure.'

'Do you know what the penalty is for treason, sir? Have you seen it?'

Thanakar said nothing, and the captain licked his lips. 'That's all right, sir,' he resumed. 'I won't beg. I've got my pride. I'm God's soldier, and I do what I'm told. But as long as you're such a humanitarian, sir, I thought you might care to imagine what your life might have been like if you had been born with my name and my tattoos. Do you think we're here on voluntary service? No offense, sir. It would be different if you could do some good up there. But as long as you can't, don't you see, it's a selfish act, and it's not you who'll bear the consequences. What can they do to you?'

'You think it's selfish of me to risk my life . . .'

'Not your life, sir,' interrupted the captain. 'My life.' A drop of perspiration ran down behind his ear and under his uniform. He swatted it as if it were a fly.

'I'm sorry to speak so blunt, sir,' he resumed. 'I'm not complaining. I do what I'm told. But I thought I'd ask.'

'I'm sorry, Captain Locke. I've made up my mind.'

The man licked his lips. 'Then that's all right, sir,' he said. 'No reason to apologize.' He stepped back towards his desk and picked up a ring of keys. 'Heretics, was it? I'll run you up myself.' He called into an inner room, and a young man came out and stared with dumb horror at the doctor and the ring of keys.

'Not to worry, Sergeant,' continued Locke. 'I'll take him up myself. Just mind the store.' Relief washed into the young man's face, but the silent question stayed unchanged until the captain answered it with a grim, almost imperceptible shake of his head.

The biter reined his horse at the gates of the Temple of Kindness and Repair. He had been riding since before dawn, and he was happy and not ready to dismount. So he pulled his horse away and spurred it savagely up a slope of loose rock to the left of the gate; after the long ride, the animal was exhausted and bewildered, and it slipped and almost stumbled at the new exertion. The biter snarled and cut it with his whip, but at the top of the slope, he could see the city in the distance and the black mountain rising to the clouds. There he relented, and reached back behind his saddle to stroke the cut skin. He loved this horse, not a miserable, beet-fed barbarian creature, but a real horse, huge, wild, carnivorous, black. He stroked its bloody flank.

He had been riding for eleven days, up from the imperial capital, with messages and a mandate for power. A barbarian would have taken a dozen retainers and a train. But it was already raining in the South; the bridges and the tracks were all washed out, and he had been glad to leave his regiment to underlings and ride on alone. Nothing ever gave him as much pleasure as riding, the horse staggering off-balance and half mad with fatigue. He stripped the glove from his hand and stroked the animal lovingly, and looked out over the city. It belonged to him. He was free.

His other hand was just a steel claw; he cursed and shook it, but in fact he remembered the city only vaguely. It had been a long time since he had seen it, and then it was only through eyes darkened by ignorance and hate, through the bars of his cage as they dragged him through the streets after the cannibal war, the barbarians spitting and shouting. He barely remembered because, as always, the past was to the present as the rider to the horse, unimpressive and mean, though it cut with the whip, kicked with the spur.

A group of monks and soldiers gathered near the gate, and he watched them with a mixture of impatience and delight. He himself bore the message of his own arrival. They gestured and talked among themselves, frightened by the giant stranger on the giant horse. Down below, he had jumped the wall. Here, he watched their faces widen and contort as he brought his horse back down the slope, and when he reached the flat he spurred it to a gallop again. The soldiers scattered, reaching for their pistols, though one stood firm, an old sergeant at the middle of the gate. A brave man, thought the biter. He would be rewarded for his bravery. But in the meantime, the biter lashed him in the face with his whip as he galloped through the gate into the first of ninety courtyards, where the guard was turned out to greet him.

They stood around him in a circle, awaiting the order to fire. He reined his horse so sharply that it almost collapsed, then sat still and glowered at them while they stared open-mouthed along their rifle barrels. The sergeant came in, limping, with the blood running from his cheek, but before he could give the order, the biter stripped his white scarf back from his collar to show the crimson star, the crimson dog's head at his throat. He dismounted stiffly, and as the sergeant came up, tossed him the reins. 'My name is Aspe,' he announced in his harsh voice. 'I have orders for the bishop.'

The elevator ride to the heretics section took twenty minutes. The captain had brought a book, so Thanakar sat silent on a stool swallowing periodically to release the pressure in his ears. When the doors opened, they were almost at the top of the mountain, near where one of four uncompleted towers broke from its base, up towards the spiderweb cathedral hidden in the clouds.

This was the Tower of Silence; to get there, the captain led Thanakar up stairs and down stone corridors, and out into an open space several acres in extent, where the air seemed different from below: wetter, colder, whiter. The sun was in the center of a swirl of mist.

Because it was unfinished, the tower had no roof. Masons worked in the open air 700 feet above Thanakar's head as he entered through a metal door. At that distance he couldn't see them, but he could hear the chink of their hammers, and occasionally some pieces of stone or mortar dust would fall down through the vast, empty cylinder, down past him into nothingness, for the void stretched down into darkness as well as up into light, until the eye was lost. He stood on a narrow metal balcony, riveted to the inside of the stone chimney, and looked up past the spiral tiers of cells. The sky was white and far away, a little white disk.

Like all parts of the prison, it was very quiet. There were no wardens or guards. No movement caught his eye. The place seemed uninhabited.

'Is there a section for antinomials?' he asked.

Without speaking, Captain Locke led the way to the end of the spiral, rising some distance away out of the circular balcony on which they stood. He unchained a steel gate, and they started up a track of welded steel, circling gradually upward along the inside of the tower. The metal rang under their footsteps. To their left was the empty void, lit from above through the open roof. At intervals below, lamps rimmed balconies similar to the one they had just left. Looking down, Thanakar could see them, rings of light, gradually diminishing in size until they resolved into an evil glow. To the right were the cells, piled three high, the top ones reached by metal ladders. Inside, they were dark, illuminated only by fitful gleams from the captain's torch. He swung it carelessly to mark their way, and occasionally the light would flit into a cell and catch some object there in its moving circle, a heap of bedding, a glint of metal, a living shape, the striped bars of the cage.

'How many people are imprisoned here?' whispered Thanakar.

'Capacity is one hundred thousand.' The captain spoke in his normal voice. In the half-dark, it sounded like shouting. 'Present occupancy is almost two,' he added expressionlessly.

'All heretics?'

'One kind or another. These are lunatics, here. Paranoids.' The captain paused and shone his light into a cell they were just passing. In the middle of a tiny room, a woman sat, completely motionless, tied to a chair. Bound hand and foot, nevertheless, she gave the impression of movement, of implacable energy, as if she were straining every muscle against the cords that confined her. They cut into her flesh. Her wrists were bound to the arms of her chair, but her fingers stretched trembling at their furthest extent. Her head was sunk low on her breast, but as they passed she raised her head slowly into the light, and Thanakar gasped because for an instant it was as if she had no mouth. The lamp had resolved her white gag into her white face, a square piece of tape stuck to her lips. Above it, her eyes stared at him, insane, malignant, her pupils bleached white in the glare. Her hair was long and neatly brushed.

'My God,' whispered Thanakar.

'Yes. My God,' said the captain in his expressionless voice.

'How long can she live like that?'

'It depends.' The captain flicked his light on to a card stuck to the bars of the cell. 'She's been here five months.'

'Five hundred days. It's not possible.'

For an answer, the captain turned his lamp away and resumed walking. Thanakar had to hurry to keep up. He gripped the guardrail spasmodically, and sometimes his feet stumbled on the rivets of the track.

They walked in silence for what seemed like hours. Several times the doctor had to stop and rest his leg, and always his companion stopped and waited for him without speaking. For some reason, it seemed warmer as they rose higher. Moisture glistened on the walls.

'We're getting close,' said the captain presently.

The cells were larger here, and there were several prisoners in each one. They squatted, crouched, and lay full length, and as the light passed, they turned to look and made small noises with their chains.

'Adventists,' said the captain.

They continued on. The cells were large enough to permit standing, and rows of men stood watching them, holding on to the bars with manacled hands. They didn't wear gags, but still they made no sound, just an occasional soft clink as they moved their feet or moved their heads to watch the passage of the lamp. They were dark men, tall and hairy, from the eastern provinces, with wide, flat faces and slitted eyes.

'Rebel Angels,' said the captain.

'Why don't they speak. Why are they so still?'

'They have no tongues.' As if to confirm the captain's words, one of the prisoners grinned as they walked past, and opened his mouth to show his toothless gums and where his tongue had been cut away.

Above them, the masons had finished work, and the sky was dark. They continued on, up into the highest reaches of the tower. The captain stopped before a long cage. 'Antinomials,' he said.

For the first time, the doctor could smell urine and human filth mixing with the sweet pervasive prison disinfectant. The captain sniffed. 'Nobody likes to come up here much,' he remarked.

In the cell, an old man sat with his legs stretched out along the floor, his back against the wall. He raised his head when the light hit him. And when he saw the doctor he snarled at him with animal malice, his eyes gleaming, his lips curled back against his gleaming carnivorous teeth;

and in the perfect silence Thanakar could swear he heard a low, throbbing growl. He took a step backward and the sound intensified, and a throaty rattle mixed with it. The antinomial was marked, a livid cross and circle branded between his brows.

'He's got something wrong with him, sir,' said the captain. 'This one does. Under his pants. Wait, you can't see it. Wait till he moves. There.' He brought the beam of light down the antinomial's right leg, and Thanakar could see part of a clumsy bandage where the cloth was ripped below his knee.

Conscious of his own sweat, he turned back towards the captain, in time to see him smile. 'Maybe you should have stayed down in Birth Defects, like before, sir. Or Perpetual Care. You won't find much gratitude up here.

'Go on, sir, please,' he continued, when Thanakar said nothing. 'I'd hate to lose my job without a reason.' He was holding out the key.

Stung, Thanakar took it and unlocked the cage. No sooner had he stepped inside when the antinomial sprang up from the floor and flung himself across the cell, but the chain around his middle jerked him back. Thanakar squatted down and opened his bag, while the antinomial glared at him malevolently. With careful fingers, he prepared a hypodermic syringe and stood up, and the antinomial stood up also, almost two feet taller, and reached out one huge hand to point at him. They stood staring at one another for a moment, and then the antinomial slowly shook his head and dropped his hands down to his waist.

'I want to help you,' said Thanakar.

The antinomial took hold of the chain around his waist. It seemed too little for his strength. He started to pull on it to test the links, and when he found one he liked, he tensed his muscles, and in a while the metal seemed to bend under his hands.

At that moment the captain turned his flashlight out. In the sudden blackness, Thanakar could hear the creak of bending metal and hear the captain smile as he said, 'They can see in the dark. You know that, sir?'

Thanakar took a step backward. 'Turn it on, Captain,' he said, as calmly as he could. 'You don't want to be reborn as a mouthful of spit on Planet Nine.'

The captain laughed. 'You're a brave one, aren't you, sir?'

'I'm a Starbridge.'

'Ooh, well said, sir. You deserve some light for that.' He flicked the torch on and then off again, but long enough for Thanakar to see where he had dropped his bag. He stooped to pick it up and took another step backward. Then he heard the sound of the breaking chain, and Locke must have heard it too, because the flashlight came back on, and Thanakar could see him draw his pistol. But the antinomial did nothing. He just stood there in the circle of light with the broken chain between his fingers. Then he spoke, in a voice rusty from disuse. He said, 'Don't play games. No games. Not with me. Go now. Now.' He pointed towards the door.

Thanakar went. He turned and walked up the ramp again, and the captain followed him, still smiling. 'Oh, come on, sir,' he said, after a little while. 'It's not as bad as that. I could have locked you in. You left the key in the door. Trusting of you. Believe me, I was tempted.'

'What's the penalty for murdering a Starbridge?'

'They can't kill me more than once, sir. Besides, the chaplain offered me a dispensation, in case the opportunity came up. Believe me, it would have been the solution to all our problems.'

Thanakar turned back. 'The captain offered you a dispensation to murder me?' he asked.

'Not murder. An accident. It was a choice between that or a court-martial.'

'Then why didn't you?'

Captain Locke smiled. 'I'm a religious man, sir. And I have my pride. Believe it or not, I respect what you are trying to do. I don't respect the method. I mean the intent.'

'Thank you, Captain.'

'Thank you too, sir, in a way. I won't be sorry to leave this place. It's not like I've got a family. My son died here, in Ward Thirty-One. He was crippled, sir. Like you.'

They walked together up the ramp. 'Where are the people from Rangriver?' asked Thanakar. 'The last crusade. Are there any left?'

'I think there are a couple.'

They walked past cages of increasing size. Some had several dozen inmates.

'Here,' said the captain. 'Try these.' He unlocked the door of one and stood aside. Thanakar forced himself to step in without looking, and when he was inside he turned around gratefully and smiled in spite of himself. It could have been worse. The captain reached in and turned on an overhead bulb. It illuminated six women against the far wall, lying or sitting in heaps of straw. They paid no attention to him.

The captain wrinkled his nose at the stench. 'No rats here, sir,' he remarked. 'They eat them.'

Thanakar looked around, relieved and encouraged by this small attempt to disgust him. The place was no worse than the worst nightmares: the smell, the sweaty walls, the women lying in rags, the oppressive silence emphasized rather than disturbed by the whine of the fluorescent light.

'These were from Rangriver?'

'Yes, sir. The males were all killed, by and large. The

171

females were brought down, I forget the reason. It was before my time. There used to be a lot more.'

They had been young girls then. Now they were fully grown, and some even looked old, or at least their bodies did, withered and wasted on their giant skeletons. But their faces still looked young, because, again, no experience had marked them – the eternal present of their childhoods, the eternal present of their cell. Because it's not pain that changes you, thought Thanakar; it's the memory of pain, the memory of happiness. No one else could have survived so long here. In a way, their childhoods had been perfect training for life in prison. Here in their cell, freedom and bondage had resolved.

'They used to sing all the time in here,' remarked the captain. 'All day and all night, when I first came. You used to hear them all the way down. They've stopped, now.'

Thanakar remembered the storyteller from Rangriver, singing to him and Abu the whole night while Abu drank. 'Even in the purest there are deep biting instincts,' he had said. Thanakar remembered the phrase now, because one of the women was looking at him with eyes full of calculation. It made her look foreign in that place: a large woman, with yellow hair and straight hard features. She seemed healthier than the others, more flesh on her bones, more supple and muscular under her ripped clothes.

'You,' she said. Her voice was low and musical, even in a single word, because music seemed to surround it, like the setting around a jewel. She might be beautiful thought Thanakar. Or perhaps she once had been, before her face was branded with the cross and circle, and marred by self-awareness. She sat cross-legged, stroking the hair of another woman, who lay with her face hidden in her lap. 'You,' she repeated.

'Yes? Please talk to me. Don't be afraid. I'm a doctor.'

'Yes, Doctor. My sister is dying.' She dropped her eyes

172

and stroked the woman's hair. Thanakar stepped to look and squatted down. The woman lay on her side, breathing softly. Her right forearm was swollen, and the skin was green and mottled purple. He could smell the rot.

'It is best to kill her. She is in pain,' said the yellow-haired woman in her luminous voice.

'She thinks I'm a parson,' muttered Thanakar. He took the sick woman's wrist in his hand, but she whimpered and pulled away.

'Look at her,' said the yellow-haired woman. 'She's in pain. She is free to live or die, but pain is something else.'

Thanakar sat back on his heels in the straw. 'She can't stay here,' he told the captain.

Spanion Locke stared at him evenly, and then shifted his eyes to look out through the bars of the cell, out into the dark.

'We've got to take her down,' said the doctor presently.

When the captain turned back, his face had changed, as if softened in the heat of the room. It was still ugly, or rather still more so, as if his deformed features were struggling with feelings even more deformed. 'You can't, sir,' he said at last. 'You just can't. You know you can't. Why do you . . .' and he broke off, his mouth still working, his eyes filled with tears.

A minute passed, and then the doctor shrugged and started to unpack his bag. He leaned over the sick woman and took her arm into his lap. She tried to pull away, and turned to face him, and opened a pair of glass-green eyes. The doctor tried to lose his misgivings in activity, arranging bottles on the floor, choosing syringes, but whenever he touched her she cried out. He took out slicing hooks, and clamps, and body shears, and incense, and a gold statuette of Angkhdt the Preserver, and he arranged them on a piece of cloth. He took out a chart of the planets and, glancing at his wristwatch, made calculations in red chalk on the stone

173

floor, and drew circles with stars inside, and diagrams of the zodiac, and abbreviated prayers in a special doctor's script. Yet every time he touched her, the woman kicked and moaned. 'Don't torture her, Doctor,' said her sister with the yellow hair. 'It's pointless, now that she is almost free.' Thanakar lit a candle and said nothing, only frowned at the hypodermic point as he prepared an anaesthetic. Then he put it down. He looked at Captain Locke. 'What do you think?' he asked.

'She'll die anyway, won't she, sir?'

'Probably. Up here.'

'Then don't be selfish, sir. Give her what she wants.'

Charity Starbridge switched on the light in her bedroom in the commissar's tower far below. At the moment when the doctor was making the first gestures of his art, had lit the incense and made a row of chalkmarks along the antinomial's forearm, representative of the Angkhdtian symbols for cleanliness and health, as well as chemical diagrams of the nine principal causes of infection – at that moment Charity was thinking about him as she lay in bed. Though not as he appeared then, stripped to his undershirt, his long face dripping sweat, but in his dark blue Starbridge uniform, as he had looked that night when her husband had invited him to dinner. He was not handsome, but that didn't matter. Her life had been so sheltered, she had never formed an image of the word. Except for Abu and the commissar, she had not seen another man of legal breeding age since before the time she found them interesting. Not even a servant, not even at a distance. Her bedroom had no windows. It contained nothing but one enormous bed. According to scripture and commentary and tradition, she was not supposed to let a single outside interest diffuse the energy of holy love. According to scripture; but her parents had married her to a man three times her age, who had already been burned to a cinder on the altar of matrimony by three dedicated wives. She had inherited their bed and their library, but the devotional literature disturbed her rest, so that sometimes she would wake up in the middle of the night, out of breath from dreaming.

Awake, her natural modesty, her simplicity, her ignorance all filled her mind with such a mist that the figures of her dreams were lost in it. They capered just beyond the limits of her imagination. And though in her dreams they had no faces, when she was awake that's all they had, or rather, one face only, the doctor's, the only face she knew. She saw it now, rising from the mist, huge, disembodied like a god, his high pale forehead, his long hair, his short black beard. That afternoon, she had fallen asleep over a book, and in the evening when she turned on the electric light beside her bed, his face was all that she had left, even though she knew her dream had not been about him.

For months she had been suffering from a kind of lethargy. She lost weight, slept twelve hours out of the day, had no interest in anything. She barely spoke. It was against law and tradition for her to have unpleasant and unhappy thoughts. That was impossible to police, but lately she found it hard to think of anything acceptable to say. She had forgotten all of the charm, all of the manners that she had learned in school. The commissar had noticed it. He was a gentle old man; too gentle. When the doctor came to see her, he stood behind her and stroked her neck, and the commissar was so kind, he didn't even stay in the same room. She had everything to make her happy, she reflected sadly.

She picked up her book from where it had fallen beside her pillow. Aspects of Religious Theory. She tried to find her place:

. . . in that area, orthodoxy has combined with an older paganism. They believe that the universe was created out of the semen of

175

Beloved Angkhdt, and, more specifically, spring rain comes from the same source, which is responsible for its color and viscosity. They worship stone idols with enormous phalluses. Sodomy and fellatio, as described in Angkhdt verses 21 through 56, among others, they regard as sacraments, though even among these people there are fierce doctrinal disputes. The most austere, or Dharimvars, regard these passages as purely symbolic. Their priests lead lives of strict asceticism. But the Kharimvars, or 'followers of the darker path', interpret these verses literally, using the crudest translations. Worshippers take the celebrant's sexual organ into their mouths when they receive the sacrament, though here again there are sectional debates: whether this is a public or a private ceremony, whether it should proceed to literal or symbolic orgasm, and so forth. The more extreme of these practices have been proscribed by the emperor, though they are thought to linger in the more backward areas of Charn. They choose their clergy democratically, from among the youngest and the most virile, which is a heresy . . .

Thanakar relaxed and sat back, and stretched out his leg. The woman's arm was off; it lay like a bleeding animal in the straw, bleeding through its open mouth. He had sewn the stump up with plastic thread and then with miraculous skill had spun a new arm for her out of memory and magic, and silver wire and rags of silver latex. He had joined it to her flesh and laid it on her breast, tied in a sling around her neck. It was lifeless still, but pulsing gently, a source of energy and light.

'It's amazing,' said Spanion Locke, squatting by his side.

'Starbridge technology,' answered Thanakar. 'We've had to specialize in battlefield injuries.'

'Will it work?'

'It should. Some people never learn to use them. The ones who try too hard.'

It had been a long operation. The blood had soaked their clothes. Spanion Locke had helped him when the woman struggled. She was unconscious now, and the two men looked at each other over her body, feeling a bond. Their hands had touched from time to time during the surgery, slippery with blood.

'Thank you,' said Thanakar, after a while.

For an answer, Spanion Locke took some cigarettes out of the breast pocket of his uniform, lit one and passed the other with his lighter, taking care not to pollute the filter end. The woman was breathing easier now, lying on her back with her head in her sister's lap, a little spit in the corner of her mouth. Though he rarely smoked marijuana, Thanakar lit the cigarette and inhaled deeply, and sat back with his shoulders against the wall. The cell was so hot, so filthy.

'Sir?'

'Yes, Captain.'

'I was wondering. Maybe you have some medicine for me. Some little pill, maybe. Something quick.'

'Don't be ridiculous. I'll see you again.'

'I doubt it, sir. The chaplain is a hard man to please. It'd have been different if you'd killed her. They might have laughed.'

'I know the bishop's secretary. Don't worry. I'll go see him in the morning.'

'Please, sir, don't make things worse. I'm not complaining. I've been God's soldier my whole life. I'm not afraid. I won't be sorry to leave. Except for . . . sometimes they're a little rough.'

'I don't carry poisons, Captain.'

'No, sir.'

'I'm sorry.'

'Yes, sir.'

Only one of the antinomials had paid the operation any attention. The rest had sat and stared out between the bars. One lay on her stomach and drew patterns in a pool of tacky blood. But the woman with the yellow hair had sat staring evenly, stroking her sister's head with gentle repetitive fingers.

'She is alive,' she said.

'Yes,' confirmed the doctor, exhaling a long stream of smoke. 'She'll live. Will you change her bandages? I'll show you how.'

'No biting, Doctor. There's no need. She is free to change them or not.'

The doctor shrugged and closed his eyes, and leaned his head back against the wall. Presently he heard the jingle of a chain, and he opened them again. The woman was pulling her manacles back along one wrist, uncovering a silver bracelet. She fumbled with the clasp. 'I can pay you,' she said.

'No. There's no need.' He smiled in spite of himself.

'No. You don't understand.' She gestured towards the captain. 'He understands. Death is the silent music, the still dancing, the dark mountain, the snow that never breaks under your feet. You're cheating her. But even so I have no wish to owe you anything. Nor does she.'

She undid the clasp and threw the bracelet to him, and he caught it. It was a beautiful thing, a circlet of carved silver, a pattern of animals devouring one another. 'Your men are very honest,' remarked Thanakar to the captain.

Locke shrugged, and stubbed his cigarette against his boot. 'It's real silver,' he said. 'I'm forbidden to touch it. It's no use to any of my men. She's offered it all round.'

'Ah yes, of course.' Silver and gold were Starbridge metals. Other people had to use stone currency. The doctor held the bracelet in his hand, examining it in the light. It made him think of something, reminded him of something. He looked at the woman curiously. What was it?

She was tall, with golden hair and yellow eyes, a shade common among her people: dark yellow, almost brown. Her skin was dark, still dark after more than eighty months' imprisonment. She was dressed in rags, as they all were, but hers had once been red and made of some softer material, maybe velvet. That also resonated in his memory. It was not that he had seen her before. But certain things about her reminded him of elements to a song.

Then he remembered. When he had gone down to the docks the first time, and Abu was drunk – it had been a long night, and the white-eyed antinomial had played and sung and talked about his childhood up above Rangriver, when all the world was snow – it had been a boring night, and much of the music Thanakar had neither heard nor understood. But one thing had touched him. There was a girl in the story, and when the antinomial had spoken about her, every time she had come into the story, a little music had come in with her and mixed with the other music. It was his way of naming her, and he had sung it sometimes with a kind of hunger and sometimes hesitantly and unsure, and then especially, listening, Thanakar had caught a glimpse of how she must have been, half delicate, half wild, running and stumbling through the crusty snow, her golden hair wild around her face, or later in the last days of the thaw, dancing under risen Paradise, or riding through that high red valley where the sun barely rose, in red velvet and a bracelet on her wrist. Just a few sweet notes, a song of hunger still unsatisfied, but later Thanakar could hear how all the other notes and music took their tone from those few notes, and he had thought that when that man had said he loved her, that was what the word meant to him, that her music had entered into his, and there was nothing he could ever do to separate them.

In the hot cell, Thanakar sat forward and tried to explain it to her, but without the notes it was useless, and the notes eluded him. She just sat there, her eyes as empty as windows, stroking her sister's hair. With music, he felt that he could break her heart; without it, it was just barbarian

179

drivel – he could hear the clattering as he tried to talk. 'The night the soldiers came . . .' and then he stopped, because she was staring at him patiently, vacantly, stroking, stroking.

The music came to him late that night. He sat up in bed, and when he lay back down, he thought he had it imprisoned in his heart. But by morning it was gone, and he ate breakfast with the rain coating the windows, trying to remember. A dozen notes, that was all, what was it? Gone. But he had kept the bracelet. And afterward he went to show Abu. He met the commissar in the hall.

'He's still in there,' complained the old man. 'Damned inconvenient. Just because I didn't . . . well. I don't know what I could have done. Pure chance that I found him at all. He was in one of those caves. Safe and sound, not a scratch. He's been in bed ever since. Only opens up for meals. You don't think,' he continued anxiously, 'that he'd try anything stupid. I haven't seen him this bad for months, damn him. Just like his father. Temperamental. Damned rain.' He was very worried. His eyes avoided the doctor's, and he sucked nervously on a sourball. The rain was cracking the slates, flooding the terraces.

The doctor asked him about Spanion Locke.

'Can't help you there,' said the old man. 'Like to. Can't. That's the purge up there. But the chaplain's deaf and blind; he might not notice. I'm the regular police. Not our jurisdiction. I'll see what I can do.'

'Would you? Thanks.'

'Stupid fools. Both of you. I'll see what I can do. Nothing, probably.'

'Thank you.'

The commissar went off muttering, and Thanakar was left alone. Thinking about Locke, he felt less patience for his cousin. The prince had suffered from morbidity ever since he was a child. Once he had tried to cut his wrists.

'Imagine him as an adult,' the commissar had grumbled then. In fact, a young Starbridge had nothing to complain of: nothing but parties and dancing lessons and indulgent schoolteachers trying to recompense their students for long lives of marriage, or short lives at the battlefront. Abu's morbidity had exempted him from the services. 'Doesn't make any sense,' remarked the commissar. 'Suicides are what they need, especially among officers.'

Abu and the doctor had both been left behind, and sometimes it was depressing when relatives came back, wounded or decorated, and sometimes Thanakar wondered whether that was the only thing that had drawn them together, the cripple and the fool. Outside Abu's room, he sat sketching furiously on an envelope – dragons, gangsters, the commissar with his piglike face. The pencil lead ripped through the paper.

Near where he sat at a desk in the hallway, a casement window blew open. He rose to close it, but it slipped from between his fingers as the wind caught it like a wing and beat it back against the wall. The window broke, so that even when he had forced it closed and bolted it, the day still spat at him through lips of broken glass. It was raining hard. He caught some water on his tongue and tasted it experimentally, even though he knew it was too early yet for the sweet rain, the sugar rain that changed the climate. Still, this was the start of it, and even though there was nothing in books or family histories but stories of disaster from this phase of spring, even so he was disappointed by the rain's thin texture, its insipid taste, and he looked forward to new weather. Then the rain would fall for months on end, and flood the city, and wash all dirt and beggary down into the swollen sea, and kill what crops there were, and cover the hills with seed, the semen of Beloved Angkhdt piled ten feet deep. And then the summer jungles, the tiger and the black adder, the gorilla

181

and the pregnant orchid, all the myths of his childhood would sprout up into life, watered by the rain.

Disappointed, he turned back into the hall. Abu's closed door enraged him. He pounded on it and grabbed the handle as if to force it, but it wasn't locked. It opened suddenly into the prince's bedroom.

Inside, Abu stood in the dark next to his huge bay window, looking out over the city. Rain fell in sheets against the glass, and it was as if he were standing in a dark aquarium looking into an enormous tank, for the weather had filled the room with shadows, while all outside the world was turbulent and wet and full of water, and the thunderclouds were dark as rocks, and colored scraps of cloud flew everywhere like fish, high up above the colored rooftops, and in the farthest distance a huge rainbow leapt against the afternoon. The sun was burning in the tempest's eye. A rainbow spanned the hills.

The prince didn't move or turn. He was in his bathrobe. 'Look, Cousin,' he cried out, and his voice was full of childish delight. Thanakar looked from where he was.

The room was padded like a child's room, the walls and ceiling hung with tapestries – pictures from Starbridge nursery rhymes or children's tales from holy scripture: innocent pastels of holy love, and Angkhdt himself still had his trousers on. The floor was thick with carpets and the room was dark, because the prince never burned electric lights. He preferred candles.

Thanakar looked around. The great four-poster bed was a tumult of soft quilts, and there was an uneaten avocado on a silver tray and undrunk liquor in a jar. The place stank sweetly of decadence and self-indulgence, because Thanakar had decided to forgive nothing this afternoon, and every little thing annoyed him more – the silver pillbox, the open book of poetry, the knife. The knife most of all. It lay on the bedstead on a silken pillow, and it angered him most because it was just a pose, like so much else, or so he thought until he saw his friend turn towards him, and saw the silken bandages all down his wrists and on his hands.

'Oh, Abu,' he said wearily. 'What is this? What the hell is this?'

'No biting, Cousin. Please, Cousin.' The prince smiled at him. 'Come look at the rainbow.'

'Oh, Abu,' repeated Thanakar. He reached out to put his arms around his friend, to comfort him, he thought, though it was he who was shaking, and the prince seemed perfectly calm, and smiled at him, and rubbed him clumsily across the back.

'Hush, Cousin,' said Abu. 'It's not what you think.'

'Not what I think? Look at you. You're not fit to be left alone,' and he pulled the prince down to the bed and sat beside him, so that he could unwrap his hands. The prince was laughing. 'Ow,' he said, 'that really hurts,' because the bandages were rough, just torn from some shirts and soaked in oil, and they stuck to his scabs. His palms and wrists were a mass of cuts. Whole pieces of flesh had been cut away.

'Let me see it in the light,' said Thanakar. He stood up and walked to the door to the lightswitch, but Abu told him there were no bulbs, and then tried to light a candle, and laughed because the movement hurt his hands, until the doctor came and lit it for him.

'I wasn't going to show you,' said the prince. 'Not until they healed better.'

'My God, look at you,' said Thanakar, examining the cuts. 'What have you done to yourself?'

'It's not what you think,' said the prince again. 'I was stupid, I know. But I wanted to see if I could cut them out. Cut them away.'

'What?'

'The tattoos.'

183

'Oh my God.'

'I couldn't,' said the prince sadly. 'They go all the way in. Down to the bone. How can you be something you're not? Every layer, there's another layer. The image just gets clearer and clearer the deeper you go, as if it were underneath and you were cutting towards it. The golden sun.' He closed his hand, and winced at the pain.

Thanakar leaned to smell his breath. 'What's wrong with you?' he asked. 'Are you drunk?'

Abu laughed. 'Not very. But I've got some really good hash. Charity put it on my tray for breakfast. I mean, the commissar got it from some priest, but he doesn't like it much.'

'From a priest?'

'Some priest in his department. Those bastards always have the best drugs.'

'You've seen Charity?'

'She's been cooking my meals.'

'Charity?'

'Sure. She puts hash in everything. I couldn't even finish the guacamole.' He reached for a silver pipe by his bedside, but his hands were still too clumsy to use. Thanakar fixed it for him and lit it, and the prince sucked in a lot of smoke. 'Do you want some?' he squeaked, still inhaling.

'No thanks,' said Thanakar, nursing the match. 'It makes me feel as if everybody hates me.'

The prince laughed until he choked and started to cough. 'What's so funny about that?' asked Thanakar.

In the end, Thanakar forgot about the bracelet. Instead, he smoked hashish, and when in late afternoon he staggered down to his car, the rain was still pouring. 'Not good, this,' remarked his driver as they idled at a crossroad where a cart was stuck in the mud, the porters striving and shouting as the rain burst along their backs. 'Rain's early.'

'It's not sugar rain.'

'No, sir. It'll come. My great-great-grandfather moved away south at the first drop last year, and didn't come home till the third July that summer, when the prince was born. Your grandfather, sir. He was an old man then.'

'Who?'

'My great-great-grandfather. My father told me.'

Thanakar was finding this hard to follow. 'So you'll go too?' he asked.

'Not now, sir. Too old. Besides, the prince used to have property down there. Your grandfather, sir. Your father too.'

'Don't rub it in.' Thanakar stared glumly out the window. The car could go no further. Imported, like all engines, from across the seas, it was feeling its age. It was a relic from the previous year, from before the winter snow had blocked the port. Thanakar felt its cylinders misfiring gently; the gunpowder was damp. Ahead, the way was blocked by skinny vagrants in their yellow clothes, shrieking and cursing and weeping at the rain.

Miles away, Colonel Aspe stood on a balcony in the Temple of Kindness and Repair, a vast sprawl of cloisters and shrines on a hill outside the city. He had been talking in the amphitheater of the Inner Ear when the storm broke, and he had stopped midword to walk out from among the shrill old men, to watch the lightning from the balcony and suck deep draughts of air while the clouds thundered and spewed. They sickened him, the priests of Charn. He turned to watch them through the window, the rain on the outside of the glass streaking their faces and their clothes. They didn't even know that he had left, most of them, and he could hear them begging with him and pleading as if he were still there to hear. The bishop's secretary, a bony-faced old man, was in the bishop's chair, a cigarette hanging from between his bloodless lips, while all around him, in

185

various attitudes of agitation and repose, reclined the members of his council. Some were clearly dead, others less clearly so, sleeping the last drugged sleep of the Starbridges. There were dozens of them lining the tiers of the amphitheater. All were dressed in red and golden robes, and since some were deaf, and most were blind, and some were dead, they communicated by means of art. A golden cord wound between them, up and down the steps. They held it in a variety of fingers, some fat and fleshy, some mummified and dry.

In the rain, the colonel snorted with contempt, and the rain ran down his uniform and down his back. He was a tall man, even for an antinomial, and old too, with long white hair. He was seamed and scarred with lines like silver in his pale skin, running like silver over his eyelids and his cheeks, his shoulders and his chest. His eyes gleamed black and empty, and his nose was beaked like the beak of a bird. He hated priests. He felt like strangling them or whipping them insensible. Partly it was the natural abhorrence of his race, and partly it was the sight of them, fat, dead, dying, arguing over foregone conclusions. He knocked his steel fist against the windowpane. Nobody noticed.

In this backward and neglected province of the empire, where the seasons came so hard, priests held sovereign power all through the spring. They were a cult of sorcerers, and they mutilated themselves and studied magic long forgotten elsewhere. Their leader was a bishop-whore, a living goddess of pornography, and Colonel Aspe itched to see her, to grasp her by the throat. He distrusted women. But already he had come to understand that she was nothing in these councils, a figurehead and not even that. All powers twined like a nervous golden serpent through the fingers of the priests.

They realized he was gone and fell silent, communicating

through the cord. Young priests gelded themselves at the time of their first vows; from then on, periodically, they would burn out one of their senses or cut off one of their limbs in a gruesome public ritual. The compensation, they believed, was in a stronger spirit, increased capacities for conjuring, telepathic power. They could summon demons, and angels from Paradise, and bring the dead to life. That was well known. It was best to take them seriously, thought Aspe.

In the courtyard below him, pilgrims waited in the rain, wrapped in sopping blankets. A monk moved among them, sheltered by a scarlet umbrella. The colonel leaned over the balustrade and spat in their direction. There was no chance of hitting them at that distance. But even so the action soothed him, prepared him for the inevitable hours of talk before his will was accomplished. He tightened the focus of his mind and re-entered the room.

Inside, the priests sat in ascending circles, or reclined on low benches around a fire sunk into the middle of the floor. The fire was magic, giving off neither smoke nor gas, nothing but a drugged perfume that made it hard to think. The colonel avoided the chair that had been set for him. He never sat when he could stand. Instead, he reached across the fire to take the golden cord into his hand. It looped down low, almost to the floor, between a skeleton wrapped in crimson silk and an obese, footless old man. The colonel stooped and took it between his fingers, and chafed it with the ball of his thumb. It was an unknown substance, between cloth and metal, and against his skin he felt the tingle of a mild electric current. He resisted the impulse to try and break it, because he knew it would not break. He let it go.

The bishop's secretary threw his marijuana cigarette into the fire. During the first part of the colonel's audience, while Aspe had recited the emperor's letter amid a whining drizzle of protest, the old man had sat as if asleep. Now he spoke. 'You're a very violent man, Colonel,' he observed. 'Very . . . violent.'

'I'm a soldier,'.croaked the colonel in his harsh empty voice.

'A soldier, yes. I wish the emperor had sent us more like you. We had petitioned him for soldiers, not staff officers.'

'He has sent you thousands, and you've butchered them all with your criminal incompetence. There are no other soldiers like me. How long has your war with Caladon been going on?'

'I believe you know the answer to that question, Colonel.'

'I know that every day the adventists grow stronger and more arrogant. As I was riding here, not fifty miles from the capital, I passed a village where a crowd had gathered to listen to an adventist preacher. Not fifty miles.'

'These are difficult times, Colonel.'

'Worse than you think. You know King Argon has had a son?'

'So we had heard.'

'You are familiar with the apocalypse of St Chrystym Polymorph?'

'There are so many different kinds of heresy,' sighed the bishop's secretary.

'This is no heresy. This is one of your saints. And the vision is a true one. Listen: 'When the rain comes, a Lion will come also, a King's son out of the North. And he will catch the Serpent in his teeth. And with the first bite all false prophets will be bitten away. And with the second bite, all tyrants and oppressors, and all those who oppress the poor. And with the third bite, all false priests and tyrants. And his horoscope will be . . .'

'Stop! Yes, we know all this. Great powers of darkness are arrayed against us. But prophecies come and go. For a long time, this new king was to have come out of your own people, Colonel, and the adventists quoted other texts. But we are still here, and where are you? Broken and scattered. Yes, it is a dismal time. But we have our own prophecies.'

'Then it must be clear to you why the emperor wishes you to win this war. He had no interest in your struggle with King Argon until this new prince was born. Now everything has changed. Now every adventist and heretic in the empire is looking northward. And if Argon wins this battle . . .'

'It is clear to us. The emperor's wishes are the same as ours. What is less clear is why he has not chosen to send us any more soldiers.'

'They have become too precious to throw away. He will send soldiers, as many as are needed, after I am installed here as commander, with or without your consent.'

As he spoke, the colonel paced the room, the only movement in it, except for the silent oscillations of the priests' necks as they followed his pacing with blind eyes. The bishop's secretary raised up his hand and, spreading the fingers, he stretched it out towards the moving figure. 'I thought so,' he muttered. 'I thought I recognized you.' Aloud he said, 'I require confirmation of the order. I don't believe it. The emperor is the defender of our faith.'

'This is a practical matter. It is not a question of religion,' said Aspe.

'All questions are religious questions. God has given his government into the hands of his ministers. It cannot be taken away.'

'But we are talking about the army.'

'Colonel, you and I are not stupid men. We know what we are talking about. But it doesn't matter. Even if you force me to submit, the army will never follow you.'

The colonel laughed. 'I have reason to believe you're

wrong. Any army tires of being slaughtered month after month, even the most devout. Your standing orders have not endeared you to the men. Medical treatment for officers only. Four thousand men murdered because you refused to issue them ammunition, even though you had it.'

'They were not the right caste to carry firearms. Warfare has laws as immutable as God's. We follow traditions of strategy beyond your comprehension.'

'True enough. Your strategy has allowed a modern army to penetrate to sixty miles from where we stand. In your own self-interest . . .'

'We have faith in God, Colonel.'

'I am relieved to hear it.'

'Yes. It must surprise you. Even if we were able to accept a new commander, do you think we could accept a man like you? I recognize you. I was here when they brought you down from the mountains, caged like an animal. Cannibal! What was your name then, Colonel?'

'I can't deny it. But I've been a long time in the emperor's service. He freed me. He raised me up. And I have accepted the true faith.'

'Have you? Every word you speak betrays your ignorance of it. A convert? No.' The old man rose from his chair and staggered foward a few paces towards the fire, his hands stretched out. The candles along the wall flickered and went out one by one, leaving the amphitheater dark except for the fire in its center. A cold draught came up from nowhere. The crooked figure of the secretary seemed to grow, augmented by its own shadow, and under his hands the air seemed to take shape, until Aspe could see a demon squatting on the coals, impudent, malignant, naked, with a tongue two feet long, curling like a serpent from his lips. The demon seized his phallus by the root between both hands, and squeezed and squeezed until it

190

grew huge, and he could curl his tongue around its head. The colonel sank into his chair. The smell of incense was overpowering.

The demon leered at him, and squeezed and licked until his erection was huge and trembling. He held it upright in both hands, and licked until it gushed sperm like a fountain, flowing over his fingers in repulsive profusion. And the room grew dark, because the flow steamed and sizzled on the fire until it was extinguished, and there was nothing but the secretary's mild voice.

'Salvation is a chemical process,' he explained. 'Do you think it is enough to believe in it? Is that what they teach now in the emperor's churches? No, Colonel. Men like you are the scourings of Paradise. You arrive on earth so deformed by sin, your flesh so hard with it, your damnation is a matter of course. Would you like to see? Would you like to see it?'

As he spoke, the fire started to glow again, and there appeared above it, as if supported on the fumes, an image of the universe, the sun in the middle, burning and changing color, while all around it, in long erratic orbits, revolved Paradise and the nine planets of hell. Slowly, as the colonel watched, they pursued their vagrant courses, some set so close together that they almost touched as they passed, the delicate circles of their orbits elongated or contracted by proximity. Some would brush the sun by a hand's breadth, and then set off on long solitary journeys to the farthest corners of the room. Eight gleamed like precious stones, lit from within by the power of the sun: amethyst, ruby, coral, jade. Two differed – Paradise, evanescent and white, tossed from one orbit to another, spinning lightly among the other planets like a bubble of milk, and Earth. Beautiful Earth. It floated almost into the colonel's grasp; he snatched at it, and his hand passed through it. Then he looked again, through the layers of cotton cloud that wrapped it, and he could see continents, mountains, oceans, cities, men, all on a sphere as small as his clenched fist.

'Beautiful, isn't it?' continued the secretary's voice. 'The most precious of all jewels. Who could believe so much pain, so much suffering, so much violence, when surely there's enough to make men happy, there, right there, within the grasp of your fist? Are you happy, Colonel? No? No, the sins that gave you flesh, transformed your spirit into earth, expelled you from a world of wonder, they are here with you. They have transformed your body and your destiny. You have grown strong; yes, you feel the life in you, but you will die. Even you. Once dead, where then? Here?' And Aspe could see the secretary's hands conjuring in the dark, describing circles around one of the small spheres. 'No. For flesh as massive as yours, as arrogant, as rebellious, this one, I think. This one.' He gestured towards a smaller planet, one that burned bright red as it brushed the sun, and then cooled to onyx at the extremity of its orbit. 'How many lifetimes here will it take to burn that flesh away? How many lifetimes before your spirit rises back to Paradise like a gassy cloud?'

The secretary was silent. Colonel Aspe sat as if in a daze, the planets revolving around him. He was only vaguely aware of the atmosphere changing, of a door opening and closing, of a sweet voice saying, 'Please don't scold me. I came as fast as I could. Is this the man?'

Nobody answered. Aspe half turned in his chair, and he saw a beautiful young woman, almost a girl, perhaps a thousand days past puberty. She was dressed in loose white clothes, and was surrounded by a cloud of light. He watched her with an unfocused mind, absorbed by little things, the play of light around her head, the sound of her breathing. She stood quite close to him. 'Is this the new commander?'

'No,' answered the secretary. 'This is the last joke of a decadent emperor, a man who has forgotten God. He has sent an atheist to laugh at us.'

'Are you sure? He looks like a real soldier. How strong he is!'

'No, ma'am. He's a savage. You are too young to remember. Before you were born, he led a band of atheists down through the snow almost to our borders. They were murdering your animals and eating human flesh. We captured him and sent him to the emperor for a cage in his garden, though if I had had my way he would have died in the topmost cell of the Tower of Silence. He may yet. I was not consulted, ma'am. Watch when he speaks. He has bewitched the emperor into freeing him, and now he has come here. It must not be. He is a dangerous man. Very . . . dangerous.'

'I can see that for myself,' came the bishop's soft, sweet voice. 'He has rejected love. It's evil, isn't it, for a man to be so hard?'

Colonel Aspe listened almost without understanding. He was staring at the bishop, because one look at the bishop's face had awakened memories he didn't know he had. Her face reminded him of a life immeasurably far away, up above Rangriver, where he had sung his music, before he lost his hand. How had he come so far? He didn't know. Stung by memory, he sprang up from his chair as she bent over him, a look of terrible compassion in her face. He seized her underneath the jaw and forced her down, until he could see her expression change. And then he let her go; she stumbled to the ground, looking up at him with such sweet and fearless eyes, he found himself stripping off his glove, and with his bare fingers he reached down to touch her face so lightly, and push her hair back so tentatively, as if asking her a question when he was afraid to hear the answer. The priests raged feebly around him. The candles had come up, and the fire burned up brightly. He turned to it, suddenly sickened by the perfumed flame, and he stamped it underfoot and kicked the cinders with his boot. 'I can't wait for your reply,' he said loudly. 'You have no choice.' He bent down and grabbed the bishop by the jaw. 'You are very beautiful,' he snarled, as she stared up at him from the floor.

Over the next few days, the colonel's soldiers started to straggle in along the river road. They were small and ferocious men. They looked as if they had spent their whole lives on horseback, on high arid plateaus under the relentless sun; they were bowlegged and hunchbacked, their skin burned dark and crisp, their hair shaved, their eyebrows plucked, their jaws powerful and always moving, because they chewed some southern narcotic and spat it everywhere. In a few days the city was full of them, and they stabled their horses in the temples and put their tents up in the marketplaces and along the streets, and took what food they wanted from the roadside stalls. Yet they were disciplined too, and didn't touch the women or break down any doors, just took what they wanted and sat in the rain inside their tents, chewing their drug with rotten teeth and whispering to each other in voiceless southern languages.

The bishop's council withdrew into the Temple of the Inner Ear, and sent impossible commands out to the captains of the garrison. But when the colonel raised the imperial standard from the top of the post office – a golden dog's head on a midnight flag so big it seemed to float in slow motion – even the young captains of the purge came down to see him and to hear him speak. The war had continued all their lives, and even though they had lost fathers, grandfathers, brothers, friends, still the war had seemed mythical and far away. There was never any news. Yet suddenly it had lumbered out of the mists of ignorance like a huge white ship out of a cloud – almost upon them, running them down – because now for the past week they had heard the enemy's artillery smashing the outlying fortifications as the Starbridge army came reeling back, and the town was full of scoundrels and deserters. So the captains came to listen. And there were rumors of some vast necromancy coming from the temple, and in fact the tower of the Inner Ear had farted out some smelly smoke, but it had dissipated in the rain, it rained so hard.

The colonel was everywhere, talking and yelling, but all day he would squeeze the town for food, and at night he had it taken in wheelbarrows down to the docks, where he was sleeping on a mat in some antinomial cave. There he prepared feasts, and people said they were eating meat down there too. He built soggy bonfires and stood out in the rain, and sang in the language of his own people, his harsh voice drawing pictures in the air, so that in the days that followed, the townspeople saw a sight that filled them with rage and fear – antinomials riding through the city on horseback, laughing and making music, and some were armed. Dogs slunk from the temples to follow them. Younger clergy – shopkeepers and bankers – hid their faces in dark doorways, making impotent gestures of purification.

It rained for seven days, and on the seventh day, Abu and Thanakar and Charity Starbridge sat on the carpet in the prince's room, smoking hashish. The prince had said something, and Thanakar was looking at his friend with a peculiar mix of tenderness and envy, because it seemed to him the prince had changed during the weeks he had spent cooped up, and not just gotten thinner. It was as if he had discovered a secret that had given him an answer, so that he didn't have to fumble quite so much. He seemed less apologetic, surer of himself. 'It's a question of truth,' he said. 'I'm sorry to disagree. You're so clever, both of you. You can say what you want with words. But you missed the point. It's not just that we should leave them alone – tolerance. It's that we should learn to think as they do. Not like that, of course. We're civilized men. Women.' He nodded to his sister. 'We can't turn back the clock. But we can learn something. Not to depend so much on other people.'

'But depending on other people, that's what civilization is,' said Thanakar.

'Yes. I've heard you say that before. You're right. So maybe I don't mean that. Maybe I mean we should learn not to settle for things. You know how antinomials are. They act as if they want something desperately that doesn't even exist, and they're not going to rest until they get it. I mean if we could learn not to settle for happiness, or goodness, or usefulness. There must be something more.'

'There is,' answered Thanakar. 'There's misery, and badness, and futility. We know all about that. Saying that you're not going to settle for happiness is like standing on Earth and saying you're not going to settle for eternity in Paradise. Why look beyond a goal you can't reach?'

'But you can. We've made it so difficult. But it's because we've kept happiness as a goal, far in the future, not even on this planet. But the antinomials are happy here and now. Or at least they were. Why do you think we hate them so much? If you look for happiness, it's always out of reach. But they never worried about the future. They were always wanting something else.'

'What?'

'Freedom,' said the prince.

'But freedom doesn't mean anything. It's just talk,'

protested Thanakar. 'Do they seem free to you? Even in their own minds?'

'No. But that's not the point. Maybe that's why they tried to cut loose from meaning, along with everything else. Why they tried to clear all that away. So that all that would be left would be that eternal hunger. That empty feeling in your heart. That's what makes you happy.'

'An empty feeling in your heart? You're on drugs. You don't have to be a rich man for that. That's within reach of the poorest.'

Abu laughed, foolish and embarrassed. 'I can't explain,' he said, passing the pipe. 'But I'm not the only one. There are a lot of people who worship them, almost. The adventists. You told me that's the only reason the bishop let them live. Because she didn't want to make them into martyrs for the adventists.'

'Yes. But that's because of what they represent, not what they are. They represent freedom, I'll grant you that. They represent a fantasy of Paradise. Freedom, equality, no property – lives of pure spirit. The adventists thought their savior would come from there. Their king. A lot still think so.

Charity Starbridge said nothing, just taking the pipe as it was passed to her. For months she had barely spoken. But, she thought, I too am happy, like an antinomial. She had gotten very thin. Her thinness had given her face an appealing, famished quality, different from beauty, but not too different. Her eyes seemed very large. 'I'm happy,' she said. 'I'm happy just to be with you, and not in my room. Both of you.'

Abu smiled and reached to touch her hair, but Thanakar looked at her pityingly. What a prison that is, he thought, only to be able to say pleasant things. No wonder she hardly speaks. As a girl, he remembered, she had had a gleeful and sarcastic tongue.

Commissar Micum knocked and entered. He carried two envelopes in his hand. 'News,' he said. He smiled at his wife, and she smiled back and tried to stand, to make the compulsory gestures of delight, but she had smoked too much. So she did them from the floor and banged her head into the carpet, and then sat up, rubbing her head and laughing. She was glad to see him, for the commissar was always kind to her, and she no longer expected more than kindness. Her sincerity showed in the way she moved her hands – not as skillfully as some wives, but happily. She clapped her hands and offered him the pipe. He shook his head. 'Business before pleasure, love,' he said.

'What's new?' asked Thanakar.

'The bishop has a new commander,' said the commissar. He was excited. He held one fist in the small of his back and walked crisply towards them, bending slightly forward at the waist. In the middle of the floor he stopped to brandish his envelopes. 'There's a new mobilization order for tomorrow. Even for old carrion like me.'

'I wish you wouldn't go,' said Charity, smiling.

'But I want to go, love.'

'Then I hope you will.'

Thanakar got to his feet. 'Congratulations, sir,' he said.

'Thank you, my boy. I'm sure it's just a baggage train. Grave-digging detail. But there's good news all round. These are your commissions.' He gestured with the envelopes.

Thanakar reached to grab them, and the commissar kept talking. 'It's something new. He wants a field hospital. The bishop must be livid. Quite illegal, of course, but it had to come. I always said it had to come, and if it takes an atheist to push it through, then God bless him for it. You're commissioned surgeon, with a provisional rank of captain. Captain Thanakar Starbridge!'

He saluted gleefully, and then he stopped. 'There's one for you too,' he said to Abu.

'They've sunk as low as that? They must be desperate. They must be going to lose,' said the prince calmly. He sat on the carpet as before, without moving, staring straight in front of him.

It crossed Thanakar's mind again that his friend had changed somehow, acquiring a sense of purpose somewhere. There was an uncomfortable silence. Then Abu's old, foolish look came back, and he smiled uncertainly, because the commissar was looking very stern. 'I'm sorry,' he stammered. 'I don't mean to sound ungrateful. We have you to thank for this, don't we?'

'No,' said the commissar. 'It's not a question of privilege. It's a question of duty,' and Thanakar thought he had never seen him angry before. 'I admit it's not much. Provisional only, and only if you behave yourself. Second-lieutenant, supply corps.'

'Thank you. I'm not going.'

'Good God, what do you expect? Lieutenant-colonel?'

'Thank you. It's better than I deserve, I know. I'm grateful to you. But I'm not going.'

'Not going?' The commissar was furious. 'You have to go.'

'I don't have to do anything. I refuse to fight for such a cause.'

'Cause? What cause? There is no cause. You'll go because you're what God made you. A damn poor excuse for a soldier. You talk as if you had a choice.'

'But I do have a choice. I hate the bishop, and I won't fight for her. Not for any of them. What I don't understand is, you hate them too.'

'The bishop is one thing; God is something else. Aspe is an atheist. The bishop had him carried through the streets in a cage He's not complaining, is he?'

There was a pause. Thanakar hadn't spoken. Then he squatted down in front of the prince. 'Come on,' he said gently. 'It's all nonsense. You have to go. Don't be afraid. I'll take care of you. We'll go together.'

Abu looked at him with loathing. 'You,' he said. 'You hypocrite! I thought you were like me. I thought you hated the world because it was unfair. Because it's cruel and corrupt and runs on lies. I thought you wanted to change it. No – you only hate it for what you think it did to you. If you had been born with a straight leg, you would have been as proud and stupid and careless as any of them.'

'I was born with a straight leg,' said Thanakar between clenched teeth. 'He dropped me.'

'Shut up!' shouted Abu. 'I don't care. If you're not brave enough to throw it back at them now, then I never want to see you again.' The prince was crying. Tears ran down his face. He got to his feet and turned away from them, and walked over to a table across the room, where there was a bottle and some glasses. He poured himself a drink.

'I'll tell you why you have to go,' said the commissar quietly. 'It's the bargain you made. A rich, pampered man; look at you. It's the bargain you make every month when you cash the bishop's check. You made it. You can't turn back on it now.'

Outside the window, it had gotten dark. The rain had stopped. Prince Abu swallowed some liquor, but his nose and throat were clogged with tears so that he coughed, and some of it slopped down his uniform. 'Thank you,' he said when he had recovered breath. 'That makes things very clear. It resolves something I've been thinking about. Now, if you don't mind, I'd like to be alone. You too, Charity.'

'By God, no. Listen to me . . .' said the commissar, but

200

Abu interrupted. 'Please,' he said, and raised his hand, and even in the half-light, through the cuts and scabs, they could see the tattoo of the golden sun. 'Do as I say.'

The commissar cursed, pale with anger, and he turned on the heel of his boot and marched out. Thanakar and Charity followed him, not without backward glances, but Abu had turned back towards the window and was looking out over the city, a glass of liquor in his hand.

4

God's Soldiers

The army of Argon Starbridge, King of Caladon, was camped that night around the monastery of St Serpentine Boylove, sixty miles north of Charn. But the king had sent out skirmishers almost to the city walls. In the morning, Colonel Aspe rode out to meet them at the head of his regiment, and accompanied by a ragged corps of antinomials: over a thousand men and women, some with babies at their breasts. He had recruited them from the docksides, where the rising water had driven them from their holes. Or rather, they had chosen to come, and he had armed them and given them horses, huge carnivorous beasts from the emperor's own stables. Once on horseback, some had simply ridden away over the hills, but most had stayed, because food was very scarce.

They rode all day through haggard countryside – not a house, or a stick, or a flower, or a blade of grass. In that season, the hills were stripped to their foundations: petrified mud and sand dunes, black, red, and a hundred shades of gray, mile after mile. The valleys were wide and desolate, and there was no water anywhere, despite the recent rain, nothing underfoot but sand, and rocks the size of eggs.

They reached a town about seven miles out, tall, stone, abandoned houses with the roofs gone and the doors groaning open. In the square was a dry fountain choked with rocks, and a huge statue of Immortal Angkhdt, squatting down on dog's haunches. His whole face had been worn away by the wind, and towards afternoon the wind began to blow, and it filled their eyes and noses with blown sand. Yet still the antinomials laughed and sang, and when they saw the flags of the enemy on a ridge over the town, they spurred their horses forward without thinking, disorganized and wasting powder. Aspe let them go. At that time he had no control over them. In a few hours they were back, in a swirl of dust, and some carried severed heads on the tops of spears. During their long captivity they had learned much, and if they hadn't yet discovered love, most had learned to hate, and hate bitterly enough to overcome their solitary pride and make it possible for them to ride together. Many deserted every day, but most of these came back after a while, hungry.

After three days, Aspe overtook some remnants of the bishop's army, leaderless since the day before, when General Cayman Starbridge and most of his staff had been captured and crucified. These soldiers watched the antinomials with open mouths, and when they saw the women, they turned and spat into the sand. But even so, most were willing to turn again and follow the colonel, especially when he threatened them with death. So Aspe's army quickly divided itself into three parts: his own silent regiment of horse soldiers, the bishop's infantry, and the antinomials. These last were terrible soldiers – undisciplined, vicious, undependable. But they were effective too, because in the month that followed they won a reputation in the hills for a kind of random savagery that made the enemy run whenever they appeared. They took no prisoners. And whenever Aspe recaptured some village, the starving people would come out, and they would beg on their knees not to be delivered to the atheists. 'Cannibals,' they called them. 'Not men, but singing devils.' They told stories of how the antinomials drank blood from their horses' necks, and made campfires at night to grill the bodies of their enemies or else ripped them raw with huge predatory teeth.

Most of the army hated the antinomials, and feared them more than the enemy. Some hated them and loved them too. It was infuriating to see them break off fighting in the middle of a skirmish for no reason and gallop back at random down the valley, like angry random gusts of wind. A man could never be sure whether they could tell barbarians apart, or recognize their allies from their foes, or even if they might turn on themselves some day and cut each other to pieces in an excess of frenzy.

But it was exhilarating, too, to see them riding, surrounded by this time by a great army of dogs come out of nowhere to follow them. It was exhilarating to hear them break the air each morning with their harsh, wild songs. They were fearless. They would ride laughing to overrun some dug-in guns, and then they would hold the place for hours, though outnumbered many times, and when their ammunition was gone, they would charge the enemy with bayonets, yelling like demons, the colonel out in front, until the enemy broke and ran. In those days, many of King Argon's soldiers were adventists; they carried the red and white cockade strapped to their helmets, though some still wore the old penis-shaped pendants their fathers and grandfathers had worn. To them the antinomials represented God's avenging scourge, and they spoke about them with a kind of superstitious awe, and they were always the first to run.

In the balance, thought Commissar Micum Starbridge, the antinomials did more good than harm, wild and undisciplined as they were. At first, Aspe was careful to keep them separate from the rest of the army, to let them fight on different days, to give them different objectives. But after a time, they answered to his call, because he bit them with his magic voice and drew them pictures in the air. In the evenings, in their camp, under the dark sky, he sang to them of home, of snowfall, of freedom, of safety from persecution, of a great journey back up above Rangriver, when all the barbarians were dead. He gave them memories of Paradise. They were easier to deceive than children. He led them in person when he could, his white hair streaming out behind him, and he took care to be the bravest and the strongest. At the battle of Halcyon Ridge, on September 99th, in the eighth phase of spring, he came back with the heads of two enemy commanders, identical twins, hanging from his saddle bow, and after that the antinomials were his, body and heart. In every man and woman, even the purest, there are deep biting instincts and an unconquerable love for destiny. They followed him without thinking.

The commissar loved them, though he hated their cruelty. Though he gestured angrily when he heard about it, he condemned it as he might have condemned viciousness in one of his own children, had he had any – angrily, yet excusing them in his heart, as if their cruelty had come out of an excess of some good quality, energy, perhaps, or courage. He forgave them because they symbolized for him the pure essence of soldiery, the way they laughed and never complained, the way they fought until they died, the way they rode those huge, savage horses as if they were part of them, careening down the scorched gullies just for the love of riding, and then all changing direction in a mass, without a word or signal, wheeling like a flock of birds.

Also, there was something in their disorganized appearance that touched the heart in his starched, polished old breast. They had no uniforms. Some rode almost naked under the white sun.

When there was wood, at night they lit bonfires and played music and danced. Then the old commissar would walk down from his tent and sit somewhere on a rock above their camp. Alone and far away, but not out of earshot, he would sit with a cigarette and listen to some saxophone rip up the night, and watch the figures of the dancers. He hadn't much to do. As he had anticipated, he was with the transport corps, bringing up ordnance from the city on the backs of dying elephants.

The commissar had gone with the first wave of reinforcements, veterans and reserves, and a few companies of the purge. Thanakar remained in the city a few days, putting together a mobile hospital with a man he had known from medical school named Creston Bile. They had seven surgeons and a muleteam, along with some episcopal spies posing as assistants. These spies were to make sure that no one but Starbridge officers got more than rudimentary first aid, certainly no anaesthetic, nothing to blunt the pain when God saw fit to wound a soldier for his sins. 'We'll ditch them first thing,' said Creston Bile. 'I had to agree. Otherwise the bishops would have locked us up.' He was a good man.

The night before they were due to leave, Thanakar got a message from Charity Starbridge. 'Please come please,' it said, in a style of calligraphy only the brightest and best-educated were allowed to use, the first percentile of the graduates from Starbridge schools. There Charity had been taught, along with physics, calculus, and astronomy, never to show discomfort or displeasure, but when Thanakar reached the commissar's tower, she was on the verge of tears. She was trying to control herself, but her famished body seemed to shake from the exertion. 'I don't mean to

206

scare you,' she said as she met him in the hall. 'Please, if you have something else to do . . .'

'What is it?'

'Please, I feel so ashamed.'

'What is it?' he repeated gently. He took her hand. It was easier to touch her than talk to her. She grabbed him by the thumb with a tightness that he never thought could have come out of such thin fingers. She led him into Abu's bedroom. The room had been swept and straightened, the quilts folded and arranged. 'He did it himself,' she said. 'The servants almost panicked when they saw.'

Abu was gone. He had left a letter on the bed, on a pile of photographic prints.

'May I read it?'

'Please.' She had not released his hand. She raised it up and pressed it hard against her dry lips.

The note was very short. It said: 'I've gone to find the man who took these. Maybe I can do some good this time. We have a chance. Even so, you don't have to hope, to try.'

The photographs were large and stiff, portraits of child laborers in episcopal industries – glass mines, steel foundries, cotton mills, dress shops, prayer farms. Some were very young. A girl posed next to her thread machine, an endless row of spools, levers, and metal gears. It was spotless, but the girl was dirty, barefoot, her dress torn and patched. Her hair was cut short, so as not to catch in the machine, and her face was smudged with dirt, or maybe just a flaw in the print, because photography was primitive in those days.

She only had ten fingers, and her hands were raw and bruised, yet even so she smiled. All the children in the pictures smiled – gaping laughter from a group of boys in caps, posing at the entrance to the coal pit; fox-faced smiles from prim little girls knitting socks; a wistful almost guilty smile from a girl standing by herself on a heap of stones in an endless field.

'I didn't know they started so young,' said Charity Starbridge.

In those days, a photographer focused a reflection on the surface of an acid pool. Then he had to wait for the image to congeal, so that he could lift it out with wooden tongs and spread it between two plates of glass. He could make the prints at home, placing the plates on paper sensitized to light, but the image itself took six minutes to harden in the pool, and if the subject moved too much, or if anything happened to disturb the perfection of the acid's surface, he had to start again. Thanakar wondered how a photographer could have been in those places for the time it took, before he was arrested. Or perhaps these were official portraits, sanctioned by the bishop, and that was the reason for the children's smiles.

The last few photographs were different. They were taken in the slums of the city, and one showed the back court of a filthy tenement, and children playing games. One showed a family of Dirty Folk, heretics who worshipped snakes, and they never washed except a few times in a generation, when Paradise rose. One photograph showed a young flagellant, a girl with angry, haunted eyes, sitting braiding a whip.

The girl was sitting in an artist's studio, photographic equipment in the background. Far in the back, showing through a doorway, there was a printing press with some blurred figures working over it, and the girl sat with one foot on a poster, one of several strewn around the floor. In the photograph you could only see a bit of it, part of a headline and a picture of the gates to the infant penitentiary, but it was enough for Thanakar to recognize a poster he had seen on the walls around the city for a few weeks, the first of their kind that spring. It had filled him with furtive hope. The bishop's secretary had ordered special patrols to go and rip them down.

'Have you shown these to anyone?'

'No.'

'Don't.' Thanakar replaced the photographs on the bed. Standing in the prince's room, looking at Charity's famished face, he felt some of that same hope. He had stood in the rain, watching a group of soldiers pulling down a line of posters on a wall, while people gathered to read ones further along.

The feeling rose in him and mixed irrationally with some of the pride he felt at being in the bishop's uniform, finally, a captain in the bishop's army. It was as if things might change for him, finally, and the world too. He stared at Charity until she dropped his hand to break the tension and walked away to the prince's wardrobe near the window. His suits hung there in a row, ten of them, one for each day of the week.

'He hasn't taken any clothes,' she said. 'What'll he wear?'

When Thanakar opened his eyes in the dark, awake and quickly sensitive, he found the shadows coalescing into unfamiliar shapes, the wall at his head instead of by his side, the window in a different place. It had been a long time since he had slept in a bed different from his own. And the sound that had woken him – the spray of rain against the glass, not that. Something else. There, again. He raised himself up on his elbow.

He had been woken by the sound of dreams. Charity Starbridge lay curled away from him. Light stretched in through the window from some distant source and drew a soft diagonal across the bed. It was enough for him to see her eyes moving under her lids, and he could hear the labor of her lungs, as if she were out of breath. Once her foot made a small kicking motion. Like her brother's, her dreams led her fast, far.

He reached out his hand towards her but then drew it back. How sweet she seemed, smelling of hashish and sleep, and perhaps even a little love, her skin pale and luminous, stretched tight over her sharp bones, her hair so black. Looking at her, he tried to remember other women – a few, older, a long time before. They had never taken off their clothes. And sometimes, later, he had gone down to the market at night, to stalls rented from the bishop by the guild of prostitutes, but from those places he remembered mostly the coloured lights and the peculiar textures of certain kinds of artificial cloth against his skin, and it was as if those things had happened to another body, not this clean one he had now, lying in this clean bed, but to another one, as if he had put on another body like a suit of old clothes to do some unmemorable and degrading chore.

Charity's breathing settled down, and she rolled over on to her back. The bones of her pelvis and the bottom of her rib cage stood out in a stark circle, filling with shadows as her belly sank down. Her skin along the ridge seemed stretched almost to breaking. Again he put his hand out to her, and again he hesitated.

In the morning, Thanakar went off to war. And in a little while he came to think: happiness, like most things, increases in value with its rarity. At first, hitching up his mules and looking at the glum faces around him, he had felt arrogant and alive, a rich man among poor. But as the weeks went by, and the wagons filled with wounded men, and the tents went up in villages of starving people, then Thanakar's happiness made him uneasy, and he guarded it like a man carrying money through an alleyway, afraid that some skinny hand might snatch it. He held it in a secret place, and only took it out from time to time when he was alone.

He had dreamed of war ever since he was a child, and been ashamed he couldn't go. God had made the Starbridges the wardens of Earth, of all the nine planets, and the two keys he had put upon their ring were the army and the church. A man not part of either found it hard to justify himself, because prison wardens have a job to do to earn their keep. And even though he had never believed much in the myth, it didn't matter. He found it hard not to see himself through other people's eyes, through the shrewd assessing glances of widows, and superannuated officers who had known his father.

But you had to be well rested, to care what people thought of you. It was strange how quickly you lost the habit of imagining. Dreaming of war, his mind had made beautiful pictures, and because he had been a realistic child, even the most beautiful were also horrifying and grotesque. Still, they were pictures, because the mind's eye is more developed than its hand or tongue or ear. But at the war itself, sitting at nightfall near the fire, drinking out of a tin can, he found that sounds, tastes, smells made up most of what he knew. Visual images were drowned in them. Coming up from the city, long black lines of soldiers had writhed like snakes over the rocks, and at first he had twisted backward in his saddle and sat gazing, trying to impress the image in his mind. But after a day he had stopped looking, and when, in camp after six weeks, he looked back on that trip, all that really came to mind was the dust at midday and the wind licking his face with its tongue coarse and dry.

Perhaps, he thought, stretching out his sore leg towards

211

the campfire, if he were ever really in a battle, it would be different. Then there would be lots to see. But he was always where a battle had just been, and sometimes he could hear it going on over the next hill. Stretching out his leg, he turned and watched the canvas tents behind him and the shadows of the surgeons still at work, made huge by the lamps inside, made grotesque by the bellying wind. Still, he thought, all he felt like remembering from this night would be the taste of the whiskey in the can, the same episcopal whiskey they were using as anaesthetic now. The taste of the whiskey and the drunken singing of the amputees. Most wouldn't know till morning that they had lost a limb. In the meantime, it would be hard to sleep.

Things you could imagine but you never saw, you could make perfect in your mind. You could control them. Yet as a child he hadn't predicted there would be opportunities for pleasure here too – the smell of his dirty uniform, slept in, worked in. The anaesthetizing taste of whiskey. Being too tired to think of consequences lining up like policemen. The coals settling down. Life seemed precious when you saw so many ways to lose it.

The doctor stretched his leg out towards the campfire and leaned back. What made him happy was another image, one he carried with him like a snapshot. Charity Starbridge lay asleep, curled up away from him, her mouth open a little. As he watched, she turned over on to her back.

'Think there'll be trouble?' asked a man.

Thanakar shrugged. It felt good not to care.

'It's no good taking that line,' said the man. 'You could have fucked this whole thing up.'

True enough, once again, thought the doctor wearily. That afternoon he had gotten into a fight.

'Not that I blame you,' said the man. 'It's just that things with the bishop are touchy enough.'

That afternoon they had been busy. Men had been stretched out all over the rocks. There had been no time for foolishness, but one of the surgeons was the bishop's spy. He had put up an altar on the ridge and performed unproductive magic most of the morning, waving a feather fan. Thanakar had gotten tired of seeing him up there, his red robes flapping underneath his apron. So he had sent word for him to stop, to go work in a shallow cave where some of the most hopeless cases had been laid out of the wind. There were three Starbridges, whose names and obligations had driven them to acts of crazy heroism. And two others, general infantry, but when Thanakar came in later to see, he found the surgeon fussing with the corpse of an officer, while right beside him lay a common soldier with the most appalling injuries. Thanakar had heard him crying from across the field. But when he knelt down over him, the surgeon stopped his hand, saying, 'Don't touch him. Don't pollute yourself.' He showed Thanakar the boy's forearm and the tattoos of his horoscope. 'Glass miner,' he said. 'Human filth. He deserves this. It'll teach him. Look at his complexion. Look how pale.' And he had stooped down to mark the boy's shoulder with his scalpel, and cut the symbol for the ninth planet into his flesh.

But as he made the incision, Thanakar had grabbed his wrist and slapped his hand away. He had stood and kicked him as he went down, and hurt his leg, so that later he could barely stand. Then he had wasted more time than he should have on the boy, who died anyway. He had given him the last of the morphine, and stopped him from crying out so loud.

This life was hard on Thanakar's leg, riding on horseback

and working all the time. Kicking priests. It felt good in a way.

'You can't go around kicking priests,' said the man at the campfire. 'Not and not hear about it.'

'He wasn't a priest.'

'Close enough. Pass the can.'

Thanakar held out the whiskey. 'Don't drink up all the anaesthetic,' he said.

'A man could use a little.' In the tents behind them, quavering voices sang the national anthem.

The surgeon spy had gone back towards the city with a train of wounded, muttering curses and threats. 'Glad to see the last of him,' said the man. 'Still, I wonder what he'll say. Not so bad for you, being a Starbridge. But he might decide to take it out on the rest of us.'

'I'm not sure the bishop has the power she once had. The colonel's an atheist.'

'Temporarily. He's not long for this world, the way he fights.'

'Still, he seems to be winning.'

'Mmph. Damned cannibal.'

Thanakar looked at Charity Starbridge through his mind's eye. She was sitting up in bed with a pillow clasped to her chest, wrinkling her nose. It was hard for him to put together a scene with her, or a conversation. He had spoken to her so rarely. In the prince's bedroom he had said almost nothing, just limped up behind her as she stood fingering the prince's suits, and put his hands around her waist. Sleeping with her once, he hadn't yet begun to touch the fantasy he had of helping her unlock the prison of her manners, so that he could coax her out, so that she could say what she felt sometimes. In the morning she had barely spoken, though she had been eager to touch him, to say goodbye.

'Good evening, Commissar,' said the man, making gestures of respect.

'Good evening, Captain. Don't get up. Is Captain Thanakar around?'

'You're stepping on him, sir.'

'Ah. My boy.'

'Micum.' The doctor roused himself. 'Where did you come from?'

'Just crossing back. I went up to listen to some music.'

'No need for that, sir,' said the man. 'We've got our own.' He jerked his thumb back towards the tents.

'So I noticed. What is that noise?'

'Choir practice, sir. Half a bottle for an arm, three-quarters for a leg. Have some.' He held out the can.

'Thank you, Captain.' Micum brushed off a rock and sat down by the fire.

'What music?' asked Thanakar.

'Antinomials. They're camped over the next ridge.'

'Damned cannibals,' muttered the man, but Thanakar sat up. In six weeks he hadn't seen one. They didn't come much to the hospital, preferring to ignore a wound or kill themselves if it got too bad. 'Are we that near to the front?' he asked.

'Not much of a front,' said the commissar. 'And we're not very near it. Aspe sent them back to rest.' He frowned. 'They've been out repacifying.'

'Murderous bastards,' said the man. 'Aspe's just as bad. Sir,' he added when he noticed the commissar's raised eyebrows.

'He's a great commander.'

'He's a lunatic. Sir.'

Micum laughed. 'Perhaps. I'd think you'd be obliged to him, getting you into uniform. Without him, you'd still be delivering babies.'

'I'm not complaining, sir,' said the man. 'But it was bound to happen. My great-great-grandfather was a doctor in this war.'

'How long ago was that?'

The man squinted. 'One full year.'

'There, you see? You're the first doctors this season. In my time, we never had such luxuries. Officers, of course, but all the rest, we just had to shoot them in rows and send them back for the priests to sort out. They'd be having parties just behind the lines. Funeral rites. You could hear them every night, and see the fireworks. It was cold, back then. This whole area was under snow, the first time I came out. Of course, we were never this close in. We were winning, that season. At one point, we almost thought we'd won.'

They were sitting around a fire, in a hollow in the rocks out of the wind: Micum and Thanakar, and the man. He was a Starbridge half-breed on his father's side, but unlike most, he had been acknowledged by his father and sent to school. That accounted for his easy manners with all classes, and he was not likely to be punished for them either, because he was a good doctor, and in the city he had been licensed to treat Starbridges, though only with his right hand. He.was a big man, and his hair was red, not one of the criminal shades, but too bright for comfort, and if he had gotten into other kinds of trouble, it might have been held against him. In the city he had dyed it, as many did. Now it was beginning to grow out. His name was Patan Bloodstar. His mother had been a nurse.

'Got a letter from Charity,' said the commissar. 'She sends her love.'

Thanakar frowned, wondering what a letter from Charity would look like. 'I am well. I hope you are well. I saw something today that made me happy, thinking of you . . .'

There were form books for all types of letters, prepared by the bishop's council for the use of wives, and if the letters varied depending on the horoscope, the season, the date, their tone never varied. Charity would follow them scrupulously, Thanakar imagined, and if she allowed in any bitterness or substance, it would take a clearer eye than the commissar's to see it. Or if there was any bitterness, perhaps she would express it in the sarcastic beauty of her calligraphy, the complicated ideographs which proclaimed her education and housed her foolish sentiments as a palace would a slave.

'Charity is my wife,' explained the commissar.

Bloodstar stared at him, and made a little circle with his lips. 'You're a liberal man, sir,' he said after a pause.

'Not at all. Thanakar is like a son to me.'

'Well, sir,' said Bloodstar. 'Here's to the end of stupidness.' He toasted with the can. 'My grandmother told me that in summer married women used to walk out in the streets. I guess it was too hot to stay inside. I'd like to live to see it.'

This kind of talk made Thanakar feel ashamed, as if he and Charity, by sleeping together, had somehow justified the bishop's regulations. There were acres of cells up on the mountain reserved for adulterers, and they were mostly empty these days. Thanakar wondered if come summer they were mostly full.

'If things are going to change at all,' the commissar was saying, 'we have to trust each other.'

From the ridge above them came the sound of gunfire, just a few shots, and then some yelling in the dark, and a dog howling. Then silence, and then the dog started to howl again, nearer now. The sound stretched and broke, suddenly, and there was silence again in the dark night, for the amputees had quieted down. And then they heard a

217

woman's voice calling out, very near. The commissar got to his feet. There were sounds of some rocks falling, and the frightened neighing of a horse, and the voice calling out again, wordless and soothing. Then they could hear the horse's hooves, down on the bedrock where they had camped, coming towards them. A dog slunk out from between two boulders and stood grinning, his tongue hanging out.

The shadow of a horse stepped out of the darkness, its hooves talking on the bare rock. It hesitated for a moment outside the circle of firelight, and then it stepped inside, suddenly diminished as it shed night's bulky cloak. On its back sat a young woman and a boy, staring down at them. They were dressed in horsehair breeches, and naked from the waist up. The woman sat behind, holding the reins in one hand and a rifle in the other, its barrel pointed to the sky. The firelight shone on her skin and her small breasts, her proud face and the bandage wrapped around her forehead.

The boy leaned back against her. In one hand he carried a small horn, a mess of copper tubing coiled like a whip. Across his knees hung the body of a rock cat, bright gold in that light, still dripping blood. Tied to the saddle horn between his legs swung a battered trophy, a man's severed head, tied up by his hair.

'Welcome,' said the commissar.

'Good hunting,' said the boy.

Behind them the singing had been quiet for a while, but then from the tents broke out a long blubbering cry, as a drunken man awoke to what he had lost. The horse shied at the sound, and the woman reined it in a narrow stamping circle. It kicked nervously at the stones, kicking up sparks.

'Dangerous, riding at night,' remarked the commissar.

'A horse lives to run,' said the boy. 'Tonight, not tomorrow.'

'Yeah, yeah,' muttered Bloodstar. 'Pedantic bastards.' He got to his feet, looking backward towards the tents, towards the weeping and the crying out, as other men cursed at being woken. 'I'll go see,' he said. He raised the can to his lips for a final drink.

The boy sniffed the air. 'Whiskey,' he said. The woman kicked the horse a few steps towards them.

'Oh, no you don't,' said Bloodstar. He put the can behind his back and stood motionless as the woman looked at him inquisitively. She sat quiet for a long moment, and when she moved, finally, it was a tiny gesture, nothing at all, except for the care that she put into it. She sat with her rifle stock in the crook of her thigh, the barrel pointed upward, and then she turned her wrist, so that the gun turned in her hand and the triggerguard faced out instead of in.

The commissar broke the silence. 'That's not very hospitable, Captain,' he said.

'Drunken savages,' muttered Bloodstar. The woman looked at him curiously, and the boy held out his hand. Still muttering, Bloodstar came down towards him and gave him the can. He needn't have worried. The boy took only a small swallow, and Thanakar admired the light on his pale skin as he stretched back his head and the liquor knotted his throat for an instant. He didn't offer any to his sister, nor did she take it. She just sat there, staring at Bloodstar until the boy finished with the can and handed it back, and then she wheeled the horse around and kicked it out into the dark. The dog got up and followed them. Behind Thanakar, the noise in the tents died down.

'Drunken savages,' repeated Bloodstar louder.

'They don't drink much,' said the commissar. 'Not like us. They don't have to. Nothing to forget.'

'Cannibals,' continued Bloodstar, making the gesture of purification, dropping his face down to each armpit in turn. 'That rock cat didn't die of old age. They murdered it. I bet they eat it.' He poured the rest of the whiskey out on to the rocks, and then dropped the can.

'I'll bet,' said the commissar sadly, looking out into the dark.

Thanakar sat cross-legged, feeding the fire. 'Our ancestors ate meat,' he said. 'Not so long ago.'

'Pedants, everywhere,' said Bloodstar, grinning. He sat back down. 'How do you know?'

'Teeth. We've got the teeth for it.'

'I guess we've evolved a little.'

'No,' said Thanakar. 'It's not a question of that. At least, not at the beginning. It was a question of property rights. The eighth bishop banned it. He said animals were God's property. His property, he meant. Starbridges used to eat meat long after that, long after it was illegal for everybody else. Then we lost the taste for it.'

'Well, that's evolution, isn't it?' asked Bloodstar. 'They're savages. Come on. They cut people's heads off and ride around with them. What do you think happens to the bodies?'

The commissar was still standing. 'Whatever they are now, they were a peaceful people once,' he said.

The next day, Aspe crossed over the escarpment down into the river valley, and here the land was more fertile, with the swollen river rushing through. The rain had had some effect here; already a thin gauze of grass had stretched over the wizened earth, grotesque somehow, like a sweet new shroud for an old corpse. This was monastic land and supported a number of villages, each grouped around a shrine. The people of each village had worked at a different cottage industry for the monks. There was a town of weavers, of tinsmiths, of tailors. And in front of each stone gate was the image of that town's product – a stone umbrella twenty feet high, a stone sock garter, intricately carved, twice the length of a man.

The inhabitants, rotten with adventism, had rebelled. They had joined King Argon as his army had come through, and many of them had abandoned everything to follow it as it receded. Others had stripped off their clothes and run naked into the hills. In an adventist delerium, expecting their savior every minute, they had burned their crops. The monks had allowed only one food in each village, turnips for one, cabbages for another, and the tattoos of the villagers had prohibited them from touching anything but that one vegetable, boiled whole. For many that had been the bitterest part of slavery, and when King Argon came, they had torched their own fields, thinking that the land would blossom under the conqueror's feet, and sprout up fruits and flowers, and need no tending. Argon had encouraged the fantasy, but even so he had had them whipped, for he was desperate for the food. They had run off terrified into the hills.

So by the time King Argon's army had retreated to the monastery at the head of the valley, and Colonel Aspe was chasing stragglers towards it up the road, these villages were almost deserted. Aspe ordered that the remnants of the population be spared, and he sent the antinomials the long way round. At one gate, he reined his horse next to the immense stone statue there, wondering what it was. For generations, the villagers had made a little wooden toy in the shape of a duck. Only a few old men and women were left now, huddled in the shadow of the gate, and some came out when they saw him and went down on their knees next to his stirrup, begging for food. They had brought as offerings a few samples of the little toy. Aspe leaned down to take one. It was a duck, and when he pushed his finger into the bottom of its base, its bill sagged open and its tail sagged down.

Aspe sat in his saddle, chewing a piece of melon. He played with the duck without looking at it as he squinted up the valley into the sun. Then he leaned and spat a few melon seeds meditatively on to the bald head of one of the villagers, and he was amazed to see the man grab them and put them into his mouth. Aspe dropped the rest of the melon rind on to a woman's back as she searched among the pebbles for a seed that might have dropped. Another man grabbed it, but there was no fight; he broke off pieces of it and handed them around, making little bowing motions with his head.

The colonel gestured with his hand and his adjutant rode up, a slick officer of the purge. 'Give them something to eat,' the colonel commanded. 'Feed them.'

The officer shrugged. 'It's a waste, sir,' he said. 'These people always die when the rains come. They're used to it.'

'Feed them,' repeated the colonel harshly, and then he spurred his horse.

But his order was ignored.

Two days later, Thanakar saw some of the battlefront. He had crossed over to the valley and road, following the army's baggage, and he had accepted an invitation from Micum Starbridge to ride his elephant. It was a hairy beast, healthier than most, but even so its shaggy back was clotted with scum, and scum hung down from its great lips, for it had caught a lung infection in the rain, in the cold nights.

Thanakar was sorry he had come. He and the commissar rode in a carriage on its back, and Thanakar resented sitting so close to the old man, not because he disliked him. In the days of the campaign, he had grown fond of him. But if he had liked him less, he would have resented him less, because if a man is a fool, perhaps you have a moral obligation to try and hurt him secretly, to sleep with his wife if you can. Not quite that, thought Thanakar, smiling. But at least you don't feel so guilty. As he rode, he looked for things about the old man to dislike, and in his mind he drew a caricature of Micum's profile against the slate-blue side of the gorge, his nose and lips protruding like a pig's snout, his eye peering out from a little puckered whirlpool of flesh, his hair cut short like bristle. Thanakar relaxed, and the man became human again. His features slid back into place; he turned and smiled, his face warm and friendly, his eyes sad. Thanakar wished that he had come another way, but his leg was too sore for him to ride a horse.

The river valley was paved with smooth white stones. It was a flat mile across, and the slopes came down sheer on either side. The river ran a dozen twisting courses over the stones, and the road skirted the cliff along the east bank, one of a great skein of roads called the Northways, which twisted like the river all over the district. The army followed it upstream, towards the monastery of St Serpentine Boylove high up ahead: spires and battlements cut into the mountain, but still out of sight from where they sat on elephantback. The view was blocked by rocks, a configuration known locally as the Keyhole. A few miles up, the cliffs on each side of the river jutted in until they almost touched, and the road led through a narrow defile while the river roared beneath it. And high above the road, the overhanging cliffs almost touched. There they were

223

joined by a span of masonry, and Thanakar could see the heads of enemy soldiers walking back and forth along it.

He borrowed the commissar's field glasses. Heads in black helmets moved back and forth, and on the rampart, someone had painted a white phoenix rising from its nest of fire, a symbol of adventism. Below that, Thanakar followed some ropes down into the blue sky below the bridge, and at the ends hung bodies. He was used to that. King Argon had decorated each hilltop in the district with a thicket of crucifixes, and nailed up loyalists and monks. Their red robes fluttered in the wind like flags, and carrion crows perched along their outstretched arms. Here and there a cartwheel had been hoisted to the top of a long pole, and a man had been spread out on it, disemboweled for the crows, while other men hung by one wrist from the rim until their arms fell off. Thanakar was used to it. As he watched the bridge above the Keyhole, another man was lifted to the rampart and pushed over, to jerk at the end of a rope. He was dressed in golden robes. Thanakar passed the glasses to the commissar, who peered through them. 'Abbot,' he said briefly, and made the customary gestures of respect.

In the shadow of a boulder up ahead, Colonel Aspe sat with some officers and antinomials. He was eating grapes and spitting out the seeds while the others argued. It was a peculiar kind of argument. The captain of his regiment, a bandy-legged southerner with a round head and false teeth, was angry. He pointed and swore at the antinomials, but his accent was thick, and his teeth clattered when he spoke. 'Schob. Thamn you. Fwerk,' he said, but nobody could understand him. And so he shook his fist, and looked up at his orderly standing near, and relapsed into his native language, all spitting sounds and growls.

The orderly saluted stiffly and translated. 'He says it was

224

for you, keeping the ridge. For you kept. No. Colonel's orders; he was telling you. I tell you! Scrape that shit off the rocks!' he gestured towards the enemy soldiers above their heads. 'Now what you do here? What are you? Where you go?'

One of the antinomials was a wide man with a shaved head and a flat, white, masklike face. He wore sunglasses, and his skin after weeks in the sun seemed to be getting paler as the others burned and tanned, bleaching like shell or bone. He turned his face away and then he smiled, humming an inquisitive little tune. He didn't understand.

The southerners glared at him, the captain spitting and cursing while his orderly clicked his heels and translated. 'You bastard, please!' he said. 'Cowardly shithead! Cannibal! Why not ridge? You, on ridge.' He saluted.

'He's saying,' said the colonel's adjutant, 'that you were supposed to follow the hills. He says those were your orders. He says if you had followed orders, we wouldn't be stuck here in the valley with those fellows above us.'

'Supposed,' said the antinomial thoughtfully. 'Supposed to do.' He frowned, and the tune he was humming changed.

The colonel smiled, 'Suggested, my brother.' He sang a little song in his harsh voice.

'Hot there,' said the antinomial, putting words together with difficulty. And he coated them with humming, which made them hard to understand. 'Too hot up there. No water. I come along the river.'

'Besides,' said the adjutant, dapper and smooth. 'I don't understand the fuss. We're not stuck here. We can ride right through. Argon's at the monastery.'

The southern captain started to spit and growl. His orderly translated, saluting. 'Fool. You are fool! Sir!' He gestured towards the bridge above their heads, and the helmets of the enemy soldiers. 'They kill us here. Too . . .' He put his palms an inch apart, indicating 'narrow'.

The antinomial looked at him with scorn. 'Slaves are afraid of death,' he said. 'Only slaves.' He got to his feet and started walking towards the road, but the colonel laughed and sang a song that made him turn around.

'Maybe you should let him go through, sir,' said the adjutant. 'We need a scout.'

'Not him,' replied Aspe. 'Get me fodder.' He squinted down the river road, where the army stretched and coiled for a mile or more. 'Starbridges. Who's on the elephant? Read me their flags.'

His adjutant lifted a pair of field glasses. Above the carriage on the elephant's back rose a pair of fluttering white ensigns. 'Thanakar and Micum Starbridge,' he said.

'I've never heard of them.'

'Transport corps,' said his adjutant. 'One's a doctor. You shouldn't waste him, sir.'

'Is he brave?'

'Of course.' A list of obligations was sewn on to each flag. 'Fourth degree, both of them. They were born under the same sign.'

'Fourth degree?'

'Up to and including loss of life.'

'Good. That's handy. What about obedience?'

'You can see it. It's that red crescent on the commissar's flag. The doctor doesn't have it. He's a . . . cynic, it says. He believes in . . . nothing.

The colonel frowned. 'He sounds like a fool.'

'No, sir. You can see from here. Fifth degree intelligence. It's that triangle right at the top of the flag.'

But Aspe was no longer listening. He was singing for his horse, and it lifted its head where it was drinking by the river. Then it neighed and came running, and Aspe seized one of its horns as it ran past and swung himself up into the saddle. When he reached the road he spurred it to a gallop, even though that part of the valley was crowded with animals, and men standing and sitting, and waiting for something to happen. Men scattered in front of him, leaping for safety off the shoulders of the road, rolling in the dirt out of reach of his flying hooves.

'Who is this madman?' asked the doctor.

The elephant took up the whole road. When it saw the black horse coming down on it so fast, it trumpeted in terror and raised its blobby nose to the sky. The commissar stood up in the carriage and prodded it with his spike, distracting it into giving up all plans to flee or die. It just stood there, trembling and sweating, while the colonel reined his horse back on its haunches in the road in front of them. He raised his whip above his head.

The colonel's voice was harshness without substance, the words like coarse dust in a breath of wind. Thanakar couldn't hear him. The noise of the army was too thick around them, and the elephant seemed to sweat vibrations of thrumming terror through its pores. Aspe cursed and dismounted stiffly. His knees moved stiffly when he walked. It was as if he were only comfortable on horseback, but he grasped the ladder that hung from the elephant's back, and swung himself up, and stood on the beast's head while it bucked and swayed, his gauntlets on his hips.

'Starbridges,' he said. 'I need spies. Ride through that notch and tell me what's behind. I am Aspe.'

Thanakar peered ahead. 'You fear an ambush, Colonel?'

'I fear nothing. I welcome an ambush.' Aspe grabbed hold of the elephant's ear, preparing to descend. 'Ride through.'

'With respect, Colonel,' said Thanakar, 'if there is an

ambush, they won't spring it for us. They'll wait for us to say the road is clear.'

Aspe shifted his hand to support himself on the doctor's flagpole. 'Intelligent,' he sneered. 'What if I go? They won't resist trying to kill me.'

'Your life is too valuable to risk,' said the doctor.

'Valuable! But I don't care if the world is destroyed this instant. Listen to me. Ride through. Take my bugle. If Argon has stones or missiles along the cliff, blow an A sharp. If there are soldiers on the other side, blow and E flat.

'I'm sorry, Colonel, I don't know how.'

'Barbarian! I'll do it myself, then. Does this beast know how to walk?'

Goaded, Thanakar grabbed the commissar's spike and pushed it into the soft flesh around the elephant's tail. The animal shambled forward, wagging its huge head, Aspe standing on its neck. But when it reached where the colonel's adjutant stood in a group of officers and men clustered around the colonel's ensign, it stopped by itself.

'I am going,' Aspe called down. 'Pass me my flag.' A man uprooted it and threw it up to him; he caught it and thrust it through the socket in the carriage rail that already held the doctor's and the commissar's. It flew above theirs, meaningless red squiggles on a black background.

Aspe shouted orders, some in speech and some in music, and soon the officers were running to their stations, rousing their men. One stood still, a handsome man in a red uniform, a priest, the bishop's liaison. 'Colonel,' he shouted. 'The abbot's body must be recovered. There are certain ceremonies I must perform to free his spirit's flight to Paradise. You must send men to cut him down.'

The colonel looked up at the abbot's body, revolving in

the last of the sun. 'But your Paradise is just a lump of rock,' he said. 'I wouldn't waste the tenth part of a second on that fat carrion. Be thankful that there is no life to come. If there were, he'd rot in hell. Ride on,' he said, and then he paused. 'Garin,' he called, and a young boy stepped out of the shadow of a boulder.

'Yes, sir.'

'I left my horse down by that arch of rock. Strip him and comb him. Give him oats mixed with red wine.'

'Yes, sir.'

'Good.'

In front of them the sandstone wall rose like a rampart. The elephant ambled up the road towards the notch where the river ran out. A hundred feet above them, enemy soldiers started to shoot as they came in range. Commissar Micum lit a cigarette, and the sweet marijuana smell was comfortable to Thanakar as he held the elephant to a walk, to pace their bravery. And in a little while, the lower rocks around the Keyhole sheltered them from the soldiers. The rock formations, petrified remnants of old sand dunes, pink and scarlet in the setting sun, blocked their fire. But there were some soldiers on the bridge between the cliffs. They threw down firebombs and bags of what seemed like excrement as the elephant passed underneath.

In the Keyhole, the rocks closed over their heads in a kind of tunnel. In the last moment before entering, Thanakar looked back towards the army. It had spread and scattered, and tents were going up. But a clump of officers still stood, arguing and staring after them through telescopes, and Thanakar could see bands of antinomials on horseback passing back and forth, and he could see the man with the shaved head and sunglasses standing in front of the rest, a trumpet in his hands.

'Do we have a plan?' he asked.

Aspe leaned backward to pluck the cigarette from the commissar's lips and puff on it himself. 'Long ago,' he said, 'my brothers and sisters found a path beyond what you call civilization. Because of what I am, I can beat these slaves,' he gestured vaguely up ahead, 'wherever I meet them, whatever the odds. My way has gone far past strategies and plans. But because I have barbarians in my army, I have to pretend.' he shrugged, expelling smoke from his nostrils. 'My brothers and sisters will camp up ahead tonight, if they want. They may hold it for the others in the morning. It is too late for them tonight. They rode all day and need their rest.'

'And us?'

'Look how beautiful it is.' They were in the Keyhole, in a long tunnel of sculptured sandstone, a hundred feet high. It was quieter here inside, and the river ran deep and placid below the road. The colonel pointed back to where a corner of the sun still shone through an arch of rock, making it glow as if translucent. 'Look,' he repeated. 'Danger gives each moment power, as if it were the only one there ever was. Don't waste it worrying. It will soon disappear. How can I describe it? It is . . .'

'Transience,' suggested Thanakar.

'Yes. Perhaps.' Aspe sighed. 'Often I can't talk to my own family. I need to talk sometimes. When I was young I tried to break away from them. But I could never break away.'

'A biter,' said Thanakar.

'Yes. A biter. It wasn't always so. I was an artist once.' He stripped off his gauntlets and showed them his hands, one flesh, one a claw of steel. 'When I lost that, it was as if all the music stayed caught inside, and it could only escape through talking, doing, making, words. I had lost the way to free myself.'

230

The elephant trudged on in silence for a while. Bullets started to flick around them.

The commissar hadn't spoken in a long time. He cleared his throat nervously. 'I'm very worried about Abu,' he said.

'Wherever he is, it's bound to be safer than where we are,' replied the doctor.

'I'm very worried. He is so vulnerable.'

'Not half so vulnerable as we are,' said the doctor, looking around for the source of the bullets.

'It's not good to run off like that. A man has responsibilities. It's not good.'

'He'll be all right,' said the doctor anxiously. They were approaching the end of the Keyhole. Through a break in the rocks up ahead, they could see the towers of St Serpentine, high on the hillside, still in sunlight. They turned a corner and the valley opened up in front of them, ringed with sharp hills. Where the road started to climb up towards the monastery, half a mile in front of them, several hundred soldiers blocked the way.

'If this is an ambush,' murmered the commissar, 'it's the most foolish one I've ever seen. Unless those troops are bait.'

Aspe grunted. 'Argon Stgarbridge has guns,' he said. 'That I know. There.' He pointed up the road, up past the soldiers, up the hillside to where it disappeared into a tunnel below the monastery gate. A series of terraces were cut into the cliff just where the road disappeared. 'There,' he said.

'I can't see. It's too far,' said the commissar.

'It's as plain as day. Field howitzers. You can see the crews.'

'I can't see it. Where?' The commissar was fumbling with his field glasses.

231

Aspe grunted. 'Let's go,' he said. 'Forward. I want to test the range.'

Thanakar prodded their elephant into a walk again, and they shambled down the road. The enemy soldiers were adventists, drawn in three lines across the road. They carried red-and-white banners, and flags of the phoenix and the rising sun. At about four hundred yards they opened fire.

'Steady,' said Aspe, but it was useless. The bullets made a sucking sound as they hit the elephant; it just stopped and refused to go any farther, though Thanakar stood up and goaded it until it bled. It just stood there, and then it knelt down solemnly. It wouldn't take another step.

'Stay here,' said Aspe. He jumped down from the elephant's back, his boots ringing on the stones. He walked forward down the road a little distance, and from the pouch at his side he produced a copper bugle. Then he raised his arms and shouted out, as if calling for silence, once, twice, three times, and perhaps it was just a trick of the rocks, but his voice seemed to fill the valley and the gunfire lessened. As he put the bugle to his lips, it almost stopped. He started to play a song, full of low notes and deep melancholy, and Thanakar noticed that some of the adventists in front had dropped their weapons, and some were praying, and some knelt down and put their foreheads to the stones. And the sound of the music seemed to carry a long way, for Thanakar thought he heard an echo from behind them, but then he looked back and saw, sitting on an outcropping of rock far above the river and the road, the white-faced antinomial with sunglasses, the sunset gathering around him, and his long trumpet lifted to the sky. Above him, the clouds had caught on fire.

For a long time the two men played, not the same song, but melodies that seemed to catch each other in a sad, loveless embrace. And underneath the music Thanakar could hear the running river, and then he could hear the sound of hoofbeats and a different kind of singing, and in this new sound he recognized for the first time the war song of the antinomials, and it wasn't wild or harsh or even loud, but instead it seemed to linger somewhere in the sky, pure, bitter, restrained, almost out of earshot, not one song but a thousand, mixing and searching high above them for harmonies among the clouds.

The commissar was studying the enemy through his field glasses. 'Incredible,' he said. 'They are weeping. You can see the tears.'

Thanakar looked back towards the Keyhole. From a gap in the rocks the first of the antinomials rode out, men and women riding on horseback, jumping over boulders. They rode and turned and mixed in a whirling pattern every moment more complex, because at every moment there were more of them. They wheeled and changed direction, spreading out around them in a spinning circle, the dying elephant at its hub, and then they turned and circled Aspe as he stood with his bugle to his lips. They carried rifles and machetes in scabbards on their saddles, but they never touched them, and if the adventists had opened fire, they could have killed great numbers. But all this time the enemy stood as if paralyzed as the antinomials spun and circled closer and closer, and it got dark. Soon light touched only the topmost towers of the monastery, and the rest of the valley filled with shadows, like a bowl filling up with ashes under the burning sky.

In time, the enemy lit torches and retreated up the road. Then the guns talked from the mountains and spat long streamers of green fire, trying to find the antinomials in their range. but they couldn't spit far enough. Up the road, they lathered the whole valley with green fire, as if to show that there was no part of it they couldn't reach. By the light of those unearthly flames, the antinomials dismounted and made camp.

'He's not an officer commanding troops. He conjures them, like a magician conjuring demons,' said Thanakar.

'Or angels,' replied the commissar.

'There's no difference,' said Thanakar airily. 'They're just as difficult to control.'

The two men were sitting outside their own careful tent, at the top of a small slope. They sat in deck chairs, looking down towards the riverside where the antinomials were camped around some bonfires. Tents stood scattered as if at random along the bottom of the valley, half erected, fallen down. A few seemed to have been set on fire, and people squatted around them warming their hands. From the river came a constant noise of splashing and yelling as men and women, naked in the cooling wind, washed themselves and splashed each other like children. Dogs ran everywhere, little barking dogs from the city temples and huge shaggy brutes picked up along the line of march. They had slunk down from the empty hills wherever the army passed, to run with the antinomials: silent beasts, slinking with their heads close to the ground, stealing food, and boys and girls ran after them, slapping at their shaggy heads and laughing when they tried to bite. There was food enough for everyone that night. As the two Starbridges had looked on, appalled, the antinomials had butchered the dead elephant, gutted it, stripped off its skin, sliced long slabs of meat from its bones, broken the skeleton apart. Thanakar was a good cook, and he had made an excellent meal for the two of them over the primus, white rice and pickled figs, served in lacquer bowls with sprigs of mint. But as they sat in deck chairs looking out over the camp, it was impossible to eat. The smell of roasting flesh rose up everywhere around them, and everywhere people yelled and reeled as if drunk with blood.

Later they had seen the colonel stand up, surrounded by a circle of his family, his steel fist raised to the sky, and they had heard some of his talking, too, a low toneless whisper. It had no words or voice. Yet still it wasn't buried among all the other sounds, the shouts, barking laughter, people ringing saucepans like gongs, people making music. It rose above those noises like a kind of vapor, like the distilled essence of all the sounds in that disordered camp. It seemed to distill what all of them evoked in different ways, a yearning for something out of reach, and the defiant joy that comes from never settling for anything less.

'I have to get back as quickly as I can,' Thanakar was saying. 'I'm the only one who can redo hands. Bloodstar gets to the wrist all right, but the fingers turn out webbed, like a fin or a flipper. Not that we have the materials to do a careful job. Still, they must be wondering where I am.'

'We'll go back in the morning,' said the commissar, half-listening. 'We'll all go back. The guns are impregnable from this side.'

The bonfires had burned low, and before long everything was dark. But tracer shells still drew occasional parabolas across the sky. They fell short, noiselessly, and flared up.

The two men heard footsteps coming up the slope, and Aspe stepped into their lamplight, carrying a bottle. He was smiling and flushed. Exultation freed his movement and the gestures of his hands, and made him seem bigger even than he was. The air was cool, yet his face shone with sweat, the seams and scars standing out in silver lines along his cheeks.

'I have come to see if you are comfortable,' he said. 'I'm going back.' He paused when they said nothing, then continued, 'I should have brought the horse. I was a fool. I have to walk, but I feel like walking. I have them,' he exulted. 'I have them in my hand.'

'What do you mean?' asked Thanakar.

'Tonight they swore to follow me. Me. They swore to obey me for one month. It's not long enough, for a long journey. It doesn't matter. What is a month to them? A word. I will make it long enough.'

'I don't understand.'

'No, of course not. Why should you? When have you ever understood anything of importance?' Aspe sprawled down heavily on the stones in front of the tent, and his bottle made a chink as he put it down. He took out his knife and made a line in the dirt. 'This is the valley,' he said. 'North and south. The guns are at this end,' he said, touching the north end with his knife. 'The guns and the monastery. We are here,' he continued, bisecting the line with a small mark. 'Just north of this notch, facing the guns. The army is here, where we left them on the other side. Tonight I go back to join them, and tomorrow morning we must circle round, out of the valley on to the ridge. I know the way.' A tracer lit the sky, and lit the valley from the monastery to the notch, and showed the escarpment on either side. 'I will meet King Argon there.' Aspe pointed with his knife to the top of the ridge northeast of where they sat. 'I know the place. But I must keep men here. Otherwise the king will try and move his guns. But when he shoots those flares, he thinks he sees my army. My brothers and sisters will stay here all day. They have given their word.'

He paused, then went on. 'No, not that. They have no word to give. I don't want that. But I have given them a symbol.' He reached into his breast and pulled out a white silk scarf. 'They will follow this, and the man who carries

236

it. And I will burn it one month from tonight, when I have led them home.'

'I don't understand,' said Thanakar.

'Then it is too hard to explain to you. ' Aspe turned to the commissar. 'Old man,' he said. 'It is a sin to try and break the unbreakable horse. So it is. But I found this horse shackled and bound, and I broke the chain and loosened the rope. Only, I must lead it for a time. I too have my obligations. But when King Argon's head is on a pole and I have sent it to the emperor, then I ride north, and my family rides with me. They follow me because of a memory I gave them. I can make pictures in the air. Have you seen it? No? Barbarians! No matter, it's a trick I have. It is a magic that I learned long ago. I have given them a memory of freedom. Every night I have sung it in their ear. But I will not betray them, not this time. North, north above Rangriver, where the grass grows, and there's fish in the water and snow on the hill. In the house where I was born, I will sing my music. I have pledgèd my word. I will not break it. One week from tonight I ride. And my people will ride with me.'

'The savior of his race,' muttered the commissar.

'Ah yes, a biter,' said Aspe, smiling viciously. 'And maybe hoping is the sharpest bite of all. But there is beauty in the heart of ugliness – I learned that from your bishop. You know she has true power, that one. All the rest are conjurers and charlatans – your priests are masters of illusion, as I am. But she has a true power. When I saw her in the center of that circle of old priests, it made me think that there was hope, for me and all of us, and that a man could change. It made me hope I had some beauty of my own. A biter, yes. But look you, Starbridge, look. We can't all keep our fingers clean. Maybe I have been ambition's slave, and worse than that, a slave to other people. But without me, my brothers and my sisters would still be stinking in your filthy slum, because sometimes it takes a man with dirt on his hands.'

'I don't deny it,' said the commissar. 'The hands don't matter, nor the dirt, nor the man. Only if you keep this clean.' He pulled the white scarf from the colonel's fist, and smoothed out its wrinkles. 'Only if you never let it drop. But I believe you are what I would call a man of honor. Otherwise you would have broken them to your own will, and not to this.'

'They would not have been fit to lead, if they had followed me,' muttered Aspe, grabbing back his scarf.

'Remember that,' said the commissar, 'and you may do some good.'

Aspe grinned. 'Tomorrow you'll see me on the ridge.' He pointed with his knife. 'Watch for my standard. Tomorrow I'll break him, by God I will. I'll take him on the flank. I'll have King Argon's head upon a pole. And his guns won't shoot one shell.' He got to his feet, and took his scarf and his bottle down the slope into the dark.

'What does he mean, "by God"?' asked Thanakar.

'He's caught between two worlds. He is the saddest man I ever saw, to talk to us like that. His own people are beyond his comprehension.' The commissar shivered. 'I feel a presentiment of death,' he said.

It rained all night, without managing to launder morning, which was neither crisp, nor fresh, nor clean. The sun peered dubiously through a damp mist, and the sky seemed full of illusions — clouds in the shape of continents and monsters as the commissar looked out, and once his mother's profile drifted by. An expression of sternness changed to surprise as the clouds lifted her eyebrows, and then she blew apart.

238

Commissar Micum sniffed the air. 'Sugar rain,' he said.

'People have been saying that for weeks,' yawned Thanakar behind him.

'It'll come.' The commissar stooped and picked up a stone from the ground, and tested it between his fingers. Perhaps it was his imagination, but it seemed a little slippery, and it seemed as if some residue was left on his fingers. When the rain came, these stones would shine like mica, and it would be hard to stand upright.

The camp was hidden by a tattered mist, but through its rents they could see parts of the river, and antinomials washing horses. And in one place they could see a gathering of people, standing gray and dispirited, and curiously still. The sight depressed them though they caught no shreds of talk. So they packed quickly, leaving most of what they had. Skirting the camp and meeting no one, they set out on foot, back through the Keyhole towards where the regular army had camped the night before. Doubtless the army was gone by now, thought Thanakar, up with Aspe before daybreak, circling round out of the valley to attack the monastery along the ridge, but the camp would still be there, and the hospital.

The rocks looked ghostly in the mist, along the road where they had passed on elephantback. Leaving the antinomials they had met no one, and there was no one on the road, yet still they were always turning to look behind them, and peering around boulders and up along the cliffs that closed in on either side. For random sounds seemed to metamorphose into footsteps, and the hissing of the river seemed like voices calling. Once they saw someone, an antinomial woman standing motionless by the water's edge, barefoot in the water. And in the misty morning she looked dark and hard as a tall pile of rocks, her pack of muscles and her small hard breasts, her hair cut short around her broken face; she was not young. She looked at them as they passed. They mumbled and bowed their heads, and hugged their cloaks around them, for her expression was at once scornful, thoughtful, and immeasurably sad, and it made them feel nervous and unclean.

'I feel a presentiment of death,' the commissar said again, after they had passed. Thanakar would remember the words, because at that moment death followed close behind them, and in a little while, when the way broadened out and the cliffs started to spread away, death called out to them, and they turned to wait for him to gather form out of the mist. He was dressed, as he so often was in those days, in the red robes of a priest.

'Wait!' he called in his shrill voice, and they turned back. It was the bishop's liaison, a thin handsome man with laughing eyes. 'Wait up,' he said, leaning on a rock to catch his breath.

They waited, and he stood before them, a handsome man with thick black hair, his hands on his hips, taller than either of them. 'I looked for you,' he said. 'Where were you? How was your night among the heathen?'

'Happy,' said the commissar.

'Then it was better than my morning. One of them touched me. Pah!' He spat on to the road. 'I washed, but nothing takes away the smell.'

'What were you doing there so early?' asked Thanakar. 'Making converts?'

The priest frowned. Thanakar had an uneasy reputation among Starbridges, but the priest could understand it, given his obligations and his leg. Any differences between them were nothing compared with what they shared, the same blood, the same duty, the same family, bonds that mere hatred could never dissolve. 'Preaching,' he answered. 'Of a kind. More effective than any I've done before, I think. Yes. They've been a scourge to this whole countryside, and flouted God's most cherished laws, but now I think we've seen the last of them.'

'What do you mean?' asked the commissar.

The priest marched past them a few steps. 'You'll find out,' he said. 'No, I'll tell you. I am triumphant. I never expected it to be easy, or even possible. Yet it was so easy.' He laughed, a shrill raw sound.

'Tell me,' said the commissar.

For an answer, the priest pulled a scrap of paper from his pocket and smoothed it out for them to see. In spidery Starbridge pictographs, it read:

Find me a way to hang these cannibals and spare me the expense of rope.

        Chrism Demiurge, episcopal secretary.
        Kindness and Repair
        Spring 8, Oct. 19, 00016

'God save us,' said the commissar quietly.

'Aspe came back late last night,' continued the priest. 'The problem was always how to separate the atheists from the rest of the army, but he took care of that. He woke us up for a council of war. Then he roused his regiment, and they were up and away long before dawn. I left as soon as he was gone.'

'To do what?'

'I confess, at first I didn't know. I thought it was an opportunity not to be missed. I thought of bringing them false orders, but Aspe can't write, and they can't read. I didn't know what I was going to say. But the problem resolved itself. God found a way. Aspe was swaggering and boasting last night. I think he was drunk. And something he said . . . I stole his scarf. The fool didn't even notice.'

'My God,' whispered the commissar.

241

'Pah!' continued the priest. 'It was as much as I could stand to touch something that belonged to him. But something he said last night . . . I confess, I underestimated the power it would give me. At first when I got there they took no notice of me. You know what they're like. But I was talking to a group of them by a bonfire, and frankly I was about to give up. They weren't even looking at me. But then one of them noticed the scarf around my arm. I took it off and gave it to him, and after that, everything was different. It was like a magic talisman. Some savage symbol. They passed it from hand to hand, and the whole crowd came to stand around me, listening to every word I said. They seemed . . . very subdued. Then at the end, one of them took the scarf and wound it round the point of a spear, as if it were a kind of flag. Nobody said a word. Of course, I can't be sure they'll do it – who can be sure? But I really think they might. When I left, they were saddling the horses.'

'What did you tell them?' asked the commissar.

The priest laughed. 'It's so simple. I gave them a message from Aspe. "When you see my standard, come meet me up the road." That's all.'

'My God,' said the commissar. 'They're going to charge the guns.'

'Yes, isn't it priceless? A fly couldn't live in that barrage. And Aspe – I thought it so appropriate that he should give the signal. My only fear is, if the mist holds, they might not see his flag.'

Thanakar looked up. The clifftops to the east were still invisible. 'It's a chance,' he said. He looked back down the Keyhole towards the antinomial camp. 'I'll go back,' he said.

'No,' said the commissar. 'That's no use. It's a decision

they have made. They're not stupid. No. You've got to go the other way. Find the colonel. Find Aspe.'

The priest squinted. 'Here,' he said. 'What do you mean?' But before he could move, the commissar pushed him in the chest, and he tripped over a rock and fell down backward.

'Damn you!' shouted the old man, standing over him. 'Damn your eyes, Gorfang Starbridge. Traitor!' And to the doctor, he said, 'Go on, my boy. Hurry. I'll keep this bastard back.'

But the priest drew a knife from his boot and lunged at him, and stabbed him through the chest. The commissar seized him by the arms as he tried to jump away, and Thanakar moved behind them, and snatched up a rock, and battered the priest's head in from behind. Then he pried him loose from the commissar's arms and flung him aside.

The commissar stood, swaying slightly in the middle of the road, his hands clasped around the knife haft, which protruded just below his breastbone. He grunted as he drew it out, and the blood poured down his chest. Thanakar went to him, but the old man pushed him away and sat down heavily on some rocks, stanching the bloodflow with one hand. 'No time.' he said. 'Hurry.'

Thanakar knelt beside him, but again he shook his head. 'No time. No. Damn you,' he said gently. 'No matter. Done for. Find Aspe.'

'Don't talk,' said Thanakar, and put his hand out, but the old man pushed it away. 'Nothing to say. Do it. Please. I'll be fine. Just sit here.' His features were set in an expression of piglike obstinacy, a caricature of stubbornness. But the melancholy in his eyes was already a little unreal, a little glazed, as if the secret fire which had always burned behind them was now hardening them from within.

'No talk,' said the commissar finally. 'They'll be cut to pieces. God's soldiers. Women too.'

Then he closed his eyes. When he opened them again, Thanakar was gone. 'Damn you,' said the old man, very gently, with the last of his breath. He looked down over his chest, where the doctor had drawn on the flap of his white shirt over his heart, in blood, the mark of Paradise. 'Damn you,' said the old man. 'Go.'

The doctor stumbled down the road, and he found the refuse of the army still sprawled in camp: wounded, unfit, noncombatant; men sitting, drunk already, playing cards with unsufficient fingers; two hundred men with dysentery from drinking river water; priests cavorting around a collapsible battlefield temple. Some people called to him and stretched out their hands, but he ignored them, and with the breath already hot and rasping in his throat, he found a horse, and pitched into the saddle, and kicked it up along the army's track. A narrow defile led up from the valley on to the eastern ridge. The way was hard, and at the top it was choked with figures of the dead and dying, and the mist had lessened too, so that when he reached the ridge he could look out east and north over the plain, and in sudden gaps of light and sunlight he could see huge masses of men and horses clashing underneath the monastery walls.

He heard noise, too, a roaring like the sea, and he could hear the voices of the drowning in it, for wounded men recognized him and called out to him as he rode past. He saw the hospital, and files of wounded men and stretcher-bearers converging on it from all over the field, like tentacles to bring it food. He saw Creston Bile in his shirtsleeves, for the sun was burning through the mist, and it was hot. 'My God, Doctor, where have you been?' the man called out, his forehead badged with blood where he had tried to wipe the sweat away. Thanakar didn't stop.

Amid endlessly repeating scenes, he searched for Aspe. And up to the very instant, he thought he might not be too late, until, through a break in the mist, he saw the black flag fluttering at the topmost pinnacle of the ridge overlooking the river, and the colonel standing in a group of officers. Yet still the guns hadn't spoken. Thanakar spurred his horse up the slope, shouting and yelling. He could see the colonel striding back and forth, eating an orange and giving dispatches with his mouth full.

Behind him, his troops spread out unimpeded over the plateau. Victory was sure. Aspe's savage face was flushed and happy, and he had taken off his helmet, and his long, white hair blew around. It was this mood that Thanakar found it most difficult to penetrate as he rode up. The circle of officers gave way before his horse. But the colonel barely looked at him. He walked back and forth with his cheeks puffed up with fruit. But when the first guns sounded from the monastery a mile away, he turned towards the noise, quizzically, and Thanakar could see him stop his chewing. The bombardment was gentle at first, a few rockets taking range, but then the great field guns opened up, and then the murderous screaming of the grape. Thanakar shouted above the noise, and this time the colonel understood, for his hand stole up around his neck, searching for his scarf, and then he ran up the small slope behind him, to seize his flag and throw it down. He stood looking out over the river, and then he opened his throat and let out a roar so terrific, it drowned out the pounding artillery. At the sound, his horse pulled its bridle loose from the hands of a soldier, and Aspe ran down to meet it and vaulted on to its back, creaking and swaying in the saddle, shouting guttural commands in a language Thanakar didn't know. Then he was gone, galloping over the open ground towards the monastery and the sound of the guns, his hair streaming out behind him.

The officers followed, and the soldiers too, and in a little while Thanakar was alone on the hillside. From where he was, he could look down and see where he had spent the night, though the upper valley was still hidden. But he could see the deserted camp where the antinomials had left it, never planning to return. And he could see the river flashing in the afternoon. He dismounted near where the colonel's black standard lay among the rocks, and he sat down with his head in his hands, to listen to the music of the guns.

North of Charn, in winter and the first phases of spring, the land is empty and cruel, striated hills of petrified mud, eroded into strange shapes and strange colors, burnt ochre, dark red. Even close to the city, the land is empty during that part of the year. But later, when the wind abates, and the air grows hot and sweet, and the trees grow tall in sweet new soil, then villages come up, and huts of bridal-weed, and naked sunburned people. But in spring before the Paradise rain, life is bare and stark. The people have grown up in the coldest times, and these questions of belief seem desperate to them. Among the twenty thousand days of spring, men are willing to die for trifles. The ancient cult of loving kindness withers and exposes harsher, more austere beliefs, like flowers withering on a rock.

The monastery of St Serpentine Boylove had been built in autumn, and it was like a mirror held to the most poignant of all seasons. It had no defenses. It clung to the hillside like a spray of flowers of delicate steel spires, and below it hung secluded terraces where in autumn the monks had sipped hot cider overlooking their orchards in the river valley, and counted their money. Now the monks were dead or scattered, and among the terraces where they had sat, Argon Starbridge's gunners worked happily, experimenting, studying the effect of different parabolas of fire. So intent were they on the practice of their art, that they had heard nothing of their own defeat until Colonel Aspe broke through the door. He had smashed the glass postern with his steel fist and rampaged through the sanctuary looking for defenders, but there were none. And when he found his way down a dozen spiral staircases and out on to the terrace, the captain of artillery was happy to surrender, and all the guns stopped bellowing together. Aspe was just one man, but the captain was an artist and had no false soldier's pride. He was conscious of his merits, and when the colonel strode clanking to the terrace lip, he stood beside him and surveyed the valley with a sense of modest satisfaction.

For more than a mile, the valley floor was littered with a wreck of corpses, broken men and women, dogs, horses. It stretched up the road, up to the monastery gates, up to the very muzzles of the guns, still seething in a thousand parts. A horse wallowed on its back, kicking its hind legs in the air. Men rose, and staggered forward, and fell down again. Children cried. That whole army of independent souls had come together in a common attitude, dressed in common uniforms of their life's blood, while above them played a quiet music. They were free.

On the lowest terrace, near where the road ran up to the gate, a single antinomial stood erect. He had cut himself loose from his fallen horse and limped forward to the gun itself, where he rested his hand on the burning metal. He was breathing heavily, and his lips were covered with a froth of blood. He wore sunglasses, and his head was shaved, and his pale, flat face had no expression, but when he looked up and saw the colonel standing on the terrace up above, he raised his fist and shook it. And from his bosom he took out a crumpled scarf, and wiped his lips, and spat into it. And though his voice was low and broken, the captain of artillery heard him distinctly from where he stood next to the colonel, a hundred feet away. 'Aspe,' he whispered. 'Aspe. Biter Aspe,' and he spat blood.

5

Sugar Rain

First there was a noise at the window, an animal scratching at the pane. Precipitation had coated the outside of the glass with sugar scum, and the animal's claws cleaned out a circle. Through it the bishop could see a circle of black night and glimpses of a small furry face. And then the casement gave way, the window swung open, and a cat jumped down into the room.

The boy had reached the temple about midnight, but it was almost four o'clock before he found a way up and through the ninety courtyards to the Bishop's Tower. No one had challenged him. The temple was almost deserted, for most of the guards had been sent away to war, and most of the rest were out patrolling the city. There was almost no one left but seminarians and priests – blind priests, fat priests, priests with no legs, inadequate as sentinels, though they never slept. Their conjuring had filled the courts with acrid fog, impenetrable except to atheists. They had sealed the gates and doorways with powerful geometry, but the boy was too ignorant to know. He was following the cat. When it leapt up on the balustrade, he followed it. Along the rooftops, the tiles were slippery in the sweet rain, and by the time he had climbed up all the gutters and drainpipes, up to the single lighted window in the bishop's tower, he was too exhausted to stand. The way had been dangerous for him, and he had kept to streambeds and ravines along the road out from the city. There had been nothing to eat. So that finally, when he found the right drainpipe and climbed up, he barely had the strength to drag himself over the sill. The bishop was standing with his cat in her arms, cleaning its fur.

This was the room where she lived. It was small and spare, with walls of quilted silk. Part of it was a private temple lit with candles, and the wind from the open window roughened the light. Outside, lightning caressed the hills, soft and thunderless. The boy was shivering with cold. He stared at her, and she could see a wish for violence mix with confusion in his eyes as she smiled and put her hand out. She released a small magic and put a little sleep into the air, so that he dropped his head. He curled up on the floor, and she could hear his breathing settle down.

For a moment she stood and looked at him, stroking the cat. Then she put it down and found a towel and dry clothes, sacred vestments from the temple. She knelt down near him on the linen mats, wiping the water from his body, touching him with a kind of wonder. Even though she was the goddess of love and mistress of the seven arts of love, this was the first man she had touched. He was the youngest, the largest, the most beautiful that she had seen, for her life had been spent within the confines of the temple, among priests and parsons. On festival days she had heard petitions in her own shrine, and she had peered at the congregation from behind the slits in her masks. But in all those shambling lines of worshipers there had never been anyone as magnificent as this, and she touched him with a kind of reverence, stripping off his clothes. The leather cloak seemed so unsuitable, so stiff, so uncomfortable. She wondered what it was made of.

She gave him a drug as he lay sleeping, a dream, and she went into it herself with a crown of flowers, for vanity's sake. She could make a dream as real as flesh. She knew what he was; she had studied all kinds of heresy. She'd had a picture book. And of all heresies, atheism had seemed to her the most fascinating, as fascinating as an empty well – dark and empty, sleep without dreams. As the boy lay sleeping, she gave him a vision, form out of darkness, the beginning of the universe, nothing at first, just mist on a gray background, and then a scattering of stars. She gave him a horizon, and in a little while the sun rose. It burned away the mist, the darkness, and the starlight. It filled the sky with radiance, and yet it didn't burn the eyes, and it invited staring, because Angkhdt the Interpreter sat on a throne among its rays in his most gorgeous clothes, with fire in his face and the crown of heaven on his brow. In one of his four hands he held an astrolabe, another grasped the collar of the dog of war. Another rested on the head of his familiar, the symbol of his poetry, a crouching dog with the face of a beautiful woman. His fourth hand lay clenched in his lap, a modest metaphor of phallic power.

The sun illuminated all secrets. You could see the earth, rolling insecurely in its enormous orbit, its seas advancing and retreating, its forests and deserts swelling and disappearing, the relentless flow of seasons. You could see glaciers, and mountains thirty miles high, and places of eternal day, eternal night. And above this chaos, this plunging flux of life and death, Angkhdt the Charioteer held in his hands the symbols of intellect, love, power, art, the four reins of the plunging chariot.

The bishop put her fingers to the head of the sleeping boy. In his dream he was lying on his stomach in the mountain grass, watching the transparent sun, and the world spread out like a map. Below him he could see countries, towns, cities, rivers, the clash of armies, the emperor walking in his garden, stopping to sniff a flower among the cages of famous philosophers. The boy was chewing on a blade of grass, and he didn't even turn his head when she came into his dream as softly as if she had not wanted to disturb him. She was barefoot, wearing a summer dress. As she walked, the grass bent away under her footsteps, and ripples of dandelions and blue chicory spread out in her wake.

Far below, in another part of the temple, Chrism Demiurge was eating. His table was spread with silver dishes piled high with vegetables stewed in wine, fruit pasties, custards, obscure salads, far too much for one old man. But he was not alone. Along the floor crawled snakes and little hairless beasts, and he rolled bread into pills to throw for them and watch them fight. Blind to form, he could still distinguish color, motion, light. Around him, the red walls blazed with light, wax tapers set in girandoles.

Demiurge was celebrating, for he had heard news from the battlefield, a victory over the forces of darkness. He lifted a goblet of water to his pale lips, then leaned to smell the marijuana smoke rising from a silver censer in the middle of the table. Around it, making messes of the food, goblins and grimalkins played leapfrog and danced impudent and vulgar dances, rubbing their fat bellies. The priest laughed out loud.

There was a knock at the door, and instantly Demiurge's face assumed an exaggerated look of guilt, like a child interrupted in some shameful act by a danger of discovery more apparent than real. It was a parody of an expression, and it mixed well with his laughter. He clapped his hands, and instantly all the gnomes and goblins stopped their sport and ran to hide themselves among his clothes, under his robes, next to his skin, so that all was in order when the door opened.

His disciple stood there, a colorless young man, almost

invisible to his blind eyes. 'Do you want something? I thought I heard you call.'

'No, I was just . . . amusing myself,' answered the priest, vestiges of laughter still on his face. 'But will you sit with me, Corydon? If you have a minute.'

The disciple sat, and the old man continued eating. When he was finished he sat back and smiled, and let an amicable silence grow around them as he prepared a long sinsemillian cigar. He lit it and passed it to his disciple, and then he said, 'My grandfather was a banker in this city. He had a relative who married young, according to the customs of the season, a pretty girl, yes, but very ignorant and naïve. Very . . .naïve. And her mouth was very small, so small that the nuns of her shrine were worried, for her bridegroom was a strong man, and a very holy man too, matrimonially speaking. At least, he had the same predilections of our Beloved Lord, as we read in Angkhdt 181 through 189, 401, 606 through 610, to cite just a few. This man had only had ten children, rare for that hot weather, very rare. Though he easily could have had many more; he was so well made, it was rumored that his first wife had choked to death.' The priest laughed noiselessly, then continued. 'It was just a rumor. Yet this lady's mouth was very small, and it worried the good nuns, so that they made her practice constantly with plaster models and many kinds of fruit. Many kinds. They taught her to stretch her lips by repeating words like "how", "where", "why", questions which otherwise might not have suggested themselves to her . . . rather uninquisitive mind. "Who", of course, was counterproductive, and as for "what" . . .' He laughed again, a noise like a dry cough. 'Catastrophic.'

His lips curled back, the same expression on his face but without the laughter, Colonel Aspe sat in his tent. The battle was over, the enemy had withdrawn and he had let them go, though he had held them as if in the clutch of his hand. At the moment of victory he had been distracted. On the terrace of St Serpentine's he had felt a great sudden pain that had left him helpless, as if the force of some new hatred, pulling suddenly in a new direction, had torn a crack in him, and the urge to move, which was like blood to him, had leaked away like blood.

Lacking the catalyst of his malice, the armies had disengaged, the enemy had withdrawn. Argon Starbridge had escaped with his life and his baggage, but now, in his tent, Aspe regretted winning for the priests of Charn even a partial victory. He thought of riding back to the city and putting it to the torch, but there were reasons, always reasons, and as always, reasons were the bit between his teeth. So instead he refused food and let his mind wander among the corpses by the river. He hummed melodies in all the modes of hatred. And he would put together melodies in his mind, sequences of events either imagined or remembered. Notes and cadences would summon up faces, actions, whole scenes. He added themes of misery and regret, low in the bass register, high in the treble, mixing them together like a symphony of hatred in his mind.

Chrism Demiurge whirled by, crucified and burning, his mouth gaping wide. He disappeared, and in his place Aspe composed, as if upon the xylophone, the bars of his cage in the emperor's garden, and the light of the setting sun on them night after night, while his body wasted and his hair changed color. In the setting sun, the golden figure of the emperor, as he paused sometimes to talk. And like the rattle of a drum, the lock and chain snapping open on his jail, the emperor releasing him into a larger jail of promises, reasons, services, consequences.

These images mixed with memories of an earlier time, of Rangriver in the snow, when he was king of the biters up above Rangriver. He remembered the day when he had lost his hand. A hateful face, a dancer, a knife fight about . . . something, some piece of music, he had forgotten. But he remembered the scene, his violin where he had left it to get up and fight, his own instrument, so difficult that no one else could ever play it after he had set it down, so perfect that people had been compelled to listen, night after night, while the music poured from him in flashing streams. Was it through musical perfection that he had first sickened of a biting illness, the need to make his mark?

He remembered the circle of hot faces in the firelight, the sudden blow, his hand half-severed, the knife stuck between his bones, his ears ringing like cymbals, the faces around him changing into masks – ah, ah, ah, his enemy receding as if lost in a black mist, only his eyes and his teeth showing as he smiled.

He remembered the stone table in the snow, the statue of dog-faced Angkhdt, the broken foot and that same smiling face, that dancer in the freezing air, dancing his last dance. In his tent Aspe's memories were deafening. He thought: other men have turned to biting out of love, or misdirection, or musical ineptitude. But with me it has been hate, always hate, and hatred is a kind of love, a way of refusing to accept the cacophony of certain kinds of music in the world.

Along the river, his sweet brothers and sisters lay as dead as meat. The images banged around his ears. And then suddenly Aspe saw, in the middle of that circle of discord, the bishop's face, a poisonous harmony of black curls, black eyes, sweet skin. So young, she was. He struck the table with his steel fist. Hatred, memories of hatred, cadenzas of hatred spun and jostled in his mind, until he cried: 'Enough! Great Angkhdt, enough. No more.'

The bishop tended the shrine in her turret chamber while the boy watched her from the bed. Unlike all but six in the city, it was a shrine not to Angkhdt but to God Himself, not to the servant but to the master. In most temples, Angkhdt the prophet stood between men and the God of Love, but not here. The room smelled of lovemaking. She filled a crystal bowl on the altar from a ewer of water, reciting lists of prayers.

She had had a tiring day. She had consecrated forty newly gelded priests, their faces lumpy from painkillers and pain. And she had performed the feather celebration on the altar of St Unity Bereft, a long, boring dance whose significance was lost, but still it was recurrent in the endless calendar of worship. She had danced it once before, as a little girl.

While she was gone, the boy had lain in bed. Today he seemed a little restless, she thought. He watched her with a curious absorption as she wrote symbols in the air above the bowl. The cat covered his lap, and he stroke the long fur under its throat and around its slitted eyes.

'Something bad happened,' he said.

The rain was pouring down. The bishop shivered in her white dress, because that day she had felt the same thing, and when she was talking to her secretary, she had thought it would be a relief to know something of the world. The heart beats in darkness, separate from the brain, the old man would say. She accepted that, but sometimes it would be a relief to know: there was a war, and it had gotten closer. She had seen a stiffening desperation in her secretary and the members of her council in their dedication to the small details of worship. But for a few days now there had been something like triumph in the old man's chicken step, and his attention had been inclined to wander. True, the feather dance was a terrible ordeal. During some of the slower movements, she had been inclined to doze herself.

But sometimes she thought that since the land, and the people, and everything that breathed belonged to her, she should be allowed to take a closer interest. Sometimes as she sat in her own temple in the clothes of the living goddess, listening to supplications, she could catch wisps of news – a mother's prayer for four sons in the army, a wife's prayer for her husband. Knowledge bred opinions, and opinions interfered with love, that's what her secretary said. He would tell her what had happened sometime when all the news was cold, when it was no longer possible to take sides. In the meantime, she read hungrily: history, natural history, theology.

The boy leaned his head back against the wall. 'It's a feeling,' he said. 'I feel . . . unhappy.'

Sympathetic, she touched his forehead. He reached up and brought her wrist down to his mouth to kiss it. 'How long have I been here?' he asked. 'I don't know why I came.'

'To kill me.'

He frowned. 'I forgot everything you said. Explain it to me once more.'

'What do you mean.'

'Your soldiers.'

'I have no soldiers.'

His grip tightened on her wrist, and there was some tired danger in his voice when he said, 'That's not true. They lit fires at the entrance of the tunnel, until the air was full of smoke.'

'God has given us many laws. Some are cruel.'

'Is it against the law for me to be here?'

'The laws aren't my concern,' she said. 'They don't apply to me.'

He closed his eyes, then opened them again. 'I don't think you understand,' he said. 'I've been so poor. I mean in my mind. My fathers and my mothers didn't need to think to fill their world. It was full already – horses, dogs, freedom, snow, things to do, feeling. I never had those things. So instead I want to learn to think. But I don't want to learn something and have it not be true.'

'Don't be afraid,' said the bishop. 'I am not allowed to lie.'

The boy stroked the cat and looked unhappy.

'There's no reason for me to be humble,' she said. 'I am the bishop of Charn.'

'Yes. There is a part of you I don't like so well. But there is another part.' He put the cat aside, and then he reached to pull her down beside him and comb the hair out of her face. He combed his fingers through her hair and ran his thumb along the underside of her ear, admiring the softness of the skin, the delicacy of the black hairs that grew along her cheek. 'You're so different from my sisters,' he said.

She made a face, but he couldn't see it, and it wouldn't have meant anything to him if he had. He couldn't read the language of expressions. He couldn't understand it. She lay down beside him and bent to take one of his testicles into her mouth, while he wrapped his hand around her tail, stroking the hair at the base of her spine. She licked carefully along his underside, using a technique described in Angkhdt 710, while he leaned back happily. 'So different,' he said.

She laughed, releasing him. 'I hope so. I've heard about

258

your sisters. Muscles like steel and monstrous teeth . . .' She dragged her incisors along his inner thigh.

He grabbed her by the neck, pushing her face into his leg. She tried to twist away, but he held tight. 'Stop hurting me!' she cried. 'Can't you tell you're hurting me?'

'I can't feel it.'

'Let go!'

Outside, night was falling, and spring rain. Lightning licked the hills around the city. It never really stopped; the silk-lined room was never absolutely dark.

'Lie to me about one single thing,' he said, 'and I'll break your neck. You know we have a music for lying. I can hear it in your voice.'

'Let go!'

He released her, and she jumped up and stood facing him, hands to her neck. 'What are you talking about? Why are you such a child?'

'Because I am.' He dropped his eyes humbly. 'I don't know anything about love. Barbarians know all about it.'

'Don't call me that.'

He was right, he didn't know anything about it. Later he fucked her with a kind of desperation, as if she held hidden inside her body some vital secret. He searched for it, his fingers locked around her tail, and fucked her until she was like a river inside, and he couldn't even feel her anymore. She cried out, exhausted, but still he kept on and on, and the sweat made their bodies skid and slip. And then, still hard, he lay on his stomach on the saturated sheet, his eyes unfocused, reflecting nothing. She let him go. It was part of what fascinated her, that enormous capacity for nothingness which stilled his soul and took the place of Angkhdt. She lay with her cheek against his back, her fingers in the groove of muscle along his spine.

* * *

259

She was a beautiful woman, and not in the normal masklike way. In some women, beauty speaks of who they are. In her it spoke eloquently, the more so because her training as a priestess and a goddess had muted other voices. She had grown up practically alone. Her skin was the color of custard or sweet cake, of something edible and good to eat. She was not tall. Her hair was Starbridge black and fell in thick untidy curls around her face and shoulders.

His form too, the shape of his features and his enormous body, seemed the most expressive part of him. Along with so much else, his race had rejected the idea that people differed, because they saw it as a way of chaining actions to reactions. So while they worshipped freedom, they rejected individuality. Free men and women resembled one another a great deal, it had turned out. They were arrogant, irrational, impulsive, humorless, ecstatic. And though this boy was trying to change, was eager to accept some shackles, still his body was the most expressive part of him, the only part he knew. He touched it often, scratching and rubbing, and he was always moving his arms and legs to stretch the muscles, and rotating his ankles and his wrists to hear the bones snap and realign.

He had been there for a week, living in secret in the bishop's chamber, eating the food she brought him, before the old man found him. The bishop's secretary limped up the stairs one night when they were half asleep. Devils and angels cavorted in his clothes, peeping with long-nosed faces out from his sleeves, hanging by their tails from his chain of office, playing hide and seek in his hair. They bounded past him up the spiral stairs, full of play. The old man reached the landing and stretched his hand out for the stone statue of the faun at the entrance to the bishop's quarters, stroking it with withered, pale fingers. Lamps burned bright here. And every angle of the corridor, every discoloration of the marble floor was known to him, illuminated by the lamp of memory for his blind eyes, for he had been a child here, a chaplain in the temple. But there was something unfamiliar now, an unfamiliar smell in this sacred place, something that made him pause, something that had brought him fumbling up the stairs from his own rooms, something. He smelled a faint, lingering smell of sin.

He shuffled forward, almost tripping on a seraph that had curled its rubber body around his ankle. At the temple doorway he hesitated again, but the smell was stronger here. He shuffled through the doorway and along the corridor, and pushed through heavy curtains into the shrine itself. He summoned all his powers of perception – it was here. His blind eyes caught the image of a boy sitting naked on the bishop's bed. The bishop herself was asleep, her mass of curls falling over the stranger's thigh.

Trembling, the old man reached out his arms, as if in supplication. 'Unclean,' he whispered, so as not to wake her. Triumphant, miserable, mad, he opened up his hands. His was the loneliest office in the world, the hardest duty. How sweet she seemed, lying asleep, and he could hear the softness of her breathing and see the blackness of her eyebrows. 'Unclean,' he whispered. From underneath his skirts, demons and cherubs uncurled and somersaulted slowly over the floor towards where the stranger sat, stroking a golden cat, his blue eyes curious.

That same night, Abu Starbridge was sitting in the taproom of a tavern in a vicious section of the city, a tangle of alleyways and rotting houses called the Beggar's Medicine. Around the walls of an episcopal prison and the gallows there, the streets seethed like worms. In those days, the sugar rain just starting, the sewers and gutters overflowed and filled the streets with caustic mud. It slopped into the first floors of the houses and bit at their foundations. Already some façades had crumbled away, exposing ruined interiors and holes for the rats to play in, uncounted thousands of them, up from the docks, fleeing the rising water. It was against the law to harm them or even to frighten them, and so they ran everywhere, over men and women sleeping in their beds, gnawing corpses in their coffins, biting the ankles of the customers in the tavern where Prince Abu sat.

Though it was not yet dark, the lamps were lit. The windows were opaque with grime, though they let in the rain. It soaked the tattered wallpaper and made it shine with the beginnings of a dull phosphorescence. Later in the season, there would be no need for lamps.

The company huddled around a coal stove, and Prince Abu sat apart, drinking, wrapped in a flannel cloak. He was listening to their voices, the high, sharp accent that the law required from the absolutely poor. It was an ugly sound, and the men and women who gathered there were ugly too – pickpockets, housebreakers, gamblers, unlicensed prostitutes, musicians, drunks. They lived outside the law, but even so, some laws still bound them when all the rest were broken, the so-called 'character laws', which had made them what they were. It was against the law for them to talk, except about themselves, their business, or their belongings. It was against the law for them to use any word describing or referring to an idea. It was against the law for them to practice courtesy or politeness, except to social superiors. It was against the law to speak kindly, except to their own children.

Five men and women sat eating around the stove, and Abu was happy to see fruit and bread on the table, and all manner of illegal delicacies. One of them had brought a rotten piece of cheese, stolen from some shop. It would have been enough to hang them; even their clothes would have been enough, for mixed with the yellow rayon of their caste, Abu saw rags of cotton, linen, even silk, in many proscribed colors.

A tall man, wearing a shirt that had once been white, sat balanced on the back legs of his chair, cleaning his teeth with a pocket knife. His hair was coarse under a black cap, and his black beard was stiff with dirt. Dirt lined the wrinkles and the cuts around his eyes, and lay smeared like a doctor's salve over his pimpled cheeks. When he laughed, his teeth flashed strong and hard and very white. They were his pride and he was always picking at them with the point of his knife or with fragments of wood. His name was Jason Mock. He was a thief.

'It tastes like shit,' he remarked, picking a piece of cheese out of his gums and scowling darkly at it on the point of his knife. He spoke in the high pitch common to them all. It seemed particularly out of place in his fierce mouth.

'You wouldn't say that,' whined another man. 'Not if you knew how slick it was. Hard to catch. Six months if you're caught, just for that one piece. Second offense. It's valuable.'

'Tastes like six months. Tastes like a year. What did you do, bury it while you were in?'

'That piece? That piece isn't two days old. I just walked in and put it in my hat, slick as anything. That blind old parson never said a word.'

'Mmm. What's it called?'

'Cheddar.'

'Mmm. Tastes like . . . excrement.'

'Hunh. You wouldn't say that. Not if you were used to it.'

'Used to it? Excrement? I've been eating excrement ever since I was a boy. An expert. That's why my teeth's so distained.' Mock forced his knifeblade in between his molars and then pulled it out and frowned at it. 'I can't find the sense in it,' he continued. 'Six months in jail, what for? It's rotten. They should make it three months and serve it every day. That way nobody'd go near it.'

'Perhaps,' said a boy, 'perhaps they don't want us to know how bad it is.'

'You shut up!' retorted Mock. Then suspiciously, 'What do you mean?'

'Perhaps it's their secret, how bad it is.'

'Don't you be smart with me. What do you mean?'

'Perhaps it's envy of them, what keeps them up and us down. Envy more than force.'

'Shut your mouth,' commanded Mock. He lowered the two front feet of his chair until his boots touched the floor, and then he leaned forward across the table, glaring at the boy. 'Are you trying to be funny?'

The boy dropped his eyes and clasped his hands around his mug of gin. He said nothing. Mock raised his knife and pointed across the table. But then he cried out, because the rats were passing back and forth along the floor, and one had bitten him in the ankle through a rip in his plastic boot. It was a slow, trusting, unsuspicious beast, and it stood on its hind legs looking up at him, as if curious of his bad language. Before he could be restrained, Mock brought his heel down and crushed its head.

'Watch that,' cried the landlady, a middle-aged slattern with painted lips and cheeks, and teeth stained blue from kaya gum. 'That's all I need. That's murder on the premises, even if it's only tenth degree.' She leaned over the stove to peer doubtfully at the furry, purselike body.

'Nothing to be afraid of,' said Mock. 'What's one more dead rat?'

'You can't be too careful,' muttered the landlady.

Mock looked around the room. 'Natural causes,' he observed. 'Five witnesses. Six,' he said, frowning at Prince Abu, who sat in a corner with his cloak pulled around him. 'Upped and died. Heart attack, I'd say. It's common enough in these sad days.' He got to his feet and picked the rat up by its tail. Then he crossed the room, unbolted the door, and threw it out into the street. Rain blew in, and mud slopped over the sill into the room.

'Don't just leave it on the doorstep,' called out the landlady. 'Throw it across next door. I don't want any questions tonight, not with you all dressed up. Not with that lot,' she said motioning to the food on the table. 'All those rats are numbered,' she muttered dubiously.

'Crap. That's what they say. It's a lie.' Mock bolted the door and turned back into the room, smiling. He limped as he came back to the table.

'You'll come to a bad end, Jason Mock,' said the woman, shaking her head.

'That's what the parson claimed when I was born,' said the thief. 'You think so too?' And without a muscle moving, his expression changed from a smile to a dark scowl. 'Will I? I tell you it's a short road for all of us, and the only thing that's never sure until you know, is whether it'll lead you to the scaffold or the stake, whether it'll be this month or next. That's all. Other than that, you can rest easy.'

During this outburst, the boy started to cry, gently, hiding his face in his hands. He put his head down in the cradle of his arms on the dirty table. The thief stood above him and clenched his fist in the air. 'Nothing to cry about,' he said. 'What's there to cry about, Boy?'

'You leave him alone,' exclaimed another woman,

younger and fresher than the landlady, but not much. 'Haven't you done enough?'

'What's the matter, Boy?' repeated Mock harshly.

'Hush,' said the woman. 'His papa swings tomorrow night.'

'What's the charge, Boy?'

'Leave him alone,' repeated the woman, but the boy lifted his head and stared defiantly at the thief until the water hardened in his eyes and he could speak. 'Robbery,' he said. 'Aggravated by violence, so they say, I don't believe it. He's an old man. They picked him up with seven dollars and a book.'

'Book? What for?'

'He just liked the gilt along the pages,' said the boy. 'It was just the pictures, that's all. No harm in it. Starbridge nursery rhymes.'

'First offense?'

'Eighth. He's been branded on both cheeks, and over his heart ten months ago. This time he'll swing for sure. The inquest is tomorrow morning.'

'And . . .?'

'And nothing,' said the boy. 'He was a drunken old pig,' he said, his eyes filling up with tears again.

'Then what's to cry about?' Mock grinned. 'Now I once had a mother and two brothers. Not recently. Larceny was in our horoscopes. Look here.' He showed his hand. His palm was covered with a strange tattoo. It looked like a spider's web.

The boy stared up at him. 'Fuck you,' he said, savoring the words in his mouth before he spat them out.

Mock grinned. 'That's all right then. That's the attitude you want. Remember that.' And he struck the boy on the ear so that his head snapped back.

Abu was sick of the high voices. He had sat there

drinking the whole afternoon, and now he made a motion with his hand to bring the landlady over to his table.

'How much do I owe?'

The woman squinted. 'Eighty cents.'

Abu picked out some coins from his pocket and selected a silver sequin. 'Can you change this?' he asked. 'I'm afraid I don't have anything smaller.' He put it down on the table, and the woman reached for it. But her fingers hesitated at the last moment, and she drew her forefinger around it in a circle on the surface of the table without touching it. 'You're a slick one,' she remarked, eyeing him closely. 'Where did you get that?' Abu was finishing his wine.

'Seven dollars change,' said the woman, still without picking up the coin. 'And my risk if it's stolen.'

'There's no risk,' answered Abu. 'Seven dollars is fine. Really, it doesn't matter.'

She was still looking at him. 'Where did you get that coat,' she asked. Then, not waiting for a reply, she called out, 'Jason. Come look at this.' And the thief came over, smiling. But when he saw the money on the table, his expression changed. Again, it changed by itself, without him moving a muscle.

'Look at that,' said the woman. 'Not particular about the rate, either.'

Mock bent down and took a fold of the prince's cloak between his finger and thumb. Then he reached out and pushed the hood back from Abu's face, and bent forward to look at him, so that Abu could smell the rotten cheese still on his breath. The man seemed puzzled momentarily, until he saw the golden earring in the prince's ear, and then his eyes took on a misty, distant expression, as if he were trying to remember something. 'Let me see your hands,' he said.

When Abu laid them out along the tabletop and Mock reached down to turn them palmside up, all the people in the little room came and stood around him in a circle. And when the prince looked up timidly into their faces, he was surprised to see no malice in their eyes, only a kind of wistful melancholy. But he could feel the tension of their interest slip around him like a net as Mock pulled back his fingers. He had not washed for days, and for days he had slept in his clothes in places like this tavern. But still, the dirt upon his palm was as insubstantial as a dirty cloud with the shining sun behind it. The people stared at him.

'What are you . . . doing here?' asked Jason Mock, finally, after a long silence. He had jerked his hand away, as if the sacred flesh could burn him. Abu could barely hear him when he spoke.

'I wanted something to drink.'

'That's true enough,' said the landlady. 'He's drunk enough to float a boat. He should thank me for diluting it. I should charge him extra for not killing him.'

The edge of this speech cut through the net around him, and Abu could feel the tension loosen as people started to whisper and talk. But Mock still stared at him, and Abu thought he could see some weary fire of hatred kindle in his eye, though he spoke as softly as before: 'You're a . . . spy, aren't you?'

'No.'

'And all the time I was just talking,' continued the thief. 'All that talk about the gallows, you must have thought: that's closer than he guesses. But a man can say a thing, and know it to be true, and still not believe it. By God, what wouldn't I give to die in bed, in a real bed?'

'I'm not a spy,' insisted Abu, but the thief talked without listening, as if to himself.

'Starbridge,' he said. 'Starbridge. Are we really such a

threat to you, that you have to search us out and find us here? Is there something in this room you think is too good for us to have?'

'You have nothing to f-f-fear from me,' said Abu. 'I'm – I'm on your side.'

'Our side.' With movements as soft and melancholy as his voice, Mock pulled a pistol from his belt, cocked it, and primed the charge.

'My God, Jason,' hissed the landlady. 'Not here . . .' But then she was quiet when the thief turned to scowl at her and show his teeth. Nobody spoke, but the circle widened around Abu to give the man room to fire.

Abu dropped his eyes and looked down at the table and the silver coin still lying there. He picked it up and rubbed it drunkenly between his fingers, wondering whether he would hear the noise first or feel the shock. He thought: the palmist said I was to die by fire. A fraud. Or perhaps not, he thought, because someone was shouting in the street outside the window, and someone hammered on the door. 'Open up!' someone shouted. 'Open. In the bishop's name!' A man was beating on the door, and not just with his fist, but with a stick or something, the sound was so loud.

Mock seemed not to hear it. He brought the gun down so that it pointed at the prince's head, but before he could shoot, the other thief had grabbed him by the wrist, and the boy stepped forward too, to restrain him. The knocking grew louder, and there were several voices shouting in the street. The landlady opened a door into the back of the house, and she and the other woman vanished through it. Abu staggered to his feet, and as the front window shattered from the blow of a stick, and as the two thieves struggled and swore over the gun, he and the boy followed the women back through the house and out the back door into an alleyway between two buildings, where the mud slopped almost to their knees. In a moment their clothes were coated with sweet rain, and Abu opened his mouth to let some in. His throat was dry.

They climbed up out of the mud on to the gutter's rim, and the boy took his hand and led him into a maze of narrow streets, where the evening was not punctured by a single lantern or a single lighted window. They ran quickly over the uneven stones, as quickly as they could, for there were sounds of pursuit behind them, and voices shouting in the dark. Someone blew a whistle, and from time to time around them whistles answered, some far away, some not so far. Episcopal patrols were talking to each other in their strident language, and they ran until they couldn't hear it any more.

Two high houses had collapsed against each other out over the street, forming a kind of arch. In the partial shelter of one wall, the boy stopped to listen. Abu listened too, but could hear nothing but his own coarse breath, and there was no light anywhere, except the phosphorescent rain. The city seemed as empty as an empty field, yet Abu knew that all the houses were stuffed with abject life, though it made no noise, lit no lantern.

Then suddenly from a tower high above them came the sound of someone laughing. It was an eerie chattering noise, out of place because laughter, though not actually forbidden, was circumscribed in Beggar's Medicine, this close to the prison. Yet even the fiercest soldier of the purge, even the most conscientious magistrate couldn't have made a case against this laughter, unless perhaps for simple disturbance of the peace, because the ratio of noise to mirth or joy or gaiety was so high. It had the form of laughter, but not the content.

Yet even so, perhaps there was still some echo of

subversion in it, because the boy started to smile. 'Now I know where we are,' he said. He plunged back into the mud, under the arch. And at a juncture in the road, where the brickfront of the houses was kept from falling by long wooden poles jammed in the opposite gutters, the boy paused. Under a triangular tunnel of scaffolding there was a crack in one wall, wide enough to admit them. But first the boy pulled a brick loose from the mortar and threw it inside. Abu could hear the rats scamper and scream, yet still when he passed in through the gap, the boy's hand around his wrist, he could feel them underfoot, stumbling clumsily against his boots. It was perfectly dark, but the boy pulled a pocket torch, and by its soft red light they groped their way inside and back through a dozen deserted rooms. The plaster on the walls had crumbled down to lath, and lay in heaps on the muddy floor.

They passed through corridors as complicated as the streets outside, up stairs, through rooms, until in that house or another they reached rooms progressively less dilapidated. They passed rooms full of people, Abu could hear soft conversation through closed doors, and occasionally voices raised as if in high-pitched anger. Light shone above the transoms. But always, out of several closed doors, the boy picked one that led, not to the sound of voices or to light, but to another dark corridor lined with closed doors. Or they would pass through a series of square unfurnished rooms with a closed door in the middle of each wall, and Abu would know there was some life behind two out of the four, but the boy always chose a door that led them through another square unfurnished room.

Finally they stopped before a door identical to all the rest, set in a wall of grimy, rose-patterned paper. Here the boy shined his flashlight over Abu and looked him carefully in the face. Then he turned and began drumming softly on the door with the heel of his hand. Abu was soberer now, but still he couldn't distinguish any rhythm to the knocking, or any effect either, for the sound of talking on the other side of the door went on uninterrupted. The boy tilted his hand so that his knuckles sounded on the wood, but still nothing happened. After a while he stopped, and shone the light in Abu's face again. He seemed unsure of what to do.

'Is the door locked?' asked the prince.

'I don't know.'

Abu reached for the knob. The door opened partway, until blocked by some obstruction inside. But the gap was wide enough to step through, and Abu could see part of a table with a few men grouped around it, talking by the light of a kerosene lamp. He stepped inside, and the boy followed.

The room was indistinct in so much darkness, but Abu got the impression of vast space. Other pools of light suggested tables farther in. All around lay piles of crates and barrels, and boxes tied in black sacking.

A man got up from the table and came towards them. He had grown his hair long, but Abu could see that part of his right ear had been cut away, and he was branded on his forehead and his cheek. His right thumb and forefinger had been sewn together in a circle, the penalty for smuggling, second offense. At the table the men were playing cards, and drinking, and smoking foreign cigarettes scented with cardamon and clove.

'Who're you?' asked the man.

'A prisoner.' Abu smiled and shrugged, and gestured towards the boy behind him.

The smuggler frowned when he heard the prince's accent. He turned to the boy. 'Who's this? Rich customer, eh? What does he want? You should bring him to the store.

Office hours – you know better than this.' He laid a rough hand on the boy's shoulder. 'Not here. You know that.'

'He's a Starbridge,' said the boy, trying to pull away. 'Where's the captain?'

'Starbridge,' repeated the smuggler after a pause, and Abu felt his courage flicker at the way he said it. When the men at the table turned to look at him, he thought he had never before seen faces so hideous, limbs so distorted. Each one carried on his face or on his body the mark of some arrest. Multiple offenders lacked eyes or hands, or their necks had been broken so that they wore steel braces and had to twist their whole bodies in their chairs to look at him.

But again, there seemed more interest than malice in their stares, so Abu took heart and stepped forward into the room, and pushed his hood back from his head. The room was warm, the air thick with smoke.

The smuggler shook the boy by the arm. 'Speak to me,' he hissed. 'You weren't followed here?'

'No, sir.'

'You took care?'

'Yes, sir.'

'The purge was out tonight. Didn't you hear the whistles?'

'Yes, sir.'

'By God, you're a fool.' He gave the boy a vicious shake and threw him down against a pile of burlap bags. 'What were you thinking of?'

'No, sir – please. We can use him. Please, sir, Where's the captain?'

'Use him? He's a spy.'

'No,' said Abu, 'I'm not.'

'No,' repeated the boy. 'Listen to him. He says he's not.'

'Of course he is. What else could he be?'

273

'He says he's not. He can't lie, can he? It's against the law for him.'

'Yes, and I supposed you never broke the law, did you? Use him? You're a fool.' The smuggler aimed a kick, but the boy twisted away. Abu laid his hand on the man's arm.

'Don't hurt him,' he said. 'It's my fault.'

The smuggler stared at him and pulled away with a curse. At the table, another man reached to turn the lamp up. Then he rose from his chair and stumped towards the prince, and peered up at him out of a battered face. 'Starbridge,' he said. 'You any relation to Scullion Starbridge?'

'Which one?'

'The magistrate here. He had my nose broken once a week for ten weeks. Broken and reset. That's not standard punishment. That's not scriptural. Second offense pick-pocketing – that's too hard. You any relation?'

'I suppose so. Not a close relation. Why?'

'Why? God damn you, that's why.'

'I suppose so. I'm sorry about your nose. I'm sorry.'

'Sorry,' the man repeated, as if unsure of the word's meaning. 'Sorry, are you? God damn you for it, I say. God damn you.'

'No blasphemy,' said another kind of voice, a large soft voice out of the darkness beyond the table lamp. 'There's no blasphemy allowed here, Mr Gnash. You know that.'

It was a woman's voice. She stepped into the light and seemed to diminish it just by standing next to it, for her skin was as black as if the shadows still clung to her. Her voice, too, contained a resonance of darkness outside the glaring lamp. The light shone on the table and on a circle of pale, miserable men. Outside the lamplight, perhaps, her voice seemed to suggest, perhaps only a little way beyond, hope and happiness might still scavenge in the dark – vague, snuffling beasts. 'No blasphemy,' she said. 'Please. Spider, who is our guest?'

'A Starbridge, ma'am,' answered the boy, getting up out of the corner and dusting himself off.

'But what is his name?' She spoke in an unfamiliar accent, and seemed to grope for words before she found them, as if misplacing them in the dark. She was tall, with hair clipped short around her head.

'Abu Starbridge,' said the prince. 'Ma'am,' he added as an afterthought. It seemed to suit her.

She smiled. 'No one but children call me that,' she said. 'It seems strange from you. Prince Abu Starbridge. I have heard you name. Come closer. I have never seen a prince before.'

He walked towards her, and when she could see him clearly, she laughed. 'Why Prince,' she said. 'You're getting bald.'

'Yes,' said Abu happily.

'I have heard your name. I heard of you among the Children of God, before the river rose.'

The man with the broken nose swore again. 'Fit company,' he said. 'Atheists and whores.'

'Sweet friend, don't say it. Atheists, certainly. They are the Children of God. A child cannot worship his own father, as other men must. It's not in nature. It is in nature to deny. Yet I am certain that when our Lord comes again, He will come from them, naked, without even a name.'

The woman said this as if it were part of a speech she had memorized in advance. As she spoke, she looked at the prince steadily, as if to measure his reaction. He smiled foolishly.

Her name was Mrs Darkheart, and she led Abu back through secret doors to rooms where she lived with her husband and her children. In the room where she made him lie down, someone had daubed crude adventist murals over the wallpaper. And when he had been left alone, Abu stretched out drunkenly on the bed. He couldn't decide if he felt worse lying back with his eyes closed, the bed seeming to recede from underneath him like a wave pulling back, or worse leaning upon one elbow watching figures of strange saints and upright prophets reel around him, formal and forbidding even while they danced. There was no window, but still the rain was beginning to leak in from somewhere, and in some places the paint had cracked and the wallpaper was loose. The spreading phosphorescence gave some scenes peculiar emphasis: Angkhdt on his deathbed, foretelling his rebirth, and the water had seeped through all around his head and glowed there like a halo. The risen Angkhdt, the new made flesh, purging the world with water and light, and the world seemed to glow between his fingers. Everywhere the walls were painted with quotations from the saints, unfurling in banners from their lips as they marched drunkenly around the room. Abu closed one eye and tried to make some sense out of the words. Captain Darkheart had picked up some literacy somewhere, and he had made the inscriptions as a present to his wife. He didn't share her heresy.

'Politically it's not productive,' he explained hours later, towards dawn, sitting at the bottom of Abu's bed with coffee in a styrofoam cup. 'People just sit around waiting for something to happen. They say God will only come again when things are at their worst, so they greet each new catastrophe with glee – famine, starvation, rain. They'll submit to anything. They hold the solutions in their own hands, but still they find it easier to sit and wait. It's tragic. There are so many of us, so few of you.'

His wife came in with a baby on her hip. His eyes

followed her around the room. 'It's different for her,' he said.

In her, he thought, because of the superior qualities of her mind, religion has been reduced to its purest form – a way of seeing justice in the world when there is none. He watched her lovingly as she lit a fire in the grate, burning trash and cardboard and splinters of lath.

Abu sat up in bed. He said, 'But there are rumors of the advent. Now. Argon Starbridge's son. The Prince of Caladon.'

'It is a lie,' responded Mrs Darkheart without pausing in her work. 'There are always rumors. A Starbridge prince – how is that possible? Can our salvation come out of a race of tyrants? Angkhdt, Angkhdt Himself was a poor man.'

'It's a trick,' continued her husband. 'A way of using us to fight their wars. Look.' He pulled out from his pocket a medallion on a chain, a painted miniature of a human baby in a golden crib. But its face was covered with hair, and its jaw stuck out almost like a dog's muzzle. 'King Argon has his spies out,' he said. 'One of them gave me this. It's Argon's son. The chain is supposed to make a man invulnerable in battle, if he fights for truth.'

Abu took the amulet into his hands. 'Is this . . . accurate?' he asked.

'The man swore so. He had seen him.'

'Poor child,' said the prince. 'He must be pitifully deformed.'

'Like all gods.'

'You're an atheist?'

Captain Darkheart looked offended. 'No,' he said. 'I'm an educated man.'

He was a rebel angel, one of an ancient sect of revolutionaries. Their cosmology was as orthodox as any parson's – predetermination, the doctrine of inevitability, the prison world. Yet they did not conclude from this, as parsons did, that the poor were damned, the rich saved. The history of their rebellions was as old as Angkhdt. Six thousand days before, they had risen in small towns along the southern coast and driven the parsons and the Starbridges out naked into the countryside. Many had died of exposure, though some were taken in by pious folk. The rebels had opened all the prisons, drawn up new constitutions, and celebrated in the streets until the army came. Even then, some had escaped in the long boats they had used to farm the sea, for they had been fishermen, harvesting sea vegetables with woven nets. Some had escaped beyond the ocean's rim, though many drowned, and boats and bodies had washed up all along the shore.

They had been a black-skinned people, and the captain, too, was very dark. He leaned toward Abu. 'The world is our prison, yes,' he said. 'But God cannot love our jailers more than He loves us. It cannot be the mark of a good man, how meekly he suffers. No. God loves the proud. He has made this world so hard a place. Does it make sense that He should love the weak more than the strong? Does it make sense that He should love the man who fails the test? But defy Him, defy them all and break away – those are the men He will choose for Paradise.'

'And if you're wrong?'

'Then He is a God to be hated. If we are wrong, and He damns us down to the ninth planet, then still He is a God to be defied. And if we can defy Him in this world, then maybe we can chance it in the next. Maybe there'll be a way there too.' His face, which had grown fierce, softened again as his wife caught his eye and smiled. 'I'm not wrong,' he said. 'I've had many blessings.'

The prince said, 'If . . .' but he was interrupted by the captain's hand upon his arm. Darkheart was smiling at his wife as if he longed to touch her; she was sitting in a corner near the door with her breast uncovered, feeding the child. 'Enough talk,' he said. 'My mind is my own. No proud man could live differently. But I don't expect you to believe me. It's not in your interest. The question is, now that I have you, how can I use you? Do you need alcohol to live? I can get you some.'

'No,' said Abu, smiling. 'It's not as bad as that.'

'Don't be ashamed. There's decadence in your blood. It's not your fault.'

'I'm afraid it is.'

'It doesn't matter,' said Darkheart. 'Show me your hands. Your tattoos.'

Prince Abu put his hands palm up on the blanket. 'I'll tell you what I'd like,' he said. 'I'd like a bath. You can barely see them under the dirt.'

Darkheart ignored him. 'What does this one mean?' he asked, pointing to the golden sun.

'All whims must be indulged, all requests granted, all commands obeyed.'

Darkheart laughed. 'That must come in handy,' he said.

'You'd be surprised how seldom.'

'You're not in the right line of work. Now I, I would find it useful. And you will too, I promise you. Spider has a plan for you. Spider!' He shouted, and the boy appeared in the doorway as if he had been listening there.

'Wait,' said Mrs Darkheart from the floor. She unplugged the baby from her breast and covered herself, but it started to whimper, so she gave it to her husband. It was a little boy, and Abu noticed it had no tattoos, no horoscope. No parson had yet touched it.

'Wait,' said Mrs Darkheart. She sat down next to Abu on the bed. 'How do you feel?' she asked.

'There's no air in here,' the prince complained. The

room seemed crowded with five people in it, now that the baby was awake. 'I have a headache,' he said.

'I'm not surprised.' She reached her hand out to touch him; her fingers were dry and cool. 'You're sweating,' she said. 'Are you hungry?'

'No. I'd like some water.'

She turned to the boy. 'Spider,' she said. 'Please bring the prince some aspirin and a glass of water.'

He went, with a puzzled expression on his face, and Darkheart, too, showed signs of impatience. 'I'm not interested in his comfort,' he muttered, trying to soothe the baby by grimacing and sticking out his tongue.

'Well, you should be,' said the woman. She took up one of the prince's hands from where it lay on the blanket. 'You're a strange man,' she said. 'Why are you here? Aren't you comfortable in your own house?'

'I have no friends.'

'It's your conscience. Look, there's the line.' She brought his palm up to her face, to study it more closely. 'Are there many like you? Rich men with consciences. I suppose there must be.'

'We are prisoners as much as you,' said the prince.

'Yes, I can see that. Your hand is much like Darkheart's. This is your way of breaking out. You don't have long to live, you know.'

'So I've been told.'

'Death by fire. Look at this.' She turned over her own hand. There, in the lap of her left thumb, someone had tattooed the mark of the gallows in white ink against her black skin. 'How can people be so cruel? You're not an informer, are you? You know enough to hang us.'

'We pay others to do that kind of work,' said Abu. 'I'm too conspicuous to be a spy.'

'Exactly,' said the woman. 'It's what I told them. One man wanted to kill you.'

'One man tried to.'

'It would have been a waste,' muttered her husband, fluttering his eyelids to amuse the child.

Many people in Beggar's Medicine seemed to have no age. Too sour to be children, too small and bent for men, too supple for old age, they seemed a race of nocturnal gnomes – smooth, hairless, yellow, as if even their faces had taken on the official urine-colored hue of poverty. Their skins seemed fragile and too small for them, and perhaps that was why they stopped and hunched their shoulders. Perhaps if they had straightened out their knees and necks, their skin might have split along the spine.

But the Darkhearts were a different kind, and so was Spider Abject. He stood up straight in the doorway, the aspirin in one hand, a glass of water in the other. There was a strength in him, not just resilience.

'Spider wants you to get his father for him,' said Darkheart as the boy came in. 'That would be easy enough for you, wouldn't it?'

Abject's eyes filled up with tears. He seemed prone to crying, but Abu liked him for it, because he never seemed to weep at blows or curses or abuse. He bore them sullenly, and sometimes he even smiled. But when he sat with his own thoughts or when he heard some words of kindness, then sometimes he would start to cry. And when Mrs Darkheart reached to comfort him, to smooth the hair back from his forehead, he pulled away as if from a blow.

That night, as the prince and Spider Abject left the house, the wind blew accumulated sugar around them in a powdery mist which whitened their faces and made it difficult to talk. It was a dangerous time, for when the weather was like this – sugar in the air with no rain to keep it wet – the mist could easily ignite. Inside their houses, people blew out their candles and sat shivering in the dark. They spoke softly to one another, for superstitious folk thought curses and obscenity gave off a kind of spark.

The prison was a small one, but it was bright with floodlights. From the four corners of the building stone towers rose up into the mist, and from their battlements huge search lamps swung in circles. At night they shone for half a mile, strands of blue light which beat down rhythmically upon the cringing streets, like the scourging of some whip. And in the fog the prison seemed to glow, and rise to many times its height, the light caught in a swirling prison of its own.

This was the center of the township, one of seven in the city of Charn. It included a chapel and a shrine, municipal offices, a bank, and, built into the prison's base, the bishop's market and dispensaries, where laborers could spend their salary receipts. The magistrate's court was a small one, for it dealt with civil offenses only. Crimes against God were handled elsewhere. But still, the gallows took up much of the square; they walked through them towards the chapel door, as if through a copse of trees. There were public executions almost every day.

As Prince Abu and the boy approached, the bells were ringing for the evening service. Worshipers crunched up to the portals through the hardened mud, their coats dusted with sugar. Abject followed them up the steps, past the great dog-headed statues guarding the gate, under the carved pediment illustrating the choices of St Terrapin the Just. At that time of night the chapel was the only entrance to the prison.

'Look there,' he whispered, standing in the narthex. He pointed down the aisle, directly underneath the pulpit, where rows of handcuffed men and women sat, interspersed with turnkeys in gray uniforms. The service had already begun, and the pews along the aisle were full, but Abject found seats for them underneath a grinning angel. On the altar, the statue of Angkhdt was surrounded by a ring of acolytes, polishing and stroking him, and oiling his phallus. They chanted lists of names. The ceremony of the lamps had been concluded – abridged, most likely, because of the dangers of the weather. The candelabra were all empty, and instead a line of glass globes hung from the vault. They burned red gas, which cast uncertain shadows and made the white mosaics of the floor glow red.

The chanting repeatedly rose and died away, and at times the congregation joined in, reciting the eighteen kinds of self-deception, the seven laws of harmony, the eleven types of civil disobedience, the sixteen phases of a woman's love. It was a beautiful performance. At certain times the sounds flowed regularly, and then they broke apart as different sections of the congregation broke away into different chants in different octaves, and all the sense was lost, only the order and the beauty remaining. They finished in a kind of round, each section coming down to silence at a different time, until only the impossibly high voices of the choir remained, and the bell-like booming of the parson in the pulpit, asking the benediction.

'Oh my children,' he roared when all was quiet, and the people sat submissively. 'Oh my children. I take my text tonight from the five-hundredth chapter of the Song of Angkhdt, which has been translated for us, by permission of the emperor, in this way.' He paused for emphasis, then continued: '"My beloved. My beloved, when I feel you under me, slippery with hunger, when you have sucked me dry, when you have sucked the sugar of my loins, then am I happy. Beloved, you have taken everything I have. If

283

this is poverty, I am content. I would not trade it for the palace of a prince. I would not trade it for a bishop's throne."'

The parson was a fat man. He recited according to an ancient tradition, whereby the words of the text were run together without spacing, in a deep monotone. At one time it had been heresy to suggest, by giving it emphasis, that one word might be holier than another. The resulting spew of syllables was hard to understand, but the text was a common one, especially in poorer neighborhoods, and Abu guessed the people knew it by heart.

The parson had recited without pausing for breath, and all through the compulsory minute of meditation, Abu could hear him wheezing. He was much mutilated. One of his eyes had been torn from its socket, not long ago, it seemed; the left side of his face was still sunken and discolored, and his cheekbones seemed to have healed improperly. It gave him a disjointed look, for though one half of his face was collapsed and hideous, the other glowed pink and fresh, the cheek fat, the eye gleaming and benign. It was as if he had made his face into an illustration of the twofold nature of his calling, and at times he would give emphasis to one side or the other as he spoke, simply by turning his head, and his audience would know whether to cringe or to be comforted.

He said: 'Oh my children, I direct your attention to the last part of this lesson, for the first part is very difficult to understand. Remember this – "I would not trade my poverty for the palace of a prince. I would not trade it for a parson's throne." Now, I can see some discontented faces among you, and perhaps you think: what idiocy is this? Perhaps you are a poor man with many children. Perhaps your horoscope forbids you to progress beyond a certain salary, so that no matter how you work – oh I know, my

284

children, I know how hard these things can seem. Such a man might cry out, seeing some Starbridge riding by in his motorcar, or feasting in a restaurant, or standing on the steps of the theater in his evening clothes, such a man might cry out, "Oh yes, gladly would I change my place with you. Gladly would I!" Oh my children, it is a natural mistake to think your own life is the hardest. But it is a mistake that Angkhdt will not permit us to make.' The parson turned the dead side of his face to his audience, and glared at them out of his unseeing eye. 'This world is a cruel place. It is a place outside the reach of God's mercy, a world we have all come to in our various ways. We have formed it with our sins. Man's fate is a hard one, and you might be excused for thinking that a little comfort, a little freedom, a little money might make it softer. But consider, is life any better for the rich? Are their women more beautiful? Do they find the joys of love more sweet? Do their children love them more? No, these questions of comfort, they are not the important ones.

'For remember, we Starbridges have a purpose. Now, even now, a great war is being waged for your safety, not sixty miles from our north gate, against heretics and tyrants. Tonight I have heard news of a great victory against the forces of our enemies.'

To make this announcement, he had presented the congregation with the living side of his face. But now he turned to look at them head on. 'My children, our victory has come at bitter cost. Many thousands of our soldiers lie dead upon that field. And of those regiments of dead, how many of my family? I hear that my own brother and my own nephew also, my sister's son, have purchased your continued safety with their blood. Now, warm in this beautiful church or safe in your homes, would you be willing to change your places with them? My children, these Starbridge officers are your bulwark and your shield. We would have no war or victory without them. The ones that still survive, do you envy them their comfort as they stretch out their blankets in the rain?'

'Or perhaps it is I you envy. Then tell me, is it my hand, my manhood, or my leg? Is it the mark of scourges on my back? Or perhaps you remember how on this very altar, on the feast of St Delphinium, I dedicated my eye.' He showed them the dead side of his face. 'That is what it means to be Starbridge,' he said. 'Don't forget it.

'Now we are at the start of a great trial. One of my predecessors in this pulpit recorded in his diary that in the ninth through nineteenth phases of last spring, it rained for seven thousand days. Many will die, rich and poor. But our survival as a nation, and a culture, and a race, depends on us. Now I have heard some of you whispering that great changes come with spring, great miracles, great new freedoms. But I say, if we cannot keep God's laws, the laws that kept our ancestors from harm during this long storm, then God will squeeze us like a sponge. Tonight from this pulpit I heard you singing, high and low together, and the beauty of it brought tears to my eyes. I tell you, I make that song a metaphor, because it is in the harmony in which we live together that we can hope to touch God's pity. And in those harmonies, there must be high and low. Without it, all the sense is lost. Without it, there is no beauty, no achievement. I tell you, high and low together, together we will raise an anthem to our God!'

When the parson had finished, the people sank down on their knees for the compulsory prayers before the next part of the service. 'Now,' whispered Spider Abject. 'Go now. They'll take him back soon.' He stood up and pointed over the bowed heads of the congregation. 'That one. There he is,' and Abu saw a hairless old man, asleep in the prisoners' pews. 'That one. Drunken fool! He's asleep, the last night of his life,' said Abject, the tears starting to his eyes.

Abu led him to the side aisle, and they hurried down the narrow row of columns and arches toward the sanctuary, where the parson was already being helped into his litter. Behind him stood the entrance to the prison, an ornamented filigree of iron bars, and all around slouched soldiers of the purge. Two stepped forward to block the prince's way. They scowled and snarled like dogs, but when they saw his hand their expressions congealed, and all their viciousness seemed to drain away from underneath, until the scowls meant nothing. Abu passed without a word, Spider Abject close behind him.

The parson had his back to them. He seemed a hill of red-robed fat, his bulk was so tremendous. Acolytes strained to lever him into his seat, but however hard they pushed, the fat seemed to flow away from underneath their hands, and they seemed no closer to lifting his essential frame than if they had stood across the room.

Abu waited, and then he cleared his throat. 'Cousin,' he began, tentatively, but one of the guards said, 'Wait. He's deaf, sir. Wait until he turns around. Then he can read your lips.'

In the sanctuary, the choir started to sing again, their castrate voices rising to the vault. Spider pulled the prince's sleeve, for in the prisoners' pews the turnkeys were getting to their feet. But still the acolytes grunted and pushed, and cursed behind the parson's back. And even when he was in place, bundled like a red bag of fat on to the velvet cushions of his chair, the prince could only catch his blind eye. Several acolytes moved to the litter poles, and some went up to open the iron gates to the prison. Behind the prince, the aisle, separated from the nave of the church by a row of columns and arches, had begun to fill with prisoners, chained in groups, waiting to pass through the same gate.

The parson's acolytes spat on their hands and bent down to the litter poles. As they did so, Abu crossed in front and stood between the foremost, and held up his hand. The parson turned his head, so that the fat living side faced forward. 'Cousin,' he said in a loud, deaf voice. The acolytes stood up again, happy to delay their burden. In the aisle, the prisoners and turnkeys waited patiently, and the guards, who had been talking among themselves, were suddenly quiet.

Abu looked around, embarrassed. Then he turned back to the parson, but when he spoke, he spoke with his lips only, making no sound. He was careful to form his words clearly, so that the parson would understand, but he was going to tell a lie, though only a small one, and he didn't want anyone else to hear. 'Cousin,' he said, forming the words, no breath escaping. 'Your sermon was very fine. It makes it easy to request a favor.'

The parson looked at him curiously. Abu had a reputation among Starbridges, and though he didn't know this man by sight, yet Abu could tell by the hardness of his smile that the man was already making guesses. 'Certainly,' he shouted. 'Come up with me into my office. Come up and have a . . . have a drink.'

The parson had heard of him. 'There is no need for that,' said Abu, still mouthing his words silently, so that only one half of their conversation was audible to the people around them. 'I don't mean to take up any of your time. The thing I want is close at hand.' He paused, then went on. 'My servant's father is condemned to death. I promised I would save him.'

The parson turned his face so that the dead half showed,

and then he turned it back. 'That was a foolish promise,' he said.

'I don't see why. It is my wish.'

'Come up to my office. We can talk.'

'No. I don't want to.'

In the sanctuary, the voices of the choir filled the vault. 'This is a very large request,' said the parson. 'Which man is it?'

'That one,' said the prince aloud, pointing at Abject's father. The old man stood apart from the other prisoners, staring dully at his son. And when he saw Prince Abu point at him, he cowered and sidled back to stand next to his jailers.

'It is a large request,' repeated the parson loudly. 'That man is rightfully condemned. He has broken literacy statute 14c and property statutes 39x and y.'

'Nevertheless, it is my wish,' said the prince. With the sound of his voice, he was conscious of a feeling rising in him that he had never known, a kind of happiness.

The parson shrugged, and smiled with the living half of his face. 'Take him,' he said, and made a gesture with his finger. Abu felt full of happiness and power. But as he stepped back towards the prisoners, he noticed Jason Mock, chained at his wrist and ankles, his cheeks swollen under his beard, as if he had been beaten. One eye was swollen shut. Yet he stood up straight, away from the rest, and his face had no submission in it, only savagery and contempt. 'Wait,' said the prince, giddy with new feelings. 'Wait. I want that one too.'

'No,' said Spider Abject, pulling at his sleeve. 'It's too much. Be satisfied with one.' But the parson was still smiling. 'Why not?' he said, making the same small gesture with his finger. 'Mercy is the virtue of princes.'

In the nave, the singing and the chanting had stopped.

Rumors had spread throughout the church, and the aisles were full of people. Excited faces peered around every pillar. Abu was the center of all eyes. 'Why not?' he cried. 'I'll take them all.' And he walked forward into the ranks of prisoners. They clustered around him, clanking their chains. He held his hand out to the jailers, and sullenly they surrendered their keys.

'Be careful, Cousin,' came the parson's smiling voice. 'Mercy is a virtue. But weakness is a crime. Be careful.' But already chains and handcuffs were falling to the stones. First free, Jason Mock strode among the others with a ring of keys, while Abu stood in a circle of panderers. They were pawing him with flaccid fingers, their faces still incredulous. He was supremely happy. With an imperious flourish, he raised his arm, and the crowd split away from him all down the aisle, and far at the end he could see the open portal, the doors pulled back, the square black night, the sugar thick on the stone lintels. But just then, as if put in motion by the prince's uplifted finger, high in the tower above them the bells began to ring, sounding the alarm. 'Enough,' said Spider Abject. 'That's enough. Leave the rest.' Among the hundred or so prisoners, perhaps forty had been freed; Abject took his father underneath the arm and dragged him towards the open door. Abu stayed behind, unable to relinquish so much power and popularity. But finally he turned, just in time to see the boy and his father vanish down the steps into the night. And in a crowd of hunchbacked, yellow people, the prince moved slowly down the aisle, an old woman hanging on to each arm. But when he was still ten paces from the portal, a young sacristan in red robes flung himself before the doorway and blocked it with his outstretched arms. It was a useless gesture, and perhaps he only meant to shine for his superiors. He could not have hoped to offer any real obstruction, for Abu's strength by then was irresistible. But as the prince raised up his hand to show his palm, Jason Mock burst past him, unable to wait, unable to judge the outcome of even such a simple test of will. He broke the young man's head in with a length of chain, and pushed him down the steps into the square.

That act of violence ended all their hopes. Mock stood in the doorway, framed by darkness, and past him the square had filled with people, summoned by the bell. Soldiers of the purge were there, and when they saw the young man fall, they came running up the steps, all doubts resolved, all weakness set aside. Mock had dared to touch a priest. Trapped, he turned back towards the church, but there too soldiers were cutting through the crowd. Wildly he looked around. There was no escape, but above his head a cross of steel hung down from a stanchion over the door, supporting four red bulbs of burning gas. With a tremendous leap, Mock seized hold of the crossbar and pulled himself up until he squatted on it, chattering his hatred like a monkey, the fog drifting around him, sweetening his clothes. He pulled his chain up after him like a monkey's tail.

Soldiers stood underneath him. The captain unbuckled his revolver. But the voice of the parson, still sitting in his litter at the back of the church, sounded above the uproar: 'Be careful! Be careful of the gas!' It gave Mock his idea. Grinning viciously, he wrapped his chain around his hand. That was the last the soldiers saw – Mock's teeth shining in the middle of his black beard as he leaned down and smashed the glass bulb with his armored fist.

With a roar, the air caught fire, following the eddies of the fog a thousand feet above their heads. In the square people scattered, but in an instant they were surrounded and engulfed in whirlwinds of flame; it was in the air they breathed. The clouds burst open, and the rain caught fire and fell in torrents on the rooftops. Back in the safety of the church, something fell on Abu from behind and knocked him cold.

6
Refugees and Pilgrims

A week later, the fire had changed consistency. It still fell unabated on the roofs of Beggar's Medicine. But after the first explosion, new rainwater had chilled it to a drizzle of cold, wet, scorching drops. The phenomenon was visible for miles, a rainstorm of light. During the day, circular rainbows formed in the upper atmosphere.

At dusk, Thanakar Starbridge stood among some corpus trees, looking back over the city. Colonel Aspe had pitched his tent among the only vegetation in the valley, and Thanakar wondered whether it was because he liked the smell. The trees bled a nauseating sap from punctures in their soft bark. It smelled like battlefields and operating rooms. Standing looking back at the lightstorm over the city, Thanakar reached for a branch; it seemed to shrink away from under his hand. The leaves rustled mournfully, though the air was still. It wasn't raining, for the moment, in the barren valley where the army camped.

There had been no fighting, for Aspe still sat sulking in his tent. The soldiers chewed narcotics around the campfires and quarreled with each other in their soft southern whispers. They played endless games of cards, games with obscure rules, cards with unfamiliar markings. They spat and cursed. But Thanakar had been busy restructuring faces, rebuilding limbs. That day he had made a golden eye for a young soldier, with nerves of golden wires, but after hours of surgery the man was still practically blind. He had lain there patiently, though the pain was terrible and the disappointment worse – a young man not six phases old. After eight hours on the table all he could see were geometric patterns of metallic yellow. In the end, Thanakar had been too discouraged to proceed. His fingers were too sore. The wire had cut into his knuckles. It was a new technique.

At the entrance to the colonel's tent, he stretched out his hand again into the corpus leaves, and again the branches seemed to evade his touch, while a tremor ran through them in the breathless air. It was a melancholy place. Thanakar ducked his head under the folds of canvas. Inside the tent, Aspe sat on a stool, hunched over a table in the shadows, his pencil moving noiselessly over a piece of paper. He drew careful circles and pentagons by the light of an oil lamp, and underneath he played at forming letters, imitations of script, imitations of printing, meaningless even at a distance.

Thanakar stood watching. The colonel took no notice of him. He didn't even raise his head, but continued his slow scratching. Even in such a childlike occupation there was nothing laughable or weak in him. He glowered at the page as if he hated it, patterns of white scars standing out along his forehead. His neck and forearms, augmented by shadow, formed a tense and menacing arc. All his muscles were taut, his hand flat on the table, the fingers of his other hand cramped around the pencil, as if with one hand he prevented the table from rising in the air, while with the other he bent the rebellious pencil to his will. Left to itself, it might have written anything. It might have formed letters that made sense.

'Go away,' said Aspe without looking up.

'You sent for me.'

'I don't recognize you,' he said, still glaring at his work.

'You sent for me.'

'Go away.'

Thanakar shrugged, irritated, and turned to go, but the harsh voice spoke again and held him back. 'Wait,' it commanded, and the doctor stood and waited until Aspe had finished his drawing. It was a complicated polygon, with a paragraph of spurious handwriting underneath. Frowning, Aspe studied it for a moment, and then he drew two lines crossing through it from corner to corner of the page and put it aside on a stack of sketches, all similarly crossed out. Then he sighed and released his pencil; it rolled a little way and stopped. He raised his steel hand from where it lay outstretched on the surface of the table. He loosened the key at his steel wrist, and bent the steel fingers forward into his customary fist before he turned the key again, locking them in place. Then he sat back. 'Captain Starbridge,' he said.

'Yes.'

Aspe looked at him for a long time without speaking, as if trying to recall why he had sent for him. If he suddenly remembered, he didn't show it by any change of expression, but instead, after a few minutes of silence, he reached into the pile of papers by his side and took out a memorandum addressed to Thanakar from his adjutant, dated the previous week. It had been passed out at a staff meeting. Thanakar was embarrassed to remember, when the colonel turned it over, that he had fought boredom during the discussion by drawing caricatures of various officers, including a savage one of the colonel himself. He had drawn it from memory, for Aspe had not attended any meeting since the battle. Still, it was quite recognizable, the heavy jaw, the hatchet face, the tangled hair.

The colonel studied it and then looked up. 'I am an ugly man,' he said. 'But you have made me uglier than I am.'

'It's a skill that I have.'

'I want this skill. What does beauty mean, Captain?'

'I don't know,' said Thanakar, yawning.

'You must know. I have seen the bishop of Charn. She is beautiful.'

'I suppose she is.'

'Suppose?' cried the colonel harshly. 'God damn your suppositions. Listen to me – your religion is a web of lies, but at the heart of it there is some truth. She is beautiful. Beauty in the heart of ugliness. What does it mean?'

'I don't know,' answered Thanakar, too tired to be anything but irritated by this kind of conversation. 'Beauty isn't so important,' he said. 'It doesn't mean so much. A woman can be beautiful and still be bad.'

'Can she? I wish I could believe that. I'm an old man. Listen.' Aspe leaned forward and spat the next words like a curse: 'This woman's face is at the center of my thoughts. My thoughts! Look there.' He pulled out some papers, and Thanakar could see that he had tried his hand at portraiture. They were like a child's drawings.

'What does it mean, Captain? Could you make a picture of her, and make it look like her, and make it ugly?'

'I suppose I could.'

'I wish I had your skill. If I had your skill, I would march back tonight and hang your priests up by their own chains and burn your city to the ground.'

'The emperor might not approve of that.'

'I am not the emperor's slave,' said Aspe sulkily.

There was a silence, and Thanakar broke it. 'Someone's sparing you the trouble,' he said. 'The city's on fire.' He yawned. 'I want to go now. I'm very tired.'

'Yes. You've been saving lives. I think you're not having much success.'

'Not much.' Thanakar had made a hospital to treat the remnants of the colonel's corps of antinomials. Aspe had not once inspected it.

296

'Yes,' he said. 'You don't surprise me. They have lost the urge to live, haven't they? Well, they are free to go.'

'That's easy for you to say,' exclaimed Thanakar bitterly. He had worked hard. But the atheists were dying, even of the slightest wounds. Men, women, children, they lay in bed, their eyes fixed on nothing.

'Yes, Very easy. Tell me, Captain. Are you also prepared to die?' Aspe picked a paper up and pushed it across the table. 'Read that,' he said. 'Read it aloud.'

It was a letter. It said:

I want a criminal – Thanakar Starbridge, of your staff – convicted in this city of adultery, murder, and attempted murder. Deliver him to the bearers of this letter. Do not thwart me in this. It is my jurisdiction. Do not thwart me.

Chrism Demiurge
Kindness and Repair
Spring 8, Oct. 42, 00016

'I thwarted him,' said the colonel grimly. 'The bearers of this letter – I stuffed their mouths with excrement and sewed them shut. I handcuffed them to their horses and sent them back.'

'It wasn't their fault,' said Thanakar.

'It was their risk, serving such a master. It doesn't matter. They came this morning. That's why I sent for you. You are free to go.'

'Thank you for warning me.'

'No. It was a debt I didn't want to think about again. You tried to save my family. Only, for the love of Angkhdt, why couldn't you have been in time? Why couldn't you have ridden faster? Then I would have paid your debt with my heart's blood.' Aspe paused, his expression mixing rage and misery, the scars standing livid across his eyelids and his cheeks. Then he continued in a lower tone, deep in his throat. 'That was the end of me, that day. That was the end.'

'I tried,' said Thanakar stiffly. 'Some wouldn't have bothered.'

'What good is that?' shouted Aspe, rising to his feet. Upright, he seemed to take up the whole tent. He loomed above Thanakar, surrounded by shadows. 'Tried!' he said. 'That's worse than useless. I tried too, to save your worthless life. Yes, and I succeeded. It is my habit. Go – the debt is paid. Take a horse and go. Ride north. There is . . . beautiful country that way, beyond the river Rang.'

'No. I'll go back to the city.'

'You see?' cried Aspe. 'And you, a doctor. Yet you wouldn't ride a mile to save such a worthless life.'

'No,' said Thanakar. 'It's not that. I have things I must do. Dependents.'

'Barbarian! Your tail hangs down your leg. I give you freedom, and you think about your slaves. Barbarian. It will mean your life.'

'Perhaps. But what did the letter say – "adultery"?'

'Ah,' replied the colonel, softening his tone. 'Does every man have some face that keeps him from himself? Even you?' He reached down to the table, to finger his childish drawing of the bishop's face.

Among the antinomials in Thanakar's hospital, there were two whose urge to live had been sustained, in one case by love, in the other by hatred. When that fierce creature, the antinomial army, had rolled upon its belly and expired under Argon Starbridge's guns, it had spat up some survivors. After the battle, Thanakar had sent men through to shoot the horses and dogs, and the desperate cases. The survivors he had gathered into a section of the field hospital, over the objections of his superiors. They claimed that such a sewer of pollution would baffle any attempts at sterilization within the radius of a mile, would infect the other patients and the staff. After several acts of semi-official sabotage, Thanakar had withdrawn across the valley, and had injected special antibodies into some strong-stomached orderlies, and employed them out of his own pocket to erect some tents. There the antinomials were dying, one by one. It was discouraging to see them, their wounds bandaged and their bleeding stopped, turn their faces into their pillows and die without a word, or perhaps just whispering the whisper of a melody as light as breath. Unable to sleep, Thanakar had wandered through the tents at night, listening to that muttered music, his lantern catching reflections from the eyes of children.

But two had kept the will to live – the heavy, white-faced antinomial who with his trumpet and his sunglasses and his shaved head had led the charge, and one other. The first healed quickly of appalling wounds, though the blood he had lost increased his pallor to a corpselike hue. Like his brothers and sisters, he never spoke, but his eyes gleamed with a fever their eyes lacked. Under the glasses they were the palest blue, the color of water over snow.

From time to time, sitting on his cot, he would take from the breast of his shirt a bloodstained scarf. And by the intensity with which he studied it, as if the pattern of the bloodstains could tell him something, Thanakar could guess the obsession that was keeping him alive. He hated Aspe. When his wounds were partly healed, he had crept out from the tent one night to prowl around the colonel's pickets. He had come back with his face bruised, his nose broken. In the morning, Thanakar tried to tell him some-thing of the scarf's true story, but he hadn't listened.

'He sang a song to us,' said the man. 'I saw a picture in

the air. A ring of mountains, and women riding in the tall grass. It was a lie.'

After that, Thanakar was reluctant to make him understand, to rob him of a delusion that was keeping him alive.

The other convalescent was the white-eyed antinomial, who had sung his memories of his childhood above Rangriver to Thanakar and Abu in the warehouse by the river. Though his wounds were superficial, he had been in danger of dying of morbid melancholia like the rest, until the doctor found a remedy. Thanakar had carried in his baggage, as a token of the hopelessness of love, the bracelet he had gotten on the Mountain of Redemption, the payment for a night's work there. The antinomial woman with the yellow hair had taken it from her wrist to give to him. It fitted neatly just above his elbow; unlike most officers, he never wore jewelry, but he had kept it as a souvenir. One day, changing the bandages on the dying man's chest, all the coincidences of the story came back to him, and the next time he made his rounds, Thanakar brought the bracelet and gave it to him with his pills. The man rubbed his thumb along the carved silver, the pattern of animals devouring one another. Thanakar waited for some sign of recollection in his white eyes, some softening of his cruel face, but there was nothing. In the morning when he came again, the man had thrown the bracelet into a corner of the tent and was nearer death than ever. Once the bracelet had meant something to him. Not any more. Time had closed its fist.

The man lay back, his eyes pulsing and expanding, and drifting in and out of focus. Discouraged, Thanakar bent over him and touched his hair, but the man was too weak even to turn away. 'Remember,' began Thanakar. 'Remember . . .' but he wasn't sure the man could hear. And as he faltered for a way of telling him his own story, the man's mouth opened and he began to sing, a song as insubstantial as a ghost, the antinomial's last song of himself, which comes with death. Thanakar bent low to listen, and as he did so, he thought he heard some last hostility creep into the tone, until the man closed his eyes and the melody ran pure again.

Thanakar waited for the part he knew would come, the sweet, despairing leitmotif of love, a dozen notes, and when he heard them, he memorized them. He waited, and when the song was interrupted by some last coughing grunts, he took it up himself, note by careful note. Memorized symbols in an unknown language, and doubtless his pronunciation was poor, because he had to repeat it twice before the antinomial opened his eyes and looked at him with an expression so miserable and sad, it made him stumble into silence. But for this moment, Thanakar had retrieved the silver bracelet from the floor, and he pushed it into the man's palm, lying open on the coverlet. His fingers curled around its rim. For several long minutes, his face held a look as if he were making a decision, and when he had made it, his mouth contorted in a snarl of anger. He had been bitten and betrayed. His eyes filled up with water, and Thanakar slunk away. But as early as the next evening, the patient was taking solid food.

These two antinomials kept company, not speaking, but playing music to each other. They kept apart from the others, out of a kind of delicacy, Thanakar fancied. He put them in a tent next to his own because he liked to hear them play late at night, an assortment of instruments at first, but after a while they had rejected all but two, a glass flute and a wooden one. When the doctor lay unsleeping on his cot, his mind racing through images of failed surgery, or of Charity or Abu Starbridge, or of Micum Starbridge repeating some simple

301

action over and over, then it soothed him to hear those soft dissonances come seeping through the canvas walls, the glass flute and the wooden one, the music as evocative as speech. They played music all the time.

But after talking to Aspe, Thanakar took a horse and went, left his hospital and rode up out of the valley back towards Charn, through lines of soggy tents. The images of Charity Starbridge had speeded up into a kind of frenzy. But once that night as he dismounted on the muddy track to stand in the shelter of a wall out of the rain, to rest his leg and watch the city burning like a candle far away over the hills, he heard the splash of horses' feet. The two antinomials sat majestic on their horses in the rain, looking down at him. They didn't speak; neither did he, and after a little while he climbed into his saddle again. They followed him all the way, riding slightly behind.

At dawn they came up to the city's gates. Thanakar had feared he might be expected. But all was pandemonium, a cursing stream of men with burdens, men on bicycles, women pushing handcarts. There was no guard. People stood in the road with no place to go, the mud up to their knees, their households on their backs.

Inside the city it was worse, the streets clogged with people shouting and struggling in the rain. The fire wouldn't spread this way for months, for here the wood was too wet to burn. Yet everywhere banks and businesses and schools were closed, the buildings empty and the streets full, the shrines jampacked with cursing worshipers. Thanakar and the antinomials abandoned their horses and continued on foot. They walked on for hours until, where two streets ran together and the houses fell away on either side, they could see the first tiers of the Mountain of Redemption rising to the sky, circles of stone battlements bulging through the mist. Thanakar felt a hand on his wrist.

'That's where she is,' said the antinomial.

'Yes,' answered Thanakar.

'Where?'

'It's called the Tower of Silence. There's a section for heretics. You can't see it from here.'

'Can you take me?' asked the antinomial.

'No.'

The man squinted, and his grip tightened on the doctor's arm.

'I can't do it,' said Thanakar. 'I've got my own things to do.'

The man gave him a long hungry look through slitted eyes. And then suddenly, as momentary sunlight tore through a rag of cloud above them, his expression cleared. He smiled up at the sky. Then, reaching out his immense hand, he put two fingers underneath Thanakar's chin, and forced his chin up in a playful gesture of encouragement, and slapped him playfully across the cheek, knocking him off balance. Then he was gone without a word, slogging up the street, his coat pulled up around his face. But at the fork, where the road led straight up to the mountain's base, he leaped forward and started to run, singing like a boy.

That was the last time Thanakar saw him. The time would come when a man could travel all through the northern provinces and all through the slums of Charn without seeing a single antinomial. They were a transient people, and soon they were all gone. Foreseeing it, standing in the mud, Thanakar chose that moment for his own. In later times, when men would ask him what the antinomials were like, he would remember not the violence, not the savagery, not the smell of roasting meat, but that moment: a man running away up to a turning in the road, running joyfully to his own death, chasing, without thinking, something that could never be.

303

The other stayed behind. He stood next to Thanakar, wiping his shaved forehead with his scarf. They were close to the Starbridge palaces. The streets were almost empty. A motorcar sped past, spewing them with mud.

Thanakar went home. But first, slinking through the corridors and up the marble stairs, his pale companion following, he stopped at the commissar's apartments. The door swung open on to empty rooms. The church had already repossessed the furniture. In the hallway a man was busy repainting; he was an idiot. When he made the gestures of respect, he kept his paintbrush in his hand, so that when he was finished his nose and hair were daubed with green.

The room smelled of antiseptic and incense. In Prince Abu's bedroom, a printed notice was pasted to one wall. It said an epidemic of immorality had broken out here, and it had already killed two people – God have mercy. The document was an official one, and pinned to the bottom corner was a snapshot of an official execution. Someone had jiggled the camera, and the faces were impossible to make out.

He walked down to his own apartment. He expected to find soldiers, but the hall was empty. His housekeeper met him at the threshold – 'Oh, sir,' she stammered. 'Thank heaven you've come back. Your mother, sir. Your mother's woke up. She killed a man.' Thanakar took off his coat and hung it up. Then he went past her through the library towards his parents' bedroom, leaving her gaping up into the antinomial's white face. 'Oh, sir,' continued Mrs Cassimer. 'You can't go in there. She's dangerous. She's killed a man. Who's this you brought home, sir?'

The antinomial unwrapped his cloak and stood dripping in his hospital clothes. Solemnly he took out his sunglasses and put them on. From his sleeve he took out his glass flute, and he examined it carefully in the light, while Mrs Cassimer gasped and wheezed. She made the sign of the unclean, ducking her head into her armpits. 'Angkhdt preserve us,' she whispered.

Hesitating at the bedroom door, Thanakar smiled. 'You can put him in the room next to mine,' he said. 'Are there clean sheets?' The door was locked, with the key in it. He unlocked it and pushed it open.

Inside, the room was wrecked. Books and pieces of furniture lay at random, and the windows were all broken. His mother sat naked on the bed next to his sleeping father, her arms around her knees, her hair loose around her shoulders, and when she raised her head to look at Thanakar, he saw her eyes had changed color from the hard black of the Starbridges to a molten red, and as he watched, they changed again, a slow reel of unnatural shades fading into one another: pink, white, yellow, orange, red, pink. It was the only movement in her face.

'Oh, sir, be careful,' remonstrated Mrs Cassimer, peeking round the doorjamb. 'She's not safe. She killed a man.'

'Who?'

'Only a sweeper. On Tuesday – he discovered her. We had a terrible time to get her off of him. Mr Gramercy, she bit his hand.'

'Mother?' he called out into the room. The woman on the bed stared at him, her eyes a swirl of color.

'She hasn't touched my father,' he remarked. The prince's long figure lay unmolested, still shrouded by her side.

'No, sir.'

'When did this happen?'

'On Tuesday, sir. Eight days ago. In the morning.'

'Did you send for the police?'

'No, sir. It was only a sweeper. Oh, sir, it was those

experiments of yours, I'm sure of it. Leave the dead alone, that's what I say. I knew it was a terrible mistake.'

'You should have said something.'

'Oh, sir.'

'I came back for other reasons. Have the police been here, or any soldiers looking for me?'

'No, sir.'

'Any parsons?'

'No . . .'

'What does she eat?'

'Oh, sir, how can you be so calm? Your own mother, back from the dead.' The housekeeper was close to tears.

'I'm thinking. She seems calm enough.' He took a step into the room.

'Please don't go any closer, sir. She's not to be trusted, back from the dead like that. She's lost her mind, and it's a small wonder. Such a good mistress, too.'

He took another step into the room. The princess opened her mouth, and he seemed to feel her cold breath from ten feet away, like a draught from an open doorway. 'Son,' she said in a cold whisper, her voice cold as death. 'I'm hungry, Thanakar.'

'Beloved God,' sobbed Mrs Cassimer. 'Look at her eyes.'

'Son,' the princess said again. 'Tell the old fool to go away. Tell her to bring food for me. Tell her to bring tumbril pie and sandwiches. Tell her to bring fishes cooked in wine. I want them.'

The doctor turned to Mrs Cassimer. 'Did you hear? Eight days – almost a week. She must be starving.'

'Oh, sir. Fishes, she says.'

'I have brought a guest here,' continued Thanakar. 'Perhaps he and the princess have tastes in common. It sounds like it. As for me, can you make me a fruit salad? I was up all night.'

306

'Beloved Angkhdt. Fishes, she wants.'

'Please, Mrs Cassimer.'

'But sir, she killed a man.'

'Yes,' whispered the princess. 'What's done is done.' She turned her eyes to the housekeeper, and the woman fled.

'Well, Mother,' said the doctor, coming forward into the room. 'You've made rather a mess.' He walked towards her, kicking through books and broken vases.

'Yes,' breathed the princess. 'Not too close, my son. That's close enough.' He stopped uncertainly, and she continued. 'Why, you're a man now, Thanakar. Are you married?'

'No.'

'No. No need. Does your leg give you much trouble?'

'Not much.'

'No.' She looked almost young. Her hair was glossy and her face unlined, but her dead white pallor and her changing eyes made her a creature out of nightmares and sick dreams, trapped between worlds. She looked around the room. 'How long?' she asked. 'What is the date?'

'October 46th, in the eighth phase of spring. It's raining.'

'So. More than fifty months, then. More than five thousand days. Are you religious, Thanakar?'

'No.'

'Good boy. They stole my life from me. I want it back. I want it.' Her eyes caught her reflection in the shards of a broken mirror on the wall; she turned away with an expression of disgust. 'Not like this. Why did you wake me? It was the heroin solution. I could feel it pulling me upward as soon as you had shot it in, but I took such a long time to reach the surface. I was down so far. Look – your father looks as young as when I married him.'

The doctor picked up a chair from off its side. 'Tell me,' he said.

His mother turned, and he watched her eyes fade from pink to white. 'No,' she whispered. 'Not now. A world of dreams, my son. Not now. I'm thirsty now. Bring me pear whiskey in a crystal glass. Bring me clusters of white grapes. I want them.'

Thanakar rubbed his nose. A sound came from somewhere else in the apartment. The antinomial blew into his flute to clear it, and then started to play a small tune. The princess heard it. She tilted her head curiously, and Thanakar watched a stain of yellow spread and darken in her eyes. 'What is that?' she asked.

He went to find Jenny Pentecost, but she was gone. The house was burned – charred timber, nothing. The police at the local station were obsequious and useless, because the mud and the ashes where the house had been still stank with perfume, and a blackened post was daubed with a cross and circle in red paint. 'I'm sorry, sir,' said the policeman, picking at a pimple underneath his lip. 'I wouldn't have touched them knowing your lordship to be interested, and a friend of the poor commissar's too. We knew they were runaways, a girl marked like that. But who isn't, nowadays? The whole district is clearing out. Evil times, sir, evil times. But look here.' He pointed out the red mark on the post, though no one could have missed it or failed to understand it. 'See that? Not our jurisdiction. That's the purge. Smell that? Now, no offense, sir, but we've heard some rumors about you too. I'd be careful, sir.'

The clouds looked bruised and swollen over a light rain. In the street, mud reached over the ankles. It was quiet here, the fire far away, the streets deserted. Thanakar sat down on a projecting beam while the policeman walked around. Near his hand, a bird huddled disconsolately among some bricks, ruffling its green feathers.

When the man had gone, Thanakar asked among the neighbors. They told him nothing, in many cringing and resentful ways. They were interested in money. They hated him. One old woman with blue teeth said, 'No good ever came from your kind. Not for poor folk. Nothing but trouble . . . sir,' and she cocked her head in the direction of the burned house.

But he found a little girl who told him. She was dressed in yellow rags. Sitting beside him on her porch, kicking her feet, wiping her nose along her arm, she told him how she had crept out that night to watch the house burn down, and how she saw the officers of the purge, in black boots and black uniforms, standing silhouetted by the flames, their horses stamping and tossing their heads. The roof had given way in an avalanche of sparks, and one of the horses had kicked back on its hind legs and pulled its bridle free. Standing on the ground, its rider had raised his whip and cursed.

'But the family?' interrupted Thanakar gently. It was starting to get dark. On the horizon, the sun had dropped below the clouds, and it glinted on the brass roofs of the pagodas and, just visible atop its pillar, the statue of Mara Starbridge wrestling the hierophant. Some women picked miserably through the mud, down towards one of the shrines at the bottom of the street, tolling hand bells.

The little girl swung and kicked her legs. Seriously, without a trace of fear, she told how she had seen a man and a woman handcuffed, gagged, led away. 'Ama came to find me,' she said. 'She told me to get back inside. But I saw them through the window.'

'There was a little girl about your age. A little younger.'

She wiped her nose along her arm. 'I know. Jenny

309

Pentecost. The freak. I called her that because she had a mark right here.' The girl gestured towards her cheek. 'A devil mark. Ama says she should have painted her face.'

'Did you see her?'

'No. Ama says it isn't right. She says it brings 'spicions down on everyone. She never went to prayer school. She never went outside.'

'You didn't see her – that night?'

'No. I just told you.'

His leg hurt. He turned his face into the sun, where it showed in a cleft between two hills. It would have been restful, he thought, to live in an antinomial country, where the laws of cause and effect had been repealed, where actions had no consequences. Here, he felt chained to many deaths – Charity Starbridge, the Pentecosts. Without his attention to distinguish them, they would have escaped notice. He thought: there is a disease in my hands which pollutes everything I touch.

The little girl beside him kicked her legs. Her upper lip was covered with a small moustache of snot. She stroked it with her forefinger.

Thanakar got to his feet. It was night by the time he reached home. A policeman had come by when he was out, but the antinomial had killed him and dragged his body into the princess's room, where he sat perched on the man's buttocks, playing his glass flute. The princess lay listening on her stomach on the bed. The little notes penetrated the walls, and Mrs Cassimer put her fingers in her ears. 'I couldn't keep the servants,' she said. 'They left. They're gone. Oh, sir, you can't leave me here with them. Promise me. The chauffeur had a pet fish. They ate it.'

Smiling, he promised, and then he broke his promise almost instantly, for when the purge came back in force that night, Thanakar let himself be taken. He met the soldiers outside in the corridor, where the music of the flute was less. They didn't search the house.

The soldiers weren't authorized to touch him, but they had brought a young curate with them, who tied a silken rope around his wrists. Thanakar's neighbor, a retired brigadier, stood in his doorway in shirtsleeves, his hands on his hips. 'What's this?' he asked.

'I'm being arrested.'

'Filthy pigs. What's the charge?'

'Adultery.'

'Lucky dog,' said the brigadier. 'Sign of the times. Never would have happened in my time. Just as well. What's the news from the front?'

They chatted about relatives until the priest pulled Thanakar away.

At nightfall, violence overtook the day's chaos in the streets, and gangs of armed men clashed at the street corners, under a light rain. The sky burned red, as if beyond every horizon the city was consumed. It was an illusion still; the houses were too wet to burn except where the fire had first started. That day the bishop's council had imposed a curfew, and every shrine had announced the news that the church would confiscate the families of rioters, looters, drunks, or absentees. Nevertheless, east, west, and south the highways were choked with runaways, running nowhere and taking their families with them. In most cases they went prematurely, fire and flood still miles from their houses. But their minds were prey to rumors from their great-grandfather's time, and his great-grandfather's, and every spring since the birth of Angkhdt. Every spring, fire and water had destroyed the city. Panic was in the smoky air. Strange sights and miracles were reported. As the purge hurried Thanakar along the street,

311

he saw an adventist preacher in the middle of a seething crowd, announcing some new and catastrophic portent of the second coming. Beside him stood a flagellant, naked to the waist, whipping himself till the blood ran down his shoulders. The torches shone on his dull, stupid face. All around, factions of heretics struggled in the mud: rebel angels, adventists, deserters, sodomites, spies. Beating great drums, dupes and agents of King Argon Starbridge marched under an effigy of the dog-headed prince. That at least would bring out the purge, thought Thanakar, but there was not even a policeman watching. His own guards hid their badges in their cloaks and kept to the shadows and the smaller alleyways.

'Where are you taking me?' asked Thanakar. They had paused to let a mob of heretics go by, rough men in from some farm, aimless and determined, carrying pikes and sickles and a symbol Thanakar didn't recognize, sheaves of cut grass hanging from the ends of poles. The curate knew it. He cowered in the shadows, making the sign of the unclean. 'My God,' he moaned. 'How many of them are there? There's not wood enough in all the world to burn them all. This month the Inquisition sat in shifts, even more since Lord Chrism made his proclamation. G-God help me. He'll never, ever catch them all. Every one he traps has made a dozen converts.' The curate was a small man with a drunkard's bloated face, a drunkard's sniveling. 'God help us all,' he said softly.

'Where are you taking me?'

'Wanhope Prison. I'm sorry, Captain. B-believe me. The case has been decided.'

'What about the other defendant?'

'The lady?'

'Yes.'

'Th-that was a mistake,' said the curate. 'A cruel mistake.

312

Since Chrism's proclamation there have been more, I-I admit it. These are sinful times. I don't judge you. With evil spread to such high places, how can ordinary men keep clean?'

'Is she still alive?'

The curate bit his lip. 'N-no,' he said. 'It was to be expected. She came from a proud family. Sister to a martyred saint.'

'A saint?'

'That's what men say.'

'Rejoice at every death,' suggested the Starbridge catechism. Thanakar turned his face away. He too was from a proud family. 'Were they burned?' he asked. The mob had passed, the street was quiet.

'Yes. N-no. I've said enough,' stammered the curate. 'A man must be careful, since Lord Chrism . . .'

'Damn you, what proclamation?'

The curate opened his mouth, astonished. 'Y-you haven't heard?'

'I've been with the army.'

'Even so.' He seemed uncertain, then he spoke. 'The bishop's secretary . . . was . . . used to be . . . Chrism Demiurge. Lord Chrism, now. He's taken a new title, while confirmation is still coming from the emperor. The bishop's been deposed.'

'What?'

'She's to be burned, they say. Witchcraft.' The curate bent close. 'They say she has a p-penis growing between her breasts. A man's p-penis. Here.' He touched Thanakar's chest. He was an alcoholic. He wore too much perfume not to be covering up some other odor. Thanakar turned away, nauseated. 'He calls himself Lord Chrism,' said the curate, bringing his face still closer. 'He's searching for a

313

wide appeal. Some of the adventists are already calling him a g-god.'

Thanakar laughed. 'That's heresy,' he said.

'He's not responsible for what they say. In a weaker man, yes, I suppose it might be heresy. But he is a strong man. He has the council behind him.' He looked away. 'It makes no difference. He was always the power in this city. It's just a matter of a name.'

'And an execution.'

'Yes. P-poor child. A p-penis.'

They were standing in the shelter of an archway. The soldiers of Thanakar's guard had waited patiently in the rain, but as the two men talked, ragged men with rifles had started gathering at the bottom of their street, carrying some flag, chanting some slogan. A second-lieutenant of the purge had waited patiently at Thanakar's side, nursing a cigarette. Now he came up and saluted. 'My lords,' he said, 'we can't stop here. It's too dangerous. It's the festival tonight, in honor of the new saint. Starting at midnight. We'll have to be at Wanhope Prison before then, sir.'

'B-but we are on a holy errand,' said the curate. 'In Lord Chrism's name.'

'Tell it to them.' The lieutenant jerked his thumb back down the street. The crowd had gotten closer. One of their banners unfurled next to a streetlight. 'October 47th,' it read. 'A Festival of Faith.' Red letters on a white ground, and underneath, a phoenix rising from a nest of flame. In front of the crowd, a man and woman danced drunkenly, waving a jug. When they saw the curate's red robes, they gave a shout.

'That's it,' said the lieutenant. 'Come on.' He set off up the street in the opposite direction. The curate followed. Thanakar tried to lag behind, but the other guards grabbed

314

him, forgetting their manners in their fright. Some shots
whistled over their heads.

The lieutenant led them cleverly, and in a few minutes
they had outdistanced all pursuit. They rested and went
on, but the streets around Wanhope Prison had been
barricaded. The rain had gotten heavier, and they stood in
the mud watching the flow of people past the checkpoint.

'Can't we go on?' asked Thanakar. 'I'm looking forward
to a nice dry cell.'

The curate ignored him. He crouched down on his
haunches next to the lieutenant, peering at the soldiers at
the barricade. 'Can you see their markings?' he asked.

'Plain red, sir. They're parsons sure enough.'

'Yes, but what congregation? Can you see?'

'No, sir. It's all one to me. We'll go on.'

The curate fingered his jaw. 'Well,' he said. 'I-it should
be. Things are so complicated since the proclamation. It's
hard to know.' He looked up at the night sky, shrugged,
and stood up. 'We'll risk it,' he said. 'There's not much
choice.' Behind them, another crowd was gathering, singing drunken songs.

The barricade was a haphazard structure of wooden
sawhorses and cinderblocks flung across the street. Wires
were strung between the houses, and bare electric bulbs
burned from the tops of poles. Soldiers and priests stood
under a corrugated iron shelter and warmed themselves
before a bonfire. All around, the rain crackled and spattered as it hit the flames, the sugar igniting, the water
putting it out. This uncertain balance made the air glow
around their heads, and as Thanakar and the rest filed past
the sentry box, the doctor heard a roaring in his ears. The
curate stood behind him, nervously shuffling, and when he
was close enough to see the man in the box, he swore and
clutched the doctor by his knotted wrists, trying to pull

315

him back into the street. But there were too many people behind them, and as the curate struggled back, soldiers crossed through the sawhorses on either side of him and plucked him out of line. They were soldiers of the purge, but Thanakar noticed that each carried an additional insignia pinned under the silver dog's head on his collar, a sprig of lily of the valley made of paper and green wire, the bishop's own symbol. Their officer wore a chain of it around his neck. He was a monk in the military order of St Lucan the Unmarred, and Thanakar recognized him – Malabar Starbridge, second cousin to Charity and the prince, and a former patient. He was a small unmutilated man in a red uniform.

'Stop, Cousin. What's your hurry?' he asked.

'P-p-prisoner for Wanhope,' stammered the curate. 'B-b-bishop's orders.'

Brother Malabar turned to look. 'Doctor,' he said. 'I hoped they wouldn't find you. I hoped you were far away.'

'I had to come back.'

The monk looked at him and nodded. 'Let me untie you,' he said. And over his shoulder, to the curate: 'Have you a warrant for this man?'

The curate shuffled underneath his robe, hesitated, and drew his hands back empty. 'I-I seem to have lost it,' he said.

'No, sir,' corrected his lieutenant, grinning. 'It's in your upper pocket, sir.'

The curate gave him a vicious look. 'Ah, y-yes. Th-thank you.' He made as if to look for it, but Brother Malabar seized him by the front of his cassock, thrust his hand in, and drew out a crumpled paper. 'Thanakar Starbridge,' he read, and flipped it over to look at the signature. 'Signed by the usurper's own hand. Chrism Demiurge. Are you familiar with this name, Doctor?'

316

'I know him well.'

'I always hated him. We'll hang him higher than a bird. This signature,' he continued, turning back to the curate, 'has no purchase here. Do you know your prisoner's identity?'

'Y-yes.'

'No. Look here.' Brother Malabar pulled back his long hair to show his silver ear, miraculously curled and delicate, and the silver hinge of his jaw, melting into skin. 'The doctor healed me when I was almost dead. Fighting for the bishop back when you were still sucking cocks in seminary. Back when you had a cock to suck. You heard about my cousins?' he asked Thanakar.

'No. I . . . have to know.'

'I'll tell you. Demiurge is murdering the old families.' He turned. 'You are free to go,' he told the curate. 'Tell your master that I'll tear down Wanhope stone by stone unless he lets them go. The usurper,' he said to Thanakar, 'has imprisoned four brothers of my order. For photographing convicts inside the Mountain of Redemption. All relatives of ours.'

'The convicts?'

'The photographers. The convicts, too, soon enough. I tell you it's critical.'

Thanakar's curate had already gone. His guard, too, seemed to have disappeared, except for the lieutenant, who stood grinning. 'Excuse me, sir,' he said. 'You wouldn't have an extra one of those flowers.'

'Certainly,' answered the monk, unpinning one from his own collar.

'Thank you. I gave my oath to the bishop herself, when I came of age. My old mother had a growth . . .'

'Good man,' said the monk absently. He pointed to the bonfire, where soldiers were roasting turnips on the ends of bayonets. 'Are you hungry?' And without waiting for an answer, he led Thanakar across the street and through a broken shopfront window into a makeshift wardroom. Officers of various services sat smoking marijuana in small groups. It was a cheerless, cavernous place, lit with dim bulbs.

Malabar Starbridge was a forceful man, but he lacked dignity. 'That piece of scum,' he remarked, lugging chairs into an empty corner. They sat down, and the monk leaned back so that his trousers rode up tight around his thighs. 'That piece of scum,' he repeated, his fingers clasped behind his neck. 'He means to burn her. Cosro Starbridge's own daughter. I saw the pyre in Kindness and Repair. It's higher than this ceiling. Witchcraft – damn!' He swiveled forward. He was constantly in motion, scratching, twisting, as if he could never find a position that was comfortable. He would contort his face into odd shapes and keep them until everyone around him was uneasy. It was a habit that made people expect him to stammer or stutter, but in fact he spoke fluidly and extremely fast. This combination of mannerisms made him a hard man to take seriously. Thanakar was grateful to him. Bad news might seem bearable from such distracting lips.

'Have you ever seen her?' demanded the monk, twisting his arm over his head to grab hold of his ear. He was talking about the bishop.

'From a distance.' Thanakar paused, then continued, 'Tell me about Charity Starbridge.'

'You're to blame for it,' exclaimed the monk severely, screwing the heel of his hand into one eye. 'By God you're to blame.' He glared at him and sat back.

'I know.'

'Don't say that. They're to blame. The evidence wasn't enough to swing a cat. A washerwoman's testimony – there

318

was something on the sheets. A laundress – her blood wasn't even good enough to make a deposition. Charity Starbridge never even could have been arrested on the evidence they had, not without a full confession. By that time she was a widow, for God's sake. And she wouldn't tell them anything. Not one word. Not her. But Chrism wanted her confession. So he lied to her. He told her you yourself had brought the charge, claiming you had been infected. Morally infected; physically . . . I don't know. He didn't care. It was you he wanted. He wanted her testimony so that he could hang you. But she refused to say a word against you. She poisoned herself. Two days ago.' The monk broke off, tears in the corners of his eyes. He flicked them away with his thumbnail, a gesture so unnatural that it absorbed all of Thanakar's attention.

'And did she confess?'

'Not one word, I tell you. Not one word,' the monk repeated, a little bitterly. 'She was a proud woman. But look at this. She left a note.' He pulled a paper from his sleeve. 'I received it this morning. Next-of-kin. It's tragic. The old families are almost gone.' He spread the paper out on his knee. It was filled with a complicated, beautiful unknown script, illuminated with gold and scarlet.

'What does it say?' asked Thanakar.

The monk peered at it. 'It's the language of the prophets,' he said doubtfully. 'She always was a clever girl. I didn't think anyone still knew it.'

'What does it say?'

'It says, "Goodbye."'

'Just . . . goodbye?' asked Thanakar, looking at the maze of paint and letters.

'Goodbye,' repeated the monk, twisting up his face. 'That is a rough translation. Those prophets never meant

319

exactly what they said.' He turned away, stroking his silver ear.

'May I have it?' asked Thanakar.

Uncomfortable, the monk got up. He paced behind his chair, making quick, random gestures with his arms. 'I'm not sure she meant it for you,' he said.

Thanakar stayed seated, looking at the floor between his feet. 'This might sound strange to you,' he said. 'But I didn't know her very well.'

The monk made an irritated gesture. 'Who knows women well?' he asked. 'Who knows anybody well? This is not the season for sentimental friendships,' he said, tears in his eyes. 'Not the weather for it. They say my grandparents loved each other. A family legend. No. Don't flatter yourself. Charity Starbridge had a fine marriage. The commissar was like a father to her.'

'He was a good man.'

'I'm glad you thought so,' said the monk bitterly. 'Did you see him die?'

'I was with him. Then I left.'

'Was it a good death?'

'Beautiful.'

'God bless him for it,' said the monk, picking his nose. 'Abu, too, they say, and who could have expected that? A prince at last, they said. Blood will tell, I suppose.'

'Tell me about Abu.'

In another corner of the room, men sat talking in low voices, passing a cigarette. Brother Malabar glanced at them moodily, and gestured past them through the window, towards the glow above the town. 'He's responsible for this fire,' he said.

'Was that the charge against him?'

'No. Drunk and disorderly.'

Thanakar smiled. 'That's not a capital offense.'

The monk shrugged and sat down. 'Homicide, then. I don't know. Seven people died in the first explosion, and more than sixty beggars. I know, it's not much of a crime, for a prince, but Demiurge is mad, I tell you. The inquisition has been sitting day and night. Ten Starbridges have been condemned, and the others in batches of a hundred. He was the first of such high rank.'

'Was it a public execution?'

'I didn't see it. Brother Lacrima says he stood up straight. The rest all begged for mercy, but he didn't. I'm glad to hear it. Of course, they'd locked a mask over his face and gloves on his hands. I'm not sure he could have spoken even if he'd wanted to. Unnecessary, really – everybody knew who he was. Anyway, he made a good impression. He never made a sound, even when the fire was around his legs, and God knows that's uncommon.'

'I heard he was canonized,' said Thanakar softly.

'That. Oh yes, well – that's just foolishness. You know how things get started. Beggars get excited in the calmest times. They're desperate now.'

'Tell me.'

The monk closed both his eyes and stuck his thumb into his ear. 'At first, when he was arrested, they didn't know who he was,' he said after a pause. 'That was last Friday. They had him in a common cell. He was so dirty, and he didn't draw attention to himself. It was only when he came to trial that he was recognized. By that time it had been five days. You know – he let them touch him. They were always touching him, even when he was asleep. You know what they're like. Most of them had never seen a Star-bridge up close before, let alone a prince. And when he was awake, they sat around him in a circle. He promised he'd take them all with him to his palace up in Paradise. He heard their confessions, gave them absolution. It was like playing with children. And when two old women were freed on some technical grounds – innocence or something – they called it a miracle. He was executed yesterday. There must have been twenty thousand people there.'

The monk leaned forward, his hands clasped in front of him. 'That much is fact,' he said. 'The rest is lies. They say they saw him drinking in a bar yesterday evening. And then these same two women spread the story that when they took him down out of the ashes, his body was as clean as if he had died in his sleep – no trace of fire on him. That's an obvious lie. But listen to this. This was unusual. A man dressed up as a parson – he had only one leg, or else it was tied up – or I don't know, maybe he was a parson. He said he was the bishop's messenger, sent to crush the rumors. He was going to exhibit the prince's ashes publicly. So he rang the bells in Durbar Square and collected a huge crowd, and broke the seal off some casket he had brought. It had birds in it. Red pigeons and white doves. Why are you laughing?'

'It's a miracle,' said Thanakar.

'It's a fucking scandal,' said the monk. It's a mockery of holiness. What are they going to call him? Abu the Inebriate?'

'Abu the Fool.'

'Don't laugh. It's not funny.'

Thanakar laughed. 'I'm happy for him,' he said. 'It's perfect for him. He was . . . such a stupid fool,' he said, putting his fingers to his forehead.

'You think he should be canonized for that? I tell you it's a mockery.'

'Don't be a prude. It's not such an exclusive club, the saints. Others have deserved it less.'

'Don't say that,' said the monk, dropping his voice, looking around.

'Come on. I thought you people were revolutionaries.'

'No. Chrism's the usurper. We're loyalists. We've got our own inquisition.' He motioned with his head towards the far corner, where some officers sat smoking. 'They've already had a man whipped for perversion. A captain of the purge.'

'What for?'

'It's not important. Something about a runaway named Pentecost. A nobody.'

This coincidence struck Thanakar so forcibly that he allowed the conversation to progress a little further before be brought it back. It seemed astonishing that this odd, twitching man had carried in his mind a name so vital; astonishing that their talk had uncovered it in such a way, when so easily he could have chosen some other combination of remarks, and Thanakar never would have known. It made him wonder how many other people that he met, at parties, perhaps, or people that he passed in the streets without a word, carried vital information with them like unopened packages, and he never knew. He was happy, now, that when this man had appeared on his table months before, almost dead, he had worked so carefully as to leave a sense of debt behind with that new ear, inserted in that new piece of brain.

'Pentecost,' he said.

'Yes, do you know him? Chrism gave special orders to have them rounded up, I don't know why. Though if you know them perhaps that explains it.'

'Yes. That explains it.'

'They were hung,' said the monk, sucking one finger.

Thanakar looked down at the floor. 'There was a little girl . . .'

'Yes. That's the point of the story. This captain saved her life. He was . . . What shall I say? Attracted to her. When he came to us, the girl was still living with him. We made him give her up. They did,' said the monk, jerking his head towards the far corner of the room. 'They had him whipped. I had nothing to do with it. I hate that sort of thing. She had a birthmark.'

'I know.'

The monk looked at him distastefully. 'Don't tell me – you too?' he asked.

'Nothing like that.'

'I'm glad to hear it. It's a filthy habit. Hard to break, too. He still visits her.'

'Nothing like that,' repeated Thanakar. 'I knew her father.'

'That explains it. The captain is a very disgusting fellow, if you want to know.' Malabar Starbridge jumped up out of his chair. Hunching his shoulders to indicate secrecy, he pulled Thanakar to the window and pointed into the mass of men around the bonfire. 'There he is,' he said, lowering his voice conspiratorially, though the man was thirty feet away.

'Which one?'

'That one.' A man stood away from the others. He wore the purple rosette of a child abuser on his uniform's lapel. His eyebrows joined over his nose.

Since the day that he had killed the bishop's liaison, on the plain below St Serpentine's, Doctor Thanakar had found it difficult to hate. He had felt no remorse. But it was as if the action of striking something foul had cracked the cavity in him where his hate was stored, and it had drained away. All his life he had hated so passionately, tenderly, articulately. All other feelings had been muffled and chaotic in comparison. Without hate, he had been left with an empty feeling, an anaesthesia for which he had been grateful in a way, for it had helped him to tolerate the death of friends. Now, watching the degenerate captain standing near the bonfire, warming his hands, he was resensitized. The man had a protruding lower lip. He would be easy to hate. And suddenly Thanakar was conscious of a new, pervasive, almost physical pain, like the pain of blood returning to a sleeping limb. Abu the Inebriate, he thought. He looked down at Charity Starbridge's last letter. Goodbye, he thought.

'I don't know how to thank you,' he said.

The monk looked away, twisting his face into a scowl. 'Don't mention it,' he muttered. 'We've got to stick together, the old families. There're not many of us left.'

'I wish I could repay you.'

'I need men,' said the monk, eyeing Thanakar's leg. 'Demiurge has fifteen hundred soldiers at the temple. He means to burn her. I wish him luck. She has powers he's never seen. Even so, if it comes to fighting . . .'

Thanakar frowned. 'Have you written to the colonel?'

'Aspe? What for? He'd be glad to see her burn.'

'No. She . . . means something to him. Just the way she looks. Some kind of symbol. Beauty in the heart of ugliness.' Outside the window, the pervert was picking his lip. It slid down over rotten teeth.

People broke into the clocktower in Durbar Square to ring the stroke of midnight: ten crashing strokes, and then a paean of joy. 'Ten o'clock,' said the pervert. Like many of his kind, he was an unimaginative man and had not responded to questions or entreaties, not to violence or the threat of violence, not to scandal or the threat of scandal, but to the promise of a fee. Thanakar had promised him eleven dollars and put a spark into his sullen eye. Thanakar hated him for it. He had a long thin face.

They stood on the steps of a dismal building – half

shrine, half labor exchange – looking out over the crowd. The pervert had taken him into the city's stews, by rickshaw, until the ways got too thick, and then on foot. Thanakar felt vital and self-confident, full of hope and hate. His mood had changed in a few hours, and around him, too, the mood had changed. The streets still seethed with people, but it had stopped raining, and in the atmosphere there was a current of joy that had been absent earlier. Only a few people carried weapons or seemed inclined to need them. With the tolling of midnight and the start of the festival, people had forgotten, not their differences, but at least their animosity. The bishop's shops were looted and burning along the major thoroughfares, but to Thanakar that was a pleasant sight. People had smiled to see him, reached out to touch him as he passed. Sustained by the example of the new saint, he had not turned away. Women yelled and pointed from upstairs windows.

Abandoning the rickshaw, they had gone on deeper into the city's muddy heart. At midnight, in the bishop's market, a crowd had gathered among the boarded stalls. A man stood on a barrel, gesticulating and shouting in a language so debased that Thanakar could only recognize one word in ten. Perhaps that wasn't it, he thought guiltily. The man was far away from where they stood on the steps of the labor exchange, and his shouting was muddled in the noises of the crowd. Even so, thought Thanakar, Abu would have had no trouble understanding.

'What is he saying?' he asked. And again, 'What is he saying?' The pervert had turned away down the steps, muttering something inaudible. 'Wait,' said Thanakar. 'I want to watch.'

The square was lit with torches and uneven fires from gutted buildings. The sky burned orange, as if traces still lingered from a malignant sunset. But as the shouting stopped and the people grew so still that Thanakar fancied he could hear them breathe, a new kind of light spread out humbly from among them. Men and women produced lumps of candles from underneath their ragged clothes. As they lit them, one from another, tentacles of light seemed to reach down the dark alleyways, and the center of the square seemed to burn up bright, the torches and the bonfires overwhelmed in a gentle golden radiance. There was no wind. People stood without talking, almost without moving. The candle flames burned straight and gentle, and then there was a slight commotion in the middle of the crowd as women unwrapped baskets of birds, red and white doves. They held them up and coaxed them into the air; having spent so long in blinded baskets, they seemed unwilling to go, and when they finally rose one by one into the dark, it was with no great rustling or flapping, but they went gently. Thanakar watched them, his heart full of a kind of happiness. Men pulled a banner to the top of a flagpole – the sun in splendor, gold silk on white. There was not a breath of air. The flag seemed to grasp the flagpole like a flaccid hand until the birds, curling up around it, fanned it with their wings, uncoiled it slightly on their living wind. Thanakar caught a glimpse of the design.

'They're celebrating the new saint,' said the pervert. 'Adventist pigs!' He stood picking his lips. Then he walked away without another word, down the concrete steps, hands in pockets, and Thanakar had to run to catch him. It was difficult. His leg was hurting him. He had worked it mercilessly for days, and now his kneecap had dried out. The joint worked mechanically, without strength, and made a strange clicking noise. Hurrying down the steps, he almost fell. 'Wait!' he commanded, but the shadow in

327

front of him flickered up the street. Enraged he hurried on, his kneecap clattering.

He paused to rest under the façade of a broken building. The sky burned redder here. The alleyway ran uphill to Beggar's Medicine; ahead, the pervert stopped under a streetlamp and leaned against the pole.

For almost an hour the man mocked him, far ahead, out of sight, hurrying onward when Thanakar hurried to catch up, stopping when he stopped, exhausted. The streets were echoing and empty, and sometimes Thanakar would recognize the same configurations and realize that the man had led him in a circle, but still the doctor kept on, muttering imprecations and promising cold murder. In the end, the pervert waited for him under a row of houses, and his face, as Thanakar limped up, was so empty that the doctor found himself doubting any motive in him but stupidity. He sat down on the gutterstone to find his breath. The pervert leaned against a wall. He chewed gum and threw the wrapper into the mud.

There was life here. Men sold food from wheeled stalls under a cluster of acetylene lamps: messes of noodles and artificial cabbage, cakes of edible plastic developed by the bishop's council. In a vacant lot, people lived under tarpaulins or in huts made of burlap and corrugated iron. People sat on plywood laid over the mud. Their bones showed, and they shivered in the warm air. Near Thanakar, some crippled women begged, their faces wrapped in white gauze. But most took no notice of him. Instead, they stared at the pervert with dull intensity, as if they were trying to remember why they found him interesting. He was an important man here with his black uniform, his cracked lips.

Across the road, another celebration had started. A barrel of gin had been broached in front of a dilapidated tavern, while the barkeep ladled out smoking dollops into cardboard cups under a red-and-white painted sign of doves copulating, their beaks twisted into leers. 'Come, gentlemen,' he called. 'It's free tonight, in honor of the festival. Free tonight, while it lasts.' On the corner under the lamp, a man vomited into the gutter.

'That's not a very good advertisement,' remarked Thanakar.

'He's not a true devotee,' laughed the barman. 'Now the saint, the saint could have drunk down this whole cask and still walked home. He once drank down a bottle in this very house and never even stopped for breath. If that's not a miracle, I don't know what is. These folks,' he gestured with his ladle down the road. 'Weak stomachs. Can't blame 'em.'

Thanakar got up and limped across the road. He reached his hand out for a cup. The barman poured him a huge portion, and with streaming eyes and burning tongue, he drank it down, in honor of the prince. He felt pollution coursing through his blood, and motioning to the barman to fill the cup again, he drank again to Abu the Undefiled. Dignity is the least important thing, he thought, drunkenness hitting him like a slap.

'Well done, sir,' said the barman. 'I can tell you're a gentleman. What's your name?'

'Thanakar Starbridge.'

The barman cocked an eye. 'My cousin,' said Thanakar, responding to the unasked question.

'Well then, God bless you, sir,' said the man, winking facetiously. 'Pretty soon, we'll have all the nobs down here. You're not with him, are you?' he asked, gesturing towards where the pervert stood picking his lips until they bled.

'Not in the sense you mean.'

'Stay away from him, sir. He's a stinker.'

'He's a scumbag,' agreed Thanakar companionably. But at that moment, as if to demonstrate their connection, the pervert took off again, and Thanakar put down his cup and followed. The pervert paused at the head of the street and climbed the steps of a house there. Thanakar climbed after him, his kneecap rattling.

It was a richly furnished house, of ill repute and bad smells, the kind the nose instinctively connects with vice. And even though Thanakar could identify only cigarettes and perfume as he stepped into the hall, the smell seemed to combine with the velvet upholstery and flowered carpets and unlock a host of dark associations as a key might unlock an armoire full of secrets. Furniture that elsewhere might have been considered sumptuous, here seemed tainted. Such elegance in such a place seemed to stink of softness and corruption, and brutal empty lives, and consciences so tender that they needed cosseting. Gilt chandeliers hung from high ceilings, blazing with light. There were no shadows anywhere. In a parlor off the hallway the pervert sat at ease in an armchair of carved wood and fat upholstery. In other parlors, poisonous well-dressed men talked in low voices or sipped pale wine.

A gong sounded as the street door closed, and a woman came into the hallway, a wineglass in her hand. She was plump and pretty, with a dress that lapped the carpet – an old-fashioned style and an autumn color that contrasted wistfully with the spring green walls. Thanakar took a few steps forward and he saw a quick sly look disturb her features, like an olive dropped into a cocktail, or a pebble dropped into a pool. His limp had gotten much worse that day. In the woman's pretty face, he saw a question quickly asked and quickly answered, and afterwards her face resumed its placid surface. She smiled.

'Sweet to see you, dearie, I insist,' she said, in the

accents and locutions of a previous generation. But the warmth of her welcome was interrupted by the pervert, who came to stand beside her. He whispered in her ear, and Thanakar could see a pebble of surprise dropped in before her face re-formed. She smiled again, but as she broke away from the pervert and came towards him Thanakar could see her hesitate, unsure of how to greet him or whether to offer him a glass of wine. They can't be used to Starbridge customers, he thought.

The woman curtsied and reached her hand out for the doctor's raincoat. 'We are honored,' she murmured, making the gestures of respect. 'You will find us . . . very clean.'

Behind her, the pervert sneered. 'He's not interested in that. Not this one. He wants to see her.' And to Thanakar, 'She's available for half an hour or an hour. Though I usually take four,' he added with a kind of bitterness.

'Hush, no need for that,' said the woman. 'No need for that, I insist. I'm sure his lordship will be . . .' She broke off, smiling.

Nauseated suddenly by the smell of perfume and cigarettes, Thanakar turned away. He wiped his mouth along the back of his hand and inhaled the odors of his own skin, liberated by the moisture. 'I won't be long,' he said. 'Be prepared to let me take her away. I am a rich man,' he said, moving his lip along his thumb towards the tattoo of the key which opened all doors. 'Where is she?'

The pervert's mouth gaped open, 'Tricked, by God – hyprocrite! Eleven dollars, my God,' he snarled, grabbing Thanakar by the forearm. 'Starbridge scum, you can't take her away from me.'

Instantly masked bouncers materialized on either side of him, as if conjured from the air. They pulled his hand away and forced his arms behind his back. 'I'm a very rich man,' repeated Thanakar mercilessly, drunkenly.

The pervert burst into hoarse weeping, though no tears came. 'Tricked!' he cried. 'By God, if I had known, I never would have led you here. Not for eleven hundred dollars.' His voice rose into a scream as the bouncers behind him tightened their grip. It shut off like water from a faucet as one of them twisted his wrist. And in the sudden silence, women appeared out of various doors of the rooms that lined the hallway. 'Mrs Silkskin,' said Thanakar's hostess to one of them. 'Could you fetch the little priestess? Pack her clothes.'

'She can't walk,' said the woman doubtfully.

'Fetch her, dearie, I insist,' repeated the hostess. 'Marco will help you.' She turned back to the doctor. 'Please, my lord, let me take you somewhere where we can talk. Would you like a glass of wine? I can open a new bottle.'

'No,' said Thanakar, smelling the back of his hand. 'Where is she? We'll settle the money later. I want to see her . . . the way you have her.'

'Hypocrite!' cried the pervert. 'Starbridge pederast! Liar! By God, the end is coming for your kind. Your airs and graces. I'll live to see you . . .' His voice rose high, and again it was shut off.

'Where is she?' asked Thanakar.

His hostess made a small gesture with her eyes, and Mrs Silkskin stepped forward. 'Come with me, sir,' she said, curtseying.

The hallway was full of appraising eyes. Passing them, climbing the twisting stairs, Thanakar cursed his limp, the rattle in his knee. His guide kept her face averted and went slowly. A kindhearted woman, he thought gratefully. She waited for him at the landings. And at the top of the stairwell, they passed through a doorway and through velvet curtains into a small room furnished like a shrine. The eternal blue flame burned across the surface of a bowl of water on an altar, and in the sanctuary a statue of Beloved Angkhdt reclined on a low dais, his tongue hanging out of his long jaw, two hands clasped around the base of his phallus. With another hand he supported himself upright, and his fourth arm stretched out in front of him. He held a curious symbol balanced on his palm, a high-arched model of a woman's foot, cut off at the ankle. Around him, the walls were painted with lascivious scenes. Ornate letters gleamed in the mosaic of the floor, a persistent mistranslation of the Song of Angkhdt: 'My love, I kiss the inside of your foot. More tender than any flower, riper than any fruit is the flesh there.' In certain southern dialects, old words for fruit and a woman's sex were spelled the same.

Jenny lay in an alcove, supported on silk pillows. Her small body was washed and perfumed; and dressed in the immodest fashion of southern priestesses. It left her chest and shoulders bare. Her hair was piled high on top of her head and fastened with a comb of sandalwood. She wore carved bracelets of the same material, and her face was painted, the mark on her face painted away. Her lips and eyelids were a shining green. And her feet were bound together at the ankles, and tied cruelly so that her naked insteps pressed together, the space between them a cruel parody of a woman's sex. She didn't raise her head when Thanakar stepped towards her, or recognize him when he knelt down.

He could see the skin had already started to grow together on her heels, and along the balls of her feet. He took his penknife out to slice the ropes apart, and Jenny looked at it with eyes so full of sadness that he paused. Mrs

333

Silkskin stood behind him. 'Doesn't she have any decent clothes?' he asked.

'No sir. Most people like her as she is.'

'Then bring me a blanket. Something to wrap her in. Have a covered rickshaw waiting at the door.' He reached into his pocket and took out a fat purse. 'Give this to your mistress,' he said. 'Silver and gold – she'll have to use gloves.'

At dawn, soldiers had attacked the Temple of Kindness and Repair, seeking to free the bishop. By evening they had broken through into the outer courts. Lord Chrism sat on his veranda under a cool, wet sky, talking to his disciple while seminarians played gongs and xylophones behind a wooden screen. This music was the softest and most soothing of the fourteen permissible types of sound. It contained a simple melody, and Lord Chrism had asked that the drums be muted, so that he could hear a young nun sing the vague and soporific story of the world's creation. She had a lovely voice, and the distant sound of gunshots and explosions seemed to mix with it and find its way among the deep-bellied gongs and cymbals like another instrument. Lord Chrism sipped a glass of wine. Underneath his robes, goblins and cherubs yawned and slumbered, invisible and forgotten.

'I have a memory of Paradise,' he was saying. 'A very faint one. The prophets tell us that the sun shines so brightly there, objects have no shape and bodies no form. Permit me to doubt it. I am blind, and objects have no shape for me. So I know that it is not there that evil resides. That is not the difference between Paradise and Earth. Blind as I am, I can still see color most precisely. My old master told me Paradise would be . . . what? We would float as if in a sea of colour.' He laughed, a dry rustle in his throat. 'Permit me to doubt it. He was completely blind in the last years of his life, as if he lived at the bottom of a well. Completely blind. I think men build the frame of heaven out of what they never had, but they furnish it with memories of what they've lost. According to the prophets, it's a place of perfect freedom.' Again Lord Chrism laughed his feathery laugh. 'I am an old man. Yet even so, when I consult my heart and not my head, I picture scenes of endless . . . procreation there. In exquisite detail. More so now, in fact. I remember when I lost my manhood. I never used to think of such things. I was an idealist. I didn't even know what I had sacrificed.'

Behind the screen, the world's prehistory pursued its gentle course, soft brass bells describing the formation of the stratosphere. The old man sipped his wine and squinted out into the waning afternoon. He looked towards the Mountain of Redemption, its impossible bulk wreathed in clouds. 'These days you hardly ever see the lights of the cathedral,' he complained. 'They're always hidden in the clouds. Every night I look for them.' He sighed. 'Perhaps it's fallen down.'

'It's a question of faith,' muttered the disciple.

'Don't be fatuous. Faith doesn't enter into it. Either it has or it hasn't. It's like everything else.' The old man paused, and when he spoke again it was in a softer tone. 'I told you I had lost my idealism. It's strange, because today I will perform the only idealistic action of my life. A paradox. No, because idealists are incapable of action. It takes an old man.' He leaned forward. 'I tell you I will burn her! I will. When I perceive the singer has to raise her voice to cover up the sound of gunfire. Because I used to think with all my heart, and now . . .' He touched his skinny forehead with his fingers. 'Now I know that if there is purity in Paradise, it is maintained by fire.'

335

On the table beside him lay some old books and diagrams. 'Look at this,' he continued, picking up a yellowed sheet. 'In my grandfather's time, a scientist estimated the surface temperature of risen Paradise at 978 degrees. And this.' He pulled out a photograph of a small bright planet passing over a dark larger one. 'It is heresy even to think of these things, but look. This was taken through the telescope at Mt Despane. Look. It is a photograph of Paradise in orbit around Planet Seven. That's the next planet to capture it when we have thrown it off. Look at this enlargement of the surface. Burning gas. What must it be like, I wonder, for our poor souls in such a furnace? Do you understand now when I say that salvation is a chemical process? What can it possibly mean, except that evil must be purged with fire?'

His voice had risen excitedly. But then he calmed himself and rubbed the ridge above his eye. 'When I chose her for my bishop,' he said, softly and sadly, 'it was because I could imagine nothing purer, nothing more innocent than a young girl. The Crystal Spark, I called her. Was I a fool? I tell you, at the beginning I was full of faith.'

The music behind them had progressed into a description of the first protozoa, exquisitely articulated on the hammer dulcimer. Lord Chrism took one of his books into his hands. 'Look at this,' he said, caressing the binding. 'Calf's skin. Two years old. For a long time, I was afraid to touch it. This writer lived before the days of cameras and telescopes. Yet he observed certain phases in the coloring of Paradise, and he concluded that the seasons must change there with incredible rapidity – two hundred, three hundred times in a single lifetime. He writes that all the differences between Paradise and Earth stem from this fact. What would it be like, he asks, if winter didn't last more than a hundred days? What would it be like if the church had no obligation to control men's labor? People could breathe freely. They don't understand. If we let go our grip, every winter they would starve. Every spring.'

'They're starving now.'

'More of them would starve. They would have starved months ago. Have you read the accounts from heathen times, when men farmed their own land? It's terrifying. Think – why should a man store up food for hard times he'll never live to see? Not one man lived out of a hundred. People complain now. What was the difference then between rich and poor?'

Lord Chrism opened up the book and lifted it to within an inch of his blind eyes. He read for a moment in silence, and then he put it down. 'In Paradise,' he said, 'men share the same experiences. Grandfather, father, son, there must be such harmony. But here, a winter mother has perhaps one child. What can she have in common with her granddaughter who has thirty or more? What does a man have in common with his father? . . . What was that?'

A bomb had exploded, not far away. Lord Chrism got slowly to his feet and walked out to the edge of the balcony. The sky was almost dark. Clouds of smoke reeled over the rooftops. The old man sniffed the air. 'It smells like gunpowder,' he said. 'Come in.'

A captain of the purge was standing hesitating in the doorway. He was holding the feet of a dead hawk – the bird stretched snowy white almost to the floor. 'Sir,' he said. 'A message from Father Orison, with the army. Aspe has moved his tent. He's not ten miles from the city walls.'

'Thank you, Captain. What's the fighting like outside?'

'Fierce, sir. We're holding them at Slaver's Gate.'

'Thank you, Is everything prepared?'

'Yes, sir.'

337

'Then let us start.' Lord Chrism lifted his hand up to his disciple. 'Will you help me downstairs?'

Men were already waiting for them in the Courtyard of the Sun and Stars. Soldiers had built a pyramid of wood. And on marble bleachers all around, the council of the Inner Ear sat in their richest clothes. The oldest, deadest ones had been propped up on golden cushions along the higher seats, their headdresses slipping from their naked skulls. Farther down, the priests were mountainous, gorgeous in their scarlet robes, the gaslight shining on their fat. Seminarians and nuns sat cross-legged on the tilestones, with scared, shaved faces and shaved heads.

Through the fingers of the council writhed their telepathic cord. It hummed and crackled, and as the bishop made her appearance it seemed to glow, a ribbon of light snaking between the seats. There was a clamor of voices. At the four corners of the pyre, soldiers held torches.

The bishop stood surrounded by parsons at the end of a long colonnade of soldiers, and Lord Chrism met her there and offered her his arm. Bombs and fireworks burst above them in the darkening sky, and by their intermittent light she appeared pale, dressed in her simplest white shift, her black curls tangled around her shoulders, her beauty undisturbed.

'You have been found guilty of an imperfection, my child,' said Lord Chrism gently. 'A chemical impurity.'

She nodded, and with slow ceremonial steps, in rhythm to the drumbeats of a hidden orchestra, they made their way down towards the pyre. In his most spidery voice, Chrism recited the invocation for the dead, and in their solemn progress, they stopped from time to time to receive offerings and blessings from the priests, and sprinklings of holy vinegar, and invitations to parties up in Paradise. But before they had progressed halfway, the council's ribbon seemed to glow even brighter, because a change could be perceived in the bishop's gait and she seemed to move hunched over, her hands hanging to her knees. Her hair seemed to change its color, and spread over her face, and mix into her clothes, until, by the time she had twisted out of Chrism's grasp and scampered away, she had become a white-maned monkey. In the open space before the pyre, she turned and squatted on her haunches, spitting, and grinning, and stuffing bits of garbage from the tiles into the pouches of her mouth. Lord Chrism spoke an order, and soldiers formed around her in a circle, but before they could come close, she selected one and leapt at him, transforming in mid-leap into a white tiger. She bore the soldier down and mauled his face between her paws; miraculously, when she left him, he jumped up unhurt. It was a game. The soldiers clustered around her, trying to grab hold, and she sank beneath their fingers into a nest of white cobras, dozens of them spreading out along the tiles. Their bites made the soldiers laugh, and in a little while some were reeling drunkenly, intoxicated by her venom, while the others scrambled over the stones, until the cobras stopped their writhing and melted into a white foam like scum along a beach, and some floated up into the air. The soldiers clapped their hands, and some of the seminarians, too, came forward to join in the fun, ignoring the hoarse imprecations of their teachers. And then the foam seemed to gather into a ball, and while the soldiers stood gaping, it spun itself into a spider, a white stag, a cloud of butterflies, and a crocodile, its white fur slick with oil, lashing its prehensile tail. No metamorphosis lasted longer than it took the eye to grasp it, and each one seemed larger than the last, until it formed into a snake again, a white python of enormous bulk. It coiled and towered above their heads, its mouth dripping milky venom. Laughing, the seminarians and nuns ran to drink it up; they sat in pools of it and splashed, while the snake wove and coiled above them. And then, twisting around them in a circle, it coiled down towards the pyre and disappeared among the logs.

Instantly Lord Chrism's voice was heard commanding torches to be laid on. Instantly the fire leapt up, for the latticework of logs had been soaked in gasoline and aromatic oil. At its apex rose a wooden stake. The bishop was to have met death there, tied to it with silken cords. Now she twisted around it in the shape of a python, illuminated by the leaping flames. But then she disappeared, and the stake itself seemed to grow, to flower and take root, roots creeping downwards through the burning logs. The stake bloated, and grew bark, and swelled into a mighty tree, its limbs stretching out over the multitude, arching into a canopy of leaves as if it were midsummer. No one there had seen a tree before, not in full flower, and they stared up at it, enchanted.

The boy could see down into the courtyard through the bars of her cell. He sat at the window while his cat played with the shadows underfoot. And when he saw the fire burning in the lower branches of the tree, he smiled. 'It's wonderful,' he said. 'Can you make oranges grow among the leaves?'

'It's a chestnut tree,' answered the bishop. She stepped from the dark behind him and looked down. Nevertheless, in an instant the boughs were heavy with strange fruits. The boy clapped his hands.

'And can you put a songbird on the topmost branch?' he asked. Instantly a bird darted down from the sky into the foliage. It had long red feathers and a silver voice. 'A firebird,' the boy exclaimed. 'Can you make her wings burst into flame?'

'That would be cruel.'

'Why? It's not a real bird.'

'No? How sweet it sings.'

The cell was in a high tower. Above, the sky shone with magnesium and grenades. 'My secretary is a fool,' said the bishop. 'The city burns down every year. Tonight he risks a fire here for the first time. I wish he had more sense. There are more treasures here than I can carry.' She had prepared knapsacks for their journey, full of warm clothing and dry food. In the bottom of one, wrapped in a bundle of old manuscripts, reposed the jewel-encrusted skull of Angkhdt.

'It doesn't matter. Let it burn.'

'Not to you. This was my home.' She stood looking for a moment over the rooftops towards the light in the bishop's tower, and then she stooped over the knapsacks. 'I have brought us fruit from my garden, and the first hibiscuses. We're going a long way.'

Behind them, the cell door swung open, slowly, quietly. 'Lord Chrism thinks I'm dead,' said the bishop. 'He has released the lock. Come with me.'

They passed through the doorway and up the stairs to the roof. At the second landing of the second stair, the way leveled out for fifty feet along a row of cells. The bishop paused. 'These have been locked all winter,' she said. 'It is time for them to open.' She moved down the line of heavy padlocks, and under her fingers the steel pulled away like taffy. The doors groaned open, and from a farther landing, they turned to watch the prisoners escape, dark spirits, some of them, half smoke and half shadow, smelling of gunpowder and sulphur. Some had hooves and curling horns, and dark heavy faces. They thundered up the stairs in clouds of roaring wind, crushing the travelers against the wall. Others seemed milder; they staggered from their

341

cells out into the corridor, blinking feebly in the light, and their flesh was soft and pink, their faces blobby and unformed. Some were old, their withered arms covered in tattoos, and they carried quadrants, and astrolabes, and telescopes, and perfect spheres, and machines in perpetual motion, and precious equations on chalk slates. And some were beautiful, radiant, aureoles glowing around their heads. They smiled shyly at each other, unsure after so long. They made stylized gestures of recognition with hands that were mostly air, while their wings stirred up fragrances of musk and attar of lavender.

The bishop laughed to see them and clapped her hands. 'Old friends,' she cried. 'Old friends.' And as they drifted up the stairwell they paused to greet her, joining their fourth fingers to their thumbs in careful ellipses and fluttering their wings. 'They are the spirits of the changing world,' said the bishop to her companion. 'New freedoms, new ideas. It's time,' she said. And when the last had disappeared, she stooped to pick up her knapsack. 'Come,' she said, and sprinted upward, not pausing, up and up until the stairwell gave out on the rooftops and a small cloister, a shrine to St Basilon Farfetched, patron of travelers. She ran lightly along the balustrade, out into the open air, while the boy followed. The image of the saint hung down over vertiginous heights, and she sat down beside it, swinging her legs over the edge. Far below her, some of the outer courtyards of the temple were already in flames, and others were full of gunfire and struggling soldiers. But for an instant the mist had cleared, and she could see the lights of the city in the distance, and the silhouette of the dark mountain, and above it a spiderweb of lights. Only for an instant. They flickered out one by one as the clouds regrouped, and then it started to rain, a sugar storm, hard and sudden, the phosphorescent drops bursting like sparks along the tiles.

The bishop jumped back into the shelter of the shrine and tried to scrape the rain out of her hair. The boy put his arms around her from behind, but she pulled free, and left the roof, and climbed a final flight of stairs up into the sanctum of the shrine, where the saint had lived. It was a barren, hive-shaped chamber, without windows or furniture, and the floor was covered with coarse sand. In the middle stood the sarcophagus of the saint, a heavy box of rotting stone. Once it had been intricately carved with scenes from distant countries, but in that room some secret force had sanded down their shapes to almost nothing, and some cancerous wind had gnawed at the stone features of the saint as he sat straddling his tomb, his arms outstretched, his hands eaten away. Sand dunes had blown around the statue's legs. A single candle burned on the coffin lid.

The bishop sat down on the ground, and there she prepared the first meal of their journey, as if they had already traveled miles. She laid out everything that was too bulky to carry far: fruits, and spiced vegetables, and a bottle of wine. They sat and ate without a word, already sharing the peculiar silence of travelers, taking their meals as if sitting on the platform of a deserted station late at night. And when they had finished, they sat without speaking, and the bishop's head nodded forward as if she were asleep. The boy sat staring at the candle flame, fingering his cat.

This animal was the first to sense the change. The candle flame, which had grown up straight and tall, seemed to tremble in a new current of air. The cat leapt out of the boy's lap, and yawned and stretched its back. The bishop raised her head. At the limit of her hearing she perceived a small rushing sound, like wind in the back of a cave or a train passing through a distant tunnel. The cat seemed not to notice. She licked her paws. But the current which disturbed the candle flame had gotten stronger, and it made their shadows flicker on the walls, though they sat without moving. The candle blew out, and the dark shut around them like a mouth, but in time it was as if their eyes had grown accustomed to it, for above them they could see the silhouette of the stone sarcophagus against some lighter color in the vault. The wind stirred the sand around them and fanned their faces, and it was dry and cool, and smelled of foreign languages, and sagebrush, and the salt sea. Above their heads, the stars came out, and for them it was a sight out of the recesses of memory, for not since the first phases of spring had they seen stars in the night sky. More miraculous than that, the finger of a moon rose above some far hills, the first time in their lives, and it touched the forehead of the battered saint, and it shone on a broad sandy valley sloping down in front of them, and in the distance glowed the lights of some small town.

The boy looked up at the moon, and then he turned away. 'There,' he said, pointing down the slope, where an animal was rooting in the dark.

The bishop reached out and put her fingers round his wrist. 'Ssh,' she said. 'How warm it is. It must be summertime.'

Mrs Cassimer had locked the demon into the princess's bedroom, but she couldn't claim to feel much safer. She held conversations with herself to keep her spirits up and stopped her ears with cotton to block out the incessant music. From time to time she took small sips from a jug of whiskey, labeled 'medicinal purposes only' in her neat hand. And to occupy herself, she cleaned the house from top to bottom, in preparation for its burning down. The fire had spread to the streets around the palaces, and even though their stone walls had withstood many springs, 'You can't be too careful,' she said to herself, sealing the spare washcloths in asbestos bags. 'You can't indeed,' she said, on her hands and knees scrubbing the floor. 'Angkhdt created work to be the consolation of the poor. Otherwise they'd have nothing to do. You can't blame the gentry for being so strange, bless their hearts. Not with the life they lead. Nothing but fancy clothes, and idleness, and horrible deaths on top of it. It's no wonder they're lugubrious. You can't blame them for what goes on. No, but I don't condone it, either,' she said severely, shaking her finger at the bedroom door. 'Back from the dead! Who ever heard of such a thing? She ought to be ashamed. As for the other one, tattooless trash, even for a demon. Doesn't belong in a decent home. I can't imagine what the mistress sees in him, all that music from the pit of hell. Some might call it vulgar.'

There was more to do when the doctor came home. The elevator man had run away during the night, so when Thanakar came home in the morning, he carried Jenny Pentecost upstairs, wrapped in blankets. His knee was creaking like a metal hinge, and he could hardly bend it. 'It's like when you were a child,' said Mrs Cassimer. 'You would go out without your crutches, and you would play kickball with the others, and then you'd come home limping like a criminal, just so the mistress would see. Well, she's past caring now. What's in the bundle? Another nasty surprise, I'm sure. Beloved Angkhdt preserve us, it's alive! Oh, sir, you're doing it on purpose.'

'This is Jenny Pentecost,' said the doctor wearily. 'She needs a bath.'

'And a change of clothes. What a get-up! Where did you get this one, the circus? If I might be permitted to ask.'

'Please, Mrs Cassimer, just do it, I've had a long night.'

'I suppose you have. Out all night, and then you stroll in with this . . . with this . . . I don't know what to call her. If she was a little older, I'd know exactly. Little strumpet.'

'Please . . .'

'I suppose you're the only one who's had a long night. I've done the work of ten around here. Not that I get any thanks. I'd like a bath myself.'

The doctor tried to lower Jenny into an armchair, but she wouldn't let go her hands from around his neck. 'Don't make me go with her,' she whispered. They were the first words that she had spoken.

Mrs Cassimer was cleaning the cotton out of her ears, and she heard them. In an instant, her anger subsided into tears. 'Oh, sir,' she sniffed. 'You left me alone. You said you wouldn't.'

'I was arrested.'

'Hmph. Easy to say. I've heard that one before.'

The doctor disengaged Jenny's fingers from around his neck and sat down on the arm of the chair. 'How's my mother?' he asked.

'A lot better than she has any business being, if you want my opinion,' retorted the housekeeper. 'And that music all night long, it's enough to drive you crazy. You can hear it now.'

But she relented when Jenny was asleep, curled up on the sofa with her thumb in her mouth. 'She's just a child,' she said. The doctor took off her headdress and bandaged her feet, and together they sponged away some of her makeup and perfume, and found a flannel nightgown for her. Then the doctor tended to himself, injecting oil into

346

his knee to soothe the joint. He wrapped it in a bandage of hot silk. 'The elevator man has run away,' he remarked.

'Some people have no pride,' said Mrs Cassimer.

'What will you do?'

She shrugged. 'I took an oath to serve your family. I wish I hadn't, but it's too late now, as the parson said when he chopped his mother's head off by mistake.'

'It will mean going away. I'm a fugitive.'

'Don't give yourself airs. It's a fine place for a fugitive, your own armchair.' She frowned. 'Most people go away this time of year,' she said. 'The whole place is burning down.'

Mrs Cassimer had locked the bedroom door and sealed it with signs and incantations written in chalk. 'You spelled it wrong,' said Thanakar. 'That wouldn't have stopped a cat.' He was sitting over a cooker in the bedroom, preparing a hypodermic full of heroin. His mother stretched out her hands for it.

'Thank you, Thanakar,' she whispered. 'I was feeling so tired.'

She also had had a busy night. She had butchered the policeman's corpse, draining off his blood into vases and flowerbowls, filling the washstand with his entrails. She had toasted strips of meat over the grate, at the end of a long skewer. Now she shot the needle and sat back on the floor next to the bed, her hands over her face.

The antinomial squatted in a corner, his flute to his lips. Though he still moved his fingers along the glass, he wasn't blowing into it anymore, just breathing quietly, so that the music had subsided into light, papery noises. He seemed asleep.

'I'm leaving the city,' said Thanakar. 'Will you come with me?'

'No,' answered the princess. Her eyes went through their slow rotation, the colors mixing and purifying in her colorless face. 'I never liked crowds. I like them less than ever now.' She looked over at the prince, where he lay under his shroud. 'I have someone to avenge,' she whispered. She had not asked Thanakar to try to wake his father, seeming to realize what a monster she'd become. 'I'm tired all the time,' she complained. 'It's the change of diet.' She smiled mournfully and showed her stained teeth. 'The passports are in the cabinet, and money too. There's a letter of credit. You can draw your salary at any Starbridge bank – that is, if things haven't changed too much.'

'Things have changed. Have you looked outside?'

She shook her head. 'I can't stand the daylight.'

'It's raining.'

'I can't stand it.' The curtains were all drawn. 'When I was asleep,' she whispered, 'I could remember things so clearly. It was like a memory of Paradise – I used to lie in the cold darkness, and I could see the world hang suspended above me out of reach. And it was full of parties, and champagne, and dances, and men in shining uniforms, and servants bowing to the floor, like when I was a girl. The bishop's palace all lit up, and the platters piled high with winter fruit, and the dancers skimming over the floor like birds. Then we used to ride home through the snow, and my father used to take the horses from the coachman just to scare us, because he used to drive them so fast, so reckless, the sleigh skidding and rattling until Mama cried out. And Jess and I sitting nestled in our furs, laughing and crying, and yelling, 'Hold on tight!' It's not like that anymore.'

'Not much.'

'When I was young, we lived outside the walls, but the house collapsed when the snow melted. Do you remember,

348

Thanakar? I was married from that house, and your father rode the most enormous stallion. Everybody said he was so handsome, and I was so proud because I'd been in suspense for weeks: Was he tall? Was he too hairy? I'd seen a portrait, but they always lie. And then when I saw him I was so relieved, but a little shy, too, because I wondered what he must be thinking. I suppose I was a pretty girl, but nothing exceptional, only my complexion was very good, Mama used to say.' The princess ran her hand over her cheek. 'I've broken every mirror in this room,' she whispered, looking around.

'Everything changes.'

'He was very kind. So very kind. Only I took so long to be pregnant, and the doctor said I could only have just one, the weather was so bad. That was the eighteenth phase of winter. I must have carried you a thousand days. And I was healthy. My grandmother had had forty-one, and even my mother had had ten. That's why it was so terrible when you . . .'

'Yes,' said Thanakar. 'It must have been a shock.'

'And after that your father changed. Oh, he was always so polite. So formal. He never raised his hand against me. Only, I think he had met some other women somewhere. I can't think where.'

'He was a cruel man.'

She turned on him. 'Don't say that! You have no right to say that. You of all people. Cripple!' She spat the word out, as if it had been a sharp piece of stone in her mouth, hurting her tongue the whole time she was talking, and she was happy to be rid of it. She paused and sat back. 'It seemed natural to blame you for his change of heart,' she said softly, leaning back against the headboard. 'What mother could do otherwise?'

'It was a long time ago,' said Thanakar.

'Yes,' she agreed, after a pause. One of the policeman's shoulders lay near her. She examined lines of red under her fingernails. 'It's hard to imagine such things ever seemed important. Will you take the motorcar?'

'The boat, I think. The roads are jammed. I'll head for Caladon,' he said. 'Along the shore. They must need doctors there.'

Thanakar stood up. He took a vial of white powder from his breast pocket. 'Let me show you how to fix it yourself,' he said. 'And there's food in the refrigerator,' he said doubtfully, looking at the remains of the policeman.

'It doesn't matter. I'll come with you for the first part. The passage underground. I know a way up to the temple. You understand. Vengeance sustains me. It will be my meat and drink. Your father and I were fooled out of our lives by lying priests. There is one who'll wish he murdered us outright. Demiurge! Tonight I'll touch your spleen.' She accompanied this peculiar threat with a peculiar cannibal gesture, gnawing at the tips of her bunched fingers.

As if woken by the name of vengeance, the antinomial raised his head and opened his eyes. They shone like pieces of blue ice. 'Aspe,' he said. He breathed some notes into his flute, and then, unwinding the white scarf from around his neck, he wiped the instrument with it, caressing it gently, and breathing on it, and rubbing away the mark of fingerprints. From his belt he drew a wooden case. 'He has arrived,' he said, and then he paused, frowning down at the instrument in his lap. 'Biter Aspe,' he said, and then it was as if he had changed his mind, because he made a little sorrowful noise between his lips, and then he took the flute by its two ends and broke it in the middle like a stick, the glass splintering in his hands.

'Lunatics,' thought Thanakar, but it got worse. The man prepared himself for battle as if for a wedding. He stripped

350

off his hospital clothes and stood naked in the middle of the floor, soaping his body and his hair while the princess eyed him thoughtfully. She commanded hot water to be brought for him in a basin. And Mrs Cassimer fetched towels as far as the threshold, sobbing, hiding her face, holding her nose, and laid out a white shirt and some white trousers, which had been abandoned by the tallest servant. They fit. The antinomial was a small man for his race. Thanakar thought he must be half barbarian at least. His fantasy of vengeance had enslaved him. And there was something ceremonial in the way he dressed himself, the way he painted his lips, his eyelids, and his ears with blood from a bucket and drew a line of blood around his jaw. He poured hot water into a silver basin and shaved his head with the prince's razor. And he painted tattoos on his empty palms, strange patterns of violence and good luck. Thanakar wondered where he had learned them.

The white scarf was his talisman. He used it to polish the blade of a hatchet, and then he knotted it around his neck. At noontime he put on his sunglasses, and stepped out on to the balcony, and stood staring towards the north gate, humming to himself. Thanakar went away to turn in his housekeys to the porter, and when he came back, the man was gone. 'And thank God for that,' said Mrs Cassimer, standing in the hallway. 'Goodbye and amen.'

Far beneath the Starbridge palace, a system of catacombs and canals spread out underneath the city. They were kept open even in springtime by ancient sluices and locks, and by a race of keepers still more ancient, still bound to their work by iron oaths long after so many servants had fled away. Even so, the tunnels and canals were rarely used. In winter, they were convenient when the streets were blocked with snow. Then families of Starbridges would keep great ceremonial barges and sleds with silver runners, and the long vaults were hung with chandeliers. Then too the crypts were always lit, for there was always a party down there somewhere, people gathering together for their return to Paradise, celebrating the end of their earthly duties. In winter, there were many funerals. By spring, whole wings of the palace stood empty; whole families had gone extinct. Perhaps a third of it was occupied, and underground, the chandeliers had long burned out. Yet still this race of boatmen kept to its work through flood and fire. And when the seasons changed, and the city grew up again, and the palace whimpered with new life, returning princes and their progeny would find the system still intact.

No child of mine, thought Thanakar, half bitter, half relieved. He stood in the dark on Starbridge Keys, far below the level of the street, watching the boatman pole his shallow craft towards them out of the tunnel's mouth. Lanterns hung above the prow and stern, and threw troubled yellow circles on the black water. The light shone dubiously on the boatman's back – he was a bent, gaunt figure, unchanged since Thanakar's youth. His head protruded down below the level of his shoulders at the end of his long neck, and it swung slowly like a pendulum as he peered to the right and to the left.

Mrs Cassimer was muttering and complaining. 'Shut up, fool,' whispered the princess.

'I don't care, ma'am. I'll say it again. It's a crime to leave him there. He wants to be put into the vault, like his father. He won't thank you for just leaving him, when you see him again. He wants a funeral like his father.'

'Old fool,' breathed the princess. 'Prince Thanakar is dying. He will die in his own bed, and I will never see him any more. As to where he dies, it makes no difference. Old

352

fool, there is no life but this one: the one that Chrism stole from him and me. But I will be avenged.'

'I don't care who says it, but that's atheism, ma'am,' retorted the housekeeper. 'Now I know you've been to hell and back. I don't blame you. But it's colored your way of thinking, ma'am, if you don't mind me saying so.'

The princess gave her a contemptuous look and leapt from the pier into the boat as it drew up, almost upsetting it. The boatman jammed his pole into the wall and looked at her from under heavy eyebrows. She was an impressive sight, standing taut against the bowstem in a rich black robe, her long black hair, her lips painted black, an onyx ring in her left nostril standing out against the bloodless pallor of her cheek. Yellow lamplight soured her white skin, polluted the brilliance of her changing eyes, but even so she was impressive.

Thanakar stepped into the belly of the boat. Mrs Cassimer handed in the girl and then got in herself, losing her balance and sitting down abruptly in the bilge. Thanakar sat also, but his mother stood upright in the bow, grasping the lantern pole. The boatman pushed off. He gave no word, no signal of greeting, or gesture of recognition, even though his race had been serving Thanakar's for all of history, ever since Angkhdt gave the world to certain families.

The princess watched the lights diminish along the key and the darkness resolve around the circles of their lanterns. 'I'm not sorry to leave,' she whispered.

'Nor I,' said Thanakar.

They passed into the tunnel's stony throat, and the last lights disappeared. 'Your father had great plans for you,' whispered the princess. 'He was a strong man. At one time he almost forced a truce on Argon Starbridge. The Inner Ear rejected it. War has always served their purpose.

Continual bloodshed keeps us weak. Otherwise we could not tolerate a man like Demiurge. Your father hated him. Your father had great plans. He could have made you bishop. The army loved him. At that time the parsons were still working on your tattoos, and the central panel of your right hand was still blank. Your father had written to the emperor for permission to have you consecrated, and Demiurge was afraid. He decided to destroy you, to make you an example.'

'Mother – I believe it was an accident.'

'It was not. I saw him throw you down. Chrism Demiurge has a ring with a poisoned barb. Once he cuts you with it, you never heal. Your bones rebel against your flesh. I didn't find it until later – the tiniest puncture under your kneecap.'

'That doesn't sound possible.'

'Quiet! What do you know about it? It broke your father's heart. He had great ambitions.'

Thanakar laughed. 'It's just as well the way it is,' he said. 'Lord Chrism had the bishop burned last night.'

'Yes. He burns them when they get too old. For a long time he has ruled through children.'

For a while they glided in silence through the still water, surrounded by hints of stonework in the dark and, from time to time, the carved entrances to other tunnels. Or at times the tunnel they were in would widen out, though the canal always maintained its width. Stone platforms would appear on either side, and small bridges arched overhead, barely clearing the tops of their lantern poles. They passed through underground temples, long disused, and Starbridge family shrines. Occasionally they would pass a kerosene taper still alight, burning among rows of tombs.

'He drank a lot,' whispered the princess. 'And when they offered him the choice of dying young, he took it. The weather was so dreadful, you remember. It was a great honor. I urged him to do it. In those days I was very devout. A married woman's life is so constrained.

'Do you remember, Thanakar? You were just home from school. It was the seventh of November, in the third phase of spring. Two young parsons came to the house, to put the needles in our arms and pump the ichor through our veins. Right away I knew it was a lie, as soon as I lay back. They had told us what to expect. Dreams within dreams, they said. But I could feel the cold in every part of me. It was a lie. Paradise! For fifty mortal months it was like lying at the bottom of this stream, watching the lights passing back and forth along the surface – perfectly conscious, Thanakar. Submerged in the icy dark with nothing but distorted memories to keep me sane. Is it any wonder that I've changed?'

It was no wonder. But Thanakar wasn't listening. They were entering another section of the catacombs, rising through a sequence of shallow locks kept by uncles and cousins of their boatman – old men, silent and misshapen, peering down at them with lanterns in their hands. The light glinted on the machinery, and once they passed a scaffold and two men working on a wall of brazen cog-wheels, replacing the belts. They stopped to peer down at the boat for an instant, and then bent back to their work again.

There was more light in these upper regions, closer to the street. It seeped down through the ventilator ducts. And the water was more turbid here because it was mixing with flood waters from the street. In some places the walls glowed as the water slid down from the holes in the vault, and the sugar spread out on the surface of the stream like phosphorescent oil. The air smelled of smoke. Other people, too, had found their way down from above, escaping fire or water. They sat shivering among the tombs.

So far the way was familiar to Thanakar. Eventually they would rise above the surface of the streets into the open air, to where a system of aqueducts would lead them to a Starbridge boathouse built on stilts above the riverbank, out of reach of the flood. There larger boats – river craft and ocean-going launches – hung from slings below the floor. Most of these would already be gone. But Thanakar's family still kept a boat there, a sleek narrow racer, useless in any storm.

But the boatman turned aside, down unfamiliar passages. It grew dark again, and the vaults were so low that they had to unstep the lanterns. 'He follows my directions,' whispered the princess. 'My way lies through the deepest crypts.' Her voice was swallowed by the sound of water being sucked away, for they had entered an ancient lock that plunged them down into the city's labyrinthine bowels, deeper than Thanakar had ever been. And when at last the sluice gates opened up to let them through, the air seemed hot and rich and wet, and they were in a maze of tunnels overgrown with vegetation. Curtains of white tendrils hung down from the ceiling and brushed their faces as they passed, while the water was overgrown with algae, and lotus pads, and strange blanched lilies. Sometimes a pale fin would break the water, and far behind they could hear something splash and cry. Mrs Cassimer sat speechless in the bottom of the boat while, in her lap, wide-eyed Jenny sucked her thumb.

They left the flowers behind and drifted out into clear water, an underground lake. Along the verges, candles flickered; they marked the circle of a vast chamber and a shore of stonework holding the water in a ring, lined with lumpish shapes. The princess turned the wick up on her lantern and lifted it as high as she could at the end of her pole, and by its light they saw curved images hanging down over their heads from the inside of the vault. The stone was covered with white moss, but even so Thanakar could recognize the signs of the zodiac, and in the center, free from overgrowth, primeval symbols of good and evil, the black snake and the white horse, grappling eternally.

The boatman pulled up his pole, and they drifted on the still water. 'Pagan kings,' whispered the princess. She raised her lantern to give articulation to the shapes along the verge: they were statues of cold kings with pale faces, gesturing to them across the water. Some seemed as if they had been turned to stone in the middle of talking, their poses were so lifelike, their faces so expressive. In the boat, Thanakar felt himself surrounded by a ring of passions, vices, virtues, each one crying out to him in a separate marble voice.

'This is where I leave you,' whispered the princess. 'From here a shaft runs straight up to the bishop's crypt below the temple. Chrism Demiurge has a private stair. I know the way.' She stood proudly in the boat's peaked bow. Her face was as white as stone, and it was as if her passions, too, had been metamorphosed into marble by the pressure of her long confinement. It was cut into every feature, the malice that had become her animating principle now that her blood was gone.

'Beloved Angkhdt defend us,' said Mrs Cassimer, and Thanakar turned back to the shore. It was strange there should be lights down here, he thought, strange that the tombs should be so carefully maintained when so much else was overgrown. And as he watched, a man came down and knelt by the lakeside to prime an oil beacon. And when the flare rose up above the lake and their poor lanterns were overwhelmed, Thanakar gasped, because they were floating in the middle of a crowd. Men and women stood silently among the statues. They were naked except for breechcloths over their sex, and their faces and their chests were painted white, their black hair streaked with white. Mrs Cassimer knew what they were. 'Pagans,' she whispered, open-mouthed, and the princess nodded. And then Thanakar also recognized them, from engravings he had seen in books.

Here in the utmost bowels of the city, among her utmost bones, the last of old earth's pagans had found sanctuary. They stood silent, as if at a vigil, their faces calm and ghostlike, staring at the intruders on the lake.

The boatman unshipped his pole and made for shore. A stone pier ran out towards them, and at the end of it stood an altar carved in the shape of a horse's head. Its horns were gilded and garlanded with flowers, and on its broad forehead was set an offering of strawberries, more precious than gold in that starving time. Men gathered here, and several of the oldest wore amber necklaces, the symbol of the ancient cult of loving kindness, relics from a distant blissful time, but whether the men who wore them had actually been members of that noble brotherhood, or whether they had picked them up as talismans from some place of execution, Thanakar couldn't judge. How could they be old enough? Yet they were very old, their brows placid, their eyes clear and kind. One snow-bearded patriarch came down to the water's edge and reached his hands out in greeting. Thanakar wished he could have come there on some better errand; there was such a difference between the old man's noble face and the princess's carved mask, his smile of welcome and her hardened disdain. 'Old fool,' she snarled, and leapt the few remaining feet on to the pier. He bowed low, and she ignored him, turning back to Thanakar to say, 'Goodbye. I won't thank you. We gave each other life, you and I, but I'm not sure we meant it kindly. We meant to settle an old debt.' She blew him a cold kiss, and the boatman pushed away with a flourish of his pole. A gulf of black water stretched between mother and son, but he sat looking backward, and she stood watching on the shore, a lantern in her hand. The old men moved around her, bowing graciously, but she stood motionless. Then, abruptly, she turned and pushed past them down the pier. Thanakar saw her pause at the altar, and take a strawberry and eat it.

Six hundred feet above, the antinomial stood in the burning street. He put on his sunglasses. The buildings were collapsing on either side of him, and the heat was intolerable, but he was unwilling to move. At the top of the street, across a square parade ground, rose the towers of the north gate, and the square was already full of Aspe's soldiers drawn up in rows, waiting for the colonel. Restive in the smoke and sparks, their horses pawed the cobblestones, and occasionally one would rear up on its hind legs, spooked by an ember or a falling beam.

Towards four o'clock, Aspe came through on his enormous horse, his head sunken on his breast. Couriers had reached him during the night, bringing news of the bishop's execution. Since then he had ridden like an old man, the reins limp between his fingers, and from time to time he seemed to doze in the saddle, his head jerking foolishly. As he rode in through the gate he was awake, but only just. His eyes were bloodshot, his face red, as if he had been drinking.

He raised his head and looked around, seeming not to recognize where he was or the faces of the officers around him. He put his hand to his face, to shield it from the heat.

'What are we doing here?' he complained. 'This street's on fire.'

His adjutant was at his side, immaculate and polished on a prancing mare. 'Yes, sir,' he said. 'Nevertheless, we believe it is still occupied by Chrism's troops.'

'What troops?' grumbled the old man. 'I haven't heard a shot all day.'

'Yes, sir. Nevertheless, you see that man there. We believe him to be some kind of advance guard.'

'You're an idiot,' grumbled Aspe. 'So is he. What is he doing there? He must be burning up.'

'Yes sir. Why don't you take a look?' The adjutant held out a pair of field glasses, and Aspe reached for them wearily. But as he stared through them down the burning street, his officers noticed that he sat up straighter. His spine stiffened, and some of the old harshness came back into his voice. 'Who is that?' he asked.

'He's in range. Shall I ask a sharpshooter to bring him down?'

'No.' Aspe adjusted the focus until the antinomial stood smiling at him in the glasses' eye. And as he watched, the man reached into his shirt and pulled out a white handkerchief, and wiped his lips with it.

'Go down and see what he wants,' said Aspe.

'Yes, sir.' The adjutant spurred his horse over the cobblestones. At the mouth of the street, the way was blocked with flames. The horse shied, terrified, but he forced her head around and kept onward, the animal resisting him at every step. Behind him in the square, Aspe was staring at the antinomial through the field glasses, his vision suddenly obscured by the officer's lurching back coming into focus halfway down the burning street. Aspe could see his silver epaulettes.

He lowered the glasses, and hawked a gob of spit up

from his throat, and leaned over to let it dribble on his boot. But he straightened up in time to see his brother jump, and seize the adjutant by his polished foot, and turn him out of the saddle so that he sprawled across the muddy stones. The horse pulled away, but the antinomial ran after her and vaulted up on to her back. And even though she kicked and reared, he kept his seat. He had lost his sunglasses, and Aspe could see his icy eyes.

He calmed the horse, though through the field glasses Aspe could see she still trembled, and when a roof caved in and filled the air with sparks, she started desperately. The antinomial reached down to stroke her neck, and through the glasses Aspe could see his lips moving. He was singing to her. She lifted up her narrow beak, and he unstrapped her bridle and her cruel bit, and threw them down into the mud. Then from his belt he took his axe, and raising it in both hands above his head, he gave a shout that Aspe could hear even at that distance, and spurred the horse up towards him up the flaming street, a bullet in the muzzle of a gun.

Aspe handed his glasses to the soldier at his side, and as he did so he noticed for the first time that, to his right and to his left, sharpshooters had dismounted, assembling their rifles. For a moment he could feel the temptations of inertia and old age, and he wondered whether he should let the soldiers shoot his brother down. But then he saw the man burst towards him over the parade ground out of the street's fiery throat, and above the roaring of the fire he could hear sweet music, the sweet song of battle, which he had never hoped to hear again. It touched his biter's heart, and filled it with singing, and filled his body and made a whirlwind in his head, and swept away all slavish thoughts and considerations. He stood up in his stirrups, and his harsh voice echoed over the parade ground. He shouted to his soldiers: 'Barbarian scum! Don't touch him. Are you deaf? It is my brother.' And he rode out to greet him, his whip in his live hand, his steel hand tightened into a steel claw.

Aspe's horse was the largest in the known universe, and the cobblestones cracked under its hooves. And its rider, too, was gigantic; he raise his whip and cut the beast in its tenderest flank, making it scream with rage and flog the air with its vestigial wings. Together, horse and man towered over their attacker, but the antinomial never spoke a word to check his gallop, nor allowed any note of doubt to creep into his song. He shot like a projectile, a thing with no will or consciousness of its own, an instrument of some larger vengeance. In the middle of the square they came together in a smash of metal and a flurry of wingbeats, and as the axe descended and the mare rushed past, Aspe caught her beak in the coils of his whip. Standing in his stirrups, he wrenched her neck around, using her own impetus to splinter her beak and snap her neckbone. She lurched and stumbled, throwing wide the stroke of the axe. It fell not on Aspe but on his horse, imbedding at the juncture of its neck and shoulder, and touched the life of the great beast. There was no time for another stroke. As the antinomial tried to wrench his axe out of the horse's neck, Aspe caught him in his claw, and held him and crushed him, the horses subsiding around them as if deflating in a gush of blood.

Aspe stepped free and stood among the wreckage of the horses, still holding his brother by the face. And then he raised his head and shouted, and at first the circle of soldiers heard nothing but a furious roar. But again he shouted, screaming from his heart, using all the rage he knew, and this time his cry was so harsh and so articulate that even that circle of barbarians could see an image taking shape above him, high up in the air, indistinct at first. And then it burst out of the clouds as if out of a wave, a great sea monster made of music, and every modulation of the colonel's voice gave it new color and new form. Fins and a tail it had, but also it seemed part lion and part bird, a mixture of distorted terrors. Aspe raised his steel fist. Shouting aloud, he shook it in the indignant face of day.

The monster stretched its talons out over the city. And then it vanished, dashed to pieces on the wind, as the colonel's singing died away. But Chrism Demiurge, standing on his balcony, still caught a glimpse of the illusion. He saw it as a blear of color in the sky. He touched his wristwatch as he left the balustrade, though he knew it wanted hours till sunset. Behind him in the marble courts, a musician stroked the hour.

'It seems later than it is,' murmured the priest. 'Is my captain there?'

'Yes, sir?' said a soldier, coming forward, his face blackened with powder and soot.

'You look tired, Captain. There's hot water on the table, and clean towels. What's the news?'

'The enemy has reached the thirty-seventh gate, sir.'

'And Aspe?'

'Is inside the city walls.'

'Thank you, Captain. Then you may tell your soldiers to stand down. I see no need for further violence. Are my lords assembled?'

'Yes, sir,' answered the soldier.

Lord Chrism turned to his disciple, who was standing in the doorway. 'Come forward, Corydon. Take my message to the Inner Ear. Tell them I think it would be wise to terminate our duties here. Tell them I will meet them all in Paradise. We will reassemble there.' He smiled. 'Most of them won't find the journey long or arduous. Most are

363

halfway there already.' He reached out his hand. 'God bless you, Corydon.'

His disciple knelt to kiss his ring, and Chrism ran his fingers through the young man's hair, over his cheek. 'Don't let them kill you,' he murmured.

'No, sir. I have my excuses planned.'

'Good boy. Say you were enchanted.'

'That would be the truth, sir.'

'Bewitched, then. Say bewitched.' The old man's smile was full of sadness. 'God bless you. Remember to strive always for purity in this life. Chemical purity. Remember that.'

He turned aside into his own apartments. He locked the door, and sealed it with a magic seal, and drew a magic circle on the floor. Then he stepped into his bedroom and stood for a while in front of the mirror. His blind eyes could distinguish motion and color, but not form, and when with a weary sigh he undid the buttons of his crimson chasuble and drew it off, in the mirror it was as if he had disappeared. Underneath, his clothing was a muted gray, blending in with the rest of the colors in the room. He shook the garment, and with a soft thump a goblin dropped to the floor. And when he bent to pick it up, it moved away, easily evading his blind groping. And then, one at a time, other spirits started to climb out of his clothes: seraphim, and cherubim, and long-tongued demons. They clambered down his arms and hung for a while by his fingers before they let go, as if to say that as far as they were capable of love, they loved him. Some licked his hands or gave his ankle a soft squeeze before they scuttled off. 'Ah,' he said, in a voice full of regret, 'slip away from me, do you? Can't you wait until the end?' And when the last one was gone and his skin was free from their pinching and their scratching for the first time since he was a young man, he felt more alone than he had ever felt in a lifetime of solitude and blindness. Yet he was not quite alone. The Princess Thanakar sat on his bed hugging her knees, her cooker and her hypodermic on the coverlet beside her, and when the priest turned towards her at last, she raised her head to look at him, and her eyes changed from pink to red.

In the middle of the square, standing in the wreck of broken horses, Aspe shouted again. Above him, the dragon spread its shining tail. For a moment, Thanakar saw it drifting in the wind, saw the sun glinting on its scales as he dropped his boat out of the belly of the boathouse. Mrs Cassimer hid her face; Jenny pointed, and as the boat hung suspended from its slings, he looked up too, but only for a moment. As the boat dropped to the water, he bent down to fill the engine from a flask of powder. And after that, he had to guide them through the flooded streets, and through all the floating debris and the tops of houses and the spires of sunken shrines, and all the complicated water till they found the river. It wasn't until they had almost reached the far shore, where the current ran deep and straight into the sea, that he looked back.

For half a mile along the river, the city was on fire. Ash fell like snow above a cluster of dark warehouses. There, on a promontory opposite the boat, flames had reached the roof of a small building, a temple or a dockside shrine. Thanakar watched it burning for a moment and then turned away downstream, just as the steeple collapsed into the water and filled the air with sparks.

The world's greatest science fiction authors now available in paperback from Grafton Books

To order direct from the publisher just tick the titles you want and fill in the order form. **SF1382**

All these books are available at your local bookshop or newsagent, or can be ordered direct from the publisher.

To order direct from the publishers just tick the titles you want and fill in the form below.

Name _____

Address _____

_____

Send to:
Grafton Cash Sales
PO Box 11, Falmouth, Cornwall TR10 9EN.

Please enclose remittance to the value of the cover price plus:

UK 60p for the first book, 25p for the second book plus 15p per copy for each additional book ordered to a maximum charge of £1.90.

BFPO 60p for the first book, 25p for the second book plus 15p per copy for the next 7 books, thereafter 9p per book.

Overseas including Eire £1.25 for the first book, 75p for second book and 28p for each additional book.

Grafton Books reserve the right to show new retail prices on covers, which may differ from those previously advertised in the text or elsewhere.